ROGUE

Xian Warriors - Book II

REGINE ABEL

COVER DESIGN BY
Regine Abel

ILLUSTRATIONS BY
Kesini
Vvevelur
Muns
Niklas Cloister

Copyright © 2023

All rights reserved. The unauthorized reproduction or distribution of this copyrighted work is illegal and punishable by law. No part of this book may be used or reproduced electronically or in print without written permission of the author, except in the case of brief quotations embodied in reviews.

This book uses mature language and explicit sexual content. It is not intended for anyone under the age of 18.

This book is a work of fiction. Names, characters, places, and incidents are either products of the author's imagination or are used fictitiously. Any resemblance to actual persons, living or dead, events, or locales is entirely coincidental.

CONTENTS

Chapter 1	1
Chapter 2	12
Chapter 3	23
Chapter 4	34
Chapter 5	45
Chapter 6	60
Chapter 7	66
Chapter 8	73
Chapter 9	80
Chapter 10	87
Chapter 11	106
Chapter 12	121
Chapter 13	139
Chapter 14	155
Chapter 15	171
Chapter 16	184
Chapter 17	197
Chapter 18	209
Chapter 19	216
Chapter 20	230
Chapter 21	239
Chapter 22	252
Chapter 23	269
Epilogue	284
Also by Regine Abel	319
About Regine	321

ROGUE

She was lost, until he found her.

For years, Shuria was a monster, the ultimate assassin created as a result of countless painful experiments. At the end of the war, she finds refuge on the Kryptid homeworld as an advisor to the Queen. But even here, she doesn't belong. When the Vanguard comes to warn them of an impending invasion by the Coalition rebels, Shuria's life takes on an unexpected turn as she reconnects with Rogue. He is everything any female could dream of. But how can he truly want someone as broken as her, especially after all the terrible things she has done?

When he embarks on this latest mission, Rogue only aims to put his scientific knowledge and combat skills to the defense of their former enemies turned allies. Instead, his mating glands awaken for the most unlikely female. After all those years knowing Shuria, why now? Are they truly soulmates or is his sudden physiological response to her a glitch?

DEDICATION

To those who fell but picked themselves up. To those who sinned but made amends and learned to forgive themselves. The errors of your past only define you if you wallow in them. But you can define yourself by learning and growing from your mistakes.

To those who see beauty where others can't… or won't.

It is easy to cast the first stone. It is harder to extend a guiding hand. Be someone's light, not their darkness.

CHAPTER 1
ROGUE

I lowered my vision screener and gazed affectionately at Janelle. She leveled her beautiful brown eyes on me, her expectant expression reflecting the one from her mate, Reaper, my younger brother.

"There has been some notable progress," I said in an encouraging tone. "I will keep looking for new treatments that can further help improve your vision. We may never be able to fully restore it, but I have faith it will get better than it is."

"I told you my baby-faced brother was the best," Reaper said in a tender tone to his mate before nuzzling her nape.

Janelle giggled and squirmed on his lap. Although I should probably give him a hard time for teasing me about my cursed baby face, I couldn't help but melt at the lovely picture the two of them made. For years, I had ached for my brother pining after a woman he couldn't have. His Dragon did not recognize Linette as his soulmate, making it impossible for him to pursue her. He had been even more distraught when she had found happiness with Varnog. But our Dragons were always right. Who would have thought he would have found the other half of himself trapped in one of the abandoned secret bases of the foul creature we'd been unfortunate enough to have as sire?

"Don't worry," Janelle said in a grateful voice. "All of you have already done so much for me. I had forgotten what it felt like to see. I never expected this much. So whatever improvements you can achieve in the future will only be an even greater blessing. But even if nothing more comes of it, you have given me far more than I could have ever hoped for."

I smiled and gently caressed her cheek, earning myself another sweet smile from her and an affectionate one from my brother.

"Well, you are free to go, young lady. Just don't overdo it," I said in a stern tone. "Word is that you and the Horned Creckels have been working overtime, getting up to speed with everything Vanguard related."

Janelle made a pretty pout, her shoulders slouching slightly while she took on a dejected expression.

"They are trying to learn all they can to prove to Legion and Chaos that they are ready to join us on the next mission," Reaper said, his tone and facial expression making it clear he, too, was unconvinced.

I struggled to keep my expression neutral and carefully chose my words. "The Horned Creckels haven't had time to properly train. All of you spent the past twenty years essentially buried alive in that base. You have been extremely sick and almost died of starvation. Your body faced a series of serious trauma. You need time to fully recover."

"I did most of my recovery on board the ship that brought us here from the Moon of Melibos," Janelle argued. "During the entire trip, Stran trained the others. You should have seen them battle the Zebiers alongside Stran. They mowed them down. Don't forget that Khutu made my parents modify the original Creckels into the Horned Creckels, making them even more powerful war machines. Based on all the reports Doom has been getting from Chaos and Legion about the types of weapons the rebels are bringing to battle, you will *need* the help of the Horned Creckels. Stran shouldn't have to be by himself for this."

Reaper pursed his lips in that typical fashion he always did when weighing an argument.

"There is no question that having the Horned Creckels' assistance would greatly help Stran," Reaper said cautiously. "However, Doom is the only Warrior who can fluently speak their language. I am half decent but still have a long way to go."

"Which is exactly why I should tag along, since I'm the only person who speaks their language fluently. Well besides Doom," Janelle amended sheepishly.

"There is no way we're taking you to a war, my mate," Reaper said in a gentle but firm tone.

"I agree," I replied. "You must stay here and fully recover."

"Aren't you going with them?" Janelle asked in a defiant tone.

I raised an eyebrow, confused as to the relevance of that statement. "Yes," I said with a nod, wondering what the point was.

"That means you will be gone for months," she continued matter-of-factly. "Am I to understand you are relinquishing my medical care to Victoria?"

I flinched while Reaper chuckled.

"That's a low blow," I muttered while glaring at her.

As much as I loved Victoria and respected her stellar medical skills, Janelle was my baby brother's mate. No one but me would be her physician.

Not intimidated in the least, Janelle lifted her chin with a smug expression. "I'm merely stating a fact. You can't heal me if you leave me behind."

"I do want my brother to take care of you, my mate. But we are going into danger," Reaper said gently.

"All the more reason for me to come," Janelle said forcefully.

"I will not remain here wondering whether I've been widowed. And nobody knows the Creckels better than me. I do not need to get on the frontline to be of help."

"I'm still not convinced," Reaper said. "But ultimately, it will be Doom's decision to make."

"Speaking of which, we should probably head to the meeting room," I said, feeling a little sorry for my brother. "The mission brief should start any minute now."

In his shoes, I would want to keep my mate in ten layers of bubble wrap, and as far away as possible from danger. And yet, like all the other Warriors mated to the wonderful women of the Vanguard, I would want my female by my side on every mission.

We entered the meeting room, minimally decorated with the standard black and gold color palette of the Vanguard. Despite the dark gray walls, dark floor, and furniture, the space didn't feel gloomy or confined. The large window looking out onto the plaza of the HQ certainly played a role in it.

My gaze zeroed in on Brees. The Horned Creckel leader was standing next to Stran. Although she was significantly younger than him, Brees appeared almost at a height with him, but only because the enhancements she received gave her longer legs than their original breed. Creckels resembled giant pangolins with a draconic head, vicious spikes beneath their scales that could be shot as lethal darts, and a wide, flat tail that could carry objects. Aside from the length of their legs, Horned Creckels also differentiated themselves with a long series of horns on top of their heads and napes, which had earned them their current name.

Judging by the expected way in which she was staring at our unit leader, Doom, Brees clearly shared her best friend Janelle's hope that they could join the mission. The way Stran's blue dragon eyes sparked with excitement, laced with an almost paternal pride, there was no doubt in my mind she had his support. I had mixed feelings about it. While I trusted Stran's judgment, wars often became extremely ugly. Both Janelle and these young Horned Creckels had much too recently recovered from a terrible lifelong ordeal. I didn't believe them ready to face what awaited us.

I settled at the large rectangular table that ate up most of the space in the room. Pitch black with an elegant golden trim around the edges, the table could accommodate twenty people. But Doom's team occupied less than half the seats.

Reaper sat down next to his Soulcatcher, Martha, who was also the team's weapons specialist. As she wasn't an official member of the Vanguard and didn't possess any soulcatching abilities, Janelle could not join us for this meeting. All the topics that would be covered were considered classified and highly sensitive, not that anyone would believe her capable of betraying us. But then Brees would fight for their cause, and in the worst-case scenario, I had no doubt my lovely sister-in-law would corner Doom somewhere around the HQ to sweet talk him into letting her tag along.

I sat next to my brother, to the right of Madeline. She was a stunning woman of African descent with albinism and breathtaking greenish-grey eyes. She was the Portal of the team, which allowed her to safely transfer the soul of a fallen warrior to a new body without the detrimental effects of rebirth sickness—an ability unique to the Black and brown psychic women of the Vanguard.

I smiled, noticing the possessive hand her husband Reklig had rested on her lap. Like all Scelks, he had dolphin-like skin, a few black chitin scales scattered on his shoulders, and thicker ones covering his otherwise bald head, almost in a trendy haircut. His large black eyes devoid of sclera glimmered with mischief. At the edge of the collar of his black Vanguard t-shirt, we could glimpse the claws of the bugs he had once been fusing with his host digging into his shoulders and neck.

I still couldn't fathom how such a sweet, prim, and proper young woman as Madeline had fallen in love with this fiendish Scelk. As with all the males of his species, Reklig was bloodthirsty and prone to violence. It wasn't out of malice, but just a trait that the monster who had sired me had genetically engineered into them. It still warmed my hearts that my oldest brother Bane had managed to free the Scelks from General Khutu and helped turn them into loyal members of the Vanguard instead of the mindless killers they had been created to be.

Jessica—the team's medical officer and Doom's Soulcatcher —entered the room with Thanh—our pilot—and they both took a seat across the table from us.

I didn't have a Soulcatcher of my own. Although I was an excellent warrior, just like all my other siblings, after we had escaped our father, I had given up battle to focus on medical work and research. As one of the leaders of the Vanguard, Doom had offered to have one assigned to me, but I had declined. The women joined the Vanguard to take part in the action, tag along with the Warriors on the field, and put years of training and hard work to good use. For me to take a Soulcatcher would be a punishment for her, as she would essentially be benched.

With everyone now seated around the table, Doom stood at the front of the large room to address us. While he was a genetically engineered Warrior like Reaper and I, he was a Xian whereas we were Dragons. Golden scales covered his body instead of the black chitin ones Reaper and I possessed. No crescent moon-shaped horn typical of the Kryptids adorned his forehead, unlike us. And he also had been spared the multifaceted bug eyes Dragons like me had inherited from our sire.

In more ways than one, instead of naming themselves Xian Warriors after their creator, Dr. Liang Xi, *they* should be the ones called Dragons. But my hundreds of brothers and I had taken that name because of the large percentage of Gomenzi Dragon DNA that ran through our veins. It had also been a way for us to further distance ourselves from the Kryptid genocidal maniac who had fathered us by forcing himself on the human Soulcatchers he'd abducted over the years.

"Thank you everyone for being here," Doom said in an apologetic tone. "I know that we've just returned from a long mission, and that many of you were likely looking forward to some well-deserved rest. However, there's a major shit show brewing that we need to handle."

"As you humans say, no rest for the wicked," Reklig said with a shit-eating grin.

"The wicked are indeed doing everything but resting," Doom said, looking slightly dejected. "What we uncovered on the Moon of Melibos after rescuing Janelle was only the tip of the iceberg. Wrath's team and Legion's team have discovered more treachery by some of our former allies. We're still piecing everything together, but we are now certain that many members of the Coalition have gone rogue and are plotting a retaliatory attack against Kryptor."

"But that makes no sense," Reaper said. "They know the Vanguard will not turn on the Kryptids after we shook hands in peace with them. This war lasted a hundred years. Without the genetically engineered Warriors, the Coalition would have never stood a chance. And now they want to attack Kryptor without us?"

"You would think they would know better," Doom said, "but they are sadly not stupid in their madness. The rebels were not just trying to steal the Kryptid technology from the abandoned secret bases Khutu had scattered throughout the Galaxy. They have appropriated what research they could, learned everything about it, recreated it, and sometimes enhanced it."

"How much enhancement are we talking about?" Jessica asked with a worried expression.

"Significant enhancements," I replied in a grim tone. I cast an inquisitive look at Doom, who nodded his assent for me to go into further detail. "The rebels have continued the research Khutu never got a chance to use during our war against him. So far, Wrath's and Legion's teams have run into Jadozors and Zombie Soldiers. Victoria, Liena, and I have been diligently working with both teams to find a way to defeat those creatures."

"Interesting names," Reklig said in his usual irreverent tone. "Sounds like they'll be fun to kill. But what exactly are they?"

A few members of the team snorted while Madeline looked at her mate with a 'You're hopeless' expression.

Prepared as always, Doom activated the large 3D holographic projector on the floor behind him to display a Jadozor. It resembled a pterodactyl with a narrower version of the head of a tyrannosaur.

"Thanks, Doom," I said with a smile. He nodded in response. "This is a Jadozor. That foul creature is an enlarged and enhanced version of the inoffensive silver phoenix."

"The silver phoenix is practically immortal," Jessica said in a concerned tone.

"Exactly," I replied. "Which is why father dearest brought them to the verge of extinction by experimenting on them to yield his latest abomination. Just like the silver phoenix, any time the Jadozors die or sustain injuries, a biochemical reaction takes place to regenerate in seconds all the damaged tissue and then set the heart back in motion if the creature died."

Reaper whistled through his teeth while staring at the creature in awe. "Tell me you found a way to keep them down for good."

"We have. It's still experimental, but it was effective enough to allow Wrath's team to wipe out the ones in the base they were created in," I replied.

My face heated at the sudden round of applause I received while my brother looked at me with pride.

"Thank you, but I don't have all the merit. Wrath's Medical Officer Nathalie helped a great deal, as well as Liena and Victoria."

It was Doom's turn to puff out his chest with pride. His wife, Victoria, was the Vanguard's Chief Medical Officer. And Liena, on top of being the granddaughter of Dr. Liang Xi—the creator of the Xian Warriors—she also became Doom's daughter-in-law after marrying his firstborn son, Raven.

"Stop being modest, big brother. Take credit when it's due," Reaper said, a mix of affection and teasing in his voice.

"Fine, but we're not yet so lucky with the Zombie Warriors," I replied grimly.

Doom switched the image to one of the Zombie Warriors.

"A human male?" Reklig exclaimed, his stunned expression reflected on every face around the table.

Doom shook his head. "A human clone with a similar type of mechanical brain that Marcelle had received. Except, just like our Shells, they are soulless."

"Surely you don't mean that they have their own version of Xian Warriors?!" Madeline exclaimed.

By the look of the others, they clearly wondered the same thing.

Doom smiled and once more shook his head. "No, they are not like us. They do not possess a soul that can be transferred from one Shell to the next upon death. They are merely Shells. Which is why they require a mechanical brain. You could say they are androids."

"But androids with the same regeneration abilities as the Jadozors," I added in a somber tone. "Legion's team encountered them on their mission to Strajuc. Thankfully, they were all in stasis. Legion and Dread simply ripped out the brains to disable them. But we are working on a more efficient method that can simultaneously affect them from a distance and on a larger scale."

"Do we know how many they have?" Madeline asked.

Doom shook his head. "We don't. Which is why we need a mass method to dispatch them. Unlike for our mission to the Moon of Melibos, both Wrath's and Legion's teams arrived at their bases after the rebels had already started scavenging. Wrath arrived while they were still there, but Legion got there after they had already sent a first shipment out with both Jadozor eggs and Zombie Warriors."

"So they're likely going to build a massive army of them," Reklig said pensively. "Do we know what they want?"

"They want revenge against the Kryptids," Doom said with a disgusted expression. "They are rallying their troops to mount an attack directly against Kryptor. And this is specifically why I have rounded you up here today. In two days, we will head out to Kryptor to warn them and help them prepare a defense if it comes to war."

"We're really going to fight against our former allies?" Madeline asked.

Doom gave her an apologetic look. "Hopefully, it won't come to that. We are working hard to track down the head of this rebellion and take him out."

"And with luck, the entire rebellion will fall apart," Madeline said with a nod.

"Exactly. And for those wondering why Rogue blessed us with his presence, I have asked him to join us for this mission. Aside from my Red and Liena, he is our most advanced medical expert. Since neither my mate nor Liena are combatants, it will be good to have someone with us who can help handle biohazards," Doom explained. "Our goal during this mission will be to prepare the Kryptids to face any of the crazy biotechnology the rebels may attempt to throw at them. But it will also be to keep the Kryptids from going into a pre-emptive strike or believing that we have reneged on our peace agreement."

"So I guess that's why my brothers and I worked on

expanding the holographic simulation of the principal cities of Kryptor," Reklig said.

Doom nodded. "Yes. Sorry we couldn't go into more detail when we forwarded the request to the Scelks. As you can guess, we are strictly controlling all information being spread around. We do not know who among the Coalition we can trust. Too much information has been leaked as of late, including the locations of the secret bases abandoned by Khutu. Therefore, you must keep our destination secret. We will send misinformation to the rest of the alliance to keep them in the dark about what we're doing."

"Good call," Reaper said with a glimmer of approval.

"We're leaving in two days. Be sure to take all you need for an extended leave. We may not return for weeks or even months. And use that time to learn everything you can about Kryptor. You are dismissed."

CHAPTER 2
SHURIA

I made my way to the Well of Knowledge to meet with Lekla. Access to this most sacred room for the Kryptid was strictly controlled. As an off-worlder, I was forbidden entry. That they even allowed me to know its location proved how much I had earned their trust.

Within that room, every single memory, discovery, and relevant bits of history of the Kryptids had been recorded inside small vials called conkrels. As one of the leaders of the Kryptid rebellion that had helped us finally defeat General Khutu, Lekla had a lot of memories and knowledge to be immortalized in the Well.

The frequency of her visits to the Well of late did not bode well. At eighty years of age, Lekla had reached the average maximum lifespan of the females of her species. And yet, looking at her, if not for the thickness of her chitin scales, you'd never guess she was this old.

As if to belie this thought, the doors of the Well of Knowledge parted, revealing a shockingly worn out Lekla. Her bronze chitin scales had taken on a dull hue. Her gait, usually sensual, like all female Kryptids, thanks to their narrow ant waists, now felt stiff and hesitant. Shoulders slightly slouched, Lekla gave me a tired smile, her small mandibles quivering.

As always, her multifaceted eyes made it impossible to read what thoughts were crossing her mind. However, she seemed genuinely pleased—if not relieved—to see me. That struck me as odd, considering she had telepathically requested I come meet her here. She ran a shaky hand over her Deynian horn—a much smaller version of the crescent moon-shaped horn that the male Kryptid and Dragon Warriors possessed.

"Lekla, are you okay?" I asked with a concerned expression.

She smiled. "Why so alarmed?"

I frowned and gave her a look as if she was asking an obvious question—which it was. "You look extremely weak and unwell."

She shrugged. "Of course, I do. My time has come. Walk with me."

I opened and closed my mouth a few times, wanting to argue. Of course, I knew her time would come any day now. But I was not ready to say goodbye just yet. Over the past couple of years, the female had become the closest thing that I ever had to a friend. Who would have thought that possible, considering she had been part of Khutu's efforts to turn my sisters and me into abominations who would serve his unholy war?

"I have done everything that I could to reverse what modifications they did to you," Lekla said in a calm voice, as if she had read the thoughts crossing my mind. "Another will continue to see if they can further assist you, but I doubt it at this point. I am sorry for the pain you and other Mimics have suffered because of what they did to you."

I nodded and swallowed hard. "You were merely obeying the orders of the General. You didn't owe me to try and undo any of this mess. So I am grateful for what you accomplished. In truth, I do not know that I want everything reversed," I admitted sheepishly. "The enhancements I received were not all bad. Only the premature aging for using the abilities of the creatures I morphed into posed the real problem."

"We handled it. You should no longer suffer from that negative side effect," Lekla said in that same tired voice.

She gave me the oddest sideways glance before turning back to look at where she was leading me. I had never gone to this area of the Royal Palace. Although the palace itself was built inside a spaceship, we were in the underground part, dug within Kryptor itself and above which the vessel seamlessly docked, giving the impression of a normal building when viewed from the outside.

"Meeting you, interacting with Varnog and the Xian Warriors, especially over the past year, has truly opened my eyes," Lekla said pensively. "You off-worlders are fascinating, but far too emotional."

"Emotions are great. They are the foundation of the greatest love stories, of art, of all the aspirations that drive every civilization to push forward and achieve greatness. However, they can sometimes be a weakness or make us act in stupid or irrational ways," I replied while a maelstrom of emotions surged through me.

Despite my efforts to always display a cold and in control demeanor, I was far too often overly sensitive and easily became an emotional wreck. I felt too deeply, too strongly, and reacted accordingly. The image of how I had murdered Bane flashed through my mind, and I quickly cast it out.

"The concept of love is the most intriguing of all these emotions off-worlders display," Lekla said with a wistful expression. "It is not something that Kryptids can feel."

"You can't or won't?" I asked with a sliver of challenge in my voice.

She gave me an indulgent smile as if I was a child misbehaving. "We can't. We feel kinship, respect, and admiration. We are not wired to feel jealousy or envy, least of all love. Our hive mind supersedes such emotions. The welfare of the colony and almost blind obedience to hierarchy makes it impossible for us to embrace the kind of feelings required for what I have witnessed as expressions of love between the Warriors and their mates."

"Does it sadden you that you can never experience this?" I asked in a commiserating tone.

Lekla chuckled and once again looked at me as if I'd asked something silly. "Sad? No, definitely not sad. Merely curious. You know how inquisitive Kryptid females are. Our entire existence is devoted to research, understanding how things work, pushing them further, and building things that will enhance the colony and strengthen it. I believe love would weaken us, and maybe even bring us onto a greater path of destruction than the one Khutu had taken us on over the past century. This notion of self can be quite dangerous."

I pursed my lips, pondering her words. A part of me acknowledged the merits of her logic, but the emotional side of me who understood the beautiful aspects of love—including self-love—wanted to argue. Nevertheless, I let it go knowing there would be no changing the mind of a Kryptid on that front.

"Don't you ever feel lonely? Don't you wish you had someone to share your life with?" I asked with genuine curiosity.

Lekla looked at me with confusion. "A Kryptid is never alone. I'm constantly surrounded by other Workers. I take great pride in my work, which provides me with a sense of fulfillment as I see how my contribution benefits the colony. And if you mean sexual loneliness, we have the Soldiers to 'scratch the itch' as humans say."

It was my turn to give her an odd look as we headed down yet another corridor deeper into the bowels of the underground network beneath the palace.

"Have you ever wanted something more with the Soldiers? Has there never been one whose company you sought more often and who occupied your mind at the oddest times?" I insisted.

Lekla snorted as if I had said something completely absurd. "Most certainly not! Soldiers are stupid. From the moment they are hatched, they are only trained to obey, fight, and destroy any threat to the colony. They are not trained to think. I could hold a far more interesting conversation with the membranes covering the walls and the floors of the hive than with one of our Soldiers."

"Surely they can't all be stupid?" I challenged.

"Yes, they pretty much are. Or at least, they have nothing to discuss that would be of any interest to us. On the other hand, getting to know a General might have been entertaining," she replied pensively. "They are raised to have a sharp mind, with great analytic and strategic thinking. While they do not have the technical knowledge that we females possess, we make sure they are well-rounded in psychology, science, politics, negotiations, leadership, history and, obviously, every form of combat. But their seed is not to be wasted on Workers. After all, like the Soldiers, we are sterile."

A thought I had often buried in the back of my mind resurfaced upon hearing those words. I chewed my bottom lip, wondering whether to ask the question that burned my tongue.

"What?" Lekla asked. "You have that look that says you're not daring to ask something. You should know by now that all questions are fair amongst Kryptids. Whether I answer merely depends on security clearance. Anything else is acceptable."

I scratched my nape right behind my gills, feeling slightly embarrassed about what most cultures would deem an inappropriate topic.

"I was just wondering… Do you all know which Queen and which General are your parents?" I asked.

Lekla slightly recoiled, clearly taken aback by the question. Then her face lit up with understanding. To my relief, rather than be offended, she seemed amused.

"Our society doesn't work like most others," she replied in a teasing tone. "We all know which Queen birthed us, based on the nursery in which we're raised. As for our sire, it is impossible to tell without a DNA test. The Generals take turns with the Queens to replenish their reserves of fertilized eggs and keep our gene pool strong."

"I see…" I said in a non-committal fashion.

This time, Lekla laughed, although the sound was weak in a way that broke my heart.

"By your standards, we are all siblings," Lekla conceded. "By ours, we're just Soldiers, Workers, Queens, and Generals. Can you imagine having hundreds of millions of siblings?"

I shuddered and shook my head. "No. That would be a nightmare."

Still, technically speaking, they were all siblings. But all such thoughts vanished from my mind as we approached a large set of doors at the end of the hallway we'd been walking down. While this area had been a lot less crowded than other sectors of the Royal Palace, there was still a considerable number of Kryptids entering the room, both Workers and Soldiers. It was unusual, as both casts rarely mingled since they had completely different duties.

It then struck me that none were coming out.

Kryptid hives had a perfect traffic system, whether indoors or outside. People constantly flowed in both directions, each in its respective half of the passageways. Not here…

A sense of dread washed over me as my companion began to slow down. She turned to face me with the softest expression I had ever seen from her.

"Where are we?" I asked, making no effort to hide my worry.

Lekla gave me something akin to a maternal smile. "I am tired. It is time for me to rest. Thank you for helping us save our people. Thank you for showing me your world. And thank you for this glimpse into true friendship."

My stomach knotted, and my throat tightened as the dread I

felt went up another notch. "Why do you speak like that? What are you saying?"

She smiled again and gently caressed my cheek. "You know why. Farewell, Shuria. I have reverted you the best that I could. May you find your happily ever after."

She dropped her hand and marched resolutely towards the massive doors. Too stunned to react, I stared at her in disbelief as the doors parted before her. She entered a nightmarish room where Soldiers and Workers alike were filing in the immense circular room reminded me far too much of the breeding chamber the captured Soulcatchers had been held in and forced to breed General Khutu's hybrid children, the Dragons.

An almost bright red membrane covered the entire room—which testified that it was extremely well-fed. All around the edges, unconscious Kryptids lay down on small platforms, also covered by the membrane.

Not unconscious. Dead and getting digested.

Horrified, I jerked my head towards my friend. With each step, Lekla appeared to falter more and more. Instead of standing in line with the others, she headed for a circular bench that vaguely reminded me of an upside-down mushroom.

I made to step inside the room after her, but a pair of younger female Workers stopped me.

"Do not enter. This place is for the dying only," one of the females said. "Digestive acids cover the floor," she added, pointing at it.

For the first time, I noticed its surface was indeed glistening and that the two females were wearing foot coverings. Kryptids never wore any types of clothing. My head jerked back towards Lekla. The acid had already begun discoloring the chitin that covered her feet.

"LEKLA!" I called, wanting her to come back out of that forsaken place.

"Hush, Mimic! Do not disturb the peace!" the female said sternly.

But my attention remained focused on my friend. Lekla sat down. She looked at me, smiled almost apologetically, and then closed her eyes. Seconds later, her body went limp.

"No!" I whispered, my vision blurring as I tried to silence the sobs rising in my throat.

The Workers looked at me with curiosity as if I were some strange creature.

"Why do you cry?" the Worker asked.

"What the fuck do you mean, why do I cry? My friend just died!" I shouted angrily.

The same female who had first addressed me shrugged; the same confusion still visible on her features. "We all eventually do," she replied, as if it was self-evident. "She has served her purpose."

I gaped at her in disbelief, fighting the urge to punch her impassive face and beat the crap out of her to vent my sorrow. But movement at the edge of my vision reclaimed my attention. Two other Workers, also with their feet covered and gloves on their hands, picked up Lekla and carried her to one of the empty platforms before throwing her on top of it like a bag of trash.

"Hey! Don't toss her like that!" I shouted angrily, while taking a step forward.

The youngest Worker in front of me placed a hand on my shoulder to keep me from advancing further.

"Control yourself, Mimic," she said in a tone that brooked no argument.

"Then tell them to treat Lekla with more respect!" I snapped back while tears continued to run down my cheeks.

"Respect?" she asked, visibly confused. "For what? Lekla is gone. This is not her," she added, pointing at Lekla's body that was slowly being covered by the membrane. "It is nothing but the empty vessel that once hosted her. This is organic waste being recycled."

I shook my head while looking at her in disbelief. "So that's it? After all that she has done for this colony, for your people, she dies, and now she's membrane food?" I asked while wiping my tears angrily with the back of my hand.

Both Workers looked at me with a strange expression. The annoyance faded from the youngest female, and she gave me a sympathetic smile.

"Lekla is not membrane food. Only her vessel is," she said in a soft voice. "Lekla served well, better than most. We immortalize her passage in the Well of Knowledge. That body isn't her. Stop weeping. She lived and died well. Celebrate that she existed instead of fretting over the inevitable that awaits us all."

Distraught, I turned around and walked away, fighting the tears that wouldn't stop running down my face. An overwhelming sense of loneliness, loss, and despair washed over me. Lekla's death cut me far deeper than the painful loss of a friend. It was a stark reminder that all of those I allowed myself to love always ended up leaving me.

First, it had been Silzi, my baby sister, who had convinced Khutu to use her as an infiltration agent rather than be modified like the rest of us. Sure, she had done so to look for a way to free us, but I had felt abandoned back then. I might have been the oldest, but she had always been my rock. Then Bane chose Tabitha over me. Granted, he didn't actually have a say in that. Like the Xian Warriors, Bane and his brothers didn't get to choose their mate. Their Dragon immediately recognized their soulmate the minute they were in her presence.

Bane's mating glands had never swelled for me. But foolishly, the moment Khutu had announced he would make me the Queen of his firstborn hybrid son, I had dreamed and fantasized about the future that I would have with Bane. I'd often seen him from a distance. I'd heard of the ways everyone spoke of him.

What the Soldiers mocked as weakness, I'd recognized as a generous, selfless heart. The way he had always subjected himself to the Soldiers' abuse in his brothers' stead to protect them had only made me fall even harder for him. That he had been so breathtakingly stunning with his golden blond hair and black scales had been a bonus.

If I were honest with myself, I had not been *in love* with him but with the idea of what could have been. The past year by his side, as we mounted the ultimate showdown against Khutu, had made me realize I could indeed have truly fallen in love with him. Seeing his happiness with his mate had only rubbed salt in the wound of my loneliness. To this day, I couldn't understand how he had so generously forgiven me for the terrible things I had done to him.

Next, I lost my sister Pahiven, transformed into an unspeakable abomination by Khutu's toxic seed. Most of the offspring he'd sired with her had been monsters. I had tried so hard to save the few that had been viable. But they, too, chose to find peace in death rather than succumb to the rabid madness that inevitably claimed them over time.

After the war, both Bane and Silzi had suggested I return to Khepri with them and join the Vanguard. I had declined first to help the new Kryptid Queen Xerath get her bearings. From her birth to the time we had defeated Khutu, I had served as one of her protectors. Like Lekla, she had made me feel wanted, needed, and valuable. But now that she had finally begun ruling over her people, her need of me increasingly lessened. Xerath had two strong and healthy young Generals by her side, with a couple more maturing. She'd been steadily laying perfect eggs, and her Soldier offspring were quickly replenishing her ranks.

It was only a matter of time, maybe even days before she, too, abandoned me. Like Lekla, I had served my purpose. Would I also die alone, my remains tossed like a vulgar meat sack for carrion to feed on?

I didn't really belong anywhere. A part of me wanted to crawl back to the Vanguard and see if they would take me in. But I made so many mistakes. When I'd volunteered to come to Kryptor with Queen Xerath, no one had fought to keep me on Khepri. And I couldn't blame them. Why would they want Bane's would-be murderer in their midst?

They were nice to me during the war.

But why? Was it because they'd been ordered to be? Were they merely tolerating me because I was useful to their war effort at the time?

Too many questions and too few answers fired off in my head as I meandered through the hallways of the Royal Palace's underground.

The sound of General Daeko's voice resonating in my mind startled me.

"We've received a message from the Vanguard. A small team is approaching and has requested permission to land. They should be here in less than an hour. Join us in the Queen's chamber at your earliest convenience."

"Understood," I mind-spoke back to him.

CHAPTER 3
SHURIA

Why in the world would the Vanguard come to Kryptor? Why had they not warned me of their impending visit? More importantly, Daeko hadn't questioned me about their possible motive. He also hadn't seemed distraught by this impromptu drop by. Had he known they were on their way here? If so, why had he not told me?

A million thoughts bubbled through my head, far too many of them negative and feeding my growing paranoia. As I was about to head for the Queen's chamber, I absentmindedly wiped the tears still dampening my face.

I can't let the Queen or the Vanguard see me in this state.

My worth to both the Kryptids and the Vanguard had been based on my image of strength, efficiency, and reliability. I was already standing on far too shaky ground to display the distress I currently felt. While the Vanguard might empathize with my loss, as the Workers had so clearly displayed moments ago, mourning a friend would be deemed irrational by the Kryptids.

I hurried back to my quarters not only to give myself an additional moment to grieve but also to freshen up and regain my composure. In a strange way, thinking of Lekla gave me the strength I needed. She had not always understood me, but she had respected me and genuinely wanted the best for me. I didn't know when or how, but I would find a way to make her final wish for me come true: I would get my happily ever after.

I slipped on my black leather suit, which could be used both for training and combat. It gave me a more intimidating appearance and helped boost my confidence. Thankfully, my eyes had not puffed too much. Like all Mimics, I didn't have any visible pupils or sclera. Where the Xian Warriors had entirely black eyes, ours were a silver-gray shade that vaguely resembled a stormy sky. Unlike humans, crying didn't give them the type of redness that would betray the sorrow I felt.

Thirty minutes had already gone by since Daeko had summoned me. I hurried back to the Queen's Chamber so that I could at least assess my hosts' stance before the Vanguard arrived. As I approached the room, I couldn't help but notice the number of Queen's Guards posted before the chamber had tripled from the normal number. It didn't bode well that they would suspect potential foul play from their incoming guests. While I held absolutely no trust in most of the species part of the Galactic Coalition, I would never doubt the word of the Vanguard. Had something soured the bond they formed with the Kryptids when they had helped rescue Queen Xerath?

The guards opened the heavy doors to let me in. Once more, as I stepped inside the chamber, a single look at my surroundings reminded me that, contrary to most other planets and cultures, everything about the Kryptids boiled down to efficiency. Hierarchy was merely defined by role and purpose. They wasted no time, energy, or resources to the ostentatious pomp world leaders embraced everywhere else. Beyond the fact that they never really received any foreign guests on Kryptor, they failed to see the point. They didn't have any currencies or concept of wealth.

Everyone had equal access to everything and anything they needed. However, most of their needs came down to whatever helped them fulfill their purpose within the colony.

The membrane fully covered the large and circular room. It could be found in almost every area of any Kryptid construction. After so much time spent living amongst them, it no longer creeped me out. The organic tissue that covered the floor and the walls allowed them to keep their dwellings clean. Slightly cushiony, but thankfully not wet or slimy, it ingurgitated any organic waste that would fall on it. Inedible waste would also be absorbed but transferred to the proper waste management area of the palace, eliminating the need for cleaning.

While the membrane couldn't be deemed sentient per se, it possessed several instinctive behaviors for self-preservation, self-maintenance, and the ability to differentiate between a dead body to be consumed and merely a wounded person to be left alone. It was a similar membrane that was consuming the remains of my friend when I left that death chamber.

Overhead, a ventilation membrane covered the ceiling. Although it had a similar reddish burgundy hue as the floor membrane, this one was pockmarked with countless little holes that behaved like the alveoli of a lung. This membrane recycled the air, ensured it maintained the proper oxygen levels, and could cleanse and filter any toxin or poison inside the room. Nonetheless, the musty scent typical of the membrane still permeated the space. In strategic areas of the ceiling, large wart-like protrusions served as organic light sources.

The only other elements present in the room were the large windows around one half of the walls. Even they were not made of glass, but out of a thin yet extremely sturdy translucent membrane. At the back, Queen Xerath stood regally with General Daeko to her right and Commander Hulax, leader of her Queen's Guard, on her left.

"There you are," Xerath said with a slightly disapproving tone when she saw me enter. "I thought you were not going to grace us with your presence."

I plastered a neutral expression on my face, pleased that I did not let them see me flinch.

"Apologies. I had a meeting with Lekla. I didn't realize she was taking me to the death chamber. As I had never been there before, I got a little turned around."

"I take it she has passed then?" Xerath asked matter-of-factly.

"Yes," I replied, proud that my voice didn't shake.

The Queen nodded. "It was her time. She served well."

I forced myself to rein in the anger blossoming inside me upon hearing the factual, almost dismissive way in which she spoke those words. If not for Lekla, she wouldn't be here today. Like her predecessors, she would have been ruined by General Khutu's toxic seed, and Daeko would have been membrane food months ago.

This is their way. Lekla is not dismissed. They merely accept the reality of her passing.

I would need to remind myself of this often in the upcoming days.

"She did, as was her duty," I replied in a similar tone. "But I understand the Vanguard is approaching," I continued, wanting to move away from this sore topic to avoid the possibility of me falling apart before them. "Do you know the purpose of their visit?"

"We do," Daeko replied in the Queen's stead, confirming what I had feared. "They're coming to warn us of an attack their allies are mounting against Kryptor."

I recoiled, this time making no effort to hide the genuine shock I felt upon hearing his words. By the way Queen Xerath's shoulders slightly slouched, I realized with even greater shock that relief had prompted this reaction. She had wondered if I had been aware of the threat and kept silent about it. What had I ever done for her to doubt my loyalty?

"The Coalition is coming to attack Kryptor?" I repeated in disbelief.

"Not the Coalition," Daeko conceded. "It appears that, after the war ended, many Coalition soldiers and military leaders defected to form a rebel army. Like the Vanguard, we have been tracking down all of Khutu's abandoned research bases, but only within Kryptid space. Many have been scavenged, but not by us. The Vanguard leaders warned us to be on the lookout for rogue attacks."

"But why would they attack Kryptor? It makes no sense," I argued. "The Coalition has been spoiling for peace for decades. Why jeopardize it now that we finally achieved it?"

"For revenge," Xerath said with a sliver of contempt in her voice. "Off-worlders are irrational and controlled by their emotions. We witnessed quite a bit of that during the war with some of them racing into battle against impossible odds merely out of rage that one of their kin got killed. What good does that serve when all they accomplish is getting themselves killed as well? And now they're coming to attack us because they are angry they suffered losses and casualties during the war? Their solution is more bloodshed?"

I groaned inwardly, cursing the rebels for their stupidity. I understood the desire for revenge. Wars were never pretty. Too many innocents died because of the hunger for power of a handful. The need to lash out, to make someone pay or answer for our losses and suffering was something I could relate to. But I also acknowledged that it wasn't a solution.

"While I cannot speak for those who have rebelled, I can see why some planets might want to retaliate," I said cautiously. "Some species, like mine, are on the verge of extinction because of all the experiments Khutu performed on us. Some actually are extinct or have so few members left that the odds of rebuilding their societies are slim to none. There isn't enough DNA left to recreate a viable population. These people have nothing to lose. And when they look at the Kryptids casually rebuilding, now that the dictator is gone, they probably feel betrayed and like your entire species got off too easy."

"Is that how you feel?" Daeko asked with a challenge in his voice.

This time I did not try to hide my anger. "Remember thanks to whom you're still standing here. When Khutu came to capture Xerath and kill you, it was under my command that my sisters took you and the others to safety. It was *I* who ventured with the Vanguard inside this very palace to save the Queen. If I wanted to destroy the Kryptid society, I would have done it a long time ago. Don't you dare question my honor and loyalty."

"It is my duty to question everything and everyone," Daeko said, showing no signs of shame or remorse. "If you were a Kryptid, you would know better than to let your emotions perceive that question as an insult. Our people are barely recovering from our own near extinction. As the Queen's Primary General, I must account for every risk to her and to the colony. So yes, that includes questioning your stance and everyone else's."

I clenched my teeth, properly chastised. Naturally, I knew better. My wretched temper had a tendency of getting the best of me.

"And that brings us to the Vanguard," Daeko continued in the same firm but calm fashion. "We have to question their motive for coming here."

I couldn't help but roll my eyes. "Look, I understand that you're taking your protector role very seriously, but this is ridiculous. The Vanguard has proven time and again that they are honorable and will not break their word. They agreed to peace with the Kryptids. If they meant to renege on their word, why warn you of the imminent threat?"

"They did warn us, but why come here?" Xerath asked.

"To help you, of course," I exclaimed, disbelievingly. "You mentioned a single vessel is approaching. This is not an army here to attack you but merely a delegation likely seeking to also mediate the situation. They protected your civilian population, your Soldiers who merely followed orders, and your species as a whole from the massive attack the Galactic Coalition had initially planned to take out Khutu. Similarly, it is fair to assume they want the same for the rebels who allowed themselves to be conned into this insane retaliation, and their respective planets who do not want to get dragged into this mess."

"You're defending them quite fiercely," Daeko said, narrowing his multifaceted eyes at me. "While I do not challenge the veracity of your initial statement and the validity of your assumptions, how do we know this is indeed their intention? How do we know they haven't reconsidered since then?"

"Why would they?" I asked, genuinely baffled.

"As you well know, like the hybrids, the Xian Warriors have a substantial percentage of Gomenzi Dragon blood. It makes them extremely loyal to those they consider as their people. This was the specific reason General Khutu created his hybrid sons thinking they would be blindly loyal to him. As proven by history, the hybrids and the Xians identify first and foremost with humans when it comes to loyalty," Daeko said, while both the Queen and Commander Hulax nodded. "Now that humans—among others—are turning against us, the Warriors will be forced to choose a side. Whose side do you believe that will be?"

I nodded slowly, finally understanding where they were coming from. While I disagreed with their conclusion, I couldn't deny the merit of their suspicions.

"Although you are correct in stating that both the hybrids and the Xians genetically feel an extremely strong bond with humans, they do not blindly obey that instinct. Stronger still is their need to protect the weak and the *innocent*. In this instance, the Kryptids may not be weak, but you are innocent of any wrongdoing. The rebels are violating the peace agreement that both sides freely entered into," I countered passionately. "Do not doubt for a minute that the Warriors of the Vanguard will literally give their lives to ensure peace and limit the number of casualties on all sides. They gave you their word, and they will honor it so long as you hold to your end of the bargain."

"Let us hope you are correct in this, Shuria," Queen Xerath said, folding both sets of her four hands in front of her. "Your counsel prior to and during the war has proven invaluable and accurate. We will give your Warriors the benefit of the doubt. But should we find out they are coming here as moles or to destroy us from within, we *will* obliterate them."

Despite the obvious threat of her statement, my stupid mind remained stuck on her far too rare acknowledgement of the value of my past performances, the praise warming me from within.

"I swore I'd do everything in my power to make sure you would reign free of Khutu's threat so that you could restore your people to their former glory," I said, lifting my chin proudly. "Nothing and no one will make a liar or oath breaker out of me."

I didn't know what response I had expected from the Queen, but certainly not for her face to soften the way it did. Her small mandibles quivered as her oddly human mouth stretched into an almost maternal smile. It was all the stranger that she was in many ways still a child, being merely a few weeks over a year old.

"Whatever treachery may or may not come from the Vanguard, you have proven your loyalty to me repeatedly, Shuria. I do trust you without any reservation."

My throat tightened, and I bowed my head in acknowledgement of her words, not trusting my voice not to tremble if I attempted to respond. However, Daeko stiffening spared me from answering.

"The Vanguard spaceship has entered our atmosphere. They will be here any minute now," Daeko said, with a subtle but undeniable tension in his voice.

The Queen gestured with her lower set of hands for me to approach. It flattered me as it clearly implied she wanted to display to the Vanguard that she deemed to me one of her close advisers. However, a nagging little voice at the back of my head couldn't help but wonder if it wasn't also a way of warning them against any attempt to use me as an informant.

The seconds stretched into minutes while my companions remained silent, at least in appearance. But the intense psychic energy swirling around the Queen, General Daeko, and Commander Hulax made it clear they were communicating, probably strategizing as to how they intended to respond to whatever the Vanguard would deliver as a message. It stung, considering the declaration of trust Xerath had just expressed to me moments prior. It also reiterated the sad reality that my time in their midst was ending.

The doors finally parted, revealing which team they had sent. I had wondered if Chaos—one of the two faces of the Vanguard and the most diplomatic of the Xian Warriors—would have come to handle this situation. Seeing Doom instead slightly took me aback. While he was undoubtedly the most talented Warrior among the Xians—having earned a reputation of being nearly unkillable, if not invincible—diplomacy had never been his strong suit. Or rather, he had always preferred the excitement of the battlefield over political mind games.

Like all the genetically engineered Xian Warriors, he was stunning, with jet black hair, oversized pitch-black eyes devoid of any sclera, and a tall, muscular body entirely covered in golden dragon scales.

My gaze skimmed over the human females who accompanied him. Each one beautiful in her own way, smart, highly skilled, and fearless. I couldn't help the envy they always stirred within me. Under different circumstances, I could have been one of them instead of the pariah failed experiment of General Khutu.

For a brief second, I locked eyes with Reklig. The Scelks remained the question mark for me. Although they had proven their loyalty to the Vanguard over the past year leading to the final war against the General, their powerful ability to read anyone's thoughts without their knowledge, and even mind controlling them was terrifying. Worse still, once they reached full maturity—which was Reklig's case—psychic disruptors no longer worked against them.

By the taunting smile that stretched his lips, I had no doubt he had guessed what thought had just crossed my mind.

Or did he read it?

I wanted to believe he would honor the code of ethics the Vanguard had imposed as a condition to them joining their ranks. Scelks were not to read other people's minds against their will, unless in the case of a sanctioned interrogation.

Shifting my gaze away from him, my heart lurched at the sight of the two Dragons in the delegation. Although neither had Bane's golden mane, for a split second I thought it had been him. But I recognized Reaper's mischievously handsome face, and then his brother Rogue. My heart soared. Of all the Dragons, Rogue had always been the nicest one, showing me unexpected kindness on a few occasions during the war.

The warm smile I had begun expressing for him froze on my lips when our eyes met. He recoiled then a shocked, almost horrified expression descended on his youthful features. Rogue stopped dead in his tracks and stared at me in disbelief. Utterly confused, I glanced down at myself, wondering what could have prompted such a strong reaction. Finding nothing unusual, I looked back up at him. Reaper had also stopped to look questioningly at his brother. Rogue swallowed hard, shook his head as if to say 'nothing', then resumed walking.

He cast a baffled glance my way, looking like he was trying to make sense of something that made none, then turned his attention to the Queen.

What the fuck just happened?

CHAPTER 4
ROGUE

Shock and disbelief warred within me. When we first entered the palace, I had tried to silence the discomfort triggered by being surrounded by walls covered in membranes. It brought back too many terrible memories, especially of our mothers ensnared by the breeding membrane for decades to the point that parts of their bodies had all but fused with it.

My mating glands painfully swelling as soon as I entered the Queen's Chamber swept away all such grim thoughts.

There was no question in my mind that Shuria had triggered this reaction. But how? She wasn't human. So far, all my brothers' and all the Xian Warriors' soulmates had been human. Moreover, I met Shuria for the first time over three years ago. We had been around each other on multiple occasions during the entire year that led to the final showdown against my father. Not once in that entire time did my mating glands awaken for her. Why now? What could possibly have changed? Was I somehow defective?

I had been looking forward to seeing how Shuria had been faring since coming to live with the Kryptids. Along with Victoria and Liena, I had worked tirelessly to try to revert some of the modifications she and her surviving sisters had undergone at the hand of the General. I had hoped to be able to give Silzi some positive news about her sister. Now, all I could think about was figuring out what could be happening.

I couldn't decide if fear or excitement dominated within me. While I had always found Shuria stunning, I never gave it further thought as my Dragon had not responded to her. For too long, I commiserated with Reaper's sorrow as he pined after Linette with his glands refusing to swell for her. I had sworn never to allow myself to care for a female that I could never be with.

Obviously, I wanted to believe I had finally found my soulmate. However, the medical doctor and scientist in me could not merely give into wishful thinking. Such a long delay before my Dragon acknowledged her as my perfect partner contradicted all the established norms. Until I could find a logical explanation to this, I had to seriously consider the possibility that I was somehow defective, or that some external factor was triggering this reaction from me.

"Doom, we meet again," Queen Xerath said in a polite tone.

She stood at the back of the room, looking regal with her black chitin scales slightly tinged with red. Unlike the other females of her species, who were all sterile and walked on two legs like us, the queen had three sets of legs on her lower body vaguely reminiscent of that of a spider. Her upper torso though greatly resembled that of a human female except for the two sets of arms. Like all Kryptids, she had sensuous human looking lips framed by a small pair of mandibles. Two tiny holes served as her nose, and she stared at us with a large pair of multifaceted eyes similar to ours, but hers slanted in a far more vertical position than our horizontal eyes. Where we had a single crescent moon-shaped horn on our foreheads, the Queen had an ornate double set.

By the way her swollen belly at her back quivered, I could tell she had detached from the egg sack she'd been laying with to come address us. She would likely want to keep this short and sweet to return to her duty. That suited me just fine as the swelling in my throat made me feel on the verge of choking.

"Queen Xerath, General Daeko, Commander Hulax," Doom replied politely as a greeting to each of our hosts, "thank you for receiving us. Shuria, it is great to see you looking so well."

The three Kryptids nodded in response while Shuria gave Doom a friendly smile before her gaze flicked back to me. I felt horrible for the instinctive way in which I had reacted to seeing her. The poor female had been taken aback by it. I would have to find a way to apologize for it. But until I understood better what was going on, it would be best not to let her know for fear of misleading her if I was truly broken.

That shame was further compounded by the instinctive unease I always felt in the presence of Daeko. I had no problem with the male himself—he was in every way the perfect Kryptid General. However, his physical resemblance to my sire knotted my insides. All sterile males—the Soldiers—had reddish-brown chitin scales, three fingers per hand, and a single crescent moon Deynian horn similar to ours. But Generals were bigger, broader, with a twin set of Deynian horns, five fingers, and thicker black chitin scales.

"I believe you have met all the members of my team during the war," Doom continued.

"We have," Daeko replied, his gaze gliding over us before settling on Reklig. "We see you've brought a mature Scelk as well. I'm guessing it is not because your breed has reconsidered the Queen's invitation to join us?" he added, this time addressing Reklig directly.

I groaned inwardly, his underlying meaning less-than-subtle.

"The Scelks certainly have not, and least of all me," Reklig replied with that eternal taunting hint in his voice. "Besides the fact that we're quite satisfied with the Vanguard, I am also very happily mated to this beautiful female," Reklig added while casting an affectionate glance at Madeline. "She's the only one I will ever couple with."

"I see," the Queen replied, while giving Madeline an assessing look.

Stoic as ever, Madeline held the Queen's gaze unwaveringly, her chin ever-so-slightly lifting with a hint of defiance.

"As for your underlying question, General Daeko," Reklig continued, "I would tell you to give me a psychic disruptor to reassure you that I'm not here to read your minds, but as you well know, they do not work on mature Scelks."

"I'm sure a Worker's touch would be effective even on a mature Scelk," Daeko retorted, a clear challenge in his voice.

Reklig's spine stiffened while the rest of us tensed. Even the Queen seemed slightly stunned by her General's comment, an emotion she quickly hid. A Worker could indeed lengthen her fingers into sharp needles that could inject a variety of chemicals she could produce at will, or to directly affect certain nervous centers. One of them had used such a method to connect directly to the brain of Varnog during the last battle against Khutu to block his psychic abilities. Aside from the cerebral and psychic bruising such methods caused, we couldn't truly know what else the Worker could be doing to his mind during that time.

"Judging by their reaction, it is fair to say they had not expected you to make such a suggestion, General," Shuria said in a reasonable tone. "So clearly, Reklig has not been reading our minds. Anyway, if he meant to do so, I'm sure he would have already plundered them by now," she added with a shrug.

"Had that been my intention, then yes, that would indeed be the case," Reklig replied, his voice slightly clipped. "But I did not. You are not our enemies."

I fought the urge to give Shuria a psychic nudge as a thank you for fear the Kryptids would perceive the psychic energy flowing between us and interpret this innocent exchange as proof of foul play or that she was somehow in cahoots with us. By their cold and distant demeanor, the blind trust they once shared with us had clearly waned.

"As you say, Shuria, if it was his intention, it is already done," Queen Xerath said with a sliver of annoyance. "So why are you here, Doom? You already warned us of the impending threat."

"We are here to provide assistance against the rebels," Doom replied calmly.

"Why?" General Daeko demanded. "Do you believe us unable to repel this invasion on our own?"

"Truth be told, we don't know whether you can," Doom said matter-of-factly. "We are still assessing the extent of their abilities. And we do not know just how much you have recovered from the damage that Khutu's madness has wreaked on your people. All that we know is that we entered into a peace agreement with the Kryptids. So far, you have honored your word. We intend to do the same."

"You would fight against your own allies to help us?" Daeko further challenged.

"The rebels are not our allies," Doom said in a tone that brooked no argument. "They are defectors and traitors. While some of them are ill-advised or have been lied to, others are fanatics that cannot be reasoned with and who will stop at nothing until blood is shed. The former, we will try to convince to stand down. The latter, we will obliterate."

By the triumphant expression Shuria cast at the General and then the Queen, subtle though it was, I immediately guessed she had already given them similar arguments. Psychic energy flowed between Daeko, Xerath, and Hulax.

"What makes you believe they are fanatics?" Queen Xerath asked.

"My team and a few others have run into some of the rebels scavenging Khutu's research, as well as enhancing some of it into lethal weapons they intend to unleash on your homeworld,"

Doom explained. "We have now identified Giles Dalton as the supreme leader of the rebels. The same way Khutu misled your people into a senseless war, Giles is lying to the rebels only to serve his own ambitions. We want to avoid, or at least limit, casualties on all sides and, if possible, find a peaceful resolution. We protected Kryptor while hunting Khutu, please give us a chance to protect the redeemable rebels while we hunt Dalton."

"What exactly do you propose?" General Daeko asked, his tone non-committal. "If they come here, we *will* defend ourselves."

"We do not seek to pry into your defenses. We just want to warn you of the rebels' new weapons and help you to counter them," Doom said before gesturing at me. "Rogue is one of our best scientific minds. He has been working on countermeasures for the rebels' new creatures we've encountered so far. He will share what knowledge we have acquired and help devise methods for you to integrate this technology to your own defenses."

Commander Hulax nodded with a glimmer of approval. More psychic energy flowed between him and the General.

"We would indeed be interested in this sharing of knowledge," Daeko conceded.

"It is poetic justice that Khutu's illegal sons turned against him and allied with the colony," Queen Xerath said, her eyes brimming with the hate she still bore my sire.

"He thought our Gomenzi Dragon blood would earn him our loyalty or that, failing that, the Kryptid hive mind would control us. But we do not have a hive mind, and our Dragon bonded with our mothers during gestation."

"It is both a blessing and a shame," the Queen replied, pensively. "These traits freed you from Khutu but also make you unfit for us."

I smiled with pretend commiseration. My brothers and I wanted nothing to do with joining the Kryptids any more than the Scelks did. Still, it was a great compliment that the Queen even contemplated that possibility. By rights, the Queen's Guard should have executed us on sight merely for existing. A General was forbidden from spending his seed with anyone but a fully mature Kryptid Queen.

"The rest of us have tactical and technological knowledge we will share as we discover more about what the rebels are up to. We are in constant contact with the other leaders of the Vanguard, and especially with a few ongoing recovery missions," Doom said. "Some of the new experiments that we've discovered so far are quite disturbing. We can go over them with you first thing in the morning."

I repressed a smile at the less-than-subtle way Doom reminded them we had indeed landed late. We had considered delaying our arrival to land at a reasonable hour in the morning, but time was of the essence. Based on the latest reports from Wrath's and Legion's teams, an attack seemed imminent. Chaos's team should reach their own secret base in the next few days. I dreaded what new abominations they would find there.

"Yes. You must be tired from your long journey. We will let you rest and reconvene in the morning," Queen Xerath said, shifting on her legs as her overflowing abdomen quivered with more intensity. "Shuria and Commander Hulax will escort you to your quarters."

For a brief second, Shuria appeared confused. Psychic energy flowed between Xerath and her, after which Shuria nodded very subtly. My hearts leapt at that news. I couldn't decide if I was more excited than panicked at the thought of talking to her before having the time to assess my current situation.

Taking the lead, Commander Hulax gestured for us to follow him. The Queen headed for a hidden passage at the back of the room, which undoubtedly led to her birthing chamber. By the relieved expression on her face, this couldn't have come soon enough.

As Shuria came closer, my airways nearly shut down from the pressure of my glands further swelling. A choked sound escaped me. I opened my mouth to swallow a big gulp of air. For a split second, I considered partially summoning a mouth dart as it automatically distended our throats so that we could spit it out. However, swallowing it back down could be extremely unpleasant. And spitting it out, even in a non-threatening way, would probably not sit well with our already suspicious hosts.

"*Your neck is swollen, brother! Your glands have awakened? Who?*"

Reaper's psychic voice in my head startled the heck out of me. I'd been so focused on my physiological response to Shuria that I utterly failed to hide my surprise, drawing my team's attention. I smiled reassuringly, my chin lowered to hide my neck.

"*Never mind that. There's something wrong with me,*" I replied telepathically to my brother.

"*What do you mean by that? Are you ill? Is—?*"

"*Reaper! Drop it. Not now!*" I snapped.

This time, my brother's back stiffened. Although he kept a neutral expression, I could feel his confusion and worry as he disconnected from my mind. I felt like a complete jerk. Reaper and I never fought. He was a gentle soul. Mischievous and playful, but never mean or stubborn. I often felt he should have been the physician as he possessed such empathy and charisma. But he loved to battle, and his prowess as a Warrior made him a force to be reckoned with.

I sighed inwardly, having yet another person to apologize to for my odd behavior. This was so unlike me. Clearly something was wrong with me. I gave Reaper a psychic nudge. He immediately returned it, letting me know he wasn't mad. But worry permeated it.

To both my dismay and utter relief, Shuria walked past me and adjusted her pace to match Doom's. The most irrational wave of jealousy surged through me as I watched them engage in a friendly conversation. As much as I wanted her attention on me, this small distance between us helped me breathe better.

To my shame, I caught myself ogling her. My gaze wandered over her slender body, the sensuous way her hips flared, their enticing sway as she walked, the firm and round mounds of her behind, and her sexy long legs. She had bound her midnight blue hair in a ponytail. The image of me freeing it before running my fingers through the silky strands flashed through my mind. I wondered if they would be as soft as her pale blue skin always appeared to be.

My steps faltered as I realized what inappropriate thoughts were coursing through my mind. To my shock, the expected nauseous feeling didn't strike me. Our Gomenzi Dragon blood made it impossible for us to lust after any female other than our soulmate. Any covetous thought or sexual interaction with anyone other than the woman meant for us caused serious physical discomfort and even pain.

And yet, I feel no such symptoms, only a powerful attraction.

Could she truly be my soulmate? All the signs were there, but it didn't make sense. Why now? Casting all these questions I wouldn't be able to answer aside, I focused on the conversation she was having with Doom.

"Silzi and your other sisters will be thrilled to hear about how well you are faring, and especially to see you again," Doom said in that gentle, almost paternal way he sometimes spoke.

Despite looking no older than my own thirty years of age, Doom was nearly sixty-five now, and his wisdom shone brightly through his obsidian eyes. The emotional expression that flitted over Shuria's face took me by surprise.

She smiled and nodded. "It will be good to see them again. The Kryptids have done a wonderful job of healing me."

"Healing you?" I interjected, my curiosity, both personal and professional, skyrocketing. I moved closer to them, ignoring the tightening of my throat again.

Shuria slightly frowned as she gave me a strange look over her shoulder. "Yes. Before dying, Lekla reversed what they did to me."

I recoiled in shock. "Reversed? How? To what extent? What—?"

"Whoa! Calm down," Shuria said with a 'What's your damage?' expression. "Those are pretty personal questions."

I flinched and gave her a sheepish smile. "My apologies. I don't mean to pry. It's just that I've been working with Liena and Victoria in trying to help revert what was done to your sisters as well. So I got a bit carried away when you said there has been some success in your case."

Another strange expression crossed Shuria's lovely features, this time laced with what looked like disappointment. She turned her face away from me as if to hide what thoughts or emotions bubbled inside her.

"Right… Have *you* met any success?" she asked, ignoring my previous flurry of questions.

"Much less than what I would like," I conceded. "I would be honored if you would tell me more about your current situation and even more if you would consider letting me examine you. But I understand if you aren't comfortable with that."

Shuria hesitated for a moment, her stormy eyes locking with mine for a brief instant that felt like an eternity. "Okay. If you want…"

I beamed at her, the oddest—but most pleasant—sensation awakening in the pit of my stomach.

She gave me a strange look then abruptly turned to look ahead again.

"Commander Hulax," Doom called out. "Our Creckel friends are aboard the vessel. We didn't bring them down as we didn't know what welcome awaited us."

"Yes, we are aware. Arrangements have been made to house them as well," Commander Hulax replied. "We can go take care of them now if you wish while Shuria takes your team to their quarters."

"Yes, that would be great," Doom replied.

Our team leader gave us a 'behave' look—which had Reklig smiling evilly—before he left with the Commander of the Queen's Guard. Walking side by side with Shuria, the rest of the team following us, we let her lead us.

CHAPTER 5
SHURIA

Feeling a little awkward, I took the members of the Vanguard to their respective quarters. I'd never been one to get easily intimidated, so this clumsy behavior from me made no sense. Words failed me. I wished one of them would say something or ask a question, preferably not about my current level of freakiness.

Shame filled me the minute that thought crossed my mind. Beyond any possible genuine concerns he might have for my well-being—not that I believed he did—Rogue had valid reasons to want to know about my health. Based on the messages Silzi had been sending me, the Vanguard's medical experts were really doing everything in their power to help my sisters who had been modified like me.

"How do you like living among the Kryptids," Rogue suddenly asked, taking me out of my misery.

"It's okay, if highly predictable," I said with a shrug. "If you want a drama-free life, this is the place. Everyone has a purpose and sticks to it. If you need to party, socialize, or do any type of cultural activities, you'll be sorely disappointed."

Rogue snorted while nodding. "Right. I remember all too

well what workaholics they are. I always wondered if it was just the Kryptids working in Khutu's secret bases or if it was the same here on Kryptor."

"It's very much the same," I said factually. "They consider entertainment as we define it as a waste of time. Every minute should be productive in one form or another."

"Sheesh. Do they feel guilty about having to sleep?" Madeline asked.

I shook my head. "No. Sleep is productive because it allows their bodies to perform properly the next day and maintain their productivity. They take power naps at specific intervals and eat high-protein meals three times a day. Even coupling is considered productive."

"What?" Reklig exclaimed. "You're talking about the Queen now, right?"

I chuckled. "No. The Workers and Soldiers couple from time to time."

"But they're sterile. How is that being productive?" Jessica asked with genuine curiosity.

"Well, when they get too horny, it's harder for them to focus. So they grab the first available Soldier to scratch that itch," I said, trying to sound nonchalant, while my throat tightened remembering my conversation about this with Lekla, not knowing she was minutes away from dying. "Their climax releases hormones that increase their productivity."

"You mean they have sex, climax, and run straight back to work?" Reklig asked, disbelieving.

"Yes," I said as we entered the 'unfinished' extension I had settled in. "Kryptids don't cuddle. They do not feel love the way we do. Sex is just a physical activity that serves a purpose."

"Well damn," Jessica whispered.

"No membrane?" Rogue asked, while glancing around us.

I smiled, relieved about the change of topic. "Yes, this area was meant to be an extension of the palace where Khutu intended to keep us, his Mimic Queens. They never finished it once he realized the experiments on us weren't yielding the result he had hoped for. When I came to settle on Kryptor, I requested to have my quarters here. I've never been comfortable at the thought of sleeping in a room covered with flesh-eating membranes."

"You and me both," Rogue said with a disgusted look that made me smile.

"Well, that will make Janelle happy," Reaper said.

"Janelle?" I asked.

"My mate. She's with the Creckels right now. She was trapped inside one of Khutu's secret labs for twenty years," Reaper explained. "They were starving and being stalked by what remained of the membrane. Had we arrived two or three days later, it would have been too late for her."

"Wow," I whispered. "What a tragedy that would have been. She must be extremely strong to have survived such an ordeal and remained sane."

Reaper puffed out his chest proudly. "She is. Janelle looks fragile, but she possesses incredible inner strength. And she's insanely smart. Her parents died when she was twelve. Despite that, she became a competent scientist on her own and is an expert in the Creckel language."

I silenced the powerful pang of envy that coursed through me. What I wouldn't give for someone to speak of me with such possessive pride.

"Impressive," I said with a smile. "Well here you are. These are your quarters," I added, gesturing at a door on the left. "If you need anything, do not hesitate to tell me. Please note that there is no locking mechanism. The Kryptids don't need to lock doors. Theft and crime aren't a thing with hive minds."

"That's different," Rogue said. "There were tons of locks everywhere in our sire's secret bases. But then we were all his prisoners."

Reaper nodded. "That we were. Thank you, Shuria."

"My pleasure. My own quarters are at the end of the corridor. Feel free to knock or message my com."

"Will do," Reaper answered before entering his quarters.

I smiled and led the rest of the team down the hallway, pointing each of them to their respective rooms, Rogue being last.

"Daeko is having a laboratory set up for you. It should be ready in the morning. If there's anything specific you need transferred from your ship, we can assist you with that task tomorrow, once you've rested," I said, sounding like the perfect host.

"Thank you," Rogue replied before swallowing painfully as I was about to leave.

I hesitated, my gaze zeroing in on his throat. My eyes widened as I finally noticed it was unusually swollen.

"Are you okay?" I asked.

He shifted on his feet, looking mightily uncomfortable. "Yes, don't mind me. I'm just tired from the trip and a little freaked out to be here on Kryptor."

"Right," I replied, making no effort to hide my dubious tone.

My eyes flicked to his neck again. This time, his skin darkened—a confession in and of itself. My heart instantly tightened with envy. Like his brothers, Rogue was stunning. From all my interactions with him, he'd always been gentle, respectful, and protective. Whoever the female was who had prompted this response from him, she was a lucky girl.

But why separate quarters?

She had to be one of his team members. I mentally reviewed the females who had been with us. Reklig had already claimed Madeline. The two of them became a couple at the start of the final war with Khutu. That left Jessica and Martha. Considering how long both had been part of the Vanguard, why had he not claimed her yet? The trip from Khepri to Kryptor alone had taken three weeks, which was plenty of time for him to have made his move.

Could his soulmate already be taken?

"Well then, I won't hold you up any longer," I said in an apologetic tone, silencing my wandering thoughts. "Rest well. I'll see you in the morning. Goodnight, Rogue."

"Goodnight, Shuria. It is *really good* to see you this well," Rogue said in a strange tone.

More confused than ever, I took my leave and headed to my own quarters a few doors down.

∾

The next morning, I rose early and gathered the Vanguard crew in an improvised cafeteria I had the Workers set up for them. Although it was yet another unfinished room, it was clean and bright, with a wide view of the rather arid landscape of Kryptor.

Everything on this planet was orange or beige, with sand and rocky formations all over the place. During my stay here, I'd explored enough to find the rare locations that could qualify as an oasis. This planet would never win any tourist award.

"I apologize for not offering you as fancy a meal as the ones you could get from your ship, but this is fairly decent replicated food," I said, gesturing at the breakfast trays I had prepared.

"Replicated?" Doom asked.

I pointed out the device on the counter of the square room I had selected. "This is my personal replicator. There isn't an official cafeteria or mess hall for you because I normally eat in my own quarters. Therefore, I moved my replicator here so that you can all have access to it whenever you wish."

"That's quite generous of you," Doom said. "But surely the Kryptids have different accommodations."

I snorted and gave him an amused look. "They do, but I can

assure you that you *do not* wish to be fed standard Kryptid food. Every single meal is the same disgusting 'porridge' regurgitated by the membrane."

"Oh, fuck that goop!" Rogue exclaimed.

"Fuck no!" Reaper said almost at the same time as his brother.

Reklig cringed and looked at me with a revolted expression.

"It can't be *that* bad," teasingly said the beautiful and delicate female with silver white hair that had been introduced to me as Janelle.

Reaper scrunched his face at his mate. "Okay, fine, you had it worse in that base, but that porridge was still dreadful. I'm going to have nightmares thinking about it."

I couldn't help but laugh at his overly traumatized expression.

"But why do they only eat that?" Jessica asked, confused. "Kryptid females are some of the most brilliant minds in the galaxy. Surely, they could come up with something more appetizing."

I shook my head while sitting at the table with them and gestured for them to dig in. "For the Kryptids, eating is just a necessity, like sleeping. Its sole purpose is to replenish their energy reserves and fortify their bodies. It is not a social activity. They consider the fancy meals off-worlders eat as a waste of time. It boggles their minds that a gastronomic meal could take hours to prepare."

"Ugh, they sure sound like a lot of fun," Madeline said with a shudder.

I snorted. "They take a bit of getting used to. While I agree that their 'goop' is less-than-tasty or appealing, it contains absolutely everything your body needs for optimal performance. As difficult as it may be for us to relate to their culture, they are a wonder to observe. Their society has no crime, no poverty, no hunger. Everyone has a place, a purpose, a value... Whatever challenge is thrown their way, they don't compete against each other to figure out who'll earn the most credits by coming up with the solution first. They work together, no matter how unrelated their fields are, because everything is about the greater good of the colony, not the individual."

"You are right, their civilization is a wonder," Doom conceded. "But I will take conflict and all the challenges of societies free of a hive mind if only for the joy of having met my Red, of having touched minds for the first time with our son Raven when we thought the Xians would face extinction, for the love I bear my brothers and the Dragons, including the sorrow of those we lost. I wouldn't want to live in a world where I cannot be moved by art, music, a poem… or a delicious meal," he added, waving at the replicated food.

"Hear, hear!" Rogue said.

"You will get no arguments from me," I said in a soft voice. "But that doesn't stop me from admiring what their strict world allows them to accomplish in record time. That said, as far as food is concerned, the replicator will remain here for any of you to use at your convenience. If you wish to get fancier meals from your vessel, I suggest you prepare large batches to last a few days to avoid the back and forth. Otherwise, there is chattel and greenhouses where you can get fresh meat and produce if you wish to cook."

"We can cook from the local produce," Doom said. "As we might be here a while, we would deplete our ship's stocks too quickly. But thank you for your generosity, it is exceedingly kind and thoughtful of you."

The others all echoed words of gratitude while casting friendly smiles at me. A most wondrous warmth spread through my chest. It was silly for me to feel so moved by this. Kryptids weren't big on compliments or praises.

"Are the Creckels comfortable?" I asked to draw the attention away from me.

"Very. Daeko has them settled in a vast terrain just outside the palace with plenty of room for them to train, and a series of caves nearby extremely similar to the types of dwellings they build on their homeworld," Doom said, looking pleased, before taking a large bite from his food.

"I'm glad to hear it," I replied in all sincerity.

Even though I wasn't the host, a part of me felt that, should the Vanguard feel poorly received, it somehow would be a failure on my part.

"From my conversation with Daeko, while we relocated the Creckels, the Kryptids' level of readiness is mind-boggling," Doom said pensively. "After the brutal war that just ended and the weak brood of Soldiers sired by whatever Khutu had become, we expected it would have taken them longer to bounce back. But they're only weeks away from having a formidable army again."

"The Queen is keeping the nurseries full for a reason," I said between two bites.

"Yes, exactly as the rebels feared. That's why they want to attack as quickly as possible, before the Kryptids become too big of a threat," Doom said. "And they are going all out to make sure they will win."

The ominous way in which he spoke those words had everyone tensing around the table.

Rogue swallowed his current mouthful with a slight wince, as if it had been painful. My gaze zeroed in on his throat, and once more, I noticed how swollen it looked. This time, however, he was wearing a Vanguard coat with a high collar that partially hid his neck. I instinctively knew he deliberately dressed this way for this reason.

The same wave of confusion swept over me. My eyes scanned the room, examining each of the females around the table as I tried to guess who was prompting such a reaction from him. None of them was paying him any particular attention. Was she deliberately ignoring his discomfort, or was she truly clueless of her effect on him?

"Did something happen?" Rogue asked with an air of worry.

"Yes. Chaos's team has reached its destination on the secret base of Aurilia," Doom said in a grim tone. "They thought to find a lot more Zombie Soldiers over there. However, they arrived a little too late. Most of the base had already been evacuated. But what they did find, we had not expected."

"Stop teasing us," Rogue said, echoing my sentiment exactly.

Doom gave him a sad smile. "I did not mean to tease. They found a great number of young Scelks."

"WHAT?!" Rogue exclaimed, his outburst echoed by the other members of the team, myself included.

"That's impossible," Reklig argued. "We destroyed all the eggs on Janaur."

"Correct, or at least so we all thought," Doom said in a calm voice. "But Nevrik was able to gather more intel from the handful of scientists they captured at that base. Apparently, the rebel leader, Giles Dalton, sent them a large supply of eggs. At this time, we can only surmise that he somehow managed to recover some undestroyed eggs during the cleanup."

"The cleanup?" I asked.

"For most missions, the Vanguard goes in to fight the main battle—if not the entire conflict—and then the Coalition follows to clean up. This includes disposing of bodies, recovering and destroying harmful technologies, freeing prisoners and hostages, helping them go back home, and assisting the local population to get back on its feet," Doom explained. "It appears that the rebels seized those opportunities to steal a lot of the Kryptid technology to use for their own purposes."

"Are you saying that the rebels used the local population on Aurilia as host for these new Scelks," I asked horrified.

Even as I spoke those words, my chest constricted at the pained expression on Reklig's face. Every Scelk was born as a parasitic bug that needed a host to evolve to its full potential. They had latched on to young male Janaurians who had been sacrificed to the cause, all of them children at the time. Each bug had attached to their spine and nervous system, slowly taking over their bodies and snuffing out the consciousness of the Janaurian until he died and only the Scelk remained as the new owner of that corporeal vessel.

At the time, the Scelks had considered this a great victory as they had been created to be cold-hearted killers. But after joining the Vanguard and developing a consciousness, every single one of them now lived with the guilt of having killed a child so that they could appropriate his body.

To my relief, Doom shook his head.

"There is no more local population on Aurilia," he explained. "The Kryptids wiped out their people early on during the war. Tabitha had the great hunch that the rebels might be using abandoned Kryptid bases after we had defeated them there over the years. There are unwilling hosts, but those were rebels who realized that Giles was just another Khutu in the making and tried to defect."

"A rebellion within the rebellion?" Rogue exclaimed.

"Yes. That is one bit of great news in this whole mess," Doom replied.

"But not such great news for those Scelks," Reklig said in a sharp tone, anger visible on his features.

"Actually, there is great news there as well thanks to Nevrik's quick thinking," Doom said in an appeasing tone.

The same surprise filled with curiosity that I felt was reflected on every face, with a hint of hope on Reklig's.

"The unwilling hosts are only a minority among the Scelk that were found. The others all have human clones as vessels," Doom continued.

"Human clones?!" Reklig exclaimed. "Like the Zombie Soldiers?"

Doom nodded with a paternal smile. "The exact same ones. As the clones are soulless vessels, these young Scelks are entitled to them."

"That's wonderful! And for the rebel defectors?" Rogue asked.

"Nevrik convinced the young Scelks to release their hosts," Doom said. "Tyonna has put them in stasis while they grow new clones for them."

"So they can all live," Reklig said.

The emotion in his voice and on his face messed me up. I had never seen a Scelk display such vulnerability before. Anger, provocative taunts, and disdain were their normal stance.

"Yes, they will. Chaos's team is working with them so that they could possibly join the rest of you in Skogoth," Doom said. "The other thing you need to know is that Giles is truly another Khutu in the making."

"What do you mean?" I asked, blown away by just how big this was turning out to be.

"Legion's team recovered a video from Giles during their own mission on Strajuc. He has clearly used some enhancements on himself," Doom said. "We believe he's made himself immortal like the Zombie Soldiers. But based on the defectors' confessions, it appears that each time a Zombie dies and regenerates, it uses their life force. One of the defectors released by a Scelk looks in his sixties but is only in his late twenties. He died too often during testing."

"Wow, so they could exhaust their life force during the attack on Kryptor if the siege lasts long enough," Reaper said.

"Yes," Doom replied. "But we want to avoid that. It turns out that many of the rebels have received the regeneration graft without their knowledge or against their will. They require a regular injection of a serum derived from Xenon's blood to prevent early aging. Dalton was initially blackmailing would-be defectors by saying they wouldn't get their rations. But now that

Legion has freed Xenon, Giles is apparently hoarding the serum to use for himself as he currently has no way of replenishing his reserves."

Rogue whistled through his teeth. "Talk about a monumental mess. Is there some data I can look over?"

Doom nodded. "Chaos's Medical Officer, Yumi, will send you, Liena, and Victoria all the data that she has gained from the human Scelks and the defectors, who also received the regeneration graft."

"Perfect, thank you," Rogue replied.

"The Kryptids will need to know all of this," I said carefully.

Doom smiled. "Yes, I am meeting with Daeko and the Queen shortly. I'm not looking forward to sharing all this information with them, especially since we don't know what else the rebels may have in store for us."

"The Queen isn't trigger happy, but Daeko might want to go on the offensive," I cautioned. "Unlike Xerath, he's not comfortable knowing that beings as powerful as the Scelks exist out there, outside of their control. Finding out that there are now immortal ones under the command of those who want Kryptids annihilated will only make matters worse."

"I will handle Daeko," Doom said reassuringly. "In the meantime, I need results from all of you. Shuria, Reklig, find me all that you can about Hehiri. Chaos believes it could be one of the rebel headquarters."

"It's quite close to Kryptor," I said, stunned. "Would they be so bold?"

"Anything is possible," Doom said. "Giles taunted Legion by saying he's been operating for a while right under our noses. There's no way it could be on Khepri. But where else? Hehiri would be right under the Kryptids' noses, not ours."

"The defectors didn't know anything?" I asked.

"No," Doom replied, dejected. "Giles is keeping his cards

close to his chest. Any information he shares is on a need-to-know basis only."

"Smart for someone who wants to keep absolute control," Rogue said.

"Indeed," Doom said.

We finished our meal and, to my pleasant surprise, everyone pitched in to clean up and wash the dishes, including all the males. As the team scattered, each going to tackle their respective duties, Rogue lingered behind so that I could accompany him to the ship to recover the equipment he needed.

We started off walking quietly. I didn't understand this awkwardness between us. It had never been like that before. We'd never been close, but our interactions had always been friendly, devoid of this weird tension.

Or had it always been there, and I never noticed?

It was hard to say. Since Lekla had reverted a lot of the changes I had undergone under Khutu's reign of terror, I perceived things and reacted to them in a much different fashion.

"You seem to have adapted really well to life on Kryptor," Rogue said at last, breaking the uncomfortable silence. "Have you considered coming back home, or do you plan on settling here permanently?"

I frowned and gave him a dubious look. "What home? Khutu destroyed my homeworld."

"I meant Khepri, of course," Rogue said as if it was obvious. "All of your sisters have moved there. Surely you know Silzi would give anything for you to be with them again."

Controlling my features, I tried to hide my true emotions and appear nonchalant. "I do not see myself ever settling on Khepri. I doubt I would be particularly welcome there."

Rogue recoiled and looked at me as if I had said something absurd. "Why in the world would you say that? Of course you would be welcome. The Vanguard has dedicated an area of Khepri exclusively for the Mimics to settle in—for *all* Mimics."

"Even the one who murdered Bane and attempted to sabotage your defection?" I asked, annoyed with the bitterness that seeped into my voice.

A strange expression flitted over Rogue's handsome face. "Don't be silly. We've all made mistakes, and we've all committed terrible deeds. Do you think us Dragons are blameless? We did horrible things to many innocents at the command of Khutu until we could defect."

"The difference is that *you* did not have a choice. He held your mothers and young siblings as hostages. But I *chose* to attack and kill your brother out of spite and jealousy."

Rogue looked troubled for a split second, his face taking on a neutral expression so quickly I wondered if I hadn't imagined it.

"Are you still in love with Bane?" he asked in a gentle voice.

I shook my head and looked away from him as we entered the membrane-covered hallway that led back into the palace.

"No. I don't believe I was ever truly in love with him," I said in all sincerity. "If I'm honest, I think I was more in love with the idea of what might have been. Don't get me wrong, I probably would have fallen in love with him had he wanted me. But he's a Dragon, and I'm not human. Therefore, he never could have been mine."

The same troubled expression crossed Rogue's features. "What if Dragons could mate with non-humans? Stranger things have happened."

I snorted. "Strange things do abound these days," I said teasingly. "However, a Dragon and a nonhuman has never happened. It probably never will."

"Never say never, Shuria," Rogue countered in a mysterious tone that had me looking at him questioningly. "As for your welcome on Khepri, no one holds what you did against you. You seem to forget how instrumental you were in ending the war. You were the bridge between the Vanguard and the Kryptids."

I shrugged dismissively, but secretly, his words deeply

touched me. "I'm sure the Vanguard would have found a way. You guys always do."

"Maybe, but probably not before both sides suffered many more unnecessary losses," Rogue replied. "We all handle loss and grief in different ways. Humans say 'Hell hath no fury like a woman scorned.' You had every right to feel betrayed by Bane after Khutu declared you were to be his Queen. From what everyone says, Tabitha was a hellish demon after Rage broke her heart. She was bitter for years until Bane came along."

I nodded. "Yes, I have heard the stories about the Dragon Queen. But she never tried to murder Rage over it," I argued, all the while wondering why I was trying to convince him of what a horrible person I was.

"True," he conceded, before continuing in a soft tone. "But she also had not been transformed into something else. You and your sisters received many splices from vicious creatures that were bound to affect your personality. I can see the difference. You always seemed to be a volcano on the verge of erupting, like you had all the rage in the world bottled up inside you, just seeking the opportunity to be unleashed."

I reflected on his words before nodding again. "Now that you mention it, I must admit that since Lekla reversed a lot of the things that were done to me, I feel a lot less aggressive, not so angry at the world all the time."

He gave me the softest smile that made me feel funny inside. "Yes, and it shows. It is good to finally get to know the real Shuria."

I gave him a timid smile and averted my eyes, a sliver of hope blossoming deep within. Was he right? Could the others accept me despite my past? Could I again be the female once loved by my sisters?

CHAPTER 6
SHURIA

Shortly thereafter, we entered the docking bay adjacent to the palace and made a beeline for their vessel. It stood out like a sore thumb amidst the liveships of the Kryptids with their organic shapes. They grew those ships over many months out of a special type of hardened membrane, which allowed them to self-repair and self-maintain.

As soon as the doors of the Vanguard's vessel parted before us, the fresh scent that slapped me in the face left me dizzy. I'd gotten so used to the musty scent of the membranes that I'd forgotten what it was like to live without it. Even the air outside had a spiciness that vaguely reminded me of incense.

I followed Rogue to the medbay, my gaze flicking this way and that while admiring the sleek lines of the hallway, with light-gray walls, dark floors, and black and gold accents matching the colors of the Gomenzi Dragons. Memories of my brief stay on Khepri after Khutu's ultimate demise flashed through my mind. It was a beautiful world with clear blue skies, crossed by the ghost of the planet's three rings, greenery everywhere, the loveliest bodies of water, and stunning state-of-the-art architecture.

Yes, I can see myself living there.

As a Mimic, I was an aquatic creature. I missed swimming in the wide rivers of my homeworld, playing with the aquatic flora and fauna. The city my sisters had built for themselves on Khepri, just across the river from Skogoth—the Scelk village—was truly a paradise. Maybe I should inquire further about possibly going 'home' to what remained of my people.

"I had already packed most of the things that I wanted to bring down," Rogue said as soon as we entered the medbay.

He gestured at a couple of crates sitting on a narrow hover cart.

"That won't take long then," I said politely.

"It won't be that fast," he amended with a sheepish grin. "I had only packed the most commonly used items, in case we did not receive the welcome we had hoped for. I'll make it quick."

"Take your time. We're not in any hurry," I said graciously. "Let me know if you need any assistance."

"Will do," he replied with a smile.

Rogue worked quickly and efficiently, unplugging a few contraptions I did not know what purpose they could possibly serve and neatly packing them in a crate. I couldn't help but discreetly ogle him.

He truly was an attractive male. Tall—at least 6'7—broad-shouldered, and with muscles for days, Rogue was one of the more imposing Dragons amidst his brothers. He matched the more massive physique of the Xian Warriors, unlike the other Dragons who were also muscular but a bit more lithe. I admired his long, deep black hair, the shiny chitin scales adorning his forehead all around his Deynian horn, his pointy ears, his noble nose, and his luscious, plump lips a shade darker than his gray skin. He did have a young-looking face that seemed at odds with his muscular frame and deep voice. But it didn't clash for me. I found it made him more unique.

The black chitin scales that covered his body hid nothing of the mesmerizing way his muscles bulged beneath them with each movement. The bone spikes on his shoulders and the length of his spine discreetly stretched the fabric of his tight Vanguard shirt.

Examining him reminded me how invincible I had felt the few times I had morphed into a Dragon. But that immediately brought me back to the day I had impersonated him specifically to try and kill Bane. I cast all such thoughts out of my mind and wandered through the medbay, examining the equipment.

As I ran my fingers over the edge of the fancy medical pod, a strong sense of being observed made me jerk my head towards Rogue. I barely managed to hide my surprise at finding him staring at me with a slight frown.

"Is something wrong?" I asked.

He shook his head. "No. I was just wondering if you would mind letting me examine you while we are here. The medical pod could give me a really good picture of just how far they reverted things for you compared to where things stand with your sisters."

For some reason I couldn't explain, I felt disappointed that this had been the reason for him staring at me like that.

"Sure," I replied before kicking off my shoes.

To my shock, Rogue helped me lie down in the medical pod, which I found strange. It wasn't so high that assistance would have been required. I felt oddly vulnerable as he towered over me with the most unreadable of expressions.

He swallowed painfully as he began closing the glass dome of the pod over me. I glanced at his throat, baffled to find it just as swollen as before, if not more. That made no sense. As far as I knew, we were alone aboard the vessel. Surely, I couldn't be...?

Of course you're not. Don't be stupid.

Rogue initiating the test wiped all those crazy thoughts out of my mind. Multiple lights ran up and down the length of my body, performing a variety of scans. Then countless prickling sensations occurred all over my body as needles took all kinds of samples for me. Horrible memories of painful needles injecting me with excruciating chemicals as the General's scientists experimented on me came back to the surface.

Lekla would often sedate me when she reverted what had been done to me. Although she claimed it was necessary to keep me stable during the procedures, I strongly suspected it was mostly to spare me further trauma or triggering the PTSD she had undoubtedly noticed in me.

Thankfully, the test didn't last long and inflicted no pain. I silenced the sigh of relief that rose in my throat when the lid finally opened to release me. Rogue stared at me with awe and a strange expression that I could not define. He helped me sit at the edge of the pod, right before he swallowed hard again.

"What's wrong with your neck," I blurted out, unable to hold my curiosity any further. "I noticed it last night, and it seems to be getting worse."

Rogue hesitated. For a split second, he almost appeared panicked. He shifted on his feet and stretched his neck as if to release the tension building in his nape.

"There's nothing wrong with my neck," he said carefully. "It's just that my mating glands have awakened."

I recoiled, my mind going blank for a second. I glanced around the room then back at him with confusion. "Doesn't this only happen when you're in the presence of your soulmate?"

"Yes," he said, his multifaceted eyes glowing with intensity.

"But… Aren't we alone here?"

"Yes, we are," Rogue replied, his gaze boring into mine. "It started last night at the very moment I entered the Queen's Chamber."

"Last night? But…" My voice trailed off as the meaning of his words sank in. I shook my head in denial. "You can't be saying—?"

"Yes, Shuria. I'm saying that you are causing it. My Dragon is claiming you."

I jumped off the edge of the medical pod and pushed him aside so that I could take a few steps away from him, shaking my head the whole time. "No. No way. I can't be your soulmate. You must be having some kind of allergic reaction to something in the air."

"I thought so as well," Rogue said in a soothing voice. "But there is no more doubt in my mind. Last night, as soon as you left me in my quarters, the swelling went down. And then I saw you again this morning, and it came back with a vengeance. There is no question you are triggering it."

"But that doesn't make sense!" I exclaimed, refusing to accept that possibility. "Why would it suddenly trigger now? We met for the first time three years ago. We spent a lot of time close to each other during the year leading to the final confrontation with Khutu. And yet nothing happened. So there has to be something wrong."

Even as I spoke those words, an irrational hope tried to blossom in my heart.

"No, Shuria. I do not believe that there's something *wrong*, but rather that there's something *right*." He took a couple of careful steps towards me, like he would a wounded animal. "Three years ago, you were not yourself. You were Khutu's creation, modified both physically and mentally. He had made you into something that my Dragon could not align with. But today, you are back to your true self."

I shook my head and took another step away from him. This was too good to be true. I couldn't allow myself to believe something like this. Once reality came crashing in, I would be left devastated.

"I hear what you're saying," I said, trying to sound reasonable. "However, you are mistaken. No Dragon has ever chosen a nonhuman, let alone a Mimic."

"And yet, here we are. I am not mistaken, Shuria," Rogue said with a conviction that left me reeling. "Last night, I didn't say anything last night because I wanted to run some tests on myself to be sure. I didn't want to get my hopes up in vain."

"*Your* hopes up? About having *me* as your soulmate?" I asked disbelievingly.

"Yes," he said as if it was self-evident. "You are strong, smart, a formidable fighter, devoted to those you love, loyal, and very beautiful. What more could I possibly want?"

I gaped at him in complete shock. "But... I killed your brother! I knocked you out on the breeding ship in order to impersonate you specifically so that I could kill Bane!"

Rogue snorted then shrugged. "You did. But you weren't yourself back then. By the way, thanks for only knocking me out instead of killing me."

Wrapping my arms around my waist, I hugged myself, feeling completely lost. I didn't know how to handle this. I wanted him to be right, but...

"You could be wrong, Rogue," I said, feeling pathetic for the needy and hopeful way in which I spoke those words.

"There is an easy way to prove it," he said in a soft voice.

"How?" I whispered, my heart nearly beating out of my chest.

"Only a soulmate can touch us without making us ill. Touch me, Shuria."

CHAPTER 7
ROGUE

I had no hidden agenda when I spoke those words. But the minute they crossed my lips, the oddest flame lit in the pit of my stomach. My two hearts started beating a little faster, and my nerve endings became acutely sensitive. I'd never experienced such a combination of sensations, and my potential mate had not even touched me yet.

Shuria stared at me in shock. Truth be told, I couldn't believe my own boldness for making that request. And yet, from a purely scientific standpoint, it was a sound test. Dragons—and now Xian Warriors since I had fixed their endocrine imbalances—could not bear to be touched sexually by someone other than their soulmate. It instantly made us physically ill or feel physical pain. Even inappropriate thoughts would trigger similar discomforts.

"You want me to touch you?" she repeated with a disbelieving expression.

My chest tightened at the almost offended look on her face. Did she find me unattractive? Did she, like so many other females, think I had too much of a baby face to take me seriously as a potential mate? Although she claimed not to still be in love with Bane, did she have lingering feelings for him and was simply in denial?

"Yes, I do," I said, proud that my voice remained neutral and professional. "I would like you to touch me to see how I react. Then we will know beyond any doubt whether we are soulmates."

Shuria shook her head and hid her hands behind her back. That hurt. I made no effort to hide how her response wounded me.

"Would it be so terrible?" I asked.

"Would what be so terrible?" she asked, confused.

"To be my mate?"

She recoiled and looked at me with a stunned expression.

"No, of course not!" she replied as if I had lost my mind. "You are Rogue! Everybody respects and admires you. You are one of the greatest scientific minds of our era. Any female in her right mind would be honored to be your mate."

"But not you?" I challenged.

She studied my features as if she was trying to assess whether I was stupid or making fun of her.

"Would *you* want *me*?" she asked instead of answering my question.

"Yes, I would," I said with conviction. "I already told you what a wonderful female I believe you are. You are exactly the type of person we want in the Vanguard. I would be proud to call you mine. Do you think we would have relied so much on you in the year leading up to the final showdown with Khutu if we didn't trust you?"

I took a couple of careful steps towards her, invading her personal space. To my relief, she didn't back away.

"I hope to be yours, Shuria," I whispered in a pressing tone. "But there's only one way to be sure. Don't you want to know if we are meant for each other?"

My pulse picked up again when a glimmer of hope sparked

in her beautiful stormy eyes again. Shuria licked her lips nervously then gave me a sharp nod. I held my breath as she carefully raised her palms and placed them on my chest. She looked up at me, a sliver of fear visible on her features as she clearly expected me to pull away.

I chuckled. "Not like this," I said in a gentle voice. "You must touch me like a lover would."

To my surprise, Shuria's dusky blue skin took on a darker shade as she blushed. She lowered her eyes, looking mightily embarrassed.

"I... I don't know how. I've never..." Her voice trailed off, and then she shrugged.

My eyes widened in understanding. She'd always been so strong and assertive, I'd assumed she had experience. I couldn't help a smile, pleased that if things turned out the way I hoped, we would embark on that new journey of discovery together.

"Well, I've never been with a female. So we're both equally clueless," I said teasingly.

Shuria blushed some more, and I felt my own skin heat with embarrassment. An awkward silence stretched between us.

Straightening my shoulders, I cleared my throat, then went for it. "May I kiss you?"

Looking relieved, Shuria gave me a timid smile and nodded. The small flame in the pit of my loins erupted in the strangest fire as I carefully placed my hands on her hips to draw her closer. My hearts pounded with the fear that my stomach might twist with revulsion the minute I kissed her. In that instant, I realized how badly I wanted her to be mine. The same fear shone brightly in her stormy gray eyes.

I slowly lowered my head, the swelling in my throat multiplying a thousandfold. And then our lips touched. A bolt of fire exploded in my nether region. For a split second, I was terrified it was the rejection manifesting itself. But the wondrous heat that spread outward from it throughout my body quickly corrected my mistaken assumption.

I wrapped my arms around Shuria, drawing her body against mine even more closely as I tightened my embrace. A delicious shiver ran down my spine as her hands glided over the chitin scales of my chest to settle on my shoulders. Tilting my head to the side, I pressed my lips a little harder against hers. Her mouth was so soft and warm beneath mine, as was her body in my arms.

Feeling emboldened by her reaction and the absence of nausea from me, I started caressing her back, my hand gliding up to her nape. She melted in my arms, the tension that had kept her stiff fading away. I combed my fingers through the silky strands of her midnight-blue hair. I broke the kiss, my lips wandering over her face. Shuria sighed, the sensuous sound resonating directly in my cock. Blood rushed there, making my shaft stiffen and press uncomfortably against my loin plate.

My hand fisted Shuria's hair on her nape. I gently pulled her head back then kissed a path down the length of her slender neck. When my lips brushed over her vertical gills, my female moaned and shivered in my arms. That reaction awakened a dull throbbing between my thighs.

I lifted my head to stare at her with awe. "You're the one," I whispered with wonder. "You truly are my soulmate!"

Her eyes misted, and she gave me a trembling smile. She caught my face with her hands, her gaze studying my features as if in an effort to memorize them. She caressed my cheeks with her thumbs, and I closed my eyes, leaning into her palm. How I had craved this, for such a tender touch from the one being in the entire universe who had been made for me and to whom I could fully belong.

Shuria placed her hands on my shoulders, fear creeping back into her expression, dampening her joy.

"What's wrong, my mate?" I asked, worried by this sudden mood change.

She licked her lips nervously, choosing her words before answering. "What if it doesn't last? I mean, you are responding to me now, but what if your glands go back to no longer reacting to my presence?"

I firmly shook my head. "That is extremely doubtful. Granted, I want to have a deeper look at how the Kryptids reverted the changes you had undergone. But the reports from the medical pod show that you are back to being a regular Mimic —for the most part—with some enhancements. And that is why I want to know as much as possible about how they went about accomplishing all of this."

She nodded slowly, a slight frown creasing her forehead. "I don't know the science of it all. You would need to speak with Toksi for all the details since Lekla appointed her as her replacement for anything else I would require. Unlike other Mimics, I can still use the abilities of the people and creatures I morph into."

I recoiled. "What?! You must not do that! Using such powers burns your lifespan!"

She shook her head reassuringly. "Not anymore. Lekla fixed it so that it no longer harms me to do so. It's just a little tiring."

I took on a mulish expression and gave her a stern look. "I don't want you using those powers."

Shuria glared at me. "Soulmate or not, if you think you're going to boss me around, you're in for a big surprise."

I opened my mouth to argue, but then took a deep breath before replying in a reasonable tone. "I'm not trying to boss you around, Shuria. But I just found you. I refuse to lose you. Just give me a chance to test this further to make sure you're going to be fine."

Her blossoming anger melted. "Fine. You can run whatever

tests you deem necessary. Anyway, it's not like I will need to use any of these types of abilities in the short term."

"Thank you, my mate," I said with a smile, loving the feel of the word on my tongue.

I caressed her cheek, a powerful possessive wave surging through me as she leaned into my touch.

My mate...

She covered the back of my hand still resting on her cheek before casting another concerned look my way.

"I don't want you to think that I am resisting this. I am truly happy that we seem to be soulmates. But there are so many uncertainties. Dragons and Xians modify their mates to make them compatible with you in order to have babies. What if it triggers some weird reaction in me that will make me revert instead into something you are no longer compatible with?"

As much as I hated the doubts that bubbled inside my female, she was being responsible about this. The validity of her questions couldn't be denied.

"Gomenzi Dragons enhance their mates," I said with confidence. "My Dragon wouldn't claim you if our bond could be harmful to either one of us. I believe that, had we bonded before your modifications were reversed, then you could have been harmed. Our coming together will only strengthen the bond."

"Are you sure?" Shuria insisted. "My sister's offspring were abominations. Even the ones who seemed half normal ended in deformed and rabid monstrosities."

"It was because of Khutu," I said forcefully. "His seed was as rotten as everything else about him. And Mimics are not meant to give birth laying eggs in a Kryptid Queen form. It won't be your case. Trust in me. Trust in *us*. This was meant to be."

She gave me a shaky smile and then nodded. I smiled back and caressed her hair while admiring her beautiful face.

"I can't believe I found you," I whispered. "I'm yours, Shuria. Forever."

Her eyes misted again as she beamed at me. I leaned down to reclaim her lips in a tender kiss. She wrapped her arms around me, holding me tightly as if she feared I would disappear or go away. As clumsy as we both were in our inexperience, I could already tell I would never tire of kissing my female, of the feel of her body against mine, of her possessive embrace.

Our lips parted and our tongues mingled for the first time, timidly making each other's acquaintances. Damn she tasted good. Just as I was about to further deepen the kiss, Doom's wretched voice resonated in my head, startling me. By the way Shuria suddenly stiffened, I guessed he formed a psychic group and broadcast the message to all of us.

"We have more updates from Legion and Chaos," Doom telepathically said. *"I need all of you back in the meeting room ASAP."*

"On our way," I replied.

Reluctantly releasing my female, I shoved the last items I needed into the crate and set the hovercart to follow before giving Shuria one last kiss.

"We'll talk more later," I said in a tender voice.

She smiled and followed me out of the ship.

CHAPTER 8
SHURIA

Rogue's mate... Rogue's mating glands had awakened for *me*... only *me*! I still couldn't believe he truly was mine. As we hurried back to the improvised laboratory the Workers had set up for him, I felt dizzy, a tsunami of emotions swirling inside of me.

He seemed happy, genuinely happy to be mine and to claim me as his. However, Rogue didn't know me well, just like I also barely knew him. We had interacted often in the past, but it had always been brief and professional. What if he ended up disliking me once we got closer? What if *I* was the one who ended up not liking him after all? That seemed impossible. Rogue was perfection on two legs. But I'd previously convinced myself that I was in love with Bane the minute Khutu declared I would be his Queen. What if the same thing was happening again with Rogue just because his glands had suddenly deemed us the perfect match?

Stop overthinking everything.

I kept stealing glances at him as we walked back. His happy smile that couldn't seem to fade did crazy things to me. I itched to hold his hand as we walked, like Reaper had done with his mate.

Maker, I'm pathetically needy.

We left the hovercart in the lab and hurried to the meeting room where everyone was already waiting for us. Doom and General Daeko sat at the head of the table. Also present were Commander Hulax, and two Workers: Toksi and Rakma. Queen Xerath had joined us through the vidscreen. With news of an impending attack, she was working overtime on laying as many eggs as possible.

"Good, everyone's here," Doom said as Rogue and I took a seat side-by-side. "You all already know General Daeko and Commander Hulax. This is Toksi, one of the bioengineers who developed the Scelks. And this is Rakma, a weapons specialist."

The team nodded at the two female Kryptids in greeting. Although I knew her, I had not interacted much with Rakma. Toksi, however, I had dealt with often as she had frequently worked with Lekla to revert my modifications and was now supposed to take over my care.

"As I mentioned, we have received more news from Chaos and Legion," Doom continued. "We already knew that the rebels had Jadozors, although not how many of them. And we knew they had Zombie Soldiers. Now we know that quite a few of them are actually unhappy rebels who have been enhanced against their will and who Giles controls via a chip in their brain. Added to that, we found out that there are apparently a thousand more of those cloned human Scelks already on their way to the rally point whence the rebels will launch their attack."

A collective gasp resonated through the room.

Doom nodded with a grim expression. "We have about six weeks before the attack. The Vanguard fleet is discreetly heading towards Kryptor, making wide detours not to alert the Coalition—and therefore potential rebels—that we are on the move. Our fleet will attempt to cripple theirs before they reach Kryptor. In the meantime, we must prepare the planet's defenses in case the Vanguard fails."

"We must eliminate those Scelk clones," Daeko declared in a tone that brooked no argument.

"NO!" Reklig snapped, while glaring at the young general. "We must get to them and free them."

"Agreed," Doom replied. "Chaos's team is already working on identifying their location and on a plan to rescue the Scelks."

"And what if they fail? I will not risk the future of the colony merely to spare a thousand Scelks," Daeko said forcefully.

"*If* they fail, there will be a contingency plan to neutralize them without bloodshed," Doom said in an appeasing tone. "Chaos's team is preparing for all eventualities."

"They are young Scelks," Rogue added in a reasonable voice. "Ours are mature, and therefore way more powerful. Even though they are individuals, the Scelks possess a hive mind, like the Kryptids. If one of our Scelks tell them to turn on the rebels—"

"It won't work because they have control chips in their heads forcing them to obey Giles," Doom said, interrupting Rogue. "Sabra's Zappers require us to be within range of the Scelks to disable the chips. This is the issue for which Chaos's team is working on an alternate plan if they do not succeed in freeing them before the attack."

"That's a lot of 'IFs'," Daeko said sternly. "We *will* have a plan ready to take out those Scelks *if* your people fail to rein them in."

Massive waves of psychic energy flowed from the Vanguard members to Reklig, who was baring his teeth. They were no doubt trying to calm him. Madeline gently caressed her husband's arm in a soothing fashion.

"Prepare as you deem necessary, General Daeko," Doom said in a neutral voice. "But I am confident we will find a way to resolve this issue without having to go to unfortunate extremes.

And *if* it truly comes to that, we will help you eliminate them. First, we will try to convert them. As Rogue mentioned, our mature Scelks are far more powerful than these younglings. Once they use the Zappers that Sabra has devised to disable the chips, our Scelks will have no problem bringing these human Scelks into the fold."

"But you mentioned earlier that both versions of those disks had a limited range," Daeko challenged.

Doom nodded and explained the functionality of the two devices, this time more in detail for the two Workers who had missed our breakfast meeting and the one he held with Daeko.

"If Legion and Chaos are right, the rebels have in excess of 100,000 Zombie Warriors, and an unknown number of Jadozors also controlled by a chip or mechanical brain," Doom said. "The Jadozors need to be obliterated. The Zombies need to be disabled and, if at all possible, without killing the sentient ones."

The way Daeko scrunched his face loudly expressed his displeasure at anything that would delay his ability to simply wipe out any potential threat. Some heavy discussion likely happened during his earlier meeting with Doom. I also believed that he was only playing along because of the vital information the Vanguard alone could provide him regarding the impending threats. At least, I had faith in the young general honoring whatever word he gave Doom.

"Fighting so many Zombie Warriors will result in heavy casualties for us before they can be disabled with those Zappers," Rakma said pensively. "We need a better delivery system. We should be able to adapt the technology from our Spitters, with a simplified artificial intelligence to control these Zappers. This way, they could reach the targets from a much greater range without putting our troops in danger."

My brows shot up in admiration. The Kryptid females were absolute geniuses. Their entire civilization rested on their shoulders. They were the brain and the backbone of their people.

Using the Spitter technology indeed made sense, if they could bring it down to an object no bigger than a coin. Spitters were one or two-passenger small organic vessels equipped with a powerful AI that allowed them to function autonomously without a pilot. You only had to point those vessels at a target for them to attack. Extremely fast, they spit an acid that could eat through the toughest ship hull. Individually, Spitters were no threat and easy to take down. However, they always attacked as a swarm, their combined firepower wrecking even the most impenetrable armored ship.

"How long would you need?" Daeko asked.

"Three weeks," Rakma said with confidence.

"Perfect. Make it so," Daeko said before turning his attention back to Doom.

"The Jadozors could also be a major issue," Doom said. "Aside from the fact that we don't know exactly how many they have, those creatures can fly in space. Rogue and our other scientists have devised a virus that destroys their regeneration abilities. But it takes time to act, and they need to be exposed to a lot of it."

"If they are flying in space, we can take them down as they enter our atmosphere," Rakma said.

Toksi nodded and turned to address Rogue. "If you share the virus with us, we can see if the Bombardier Beetles can fire them directly at the Jadozors."

"Gladly," Rogue said. "Actually, we should try to see if the Spitter technology you want to adapt to the Zappers could also work to deliver the virus. It would be safer to inject it in a more surgical fashion than to blanket your atmosphere with it."

"That should be feasible," Rakma said.

"Martha is our Weapons Specialist and Jessica is our Medical Officer," Doom said. "They can assist you with the technology that was used on our side for both the Zappers and the virus. Madeline is our Science Officer. Along with Reaper and myself, we can help you with air and ground defenses. Reklig and Shuria can work with your intelligence team to track down the rebel HQ based on the information Chaos provided us."

Daeko cast a glance at the Queen in the vidscreen. She blinked her assent.

"This is acceptable," Daeko said to Doom.

"Excellent," Doom replied with what I believe to be a hint of relief. "You know your tasks. You're all dismissed."

We rose from our chairs and prepared to leave. But before we could take a couple of steps, Reaper intercepted us.

"Your throat is no longer swollen, brother," Reaper said factually. "Am I to understand that everything is resolved?"

The way his gaze briefly flicked my way spoke volumes as to the fact that he had guessed at the cause. Or had Rogue told him? Instant panic settled within me. We had not discussed when and how we wanted to reveal this to the rest of his team. Everything was happening too fast.

To my shock, Rogue slipped a possessive arm around my waist and drew me against his side, his face glowing with pride.

"Yes, brother. It is resolved."

I held my breath as Reaper refocused on me, my blossoming panic cranking up a notch.

"But how? Why now?" Reaper asked.

"The mutations Khutu had subjected her to had prevented my Dragon from claiming her. But thanks to Lekla's efforts, we are compatible again," Rogue explained.

I didn't know what reaction I had expected from Reaper, but not for him to beam at me in the most affectionate fashion.

"That's wonderful! Welcome to the family, my sister. My baby-faced big brother was overdue to find you."

My throat tightened, and emotions overwhelmed me when he cupped my face between his hands then tenderly kissed my forehead.

"This is amazing news, indeed," Doom said, smiling warmly

at us. "We not only get to celebrate Rogue finding his soulmate but also you coming home at last to your sisters."

The rest of the team took turns hugging me and congratulating us. Nothing had prepared me for this warm welcome. To think I had so feared they would reject me for what I had done, for what I had become.

As Madeline was releasing me from her embrace, I noticed the Kryptids looking at us as if we were strange creatures that defied logic. In that instant, Doom's words replayed in my mind about the beauty of emotions and love, despite the pain they could inflict. I suddenly felt sorry for the Kryptids. Many uncertainties remained about Rogue and me, and how my mutations could affect our bond. But I knew now that whatever pain or challenges he and I might encounter, the happiness I felt right at this moment was worth the risk and was worth fighting for.

CHAPTER 9
ROGUE

Dressed in a hazmat suit, I circled around the many Bombardier Beetles lined up on one of the many strategically designed plateaus within the city. They served as air defense—living ground to air missile launchers.

As much as I had been sad to part from Shuria so soon after confirming she was my other half, the Kryptids' biotechnology now held my full attention. Despite how morally questionable a lot of the research had been under the command of General Khutu, the brilliance of their achievements couldn't be denied.

These Beetles in particular fascinated me. At least three meters high, almost five meters long and about two meters wide, they made me feel tiny. They kept their torsos held up with three sets of legs. Above their big mandibles, multiple small eyes covered their faces in three lines vaguely reminiscent of a bird's foot. A pair of massive, arched horns towered at the top of their heads. However, their humongous bellies made up for most of their mass. A thick, translucent membrane covered it, allowing us to see the glowing plasma within.

Although the small amount of radiation emitted by the

Beetles had little chance of negatively affecting me, I wasn't taking any risk.

"How do you get all this plasma inside them?" I asked Rakma.

"Simply by feeding them," she replied in a factual manner. "All that they consume gets transformed into gas in their bellies, aside from what their bodies use for regular maintenance. They heat their stomachs to strip the electrons from the atoms, which ionizes the gas into plasma."

"Do you need to feed them something in particular to achieve this?" I asked, fascinated.

"Mostly starchy and fermented foods." She then pointed at the large set of wings around the base of their enormous bellies. "The primary wings allow them to fly at a very low altitude over relatively short distances to move to a new position. We avoid making them fly as their weight is quite strenuous. The last thing you want is for them to crash and their bellies exploding, spilling out all that plasma."

I couldn't help but laugh at the grim way in which she spoke those words. "Why does this sound like you've experienced this before?"

She nodded. "It has happened a few times, each of them one too many. These Beetles take a long time to mature. Aside from the wasteful loss, it is also a nightmare to clean all the plasma and deal with the radioactive fallout, especially in residential areas."

"I can imagine. And what about this smaller set of wings on top?" I asked.

"These wings are triggers," Rakma explained. "They are magnetized, which allows them to move small amounts of plasma up the tunnel of the cannon. The plasma is then launched as missiles through the horns with enough speed and power to hit a target in orbit or at a close enough distance from the planet."

"This is quite amazing," I said with genuine admiration.

"However, this also poses a problem if we wanted to attach the zombie virus to the plasma. The virus would not survive the great heat the Beetles generate to ionize the gas."

Rakma nodded. "Yes, that is the main issue. We will need to test casings for the virus so that it can withstand the heat. The question is how long the casings can remain inside the plasma without melting? And what reaction the Beetles will have should the casings break and the virus mix with the plasma inside their bellies?"

I frowned while reflecting on alternative solutions. "Ideally, the virus should never go inside the belly," I mused out loud. "If we could get the plasma missile to grab the virus on its way out..."

My voice trailed off as I examined the opening of the cannon on top of the creature's back, my wheels spinning. As I observed the Beetle's horns—which looked and behaved almost like the sights of a weapon, an idea blossomed at the back of my head.

"What if we could get the virus casings to attach to the missile as it is launched?" I asked. "If plasma is ionized, magnetic casings filled with the virus could attach to the plasma on its way out. For example, if we had virus grenade distributors alongside the horns, when the missile shoots through them, the grenades would attach. Could that work?"

Rakma pursed her incredibly human-looking lips as she pondered. "This idea has merit. Attaching the virus casing only as the missile launches would solve a lot of integrity issues. However, while plasma has some magnetism, it is very weak. We normally use magnetic fields to contain plasma."

She studied the horns of the Beetle, her small mandibles moving in what I believed to be an absent-minded nervous tic when in deep reflection.

"Yes, there might be a way," Rakma said at last. "The casings could form a magnetic ring around the plasma missile. We will immediately start working on a prototype. If this works, we could begin production in just one week. But we will also work on an alternative plan as a backup if this fails."

"That sounds great," I replied with a smile. "I'll leave you to it then. I'll be with Toksi if you need me."

Although she nodded, Rakma had already dismissed me. Her long, chitin covered fingers were flying over the interface of her datapad as she began working on a solution. I smiled and headed back inside the palace.

It felt strange interacting with Kryptid Workers in a collaborative fashion. Growing up, both Workers and Soldiers who knew of our illegal existence had made our lives hell. As much as I had hated them back then, today I only felt pity. Kryptids lived according to strict instinctive rules. They blindly obeyed hierarchy, even if they disagreed with the commands. The Workers who raised us were appalled by our existence but couldn't disobey General Khutu.

They were in constant battles with themselves not to smother us, knowing we were an abomination as only the Kryptid Queens should birth the offspring of any General. Lucky for us, without a direct command from the Queen for them to execute us, they had to abide by the word of the second in command—General Khutu. That was specifically why our sire kept our existence a secret from everyone, especially the Queen, except those under his thumb.

As soon as I entered the palace through the science wing, I stripped out of the hazmat suit in the decontamination area, showered, then put my regular clothes back on. Moments later, I entered the lab where Toksi and an army of other scientists were hard at work.

Sadly, this was one of the labs where membranes covered the entire room, floor, walls, and ceilings included. They usually didn't use membranes in labs to avoid contamination. In this area, as the females worked on organic vessels made of the same organic material, denying themselves of the benefits of the membranes didn't make sense.

Large vats filled with writhing masses of organic tissue lined the walls. On multiple tables, the scientist had containment chambers of varying sizes within which they shaped or manipulated more of the same tissue.

As soon as she saw me enter, Toksi waved me over. Five petri dishes in front of her each contained an organic network of tendrils attached to a small brain-like bulb in the center.

"Perfect timing," Toksi said to me. "We've been debating the best way to deliver those Zappers and viruses to the Zombies. These are different artificial intelligences that could control the miniature Spitters to deliver the payload. But now we're unsure if a mechanical brain wouldn't be better."

"What are the differences?" I asked, intrigued.

"The mechanical brain can learn and adapt faster to changing situations and the events it will encounter before disseminating it to the network," Toksi explained. "But its learning capacity is limited by storage and by the complexity of its algorithms. As far as the organic A.I., it learns a bit slower, but can come up with truly creative solutions, and its ability to grow is infinite."

I frowned as I weighed the two options. "Quick adaptation would be ideal in the context of the upcoming battle. But creative thinking could be even more valuable since many of the Zombies will be sentient."

"That was also our thought," Toksi replied.

"How long would it take to have the organic A.I. fully operational?" I asked.

"The A.I. itself we can grow in two days. It's the rest of the muscles to carry the Zappers and the virus casings that will take longer. Probably over a week..." she said.

"Can we do both in parallel?" I asked. "The mechanical brain will require a chassis to clip onto the Zapper or the virus casings. Could we temporarily use the same chassis with the organic A.I.

while it grows muscles to be able to hang onto the payload on its own?"

Toksi's face brightened. "Yes... Yes, that would be an option. We can adjust the chassis to provide room for the organic A.I. to grow. This would give us more time to train them through simulations against our Soldiers and your teammates. Then we can see whether the mechanical brain or the organic one is more efficient before we start production."

"That sounds like a plan," I replied, excited. "However, I would like to explore a third possibility."

The Kryptid female leaned against the counter of her workstation to eye me with curiosity. I repressed a smile. Whatever issues I had with the Kryptid culture in general, working alongside their females was always invigorating. They never considered any question as stupid. Any idea, however far-fetched, deserved consideration until proven useless, unachievable, or not worth the effort. They loved challenges, the more improbable to achieve, the better. There was nothing more inspiring than working with people without ego, open to any possibility, and always willing to push the envelope.

"We're currently trying to manage the needs of different elements when it comes to delivering the virus," I said pensively. "There's the A.I., the chassis, the casing, and then the virus itself. The organic chassis you will grow is of the same impenetrable tissue as the one for the hull of the Spitters and of all your other liveships."

"Correct," Toksi replied.

"So why not make the organic chassis also the casing for the virus?" I asked. "The same way the Bombardier Beetles hold the plasma inside their bellies, this organic construct could hold the virus within itself and act like a bee's stinger."

"Stingers... An apt comparison and a good name," Toksi said. "I like this concept. We wouldn't be able to grow enough of them to match the size of your current virus canisters in the six to eight weeks Doom said we had left before the attack. However, if we can begin production of Stingers half that size, we could have two or three hundred thousand of them by that deadline."

I whistled through my teeth, impressed. "That's amazing! What can I do to help?"

"A lot," she said matter-of-factly. "You already know this virus well, and you are familiar with our membranes. I would need you to assess what modifications might be required to the membrane's DNA or what special inner coating is needed for it to remain impervious to the virus."

"Certainly. I'll get right on it as soon as I'm done setting up my lab," I replied, the usual thrill prior to embarking on a challenging research process coursing through me.

"I won't hold you any further then. You can take tissue samples in this cooling unit," she said pointing at it. "I will transfer all the necessary data to your computer."

"Thank you," I replied, readying to leave.

"You have a sound scientific mind for a male," she said pensively. "Too bad your kind doesn't mesh well with our hive mind. Your offspring with our Queens could have provided an interesting boost to our intellectual evolution."

"Too bad, indeed," I replied politely, my stomach roiling at that mere prospect.

Thankfully, as was the Kryptid Workers' wont, the minute they deemed the conversation concluded, they dismissed you from their thoughts. Without another word, Toksi turned back to her petri dishes to resume her work. Relieved, I fetched a few membrane tissue samples and headed to my improvised lab.

CHAPTER 10
ROGUE

Embarrassment surged through me as I once more caught myself stealing glances at my female while she flew us to a little romantic getaway. I couldn't seem to keep my eyes off Shuria. Every time I saw her, I noticed something new about her unique beauty. Right now, it was the swirling, embossed patterns on her skin that held all my attention.

To humans, they would resemble intricate scarification tattoos. But Mimics were naturally born with them. They held no particular meaning, although certain patterns appeared more often in specific bloodlines. Tiny scales covered them. From my research on the Mimics' anatomy and physiology, those patterns —called undars—acted as both a backup respiratory system and an additional feeding system. The slightly bigger pores of her undars could absorb nutrients from the water, even should she be unconscious or asleep while submerged.

"The Workers didn't give you too much of a hard time?" Shuria asked, a teasing edge in her voice as she flew our personal shuttle with the ease of great experience.

"No. They were very… efficient and to the point," I replied with amusement.

Shuria snorted. "Efficient and to the point... Quite the apt description. They excel at making you feel dismissed."

I chuckled while nodding. "They do, but I admit that I'll take that over trying to get rid of someone who won't stop talking your ears off when you just want to get back to work."

Shuria smiled. "Agreed. Dare I hope things were productive?"

"They certainly were. The Workers are incredibly brilliant. It is a shame that we cannot recruit them into the Vanguard. There are no limits to what we could achieve with them working alongside us," I mused out loud.

My female took on a strange expression. "I don't know if it would work. Their mentality is too different from ours. Unless a field of research directly benefits the colony, they deemed it a waste of time. Spending years trying to find a cure for an endangered species would never happen here unless that species was essential to maintaining the balance of an important ecosystem. Otherwise, they'd let it become extinct. Survival of the fittest. They would be fine crossing the line from morally gray to downright immoral if it served the interests of the colony."

I nodded slowly. "That's sadly very accurate. It's all the sadder that they're not actually doing any of this out of malice or cruelty. It is just their way."

I heaved a sigh before smiling at my female and giving her a quick summary of what we had accomplished today and would work on in the upcoming days.

"That was a brilliant idea you had with the Beetles. I'm sure you impressed them," Shuria said, her face glowing with pride.

It did funny things to me that my female should derive so much pleasure from my success. Now I wanted to perform even better to continue making her proud of me.

"They said something to that effect," I replied, feeling a little shy.

"They must hate not being able to get you to mate with the Queen," Shuria said smugly.

My face heated, and my skin darkened, giving me away.

"Oh, shit! They said that, too, didn't they?!" Shuria exclaimed.

To my relief, there was no anger or outrage in her voice. "Yes, they did," I admitted, feeling myself blush some more. "But they are well aware that it will never happen."

"That's right," Shuria said, puffing out her chest. "Not only are you not compatible with their hive mind, but you are also already spoken for. And I don't share."

"Good, because I do not wish to be shared," I replied. "I'm yours alone."

A powerful emotion mixed with the most adorable timidity flitted over my mate's beautiful face. Shuria still struggled to believe that we were soulmates. Life had not been kind to her, and my female had convinced herself that she didn't deserve happiness. I would remind her daily that we truly were the two halves of the same whole, and that she deserved every bit of the joy I intended to fill her life with.

"How have things gone on your end? Any progress," I asked.

She nodded, taking on a serious expression. "Reklig and I have made some substantial progress. We managed to eliminate quite a few planets and moons in the sector as the rebel leader's potential hiding place. The Kryptid technology definitely helped on that front. As far as Hehiri is concerned, our hopes aren't too high."

My brows shot up. "Really? Tabitha's analyses seemed to indicate there was a strong probability of activity there."

To my relief, Shuria didn't take umbrage at my comment. For the longest time, she'd resented Tabitha for being Bane's soulmate. While they had overcome their differences during the final war leading to Khutu's demise, they had never grown close.

Now that she was my mate, I hoped Shuria and Tabitha could become friends.

"Which was correct," Shuria admitted, matter-of-factly. "There had indeed been a lot of activity, but it's currently non-existent. Reklig and I have sent stealth drones to canvas the sector and the planet. But we suspect whoever had been there evacuated already, likely to join the rest of the rebels at their rally point."

"That's not good," I replied with mounting worry.

"It's not, but the upside is that once we've pinpointed that base, we can send a team to investigate it unimpeded and gather intel that could help us defeat them," Shuria countered. "According to Chaos, we still have four weeks before the attack. That leaves us plenty of time to go there and return if Doom so decides. But I doubt it's their HQ, and that's what I want to find."

Although I shared the sentiment, I couldn't help but pry further. "What makes you think that?"

"Dalton told Legion that he's been operating right under the Vanguard's noses," Shuria explained. "Hehiri is a mostly abandoned planet. No one bothers with it. I've been studying Giles Dalton, everything from his appearance, speech, and behavior. He's a narcissist and psychopath. He will want the Vanguard to be humiliated once they discover where he's been located this whole time."

"When *we* discover where he's been hiding, my mate. You are of the Vanguard, too," I gently corrected.

She smiled, her face softening with that hint of shyness again. That was another thing I needed to help her with. Shuria feared she wouldn't belong or be welcome on Khepri. If she only knew... I couldn't wait for my brothers and the other members of the Vanguard to rally here on Kryptor so my female could experience firsthand how they would rejoice for us and embrace her. In the meantime, I'd chip away at her insecurities until they were but a distant memory.

"But enough about work. Right now, it's just you and me, two soulmates getting better acquainted," I said in a cheerful tone. "So where are you taking me?"

Shuria beamed at me. "We're going to the Ekzen Valley, it's just a few more minutes from here. It has the best natural hot springs, and lovely vegetation that reminds me of Thaga, my homeworld."

My eyes widened in shock, and I glanced at the barren landscape of Kryptor with confusion. The planet was nothing but sand, rocky formations, and arid land all in the same reddish-orange hue. The occasional plant and shrub qualified more as cacti than anything else.

For all that, Kryptor wasn't actually a desert. Below the apparently parched sand and rocks, rich soil hid a short distance away. The frequent strong winds and glaring twin suns had convinced the flora and most of the fauna to live underground, just like the dominant species of the planet. Although I hadn't experienced it firsthand, I witnessed the wonders of the underground world of Kryptor where wildlife thrived thanks to the dream walks organized by the Scelks. Before we left this planet, I hoped to visit a few in person.

Shuria chuckled at my baffled expression and pointed at yet another rocky hill ahead. "Right there, on the other side…"

I pointlessly stretched my neck to try and see beyond the hill. But the wait wasn't long. My jaw dropped at the mesmerizing sight of a paradisiacal oasis in the middle of nowhere. It appeared to be surrounded by the rocky formation, as if a lake had settled inside an old volcano. The oddest vegetation grew all around, its colors still fairly muted, mostly beige, ochres, some dark blues, and greens.

The flora looked nothing like the one from Thaga, let alone Khepri or Earth. By the general size, height, and texture, we could recognize the trees from the plants and flowers. But their shapes were far too different to even try to compare them to anything I knew. While beautiful in their strangeness, I suspected a few to be venomous.

Shuria landed our shuttle on a little plateau a short distance from the pristine water. The colorful stones covering the riverbed made it difficult to be certain about the natural color of the water. But I suspected it to be clear. The freshest air slapped my nose as soon as we disembarked. Instead of the heavy, spicy aroma that permeated Kryptor, the air here had a slightly fruity fragrance and felt lighter, easier to breathe in.

What I'd initially thought to be khaki grass turned out to be some kind of spongy surface covering the ground. It slightly sank under our weight with each step, bouncing back without leaving a footprint, but making a discreet sigh as it deflated. I wanted to grab a few samples to analyze it and the plants around us. But I cast that thought out of my head. Today was about bonding with my mate. Science could wait.

I grabbed Shuria's hand as she led the way to the lake. She immediately beamed at me, joy radiating from her face. I'd make sure to multiply those little displays of affection, especially in public.

"Well, Mister Dragon, I hope you know how to swim," she said in a taunting tone.

I snorted and gave her a falsely outraged look. "I most certainly do. Land, water, or air, nothing defeats a Dragon."

Even as I spoke those words, I removed my shirt without stopping my advance towards the lake. After tossing the garment to the ground, I stepped out of my boots before discarding my pants. Seeing Shuria's stormy eyes darken as she observed me had blood rushing to my groin. Fuck, I loved the lustful and possessive way she looked at me.

To my surprise, the smart repartee I expected from her never came. Casting a glance at my female, I noticed her unusual nervousness as she stripped out of her clothes. That baffled me. I had seen Shuria naked before. Like Dragons and Xians, Mimics' naughty bits were naturally covered. A scaly membrane hid her sex from view, while a series of small blue scales on her chest—the same shade as her skin—hid her nipples. As clothes would impede her morphing during battle, she only wore some tactical accessories the same way we Dragons and Xians did.

During the long final battle against Khutu, I'd had plenty of occasions to admire her beauty. But then, I had not taken a good look as my Dragon had not stirred in her presence at the time. Of course, she would be self-conscious now that I'd be looking at her with completely new eyes and with totally different intentions.

"You're so beautiful, you take my breath away," I whispered in all sincerity.

And beautiful, she was. Tall and slender, Shuria had the longest and sexiest legs I'd ever seen. Her firm body possessed just the right amount of muscles to scream of her strength and fitness without losing its feminine curves. And such wondrous curves she had, with her narrow waist flaring into the most enticing hips.

Her dusky blue skin took on a darker shade around her face and chest as she blushed at the compliment. The timid way she lowered her eyes, tucked her midnight blue hair behind her ear, and smiled shyly messed with my head. Aside from the fact that she looked beyond adorable, it clashed so much with the tough, fierce, and uncompromising image I'd always had of Shuria. I loved a strong female, but this soft side stirred my protective instinct and made me melt from the inside out.

Closing the distance between us, I drew her into my embrace. She lifted her face to look at me. I kissed her forehead before nuzzling her nose. She chuckled and beamed at me, her stormy eyes filled with stars.

"Being with you makes me happy," I whispered, my hearts filling to bursting. "I've dreamt of finding you for so long."

Shuria melted against me, and a delicious flame lit in the pit of my stomach at the feel of her naked body against mine. Fuck, she was so soft. The ridges of her undars tickled my palms as I caressed her back in an upward movement until I cupped her nape. Our lips met, and a mix of desire and tenderness flooded through me. Despite our lack of experience, my female and I were quickly adjusting to each other, our tongues moving harmoniously in a sensual dance.

With an unusual boldness for me, I settled my other hand on the plump left cheek of Shuria's behind before giving it a little squeeze. She didn't rebel, pressing herself further against me with a soft sigh. A powerful shiver ran down my spine when my mate gently raked her nails over the scales of my back. A bolt of lust exploded in the pit of my stomach, and I moaned, barely keeping myself from asking her to do it again, but harder.

I shifted on my feet to lessen the growing discomfort of my blossoming erection as my shaft pressed against my loin plate. I broke the kiss, wanting to put a bit of distance between us to regain control of my desires. However, Shuria had a different idea in mind.

As soon as our lips parted, she began kissing my face and my neck. She fisted my hair at the nape, pulling my head back to expose my neck—not that she really needed to. Despite her height of 6'1, she still fell short of my 6'8. Shuria kissed, nipped, and sucked on my neck, while her free hand roamed over me. A pool of lava swirled in my loins as she touched me with a heat and possessiveness that further fanned the flames of my desire.

When her hand ventured lower towards my navel, my abdominal muscles contracted with lust while my cock strained painfully against its confines. I yanked Shuria's hand away and took a step back with a hissing breath. She jerked her head up to look at me. A million emotions flitted over her features, mainly shock and worry. It struck me then that she'd probably interpreted my actions as a sign my Dragon was rejecting her touch.

Thankfully, some of her tension lessened as she could undoubtedly see the burning passion she'd awakened in me on my face.

"You're setting my blood ablaze, female," I said, my voice thick with need. "Let's get in the water before I burst into flames and combust. You're far too tempting for your own good."

Shuria giggled in the loveliest fashion and took the hand I was extending to her. To my shock, when I tried to interlace my fingers with hers, fleshy membranes got in the way. I lifted her hand to glance at it. She immediately looked self-conscious as I gazed at the delicate, translucent membrane between her fingers.

"I don't recall ever noticing you had webbing," I said, stunned.

She looked incredibly uncomfortable, which baffled me. "Every Mimic has webbed fingers and toes," she explained in an almost apologetic tone. "We usually resorb them into our skin unless we are swimming. It weirds out some people and makes manipulating certain things a little awkward."

Although it bothered me that she would have self-image issues, I couldn't fault her for it. My brothers and I also struggled with some of the physical traits we'd inherited from our sire.

"I can see how they could get in the way of some manual activities, like firing a blaster," I mused out loud. "But they are otherwise lovely."

I gently caressed the thin membrane with my thumb before lifting her hand to my face and kissing the larger webbing between her thumb and index finger. She smiled with an air of gratitude.

"As you know, Dragons also resorb part of our anatomy into our skin," I confessed sheepishly. It was my turn to feel self-conscious as I gave my mate a sideways glance. "We hate our multifaceted eyes, and our chitin scales. But there's nothing we can do about that. We wished we had golden dragon scales like the Xians, and no Deynian horn. However, our mandibles we can hide. We resented having to keep them out while Khutu still controlled us."

Shuria stared at me with a shocked expression, her gaze locking on my crescent-moon shaped Deynian horn, slipping down to my eyes, and then settling on my mouth.

"Wow, it's true. It's been so long since I've seen any of you with mandibles out that I'd actually forgotten you used to have them—not that I had spent much time with your brothers before your defection. Although I didn't mind them back then, I will not complain about you keeping them tucked away."

"Oh?" I asked, raising a curious eyebrow.

She nodded with a mischievous glimmer in her eyes. "Mmhmm. I've become addicted to kissing you. Mandibles would get in the way of that."

I burst out laughing, and her stormy eyes sparkled with delight. "Great answer, my mate. I fully share the sentiment."

She puffed out her chest before studying my features again. "As for your eyes, I love them just the way they are. The Xians' smooth, obsidian eyes are cool, but your multifaceted ones make you look even more fierce. Your horn gives you a regal air. It always made me think of a crown. And don't you dare disparage your black scales. In case you haven't noticed, the Xians—and the Vanguard as a whole—always dress in black. It's elegant and badass—like the humans like to say. I love everything about your appearance."

I smiled, my chest warming for my female. "You're wonderful for my ego," I said for lack of a better response, then leaned forward to kiss her.

I felt her smile against my lips. That, too, messed with me. It boggled my mind how so many little things involving her made me happy.

Hand in hand, we ran into the water. To my surprise, the

water turned out to be cooler than the light steam crawling over it led me to expect. It wasn't cold by any means, but just a smidge over lukewarm. My scientific mind immediately itched to study the reason behind this phenomenon, but I forced myself to focus on my female.

Not that she gave me much of a choice in the matter.

Shuria was literally swimming circles around me. With her being an amphibian, it didn't surprise me, but I couldn't deny a certain level of awe. She mostly moved her legs, closed tightly together, like a mermaid's tail, but she would also sometimes alternate their movement, especially when performing acrobatic maneuvers both under and out of the water.

It didn't take long for me to realize my mate wasn't just teasing me by swiftly swimming by, tapping or poking me on the way, before darting out of range. Shuria was showing off her skills and putting on quite the spectacle. She would dive deep then shoot back up to the surface, performing some breathtaking aerial pirouette before diving back.

When she finally tired of making me chase after her, my female slipped her arms around me, and we began swirling in the water in a sensual dance. Shuria immediately took the lead. Although it felt a little strange to me, I happily yielded. After all, we were in her element.

"Take a deep breath," Shuria suddenly said telepathically to me.

I didn't question the request and complied. Seconds later, she pulled me underwater with her. Aligning my body with hers, I followed her movements as she made us glide through the waves barely a meter below the surface.

"Let me be your lungs," Shuria added before leaning forward and pressing her lips to mine.

Even as I once more complied, I was struck by a sudden realization. Aside from being practical, mind speak also made it harder for one to lie or attempt to deceive, as the speaker's emotions often seeped through the connection unless they possessed great control over them. And right now, my female was asking me for a leap of faith... in her.

"Breathe," she commanded, her lips parting against mine.

I first exhaled through the nose, then inhaled through my mouth, my lungs filling with the fresh oxygen Shuria had extracted through her gills. When she closed her mouth, I guessed she was breathing for herself, before opening her lips again. After the fourth time, a powerful wave of emotion flooded into me through our mental connection: affection and gratitude dominating. My mate had needed me to show I trusted her with my life, and I genuinely did.

"Deeper," I mind spoke to her.

Shuria's arms tightened around my back, and another wave of tenderness emanating from her crashed over me. Eyes locked with my female, I couldn't say how long we remained in the depths of the lake. Although my multifaceted eyes allowed me to see underwater, the pressure eventually forced me to close them. But I didn't care. We didn't speak, too busy reveling in our mental connection, our mutual feelings flowing through each other, the warmth of our intertwined bodies, and the caress of the water as it glided on our skin.

By the time we resurfaced, an undeniable bond had formed between us.

We settled on the beach—if it could qualify as such—to enjoy the picnic Shuria had prepared for us. To see all my favorite dishes, and an outrageous amount of sweet bites had my hearts further melting for my female. I didn't doubt for a minute Shuria had interrogated Reaper about my preferences, and he had passed on the fact that I had quite the sweet tooth. I needed to do the same with Silzi to return this kind of lovely surprise to my female. But Silzi and two of the other modified Mimics were on a critical mission with Chaos and Wrath. Right this instant, they were dealing with the newly discovered Scelk clones and trying to sabotage the rebels' efforts before they could reach their rally point to launch their assault on Kryptor.

Shuria sighed wistfully.

"What are you thinking?" I asked, curious.

She smiled sheepishly. "I was just thinking how nice this is. It almost feels like being back on my homeworld Thaga. Things were simple back then. We were all so carefree. Mimics often ate like this by the water after an intense swimming session. It was more of a potluck type of deal, everyone just bringing something. As it was never planned ahead, we sometimes ended up with nothing but proteins, or nothing but fruits and vegetables, but occasionally, we had a nice mix."

Shuria's nostalgic smile faded, and an air of sadness flitted over her beautiful face, her stormy eyes darkening as she reminisced. My hearts constricted as I instantly guessed where her thoughts had wandered. Although I'd had no control over the atrocities performed against innocent species like hers, I couldn't help the surge of guilt within me each time I heard about what my sire had done.

"I'd just turned nineteen when the Kryptids raided Thaga. We were at the end of a similar meal. The younglings had already requested to be excused and were off playing by the water. Between the happy shouts and screams, it took us a while to realize a different type of screams were echoing in the distance. There was no explosion, no smoke, no enemy vessels in the sky."

"They were camouflaged," I replied matter-of-factly in a soft voice.

Shuria nodded, her face taking on a bitter expression. "By the time we finally caught on, people were running past us, shouting for everyone to get in the water. No one questioned those orders. We just ran, still blind as to the source of the threat. And then some of my sisters started falling before they could reach the water, as if a projectile had struck them. But there was no blood, no visible wound. I tried to go help one of them but the people behind me pushed me forward. And then I saw the first Soldier."

My throat tightened at the haunted look in her eyes. I couldn't begin to imagine how terrified she must have been. By intergalactic standards, Mimics were considered primitive. They were a peaceful people, who hadn't pursued technology by choice as they felt no desire to visit other worlds. With no real predators to threaten them in their inhabited areas, they had not developed any weapons or defense that could have held invaders at bay.

"We hid deep in the water. Even without advanced technology, we could easily defeat the Kryptids there. And we did at first. They were too slow, didn't know the area like we did, including the treacherous undercurrents, and were quite vulnerable to our ultrasonic pulses. We were wrecking them. And for a while, we had hoped they would give up and leave. After all, Mimics can survive underwater for months, years even if we hibernate and rely on our undars for food and oxygen," she said, absentmindedly caressing the ridges of the patterns on her skin.

I nodded grimly. "Kryptids don't fare well in water. Their chitin repels water, and their legs are not suitable for swimming. They make great buoys though as they naturally tend to float on the surface. But obviously, they found a workaround to their shortcomings, as is their wont."

"Did they ever," Shuria said through her teeth, resentment seeping into her voice. "After eight days of us systematically spanking them, they stopped their attacks. By the fourth day of peace, we thought they had given up and left. We couldn't have been more wrong. On the sixth day—exactly two weeks after the initial raid—the assaults resumed. They set up energy fields that ran deep, down to the riverbed, creating small sections with groups of us trapped within. And then they poisoned the water to force us out."

I recoiled. "Poisoned?"

The Kryptids had many faults, but even under my demented father's command, they didn't kill just for the fun of it. With the morphing abilities of the Mimics, they wouldn't have wasted a single one of them. Even those too old would have served a purpose, whether for their organs or to run riskier experiments on, or as food for the Swarm Drone breeding swamps.

Shuria pursed her lips before shrugging. "I guess poisoned isn't the right term," she conceded. "But they put something in the water that blocked our ability to breathe. It was like they had sucked the oxygen right out of the river. We were suffocating. After we used the oxygen reserves from our undars, we had no choice but to get out or drown."

I flinched, my hearts constricting with sympathy. "They likely spent those six days designing nanobots that would disable your gills and undars. With all the Mimics they had previously captured, they were able to test which receptors to target. I'm assuming whatever they dropped in the water did not affect the other aquatic creatures?"

Shuria stiffened, her eyes widening in shock. "Maker! You're right. None of the fish were affected."

I nodded with an apologetic smile. "They made sure to remove your ability to stay in a safe environment, without impeding your actual ability to breathe once on their playground. The Kryptids wanted you alive and healthy."

"And it sure was their playground," Shuria said angrily. "We were helpless against their blasters. I was so furious when Silzi and many of my younger sisters surrendered. I wanted to fight. As the eldest, it was my duty to protect them all. But as always, Silzi was the wise one."

Shuria snorted with self-derision before folding her legs and hugging her knees to her chest. Her eyes went out of focus as the terrible events of that day likely replayed in her mind.

"Those of us who wanted to fight morphed into the most lethal creatures of our homeworld. Sure, we did a lot of damage, killed many Kryptids, but in the end, they slaughtered us because we didn't know how to use those creature's abilities properly. Mimics used to morph for fun, not for battle. We never trained on fighting in those bodies."

I nodded grimly. Back when Shuria had first killed Bane out of jealousy, she'd taken on my appearance to fool him, then taken on my battle form to try to kill Tabitha and Dread. The only reason she had failed was that she didn't master battling as one of us.

"The last thing I remember was a really loud boom, then a swarm of insects I'd never seen before stinging us. I went numb in seconds. When next I awakened, I was in a lab, screaming in pain while they experimented on us."

Pushing my empty plate aside, I drew Shuria into my embrace, and caressed her arm in a soothing fashion, encouraging her to continue. She snuggled against me and rested her head on my shoulder.

"From that moment on, I only saw my sisters from a distance. Most of the time, they were bound by membranes, some floated inside medical tanks, and others were strapped to examination tables while screaming in agony. Too many got carried away on hover platforms, their bodies just tossed in a pile. I didn't need an explanation as to why. I just wondered how long before I ended up dead as well."

Shuria took a shuddering breath and blinked rapidly to stem the tears that threatened to come out. I tightened my hold around her, kissed her temple, and gently rocked her. She reached for my free hand, squeezing it tightly as if to draw strength from me. I squeezed her hand right back and kissed her temple again.

"I don't know how long this went on. It was many months, maybe even a couple of years. One day, the experiments just stopped. I no longer felt sick or in pain. For that alone, I did everything I was told so the torture wouldn't resume. They were training me, teaching me how to fight, showing me combat technology I never could have imagined. And then the General started visiting me."

My back stiffened, and my stomach roiled at the dreadful visual those words elicited in me. The thought that my sire might have touched my female made me want to vomit. But Shuria said she was still a virgin. And as much of a monster as my sire had been, Khutu had never coupled with a female unless it was for breeding purposes. Shuria had not been ready for that.

"Khutu showered me with praises for what I'd become, for my combat prowess, and for being so obedient and disciplined. He said I'd be a Queen, Bane's Queen, and the mother of the first new powerful breed of Kryptids." She snorted again with disgust and in a way that screamed of self-recrimination. "By then, I believed everything he said. I'd even begun seeing him as a benevolent ruler. How fucking stupid was I?"

"Do not blame yourself," I said sternly. "You were tortured for years before being put through an intense indoctrination protocol. No one could have resisted that. You were not stupid, and even less at fault."

Shuria lifted her head to look at me, her eyes filled with gratitude. "Yeah," she conceded. "I don't remember when it happened, but Lekla confirmed that my sisters and I had been brainwashed and conditioned to hate the Xians and make the General's cause our own."

I nodded slowly. "The Workers are excellent at what they do, especially when they have plenty of time to work on a subject."

"Indeed. Frankly, if not for Bane rejecting me, I might still have been Khutu's most loyal soldier," Shuria said with a haunted look. "If the General had been so wrong about the golden future he'd promise me with Bane, what else was he wrong about? And then he chose my sister Pahiven as his new Queen over me. *I* was supposed to be the first Queen giving birth to the new breed. I had not been good enough for his son, and now I wasn't good enough for him either?"

Once again, I swallowed back the bile rising in my throat at the thought of Khutu touching Shuria and impregnating her.

"It had nothing to do with your worth," I countered forcefully. "Quite the opposite. Bane couldn't have claimed you because his Dragon had already claimed another. And Khutu knew you were too strong for him to control as he saw fit. He needed someone weaker and more submissive."

Shuria nodded. "Pahiven was the sweet one. She always did what she was told. Seeing what his foul seed did to her, how it ruined her finally opened my eyes. It should have been me, not her. As the eldest, I should have protected her. Once she started birthing those abominations, I knew I had to act. I couldn't save Pahiven or her offspring, but I wouldn't let any of my other sisters be next. At that moment, I finally understood Bane and his determination to save his younger brothers, to save all of you."

She caressed my cheek as she spoke those words. I covered the back of her hand with mine before turning my face to kiss her palm. A pleasant heat spread through my chest as I thought of my oldest brother. As the firstborn hybrid son of the General, Bane had sacrificed everything to protect us, taking beatings meant for us, diverting Khutu's ire or the attention of the Soldiers abusing us so that we could flee.

"But I was angry... Always angry. So very angry, hurt, and lonely," Shuria continued, bitterness returning in her voice. "Khutu had turned me into a monster who didn't belong anywhere anymore."

"No, Shuria. You were never a monster," I countered in a tone that brooked no argument. "You were an experimental subject. He turned you into something you weren't, fed your anger and primal instincts to turn you into a killing machine. Despite that, your goodness always shone through, if only in your devotion to your sisters, nieces, and nephews. It takes an extremely strong person to break free of the Kryptids' indoctrination. It took months of us working with your modified sisters to revert their brainwashing. You achieved it on your own and then rose to the moment by rallying the Workers into turning against Khutu. Do you not realize just how amazing you are?"

Shuria stared at me in shock, then her eyes misted, and her lips quivered. "Maker, you mean it. You really mean it," she whispered, incredulous.

"Yes, Shuria. I mean every single word of it. I am in awe of you. You're not a monster. You're my soulmate. No one deserves love and happiness more than you do. And I can promise you, I will devote the rest of my days making sure you get plenty of both."

CHAPTER 11
SHURIA

For the hundredth time, I chastised myself for my lack of focus. Any minute now, the others would arrive for the meeting update on what Reklig and I had found. But how was I supposed to concentrate when Rogue filled my every thought?

A week had already gone by since the Vanguard's arrival on Kryptor. While we both had tons of work that kept us busy, we still spent as much time as possible together. He was so freaking amazing to me. The way he looked at me, talked to me, and touched me with such respect, affection, and almost reverence had become my latest addiction. I couldn't get enough of him, and constantly wanted more.

And that scared me...

Good things never happened to me, and this more than qualified as too good to be true. I didn't doubt the sincerity of his feelings. His Dragon wouldn't allow him to lie about this. Yet I kept dreading the moment whatever had allowed him to recognize me as his mate would revert, and we'd lose that connection. Worse still, I feared that he'd eventually find me too clingy and become annoyed.

And yet, he's always happy to see me.

That he was. Maker, how I loved feeling so wanted, just for who I was, not for how he could use me for his own benefit. I hated feeling so insecure, and especially that he could see it. Rogue was going out of his way proving in words and actions that he genuinely liked me and deemed me worthy. I didn't want to be that needy female. This shit was all the more annoying that I wanted to push things further with him. But Rogue was holding himself back because he could sense my uncertainties and wanted me to have no misgivings or reservations about us on our first night together. So these fucking insecurities seriously needed to take a hike.

I'm beyond ready!

"That bad, huh?" Reklig asked in his insufferably taunting voice.

I jerked my head up to look at him, confused as to what he was referring to. Although Scelks could read minds without their targets even realizing it, I implicitly trusted him not to violate my privacy.

"What do you mean?"

"You've sighed three times, and grunted twice, the second time with a hefty dose of aggravation. Is your mate so difficult to handle?" he mocked.

My skin heated with embarrassment, and I glared at him, despite being mostly annoyed at myself.

"Rogue is the sweetest and most easy-going male in the universe," I snarled.

"Ah, then *you* are the source of your own aggravation," he said far too accurately in the same obnoxious tone.

I scrunched my face at him, a million thoughts of all the ways I wanted to smack him flitting through my mind. By the way his smile broadened, he knew exactly what type of uncharitable urges coursed through me. To my surprise, instead of needling me further, his face took on a soft, sympathetic—almost fraternal—expression that threw me for a loop.

"Stop overthinking everything, Shuria. You are right in saying Rogue is the sweetest male in the universe. You are his soulmate. I've never seen him so happy since he found you. Do not let whatever unfounded negative image you have of yourself get in the way of your happiness. I did the same with my Madeline, thinking myself unworthy, until Varnog shamed me into pursuing her. Do not waste time on such useless insecurities. His Dragon wouldn't have claimed you if you weren't a beautiful soul."

Between shock and overwhelming emotions, words failed me. Moved to my core, I opened and closed my mouth, my throat too constricted to speak. As a Scelk, he understood all too well what it felt like to be seen as a monster and an abomination. The Dragons—and especially Bane—had been the first to recognize their worth. It was thanks to him that the Vanguard had welcomed them among their ranks. And yet, to this day, the rest of the Coalition continued to perceive them as evil. No wonder he'd dreaded approaching Madeline with his feelings for her.

But as was his wont, Reklig spared me from having to respond by reverting to his insufferable self just as quickly as he'd become gentle.

"Now stop daydreaming about horny-head and get back to work," he said in a provocative tone.

"Ugh, you're impossible!" I snarled, finding my voice again.

"I know," Reklig retorted proudly. "But save your flattery for your mate."

Even as I rolled my eyes, I fought both to hold back a chuckle and the urge to hurl something at the back of his head.

The meeting room door opened on my mate, quickly followed by the rest of our team, Daeko, and Commander Hulax. Rogue's gaze connected with mine, and he winked at me. I smiled at him, my heart melting in my chest. I wanted to go snuggle in his embrace but forced myself to stay put. Reklig clearing his throat drew my attention. To my utter annoyance, he wiggled the scaly ridges that served him as eyebrows. Maker! How I wanted to drop-kick him.

Not to worry. I'd get even at some point.

The large vidcom on the wall came to life, displaying Queen Xerath, still in her birthing chamber. I felt exhausted *for* her, laying eggs around the clock. But as a proper Kryptid, she didn't consider it a chore, merely a duty.

Once everyone had taken their seat, Doom opened the meeting.

"Sorry for pulling you away from your respective tasks. Shuria and Reklig have some important updates to share with us, which I believe we need to act on," Doom said. "I will let them share their discoveries with you, and then we can decide on a course of action."

Doom nodded at Reklig and me, then took a seat. I exchanged a look with Reklig, and he blinked to confirm he would go first.

"We have performed a thorough analysis of the data provided by the drones which regularly patrol the area, as well as those we sent specifically to scan Hehiri," Reklig said, his tone serious and devoid of his usual mischief. "Although there has been significant activity there over the past few months, it is currently non-existent. Whatever was happening there, we're too late. Even deep scans reveal nothing. Granted, there is a small possibility that they have powerful disruptors fooling our surveys, but it is doubtful. If they were still traveling back and forth from the planet in stealth mode, our drones would have picked up some kind of residual energy signature."

"They have abandoned the planet then?" Daeko asked.

"We believe so," Reklig replied. "Based on what we've been observing at all the secret bases our teams have been visiting, the Rebels are evacuating their respective locations to meet at a rally point. As you know, Chaos's team is currently on Aurilia. Had they arrived just a couple of weeks later than they did, the place would have been empty, and all the rebels' data wiped."

"We should still investigate it," Daeko insisted.

"Agreed," Doom intervened. "We should send people there to make sure our readings are correct and see if there is anything to be recovered or that might give us an edge against the rebels. But we can discuss it after they are done sharing what they found."

I repressed a smile at the polite but efficient way Doom told Daeko to relax and not get ahead of himself. The young Kryptid General easily came across as abrasive. And yet, he wasn't a bad sort. He just liked getting straight to the point, which could make him seem curt.

Daeko gave Doom a stiff nod then turned back to Reklig with an expectant look.

"We were able to narrow down a location where most of the traffic seemed to originate," Reklig continued. "It was an old biomedical factory where they grew replacement organs and limbs for various species using the stem cells of a local cephalopod. The creature not only quickly regrew any severed limbs, it could adapt to the surface antigen of any DNA without having to worry about graft rejection. It was abandoned fifteen years ago when new technological advances found an even more efficient way of producing replacement organs."

"An organ factory?" Rogue echoed, pensively. "This could be where they grew the clones for their Zombie Soldiers. If the rebels truly have the kind of numbers Chaos mentioned, they would have needed a place dedicated to mass producing them."

I smiled, pride surging through me for my mate.

"That is exactly what we think," Reklig concurred. "As the new organ production system is strictly regulated and the stem cells can only be acquired through the Galactic Medical Board, it would make sense for the rebels to fall back on an old method that no one would suspect or track."

"It will be good to see if we can find any of the research they performed on those clones, in case they added recent improvements," Rogue said. "However, Wrath and Legion already sent us DNA samples and complete blood work from the clones they encountered. I'd be surprised if we find anything revolutionary there."

Everyone nodded.

"Which brings us to the second part of this meeting," I said, taking over. "We also believe there is nothing of importance left on Hehiri. So where is their headquarters? The biggest clue we had was Giles Dalton's claim that he was operating right under the nose of the Vanguard. The obvious assumption was that he was right on Khepri. But that was impossible. All traffic to and from the Vanguard's homeworld is too strictly monitored."

"Be that as it may, your Coalition members can still come and go with relative freedom on Khepri, don't they?" Daeko challenged.

"They do," Doom conceded. "But they aren't able to operate a secret lab on Khepri. Authorized personnel can come and go as they please, but entry of any shipment, especially electronics, weaponry, chemicals, or foreign life forms that could become a biohazard is strictly controlled. They could never build or equip a lab without us knowing."

Daeko slowly nodded, although he still looked unconvinced.

"Khepri is impossible," I reiterated. "Even assuming they'd found a way to sneak in bio samples and lab materials, the rest of their operations could never have worked. Remember that the rebels appropriated tons of Kryptid technology. Each time the Vanguard won a battle against Khutu, the Coalition would go in to do the cleanup. That included helping the surviving locals relocate or rebuild, return kidnapped victims to their homeworlds, and either destroy or bring to Khepri anything left behind by the Kryptids. Instead, the rebels stole entire liveships, Spitters, and other Kryptid vessels. They kidnapped Workers to steal their knowledge. They kept the creatures from Khutu's experiments to pursue the work for their own benefit. There is no possible way they could have brought all of that to Khepri in secret."

Daeko's mandibles clacked in a nervous tick I associated with him intensely thinking.

"Those are valid arguments," Queen Xerath said. "So if not Khepri, where else?"

"I pondered that. If it was right under the Vanguard's nose, it had to be at a relatively short distance. I figured no more than two to three days at warp speed. It needed to be a place where a lot of traffic would be expected, and where no one would pry into who and what you had onboard. And especially, they'd want a place where you could operate with complete privacy."

"That seems rather difficult to achieve. Are you saying that you found such a place?" Daeko asked.

"Yes. It was so obvious, it's shocking that we didn't realize it sooner," I said before activating the 3D projector on the floor by the head of the table.

It displayed a star map with markers over three planets.

"This is Khepri, and this is Kryptor," I said, indicating the two planets at opposing edges of the sector displayed. "And this small planet right here, a short distance from Khepri is—"

"No fucking way!" Reaper whispered, the shock in his voice reflected on the faces of every other member of the Vanguard.

Daeko, Commander Hulax, and Queen Xerath all seemed confused by their reaction.

"Yes, I am beyond certain that the rebel HQ is on Wyngenia," I said with confidence before turning my attention to the Queen. "Wyngenia is an uninhabited planet which the Vanguard often refers to as the honeymoon world. It has breathtaking landscapes, a mesmerizing sky, stunning rivers, and the perfect weather year-round. It is where every Xian—and now Dragons and Scelks—take their mates for a romantic getaway. While some common areas have been built over the years for group activities, most couples go there to be isolated for a few days."

"But how does that guarantee privacy?" Daeko argued. "New couples landing on the planet could accidentally stumble on another one. It only takes a brief glimpse to see something wrong is taking place."

"The beacons system prevents that," I explained. "The minute you claim an area, you turn on its beacon. It will warn others to stay away. Anyone who enters Wyngenia's atmosphere receives a message showing the free areas. They just go there."

"So someone could have the same beacon active for months or years, and none would be the wiser," Daeko said with sudden understanding.

"Exactly."

Reaper cursed under his breath, fire burning in his eyes. "We need to go ferret those rats out."

"Agreed," I replied, while gesturing at the star map to zoom in on Wyngenia. I then pointed at an area in the northern hemisphere. "After analyzing the occupation data from the beacons, one large sector has remained uninterruptedly occupied for the past six years."

"Which matches the beginning of the rebellion," Madeline mused out loud.

"Correct. Although we have no recordings or sightings of massive ships—let alone Kryptid ones—entering that area, we are confident they indeed landed in stealth mode," I continued. "We didn't dare perform more intrusive scans for fear they might detect us and flee."

"Excellent thinking," Doom said. "We need the element of surprise."

"Good thinking, indeed," Daeko said with an approving glimmer in his multifaceted eyes as he looked at me.

It was stupid, especially considering that—by Mimics standard—he was just a one-year-old child. But that touched me.

Kryptids were quite stingy with compliments as good performance was always expected.

"When do we leave?" he asked.

I hesitated, casting a questioning look at Doom.

"Well, this is the decision-making part," Doom said cautiously. "There is Hehiri and Wyngenia."

"Wyngenia is the important one," Daeko interrupted.

"Agreed. However, if the intel Chaos shared with us is correct—and we have no reason to doubt it—the rebels will attack in four weeks from now. It will take three days to reach Hehiri, but at least a week for Wyngenia. One of my brothers, Fury, could take his team to investigate Hehiri. And Steele could take his own team to Wyngenia."

"No," Daeko said in a tone that brooked no argument. "These rebels are targeting Kryptor. We will take part in those raids to see exactly what attacks are being mounted against us. I have no issue with Fury heading to Hehiri. But he will rendezvous with our Soldiers beforehand."

I held my breath at the commanding way in which Daeko made his demands. Doom was many things but not a pushover. He also frequently stated that he hated diplomacy.

He tilted his head to the side as he observed Daeko. "If you can spare the Soldiers, that is acceptable," Doom replied calmly.

"Yes, I can. And I will go meet Steele for the raid on Wyngenia," Daeko added.

My back stiffened at those words. By the way Doom's face closed off, I already knew what his response would be.

"*That* is *not* acceptable," Doom said with a finality that knotted my insides. "You *cannot* leave Kryptor with an imminent massive onslaught. In theory, fifteen or sixteen days should suffice to go to Wyngenia and return. That would leave us with a couple of weeks before the attack. But that's assuming nothing goes wrong. We need you to lead your troops. Believe me, *I* want to go to Wyngenia. But my mission here was to make sure

Kryptor will be ready to fend off its attackers. And so here I'll stay as well."

Although clearly displeased, Daeko couldn't challenge Doom's arguments. A glance at Xerath confirmed that her General even considering leaving Kryptor had displeased her. And yet, I could see his logic. If he found Giles Dalton on Wyngenia and took him out, the rebellion would fall apart without its leader, averting unnecessary bloodshed on all sides.

"I could lead the Kryptid troops on that mission," Commander Hulax offered, before casting a questioning look at Xerath.

As the Commander of her Queen's Guard, he should also stay by her side. But if not for Daeko, Hulax was the best second choice for this role. The other Generals were still too young to assume any type of command.

The Queen gave a subtle nod, and Daeko echoed her gesture with more stiffness.

"I should go as well," Rogue added to my complete shock. "Steele's team doesn't have the expertise needed to handle the type of experiments we might find on Wyngenia."

"But what about your tasks here with our Workers?" Xerath interjected.

"My tasks do not require me to be physically here. I already have all the samples I require to pursue my work, and the rest I can communicate through vidcom with Toksi and Rakma."

"I should go as well," Reklig said. "Steel doesn't have a Scelk in his team. Based on the intel Chaos gathered from the rebel scientists they captured on Aurilia, Giles was sending them the Scelk bugs. Which means there's likely a Scelk Queen in that base, or at least Scelk eggs, some of them likely hatched."

Reklig's statement earned him the same nods of agreement from the others as Rogue's had. Panic settled inside me as I tried to come up with arguments as to why I should go as well. I didn't want to part from Rogue. But more importantly, I didn't want him to go into danger without me by his side. Every mated member of the Vanguard went into missions with their spouse. Did that automatically imply I would go as well?

"If I may be so bold, I do not believe that it would make sense to send Steele's team to Wyngenia," Madeline countered in a soft voice. "Since Rogue and Reklig will go, that means Shuria and I will tag along. We will want Thanh to come as well as our pilot as showing up to Wyngenia in a Kryptid vessel would be too risky. And Rogue has been sharing Reaper's Soulcatcher, since he doesn't have one. That means Martha also needs to come... with Reaper?"

I could have kissed her right now.

"That's almost our entire team," Doom argued.

"Yes but, like Rogue, we can perform our tasks remotely," I blurted. "Well, we will if we leave in three days."

"Three days is too long," Daeko interjected.

"Actually, three days makes sense," Rogue countered. "It will give Rakma the time needed to complete the Stingers we've been working on. Depending on what we find on Wyngenia, it might make a difference between winning and losing. It will be an excellent opportunity for us to test their efficiency."

"Anyway, Steele would take longer to reach Wyngenia than we could, even if we leave in three days," Thanh said. "Steele recently rendezvoused with Legion on Strajuc to recover their rebel prisoners, some Zombie clones, and Xenon's DNA to create new Shells for him. He's on his way back to drop all of that off on Khepri before he can come to Wyngenia. It will take about two weeks for him to get there. We'll be there at least four days before he could."

The discussion went on for a while longer until we finally reached an agreement that more than suited me. Reaper would lead our team with Martha serving as both his and Rogue's Soulcatcher and as our weapons expert. Reklig would deal with whatever Scelks we may find as well as mind-control potential rebels left behind, with his wife Madeline handling all hacking and technical needs. Rogue would be our science and xenobiologist expert. As for me, the Kryptids tried hard to make me stay behind, claiming the Soldiers who would accompany Commander Hulax would more than compensate for whatever combat skills I could offer.

But they couldn't morph like I did. And if my suspicions were right, we'd need my abilities.

"We'll depart in four days," Doom said, concluding the meeting. "Make sure you've wrapped up everything you need to get done here."

Everyone got up to leave. I intended to make a beeline for Rogue, but the Queen's voice stopped me.

"Shuria, please stay a moment. I would have a word with you."

Stunned, I stared at the Queen through the vidscreen then nodded. A troubled expression flitted over Rogue's face, quickly hidden, before he smiled at me with understanding.

"I'll see you later," Rogue said while gently caressing my cheek.

I smiled, my heart fluttering as I watched him exit the room with the others. When I turned back to look at Queen Xerath through the vidscreen, the intensity with which I caught her staring unnerved me.

"You wished to speak with me?" I asked to hide my unease.

"Congratulations on finding your mate. It is a rare occurrence for a Dragon to claim a female. Even a Kryptid Queen finds no grace in their eyes," Xerath said matter-of-factly.

My blood turned to ice upon hearing those words, and my stomach roiled at that thought. Was she jealous or resentful that Rogue had chosen me over her? The Kryptids had made no mystery that they would have liked to include the Dragon DNA into a new breed of Kryptids.

"It was quite unexpected for both Rogue and me. But their

Dragon decides. Their personal feelings have no control over who they can mate with," I carefully reminded her.

Speaking those words scorched my tongue. As much as I loved that Rogue was mine, the insecure voice at the back of my head kept harping about the fact that he hadn't chosen me. His Dragon had imposed me as his mate. Without this trait, would Rogue have ever courted me of his free will?

Xerath made a dismissive gesture before clasping the lower set of her four hands in front of her. "I'm well-aware of this. Lekla would have been pleased to know her efforts granted you the happiness she wished for you."

My throat tightened, and I blinked rapidly to stem the tears that wanted to well in my eyes at the thought of my old friend, and at the waves of gratitude that continued to swell within me every time I remembered how I indeed owed her my newfound happiness.

"I definitely owe her for that. Her last words to me had indeed been that she hoped I'd find my happily ever after," I said, proud that my voice didn't shake despite the emotions threatening to overwhelm me.

"As I doubt Rogue will wish to remain on Kryptor once the rebellion has been quelled, I take it you will leave us as well to be with him?"

Although she phrased it as a question, Xerath's words were more of a statement.

I gave her an apologetic smile and nodded. "Yes, I will."

"Good," Xerath replied in a neutral tone. "You have fulfilled your duty and served your purpose."

Despite my best efforts, I couldn't help but flinch. Even though I understood the nature of the Kryptids, her words cut me raw. I didn't expect her to love me or have deep feelings for me. But I would have at least wanted her to express some sort of regret to see me go, some sign that I had mattered.

Xerath tilted her head, a curious expression settling on her features as she studied me as if I was an illogical enigma.

"My words upset you," she said, sounding a little surprised, if not baffled, with a hint of disappointment.

I shrugged, trying to act indifferent. "Why would they?"

This time, Xerath took on a stern expression, like a parent would with a misbehaving child.

"You're a terrible liar, Shuria. My words hurt you, but they shouldn't. By now, you know our ways well enough. And yet, you remain too emotional."

I pressed my lips together and bit my tongue to hold back the indeed emotional diatribe I itched to launch into about what a cold bitch she was—even though she didn't deserve it. She was right: I knew their ways.

"I am not dismissive of you, Shuria," Xerath added, her voice taking on a surprisingly soft edge. "My people owe you our survival. Without you, the Workers wouldn't have rebelled, and Daeko would be dead. It was your quick thinking that got him to safety before Khutu could get to him. It was you who made possible the alliance with the Vanguard to defeat the abomination that would have destroyed my people. Do you think I will ever forget that?"

Shock crashed over me from finally hearing this acknowledgement from her. I hugged myself, choked by too many feelings.

"I cannot feel emotions the way you do. A part of me wishes that I could. But that doesn't make me indifferent. You served me well, Shuria, in more ways than you realize. The day General Khutu abducted me, you telepathically soothed me and lent me your strength. I'd never felt anything like it. It gave me comfort and the courage to face what laid ahead."

"Even back then, as the child you still were, you possessed the strength of a true queen. But I'm glad I was able to help," I said, this time making little effort to hide the tears in my eyes.

Xerath smiled with that oddly human mouth of hers, her

small mandibles chittering. "You have been loyal beyond anything I would have ever expected from an off-worlder, especially one who has suffered at the hand of my people. For that, you have my friendship and gratitude. But once this impending war is over, you will have served your purpose with us. Therefore, I am glad you now have a new purpose among your people, where you belong. Know that you will not be forgotten. Your name will forever figure in the Well of Knowledge alongside Lekla's as one of the eminent members of our society."

My lips quivered, and I pressed a palm to my chest as if to keep my heart from leaping out. "You honor me," I whispered in a shaky voice.

She gave me a discreet smile in response. "One last thing, I do not see his mark on you. The Workers have not perceived his scent on you either. Why have you not mated with Rogue?"

My jaw dropped and my skin darkened in embarrassment. I couldn't even feel outraged as our delay in coupling would be deemed irrational by the Kryptids.

"It's... It's complicated," I mumbled.

"No, it's not. But I suspect those silly off-worlder emotions are the reason," Xerath said in a clearly disapproving tone. "Do not waste the time you have with your mate. His seed will enhance you and fix more of what Khutu had done to you. This delay serves nothing and no one. I do not know if or when I'll get to see you again. So I'll tell you now. Enjoy your mate and be happy Shuria. You deserve it. Now, I must go back to laying eggs."

She pressed a hand to her quivering abdomen, no doubt cramping from her heavy charge eager to be set free. Xerath didn't even give me a chance to respond, merely turning off the communication.

I remained there staring at the screen, a silly smile on my face while affection swelled in my heart. She didn't love the way we did, but in her way, she loved me.

CHAPTER 12
ROGUE

The three days before our departure were pure insanity. The Kryptids were almost acting as if we were leaving forever. Granted, every mission was a gamble, and we did not know how much hostility we would encounter at the rebel base, but with such a large contingent of Kryptid Soldiers, we should be able to mow through whatever Giles threw our way, assuming he was even there.

My gut told me that, like with the other bases, the rebel leader was already on the move to join his minions at the staging area. From all indications, he'd also been extremely secretive with the rebels, sharing only the necessary information, like Khutu had done with the Kryptids. The less people knew, the more control these types of narcissists held over those they sought to use and subjugate.

Still, this mission would be a strange one. Aside from it being weird having my baby brother be in charge of the mission, having a bunch of Soldiers as my temporary teammates unsettled me. You'd think after the final war against Khutu, I would have grown used to it. However, too many terrible memories of the abuse my brothers and I suffered at their hands had permanently scarred me.

Reaper, I didn't worry about. He might be younger than me, he was one of the best Warriors in the Vanguard, maybe only second to Doom. He had a sound judgment, and I fully trusted him to handle his duties with brio. The Kryptids only worried me to the extent they'd wanted to go in like bulldozers and just wipe out everything and everyone. To them, any experiment that threatened their colony was deemed an abomination to be eliminated. To us, they were victims who deserved a chance to be rescued and redeemed if at all possible.

However, my biggest worry was about Shuria being part of the mission. Considering what a badass fighter she'd become, my misgivings were totally unfair. But I was falling for my female, and the thought of losing her freaked me out. I had thoroughly tested and studied all the remarkable reversal work Lekla had performed on Shuria. It all confirmed that she would be safe even if she used the full extent of her mimicking abilities. I may not be in love with Shuria just yet, but I could see myself getting there fast.

Although we'd been steadily growing closer, something had shifted the day we'd agreed to go on this Wyngenia mission. I suspected it had to do with whatever discussion she had with the Queen. Shuria had merely mentioned that she'd be featured in the Well of Knowledge, but I suspected something deeper had gone on between them. As much as curiosity gnawed at me, I wouldn't pry. Either way, it had a positive effect on my mate. Shuria seemed more secure about us, even though we'd had even less time together.

Now that we'd finally embarked on the journey to Wyngenia, I hoped she and I could spend a bit more personal moments together. I was beyond ready to take our relationship to the next level, but I couldn't say for sure if she was ready. Shuria wanted me, and the chemistry between us was off the charts. But was she mentally there yet?

I hated all the uncertainty around romance. Science had clear protocols and methodologies to follow. If you understood how to read and interpret the results, you knew exactly where you stood, what you did wrong, and how to fix it. With love, everything was a guessing game that you were likely to fail at more often than not.

As if summoned by those thoughts, Shuria entered the lab as I was finishing reviewing the latest report from Victoria. My female looked delicious in the Vanguard black dress uniform she'd started wearing, courtesy of Madeline. The short skirt of the formfitting dress hugged every single one of her delicious curves and hid nothing of her endless, shapely legs. The thought of them wrapped around my waist as I lost myself inside of her flashed through my mind.

Casting the naughty vision aside, I straightened from leaning over the workstation. "Well, well… Look who's here," I said with a broad grin.

"Who?" Shuria asked with pretend curiosity, while looking left and right as if seeking who I was referring to.

I snorted and made my way to her. "The most beautiful female in the galaxy, of course. My gorgeous mate…"

She smiled in that slightly timid way I loved. Thankfully, it was no longer laced with self-doubt and uncertainty. Shuria leaned against me as I drew her into my embrace, her hands clasping behind my neck. We exchanged a deep kiss, which once again set my blood ablaze. Reining myself in, I ended it and buried my face in the crook of her neck before inhaling deeply.

"Mmmm, you smell so good," I whispered, before inhaling again.

"Stop, it tickles!" Shuria exclaimed, trying to pull her neck away from me.

I nipped her neck, soothed it with a small kiss, then relented while she continued to giggle.

"Your fault for smelling so good," I grumbled.

She beamed at me. "No, more like the Vanguard's fault!"

I blinked, taken aback by that response. "The Vanguard?"

Shuria nodded. "I wanted to take a bath in that insanely huge tub in my quarters. And what do I find on the shelves? Some Tavis salts! The rivers in my homeworld contain it. The salts react with our skin and enhance our natural fragrance. How in the world do you have that onboard?"

I grinned smugly. "Actually, the Vanguard bathtubs on board their ships were already large, but I convinced Legion and Chaos to have them enlarged a bit after some of the Mimics agreed to join us. Then I asked the salts be added as well since they help with your hydration. Every Vanguard vessel carries a stock in case a Mimic joins the mission."

"You're so amazing," she said, looking at me with affection.

"I know," I replied teasingly, which earned me a playful tap on the shoulder.

Leaning forward, I kissed her lips and gently rubbed my nose against hers while caressing her back.

"I missed you," she whispered, eyes locked with mine.

"You'd better, because I missed you, too," I replied in a seductive tone, although the words couldn't have been truer.

"Good! Because I intend to kidnap you for the rest of the evening. Are you still busy?" she asked, casting an inquisitive look at the laptop on my workstation.

I shook my head. "No. I was finishing up when you arrived. Victoria sent me an updated report about your sisters. We initiated the reversal procedure on them that Toksi shared with us. So far, your sisters are responding extremely well. We have every reason to believe we'll be able to revert the modification they sustained the same way Lekla did with you."

Shuria's eyes widened, joy and disbelief etched on her face. "Are you serious?!"

I nodded. "Mmhm. They're on the way to recovery."

"You're the best!" my mate exclaimed, burying her face in my neck while giving me a bone-crushing hug.

... and bone crushing it truly was.

While I couldn't bear any type of sexual contact with a female other than my mate, I could hug a female in a fraternal or friendly way. The women of the Vanguard had hugged me plenty of times. But none of them possessed even a third of Shuria's strength. Mimics were naturally stronger than humans, but with the enhancement the Kryptids gave her, my female's strength rivaled that of a Xian or Dragon. With the combat training she'd undergone, and her mimicking abilities, in one-on-one combat, Shuria could probably kick my ass.

It was humbling, to say the least.

I chuckled and caressed her hair, reveling in the softness of its midnight-blue strands and their unusual water-resistant texture.

"So, you were mentioning something about kidnapping me," I said in a purring voice. "I'm happy to be taken."

She lifted her head to look at me with the oddest expression. "Are you?"

My stomach did a backflip at the way she said those words, the challenge in her voice, and the intensity in her eyes. With a certainty I couldn't explain, my gut told me Shuria was hinting at far more than just me submitting to whatever sweet activity couples normally did.

"I am. What mischievous plans do you have in store for me?"

"Actually, I do have plans for you later tonight, but I believe you had something you wanted to show me?" she replied in a mysterious fashion.

"I do!"

Taking Shuria's hand, I led her out of the medbay. We

walked past Reaper in the hallway, who smiled at us. However, I didn't miss the envious way in which his gaze flicked towards our bound hands. Although we'd only left Kryptor this morning, my brother was missing his mate terribly. Leaving her behind had been a difficult decision. However, no one else mastered the image-based language of the Creckels like Janelle. Over the handful of weeks remaining before the attack, teaching the Creckels how to fight on Kryptor's treacherous landscape was primordial. With Doom busy handling the diplomatic and strategic side of things, having Janelle handling communications with the trainers was essential.

I gave Reaper a gentle psychic nudge, which he affectionately returned. For having spent months and years envying Bane's happiness with Tabitha, and then Reaper's with Janelle, I understood all too well what he felt wishing for his female by his side.

Shuria eyed me with undisguised curiosity when I stopped in front of the biggest of the two holodecks on board.

"What are we doing? Hunting?" she asked.

"Not exactly. You took me picnicking by the river on Kryptor. I'm returning the favor in a special setting," I replied in a mysterious tone.

Her curiosity piqued, Shuria followed me inside, her excitement almost palpable. I had set up everything beforehand and had the program already running when we entered. My female's eyes widened in shock as the doors parted to reveal the Mistral River on Khepri.

The crystalline water sang as it ran lazily in front of us. The ghostly silhouettes of the planet's three rings graced the clear blue sky of the Vanguard's homeworld. On the other side of the river, the mountain range of Skogoth, the Scelk city, rose proudly a short distance away from the shore. Although we could see some of the buildings they'd built directly on the ground, most of the Scelks had carved their hive inside the mountain itself.

"If you recall, the Mimic village is a short way over there," I said, pointing south. "The construction of their underwater city is complete. But there are still more ground dwellings being built. I figured now might be a good time for you and me to start thinking about what kind of house we want, pick a lot, and get the construction going."

Although I tried to sound nonchalant as I spoke those words, I suddenly felt extremely nervous that she would turn me down.

"So I took the liberty to pre-program a few designs. Hopefully, one of them will inspire you. And of course, we can modify and customize anything to make it more to your liking," I added quickly when Shuria gaped at me with visible shock.

"But... You already have a house," she argued.

"Yes, but I can move," I said with a dismissive hand gesture. "My house is in Dragon City. Picking a lot here by the Mistral River will allow you to be with your people. You've been separated from them for too long."

Shuria's eyes misted. "But what about you? Don't you want to be with your brothers?"

I snorted and made a face at her. "My brothers are all brats. Putting a bit of distance between us cannot hurt," I said teasingly, mostly to hide my nervousness. "But no, that's not a problem. Dragon City and the HQ are both a short, winged flight away. So is Dragon's Rise, where we teach our young brothers how to fly. The Mistral River is perfectly centrally located."

She studied my features for a few seconds, as if she was seeing me for the first time. I'd be freaking out right now if not for the air of wonder on her face.

"You're really serious about us," she whispered, more to herself than for me.

"Of course, I am," I responded, nonetheless. "I've waited for you my whole life, and I'm never letting you go."

I couldn't say which one of us made a move towards the other first, but seconds later, Shuria was once more in my arms, our tongues mingling. The unsated lust and passion that often flared between us didn't manifest themselves this time around. Pure tenderness and the growing deeper feelings binding us wrapped around us like a warm blanket.

With much reluctance, I released my female.

"Come. Let's go have a look at the houses, and then we can discuss them while enjoying a Mimic brunch by the river," I said, taking her hand.

"A Mimic brunch?" Shuria asked, stunned.

"Mmhmm. I may have thoroughly interrogated Silzi about the most popular Mimic recipes and especially about your favorite dishes," I said smugly.

"If you're trying to make me like you, dear Rogue, you are doing a fine job," Shuria said, playfully bumping her shoulder against mine.

"Good, because I am!"

We headed towards the first house—the only one currently visible of the three I had created. Of traditional Mimic design, it was a U-shaped sandstone house, with a slightly slanted roof reminiscent of ancient Earth's Mayan architecture. Intricate, painted tribal carvings adorned the outer walls, and especially the thick edges of the roof. Large reflective windows allowed plenty of light inside. All around, brightly colored plants, vaguely reminiscent of the coral reefs of Thaga, rose proudly in the flowerbeds.

"Maker!" Shuria whispered. "This looks exactly like our dwellings back on my homeworld. Can you even get these plants?"

I smiled at her incredulous tone. "They differ from the ones on Thaga, but they are genetically modified to resemble them, and are adapted to Khepri's weather and ecosystem. We can't bring back Thaga, but we can make sure you and your sisters feel fully at home on Khepri."

Looking overwhelmed with emotion, Shuria followed me inside.

"Don't mind the decoration," I added quickly, once more feeling nervous. "I threw in things in various styles to get a sense of what you like and dislike. We can change absolutely anything you want to something you find more appealing."

She gave me a sideways glance, a mysterious smile playing on her lips. That messed with my head. But Shuria's total silence as she explored each room, her long fingers occasionally sliding over the smooth surface of a piece of furniture drove me even more crazy. She was doing it on purpose. I'd discovered that my female had a bit of a sadistic streak that I found quite enticing.

More than once, I opened my mouth to break the thick silence, but words failed me. When we finally reached the master bedroom at the other end of the house, Shuria barely looked at the massive bed propped against the center of the back wall, going instead to observe the private garden through the large patio doors.

When the silence stretched again, I approached her to see what was holding her attention outside. But she turned around before I could reach her and went on exploring the rest of the room.

"You hate it," I said in a factual manner, finding my voice at last.

To my relief, the disappointment I felt didn't show—or at least I didn't think it did. Of the three models I had designed, this one was my favorite. I'd been so sure she would have loved it, too.

Shuria closed the door to the walk-in closet she'd been peering into, then turned around to look at me. Her raised eyebrow had that taunting edge that preceded mischief.

"What makes you think I hate it?" she asked, sounding overly innocent.

"You're awfully quiet and not showing much emotion," I replied.

"Because my mind is busy thinking," she added, taking a few steps towards the center of the large room.

"Thinking about what?" I asked, closing the distance between us.

"About how I want to give it the feminine touch it seriously lacks," she added teasingly.

"Feminine is definitely not an adjective usually associated with me," I quipped in a grumbling tone that had her chuckling.

Just as I was going to place my hands on her hips to draw her to me, Shuria skillfully dodged, spinning out of reach before moving towards the bed. I gave her a confused look only to see my mate let herself drop at the edge. She rubbed her palms on each side of her, over the soft dark-gray blanket covering the mattress, before glancing back up at me, her gaze intense.

"You're everything but feminine, which I approve of. That said, I like the furniture style you chose. But before we make a decision, I think we should test them first."

My brain froze when Shuria rested her palms on the mattress and slightly leaned back, looking at me in a provocative fashion.

"Test?" I echoed, my mouth going dry.

She nodded, slightly arching her back, pushing her chest forward to erase any doubt as to her meaning. I'd pictured a million different ways in which *I* would initiate us taking the next step, but I'd never seen this coming. Too stunned for words, I stood there like an idiot, just gaping at Shuria. It took for her skin to begin darkening in embarrassment and for uncertainty to seep into her seductive expression for me to realize how my sudden turning into a statue could come across as a rejection.

It snapped me right out of my daze.

A predatory smile settled on my face as I prowled towards my female. "The scientist in me is always down for *thoroughly* testing every mystery. Some more than others…" I added, giving her a meaningful glance.

I wanted to kick myself for my initial dumb reaction when relief flashed through her eyes. She relaxed, and her stormy eyes sparkled as I came to stand in front of her.

I leaned down to claim her mouth. Shuria immediately placed a hand behind my nape, responding greedily to my kiss. Her other hand slipped under my Vanguard shirt, lifting it up even as she caressed my side and then my back. I interrupted the kiss for the brief time it took me to yank my shirt off and toss it to the floor. Reclaiming Shuria's lips, I gently forced her to lie down while my tongue invaded her mouth.

Half lying on top of her—still standing on one foot and my left knee resting at the edge of the bed—I caressed my female's firm body over her uniform dress. When my hand reached her thigh, I snuck it under the hem of the short skirt. Despite the tiny scales of her undars gently scraping my palm, my mate's skin was incredibly soft and warm to the touch. Like us, Xians and Dragons, Shuria didn't bother with underwear. The fewer layers of clothing we wore, the faster we could shed them to shift when needed.

Right now, I couldn't have approved more.

My fingers teased the swirling patterns of her undars as I trailed a path upwards, dragging her dress in the process like she had done with my shirt. Shuria lifted her pelvis to ease my task of ridding her of the garment. Once more, we interrupted the kiss as she partially sat up so that I could pull the dress over her head. As I tossed it in the same general direction my shirt had gone, Shuria wrapped her arms around me, holding me firmly against her body while letting herself fall back down onto the mattress.

The searing heat of her naked skin against mine had my blood instantly heating. Whatever nervousness I feared would paralyze me because of my inexperience thankfully remained at bay. Instead, an eager anticipation burned deep within, yet tempered by the need to explore and savor every second of this moment and make it memorable for us both. There could never be another first time.

Apparently in sync with my thoughts, Shuria also didn't rush through discovering my body with her hands and lips, attentive to the way I responded to each of her caresses, kisses, and nips. As she'd previously found out how much I loved when she raked her nails over my scales, my female went all out. In the process, she discovered how incredibly erogenous it was for me when she clawed at the small scales at the base of the bone spikes which lined my shoulders and my spine.

Fuck, how I loved the way she touched me!

Our sighs of pleasure mingled as we continued to kiss and caress each other with a tenderness that gradually intensified with a more passionate edge. Just as I was readying to push things further, Shuria wrapped her legs around my waist and, pushing on my shoulder, flipped us around with the ease and speed of an experienced warrior.

I tensed, instinctively wanting to resist and express my dominance. But I silenced the urge and yielded to my female. The look she gave me when my body relaxed confirmed I had made the right choice.

Shuria resumed her exploration with a possessiveness that did weird things to me. I loved being so thoroughly claimed. Her lips and hands roaming over my body in a downward path had my abdominal muscles contracting spasmodically. I kicked off my boots and held my breath when my female finally rid me of the pants I was still wearing. In seconds, her mouth kissing a path up my legs had me panting.

When Shuria reached the apex of my thighs, she glanced up at me, her stormy eyes almost black from arousal. A bolt of desire exploded in the pit of my stomach at the sight of her claws extruding from the tips of her fingers before she started clawing at my loin plate.

A part of me wanted to resist that clear demand. As a male, I felt compelled to pleasure my female first before seeking my own gratification. But Shuria needed me to allow her to express and assert herself, to reclaim the confidence her traumatic past had nearly shattered. Therefore, I complied.

Her triumphant, greedy smile had my stomach doing a couple of backflips as my loin plate parted to reveal my shaft. I almost groaned in relief to finally set it free from its confines. The scent of cinnamon from my natural lubricant wafted to me. I considered releasing some of my pheromones. It shared a similar aroma and acted as a potent aphrodisiac. But I would wait a short while longer. Once I had Shuria at my mercy, I would unleash all my seduction abilities to drive her insane with lust and give her chain orgasms.

A throaty moan escaped me when Shuria's hand closed around my length, causing another explosion of heat in my nether region. No one had ever touched me in such an intimate fashion. I had feared my non-negligible girth would intimidate her. But my female started stroking me with an air of pure fascination laced with desire. I hissed through my teeth as pleasure built in an exquisite crescendo with each movement of her hand. I sank my claws into the mattress on each side of me while my pelvic muscles spasmed from my efforts to remain in control.

When Shuria finally took me in her mouth, I cried out, my body jerking up into a half sitting position. Without missing a beat, my female placed her free palm on my chest, pushing me back down. Her hand still stroking me in counterpoint to the movement of her mouth tightened its grip around my shaft. I threw my head back with an almost animalistic shout.

"Yes. Harder," I growled, my voice so thick with need my words sounded barely intelligible to my own ears.

But Shuria understood me perfectly. Squeezing the base of my cock almost painfully, she accelerated the movements of her hand while sucking the head with greater intensity. I roared, one of my hands fisting her hair as she continued to work me in a frenzy. Eyes closed shut, I released a string of strangled moans in between labored breaths. A volcano threatened to erupt within. I needed her to stop, but it felt so good... so fucking good!

With an almost enraged shout, I pulled Shuria away from me. She yelped in surprise, then glared at me with something akin to outrage to have been denied her victory over me. I'd make it up to her later. Granted, I could have climaxed and been ready right away again to pleasure her. After all, every male with Kryptid DNA could get an erection at will. But I wanted to see my mate fall apart for me first.

Grabbing her wrists, I pinned them on each side of her body before I started kissing and tasting every inch of her skin. I loved its slightly rough texture on my tongue when I licked the scales of her undars in the opposite direction. Although she had round breasts like a woman, they weren't more erogenous than any other part of her skin, aside from the actual nipples. I nipped at the small scales hiding them until they parted, opening like a blossoming flower to reveal the taut little buds.

I greedily sucked one into my mouth. Shuria rewarded me with a throaty moan that resonated directly in my groin. She tried to reach for me, but I tightened my grip around her wrists, keeping her at my mercy. To my delight, she didn't resist letting me lick and lave her nipples before I resumed my journey downward. While doing so, I released my pheromones. Within seconds, my female's dusky blue skin erupted in goosebumps. A violent shiver coursed through her as I licked and nipped her navel.

With much reluctance, I released one of her wrists to slip a hand between her thighs. Shuria's breath hitched. The intoxicating natural scent of her skin intensified seconds before she willingly parted the veil of scales covering her modesty. My mouth immediately watered as her musk wafted to me.

Although Mimics shared many anatomical similarities with

human women, they had a single set of labia, a slightly paler shade of blue than her skin, and no clitoris. But their inner walls more than compensated for that absence. The entire lining was covered in rippling ridges called ollia, somewhat similar in appearance to her undars, but each one was highly sensitive and acted like a woman's G-spot. With Mimics, there was no hoping you would find the right angle. Her pleasure was guaranteed. In a way, I almost felt cheated out of proving what a talented lover I would grow to be.

But my need to taste my female silenced those wandering thoughts.

Sticking my tongue out, I flicked the tip along the seam of Shuria's opening, teasing her. A bolt of desire struck low in my loins as the salty-sweet taste of her essence exploded on my taste buds. With a hungry growl, I placed her right leg over my shoulder and stabbed my tongue inside her. Shuria emitted a strangled cry, followed by a needy moan as I sank my tongue deeper within her sheath, extending it to its full length of nearly thirty centimeters. Simultaneously, I gently raked my claws over the undars on the side of her thighs.

Shuria called out my name, her free hand closing around the right side of my crescent-moon-shaped Deynian horn. That further fanned the flame burning in the pit of my stomach. I released a bit more of my pheromones, which would not only further arouse her but also make her more sensitive to my ministrations.

My mate lifted her pelvis, her hips gyrating as my tongue moved in and out of her. I narrowed its thickness going in and made it swell coming out to enhance her sensations. In no time, Shuria was chanting my name, her hand holding my horn tugging at it in the most exquisite fashion. I couldn't wait to be buried deep inside her while she held both tips of my horn.

Too lost in feasting on my female, I never saw her climax coming. Her back arched so abruptly, and her leg over my shoulder jerked so violently, she nearly knocked me off. Shuria shouted my name, her body shaking from ecstasy. I almost resumed licking her, but slipped two fingers inside her instead, rubbing the sensitive lining of her inner walls to prolong her pleasure while admiring her beautiful face dissolved in an air of pure bliss.

My cocked ached and throbbed with the need to make her mine at long last. As Shuria started coming back down to reality, I settled over her. She immediately parted her legs for me to lie between them. A powerful emotion washed over me while my twin hearts filled to bursting with affection for my mate.

I reclaimed her mouth as she possessively wrapped her arms around my back. Fuck me, I would never tire of this. It was deep, tender, and screamed of the bond that was blossoming between us. I lifted my head to lock eyes with her.

"Do you accept me, my love?" I whispered against her lips.

She blinked rapidly, as if to hold back tears, and gave me a trembling smile. "Yes, Rogue, I do. I am yours."

"My beautiful mate," I replied in a breathy voice before kissing her again.

I carefully started pushing myself inside of her. To my shock, her body, naturally resisting my invasion, suddenly yielded after my third shallow thrust. I stared in surprise at Shuria, who shivered with pleasure before giving me a smug smile. I snorted and shook my head at her as understanding dawned on me. She had partially shifted to accommodate my girth without us having to wait for her body to adjust to me.

But I, too, had some tricks left. My female gasped against my lips when I made my chest vibrate with my mating song. The discrete, subtonal melody would resonate directly in each of her nerve endings, sending them into overdrive. Every touch, every kiss, every caress would set her skin ablaze and multiply each sensation a thousandfold.

Our bodies began moving in harmony. I thought I would die

with pleasure as the searing heat of her inner walls squeezed me from all sides. Liquid fire coursed through my veins, each thrust sending electric sparks through each of my nerve endings. Shuria writhed beneath me, her claws digging into my back, the wondrous sting tearing another moan from me. I never thought I would crave a bit of pain during intimacy. But the thought of my female clawing and biting me hard enough to draw some blood drove me insane with lust.

I picked up the pace, taking my mate harder, deeper as wave upon wave of pleasure crashed over me. We didn't speak, our labored breaths, our blissful moans, and the sounds of our flesh meeting doing all the talking for us.

The first time Shuria climaxed around my cock, I almost gave in to my own climax. But it felt too good inside her. I wasn't ready to stop just yet. Instead, I unleashed my passion on her, pounding into my female with near savagery. Her voluptuous moans, the bruising force with which she held me, and her pelvis lifting to meet me thrust for thrust, spurred me on. I couldn't get close enough to my mate. I wanted to drown in her, become one in every way. My fangs burned with the need to extrude and inject her with my bonding hormone which would bind us for eternity. But she wasn't ready for that commitment yet.

As I felt myself nearing the edge, my consciousness reached for her. Shuria immediately dropped her psychic walls, welcoming me in. A tsunami of pleasure, joy, and adoration slammed into me. I was inside her, surrounded by her, and joined with her both physically and spiritually.

Shuria cried out, once more swept away by bliss. This time, I followed her. My spine seized violently. I slammed myself home, one hand gripping her waist as my seed shot out into her in searing spurts of liquid ecstasy. I felt dizzy, my skin tingling as my body shuddered with sensory overload.

I collapsed, feeling on the verge of combusting. Rolling onto my back, I drew Shuria on top of me. She still trembled against me, her feverish skin radiating like the sun in my arms. She rested her head on my chest.

"You are mine, now and always," I said, tightening my embrace around her.

Shuria pressed herself harder against me. "Always," she echoed, her voice barely a whisper.

CHAPTER 13
SHURIA

The next few days flew by way too fast. There were never enough hours in the day to spend with my mate. Focusing on my work—or at least trying to—was the only thing that kept me sane while Rogue tackled his own tasks. I simply couldn't get enough of him. Keeping out the memory of our passionate nights together was flat out impossible. I wanted to blame my insatiable craving for my mate on the novelty of it all and to him being such a fantastic and generous lover.

But what if it doesn't calm down?

While we were fertile year-round, mature Mimics went into heat four times a year. Then, I would truly be relentless, unless I ate jawey nuts to control the urges. Right now, since our first night, I was almost constantly hounding Rogue for more. Admittedly, he didn't seem to mind, quite the opposite. His sex drive appeared to match mine, and his Kryptid blood basically allowed him to get it up on demand to impregnate his 'Queen'. But I feared he'd eventually grow to find me too clingy and needy.

In truth, I wished he would be more aggressive in pursuing me. I had no qualms initiating our encounters, but the thought of being his prey, hunted for his pleasure, turned me on beyond words. Considering how he'd been conceived, with his sire forcing himself on his mother, Rogue—and the Dragons as a whole—were extremely sensitive about not acting in a way that could be even remotely construed as non-consent or pressure on the female. However, I wanted him to get a little rougher, dominant, and especially freaky.

My face heated at that thought. I cast a nervous look around, even though I knew no one could witness my embarrassment as I walked down the hallway to the bridge. We Mimics tended to get creative in most forms of play, social activities, and lovemaking because of our shifting abilities. Nothing was too bizarre, our imagination setting the only limits. I'd been looking forward to going wild with my partner once I finally mated. Would Rogue be up for it or be horrified?

He always acted pretty laid back about pretty much everything. But his constant restraint made me wonder. There would be plenty of time after this brewing war for me to test his limits. The various forms and creatures I wanted to shift into while we played naughty kept flashing through my mind.

Shaking my head, I forced myself to refocus on the mission at hand as the doors to the bridge swished open before me. My gaze automatically zeroed in on the object of my every thought. Standing next to his brother near our pilot, Thanh, Rogue looked beyond scrumptious. He almost looked heroic with the large silhouette of Wyngenia in the backdrop as our ship closed in on the planet. His black scales hid nothing of every single bulging muscle of Rogue's broad chest and thick arms. My dirty mind immediately went back to how it felt to be held by him, the gentle way his scales scraped my skin, and how vulnerable I felt in his embrace.

Once more, I clamped down on my wandering thoughts. Noticing my approach, Rogue turned to look at me. The tender happiness that instantly settled on his face had my skin tingling. Maker, I never thought such a magnificent male would ever gaze upon me with such pride and affection. I still didn't understand what I had done to deserve him, but I would pray every day of my life to keep him forever.

As soon as I reached him, Rogue slipped a possessive arm around my waist and kissed my temple. Despite his obvious joy, I did not miss the worry in his eyes. Like Reaper and me, Rogue was fully naked, but for his weapons, armband, and combat accessories. In the next few minutes, we would land on Wyngenia to raid what we believed to be the rebels' HQ. Clothes and armor would interfere with my ability to morph, and for the Dragons to shift into their battle form.

Nevertheless, I loved that Rogue wasn't trying to control me or force me to stay behind. Still, I suspected he would expend extra effort keeping an eye on me, ready to intervene if things got heated. I didn't mind as I fully intended to do the same with him.

Martha and Commander Hulax were also standing on the bridge on the other side from Thanh, while Madeline sat at the Science Officer's station. Moments later, the door opened on her husband Reklig.

"Good, everyone's here," Reaper said. "We will reach our destination in the next twenty minutes. As agreed, Thanh will remain airborne, and we will land in camouflaged shuttles. Despite the signals continuing to claim this area as occupied, our surface scans show no activity whatsoever."

"We're already too late?" I asked, crestfallen.

Reaper shook his head, looking frustrated. "I doubt it. Madeline has been running some deep scans. There is definitely a much bigger structure below—actually more like a massive underground facility. But we can't see through it. They're using some kind of disruptor that we can't seem to override."

"A disruptor?" Hulax echoed, suddenly perking up. "Show me?"

Reaper made no effort to hide his surprise at that request—

the sentiment reflected on the faces of the rest of the crew. Nevertheless, he nodded and gestured at the Kryptid Commander to approach Madeline. She flicked her silver-white hair over her shoulder before typing a few instructions on her computer. An overlay of her monitor appeared on the bridge's giant screen, not hiding the view of the planet as we prepared to enter its atmosphere.

An odd expression flitted over Hulax's insectoid features as he examined the scan results.

"If my suspicions are correct, this could be a good thing," the Commander said with an almost malicious glee. "Please send the signal to my armband."

Stunned, Madeline flicked her green eyes towards Reaper. Although slightly frowning, he gave his assent with a single stiff nod. Madeline complied and tapped a few more instructions on her keyboard before looking back at Hulax. Left arm raised in front of him, the Commander was typing on the interface of his armband. Within seconds of Madeline transferring the signal to him, a triumphant grin stretched Hulax's human-looking mouth. Baffled, I stretched my neck to try and see what was on the interface that could have prompted such a reaction from him. I could see the same confusion on the rest of our team's faces.

Swiping two fingers on the interface, as if to flick off some bug or dirt, Hulax transferred the image from his armband back to the bridge's giant screen. To our shock, it was the same scan of the structure, but this time showing multiple rooms, populated with several people and creatures.

"How in the world...?" Madeline whispered, her head jerking between the giant screen display and the monitor of her computer.

I didn't have to ask to guess that her device continued to show a bigger structure, but one that our scans couldn't penetrate.

"What the fuck?" Reaper said, echoing my thoughts.

"It appears your assumptions were correct, Shuria," Commander Hulax said, casting an approving glance my way.

"They were?" I repeated, completely lost. "And what assumptions were they? How did you do this?"

"They have Kryptid Workers in that base," he replied, matter-of-factly.

"What?" Reaper exclaimed, while the rest of us recoiled. "What makes you say that?"

"The disruptor is of Kryptid technology, which is why I could so easily bypass it. As you can guess, I cannot share the functionality with you. However, once we get on the surface, just have a Soldier by your side, and you will have no problem seeing through the disruptors."

That made sense. Legion had mentioned finding kidnapped Workers forced to continue General Khutu's demented research, but this time for the benefit of the rebels.

"Haven't your actions alerted them?" Reklig asked, voicing the same concern I felt.

"They most certainly have been. I made sure of it. But fear not, they won't tell. This is a defensive protocol the Workers follow in case they become stranded in hostile territory," Hulax explained. "This also means we may have allies inside."

"Allies?" Reaper asked.

"The Workers encoded a help request message in the disruptor," Hulax said. "Had I not found it, we'd be having a very different conversation. However, the primary concern is that there is indeed a Scelk Queen in there with a full nursery, a contingent of Zombie Soldiers, at least a couple of unidentified life forms, and five Workers."

"Fuck me," Reklig whispered, shock and hope mixed in his voice. "We need to rescue her and her hatchlings."

Naturally, he would be thrilled at the prospect of being able to have more of his people. With their currently low population, their genetic pool was too limited. The Scelks Chaos's team found on Aurilia would do wonders in injecting fresh blood in their ranks. But a Queen implied endless possibilities.

Possibilities the Kryptids and the rest of the Coalition will not be too pleased with.

"You don't know that it is safe to rescue her and whatever she spawned," Hulax retorted in a hard tone, as if in response to my thoughts.

Reklig immediately tensed and took on a threatening expression.

"We will assess the situation once we're inside," Reaper quickly intervened, placing an appeasing hand on Reklig's shoulder before things could escalate. He then turned to face Commander Hulax. "The Vanguard *always* goes into any mission with the goal of freeing and rescuing any victim or innocent beings we may encounter. That has not changed. If whatever experiment within that base can be saved without representing an uncontrollable risk to the welfare of other worlds, we *will* save them."

Hulax stared at Reaper with obvious displeasure laced with a mix of disgust and incomprehension. "You off-worlders and that irrational need to show empathy. You are intergalactic peacekeepers. Eradicating everything in that base would be the safest way to ensure everyone's safety. Why even *allow* the risk that those you rescue could turn on you?"

"The Kryptids sure were grateful for the Vanguard's empathy when Khutu nearly ruined your last healthy Queen and was trying to murder General Daeko. Without that 'irrational need to show empathy' your entire species would only be months away from total extinction," Reklig snarled.

I bit the inside of my cheeks to keep from snorting. You didn't want to mess with a Scelk. Their tongues could cut you deeper than any blade. And this was Reklig making massive efforts to restrain himself. However, where most other species of the Coalition would have either bristled at his comment or been shamed by it, Hulax reacted in a typical Kryptid fashion.

He tilted his head to the side as he gave Reklig a pensive look. "You are correct. Without our unexpected alliance, there is a great probability that my people would be taking its dying breath as we speak. We will never know if we could have achieved victory on our own. Are we grateful? Obviously. Would we have resented you for not aiding us? Absolutely not. Frankly, the Vanguard's desire to help us is completely illogical. We've been at war for a hundred years, destroyed countless numbers of your worlds, and slaughtered their populations. Leaving us to self-destruct should have been your natural response. *We* would *not* have aided *you* had our roles been reversed."

I flinched inwardly while the rest of the team gaped at the Kryptid Commander. I'd lived long enough with his people to understand their bluntness, which often bordered on rudeness or callousness when seen through the eyes of off-worlders.

"Are you saying we should abandon you now and let the rebels have their way?" Reklig challenged, earning himself a stern look from Reaper.

"Of course not. It would not benefit us to fight this impending war on our own. But it would have been fair for you to let us fend for ourselves. Kryptids believe in the survival of the fittest. Had we not managed to fight back the threat that menaced our colony—with or without your help—then our extinction would have been fair. Anyway, this is irrelevant now. It is past. All that matters is what we learned, and the safeguards we've set in place to avoid such a bloody deception from happening again."

Just as he spoke those words, I realized our vessel had entered Wyngenia's atmosphere.

"Landing in fifteen minutes," Thanh announced, as if she'd read my thoughts.

"Let's get ready," Reaper said, seeming as relieved as I felt to put this topic to rest.

I didn't worry about the Dragons' reaction to Hulax's words. They grew up surrounded by Kryptids. They understood their ways. While it had also partially been the case with the Scelks, they had a more volatile temper that could be harder to control, especially when one of theirs was threatened. But the humans would struggle the most to relate with the Kryptid mentality.

"Thanh, Shield Rogue and me. And as soon as our shuttle leaves the ship, block all communications in and out of this area," Reaper added.

"Understood," Thanh replied.

We headed to the ship hangar. As soon as we entered the room, psychic energy swirled between Commander Hulax and the ten Soldiers who had joined the mission with him. They were already waiting by their shuttle of Kryptid design. From the outside, it resembled an elongated, reddish-brown, giant walnut with some kind of appendages along the sides.

Organic ships always freaked me out. Made of the same membrane that covered the walls of every Kryptid dwelling—but with a hardened outer shell—those vessels self-maintained by eating any organic waste lying around. Bleeding near a membrane would immediately have it sniffing your way to see if you're about to keel over, which would make you fair game.

As we reached their shuttle, one Soldier stepped forward.

"Rosdi will accompany you to bypass any Kryptid disruptor or security system you may encounter," Hulax said to Reaper.

He nodded, although I didn't miss his subtle frown. We were supposed to move as a single unit, not split up inside. With Hulax's unfavorable disposition towards the Scelk Queen, we'd want to keep an even closer eye on him. However, it made sense to assign that duty to a Soldier to make sure we always had someone handy.

We boarded the Kryptid shuttle. It had been a last-minute

decision, but one that made sense. Giles wouldn't be on the lookout for Kryptid vessels here. He'd be scanning for Vanguard or Coalition ships. This increased the probability of us being able to sneak in undetected. With the Workers having already embedded help request signals in the rebel base's defense system, we had reason to believe they would also make sure that even if their scanners detected our vessel, they wouldn't trigger an alarm.

The typical musty scent that welcomed us when we entered the shuttle made me slightly nauseous. After all this time living on Kryptor and surrounded by the membrane, you'd think I'd be used to it by now. But the week spent traveling here aboard the Vanguard vessel seemed to reinforce the fact that I was ready to move back to a world more like my own. By the unenthused expression of the other Vanguard members, they weren't too thrilled at being inside the belly of a liveship.

Thankfully, it was a short flight until we landed. As we prepared to disembark, Rogue drew me into his embrace and gave me a brief but intense kiss. He caressed my cheek, his gaze boring into mine. He didn't need to speak for me to understand his unspoken words. I had no intention of getting hurt.

Our pilot settled the shuttle barely ten meters away from what would qualify as one of four fancy-looking cabins. They offered the perfect honeymoon retreat with their soft sandstone walls, large reflective windows, and huge deck facing the rainbow-colored river. It owed its unusual hue to the colorful stones lining its bed. Overhead, a white and green sky shimmered around the fat, ghostly silhouette of a giant moon. Not a soul could be seen anywhere, and the only sound came from our feet treading the white sand beneath us.

The Kryptids, Reaper, Rogue, Reklig, and I silently approached the buildings. As agreed, Martha and Madeline would remain onboard the shuttle until we'd secured the premises enough to bring them out. Technically, I should have remained with the humans, as I also didn't possess any rebirth abilities like the Xians and the Dragons. But my other skills were required.

Thanh having given a psychic Shield to both Reaper and Rogue, should things go sideways, Madeline and Martha would be able to catch the souls of the Warriors. As we couldn't be certain that Hulax's current ability to bypass the disruptors in the base wasn't a trap set up by Giles, we wouldn't gamble with the Dragons' lives.

"The underground entrance appears to be in the cabin at the back, on the right," Hulax telepathically said to our group. *"I suggest we head there directly. My Soldiers can secure the other three cabins. But our scanners indicate they are empty."*

"Agreed," Reaper replied.

Six of the ten Soldiers peeled off, splitting in three pairs to go check inside the other three cabins while we made a beeline for the one in the back. It was a perfect copy of the others, aside from the discreet bioscan controlling the locking mechanism of the front door.

"The other cabins do not have these bioscanners and are unlocked," Hulax suddenly said telepathically to our group, having no doubt received that information from his Soldiers. *"They have entered the buildings and are sweeping through. So far, they are completely empty."*

"I wonder why he bothered with those extra cabins then," Reaper mused back. *"He didn't need to pretend he had lodging for guests as no one would have come here spying on his activities."*

"My Soldiers have detected traces of the DNA of a Lenusian female in one of the cabins, and that of a Tegorian male in another. The third cabin had a mix of both species plus a human's DNA."

"Sounds like the other two leaders of the rebellion from the video Legion's team recovered on Ostruria," Rogue said.

"*Agreed. That they have already left means they are getting ready for the attack.* Hopefully, not sooner than Chaos assumed based on the information he gathered from the prisoners on his mission," Reaper said with a frown. He turned to Hulax then gestured with his chin at the bioscan on the fourth cabin before us. "*Can you override it?*"

The Commander shook his head. "*Not without a high risk of triggering their security system. The Workers didn't encode this one. Based on our current scans, there are many Zombie Soldiers right below the entrance. I would rather not give them too early of a warning of our presence.*"

"*I believe I can open the door,*" I interjected.

Although we all wore stealth shields, their synchronized frequencies allowed us to see each other. Every head turned my way as my team stared at me in surprise. Well, except for Rogue. Pride mixed with wariness shone in his eyes instead of curiosity, as he guessed my intention.

"*It's a bioscan. There's no question they configured it to authorize Giles Dalton,*" I explained. "*So, let's give it Giles.*"

Without waiting for their response, I immediately began morphing into the leader of the rebellion. The familiar pain of shifting, mixed with an undefinable sensual pleasure, washed over me as every part of my body reorganized itself. The internal organs caused the most stress. For a split second, my heart and lungs ceased functioning as they took on the form of those from the being I was mimicking. As a youngling, it had been a terrifying process. It almost felt like dying for a few seconds.

For anyone observing me, I would appear stoic as my skin waved and puffed, its texture changing and its shape swelling from my muscles emulating those of my model. They had no idea what depth of concentration the process required. One wrongly recreated organ could lead to violent seizures, even death. For this reason, Mimics usually stuck to superficial shifts, where we only changed our external appearance but not the inner organs.

As a peaceful species living in mostly safe regions of our homeworld, more advanced shifting had rarely been required. Only those pursuing a hunter's career would fully develop that skill. But Khutu had not given a choice to Modified Mimics like me. Countless numbers of my sisters had died in failed shifts during those experiments.

As much as I hated Khutu for what he had done to my people and me, I welcomed the shifting mastery I had achieved. I could not only easily morph into almost any living creature, I could now also immediately make use of whatever special abilities that being possessed. Normal Mimics could turn into a Dragon, but not breathe fire. They could merely use physical attributes, such as its strength and ability to fly.

I could do everything.

The best part, where my sisters would need to spend hours—if not days—studying and memorizing the anatomy of their target before attempting a full shift, I simply needed to absorb anything with my target's DNA to assimilate them. A drop of blood, tears, and hair, to name a few. But I could also do it more inconspicuously with dead skin cells gathered by a kiss on the cheek, a handshake, a friendly caress, etc.

The nanites of the bands and belts of my accessories kicked into action, adjusting their sizes to fit my now more muscular and taller body as the elite military human male that was Giles Dalton. As a Mimic, I could increase my size in an almost unlimited fashion while morphing, but I couldn't shrink my shape down by more than fifteen percent of my natural body. This meant I could turn into a two-story behemoth but not into an infant. And right now, judging by the impressed looks on my companions' faces, I perfectly resembled the short blond haired, blue eyed, trappy, forty-one-year-old male that was Giles.

In Giles's case, I had not been able to absorb any of his

DNA. While the Coalition did have samples of it, the rebel leader had undergone too many modifications on himself for it to still be valid. I had to use the traditional method through observation to mimic him, based on various images and recordings in the Vanguard database. From the video Legion had recovered from the rebel base on Ostruria, I'd copied the oversized eyes that betrayed the fact that Giles had used some of the experiments on himself.

The only downside was that Mimics couldn't materialize clothes or anything non-organic. So, here I was, standing in Giles's glorious nudity, wearing nothing else than my accessories. I didn't mind being naked. It only made things complicated when I had to morph into a species like the humans who required some kind of outfit.

In this instance, it didn't matter. This bioscan model would focus on my face.

Still standing outside of the scanner's detection range, I deactivated my stealth shield. The six Soldiers who had secured the other cabins returned at that moment. Ignoring them, I marched with determined steps towards the cabin. I stopped in front of the door and looked straight at the camera while a blue laser scanned my face.

"Welcome back, Giles Dalton," a synthetic feminine voice said in greeting as the door parted before me with a soft swish.

I took a step inside, remaining partially in the doorway to keep the door from closing while my companions swiftly filed in. Once again, the Kryptid Soldiers fanned out inside the cabin to secure the rooms. The place was clean but completely bare. Giles had made no effort at even making it look like it was inhabited, so certain had he been that no one would come disturb him.

The cabins were a pre-built model that came with one, two, or three bedrooms. While some were already positioned in the most popular sectors of Wyngenia, some could be borrowed from the automated rental and support center on the planet, or visitors could bring their own. These cabins automatically deployed when placed in a wide enough, flat space and activated.

Most visitors chose the already available cabins, which were fully furnished, including bedding, linen, dishes, and all the basic necessities. But a single glance inside this specific cabin confirmed it had been custom made. Three rooms formed a L, lining the left and back wall of the building. The last quarter of the space, which occupied the front right corner of the cabin, acted as a giant lift.

To our pleasant surprise, the bioscanner above the panel of the lift wasn't active. This hinted that Giles had grown overconfident—which would play in our favor.

The Soldiers returned moments later from securing the three rooms on the main floor.

"The rooms are empty," Rosdi said in our psychic group, although he was looking at Commander Hulax. *"They clearly served as storage areas before they removed their contents. Our scanners didn't pick up anything that could reveal what they had kept there."*

With our stealth shields still activated—except for mine—we gathered on the right side of the entrance. Reaper pressed the button to the basement. An energy field immediately appeared around the edges of that open space, and the entire floor began lowering down the shaft.

Reaper and Rogue shifted into their battle form, the rest of us giving them a wide berth. It fascinated me to watch my mate morph. In many ways, it reinforced the bond between us, at least in my mind. He was a shifter, almost like me. He'd explained the sweet pain of the morph, and how powerful it made him feel.

Like the Xians, once the Dragons entered their battle form, their scales became thicker, spreading over their entire bodies like armor. The ones around their cheeks and forehead expanded, forming almost a facial mask, and covering their hair like a helmet. Vicious, thick needle spikes jutted out from their scales, all over their heads, foreheads, arms, and length of their legs. Anyone stupid enough to try to hold or headbutt them would stab themselves to death. The pair of giant scorpion tails extruding from their shoulder blades always fascinated me. Unlike with the Xian Warriors, the tips of the Dragons' scorpion tails were hollow, allowing them to shoot poisoned darts at their enemies. At close range, they could simply stab them with the needle of the tail or use the hard ball below it to crack and smash their target's armor.

However, it was their arm blades that I envied the most. Just below the elbow, on the upper sides of their forearms, a one-meter-long blade extruded, sharp enough to pierce through most armor. While the Dragons' arm blades resembled long spears, the Xians' version slightly recurved like a scythe. The dagger claws coming out of their fingers and their long, bug wings completed the tableau. Deceivingly fragile looking, the diaphanous wings of the Dragons had sharp edges strong enough to behead an enemy with a single swipe.

My mate was a freaking badass...

And that was even without mentioning the mouth darts he could shoot with the speed and strength of a bullet, coating them with venom to do greater damage, or the acid he could spit over a five-meter range.

I bit back a smug grin at the discreet envious glances the Kryptids cast towards Reaper and Rogue, even as they extruded their own arm blades. The only other traits they shared with the Dragons were the mouth darts and spitting acid.

"Status?" Reaper telepathically asked Hulax.

"Unchanged. Our scanners still show the room to be full of Zombie Soldiers. But the readings hint that they are unconscious or in stasis. There is no one else in the room. Our override on their disruptor should also freeze the camera feed in the room," replied the Kryptid Commander.

Moments later, a large set of doors slipped up into view, right before the lift came to a smooth stop. A part of me wished I had shifted back to my natural form or to one of my favorite combat creatures. But Giles's likeness was more likely to serve us in the short-term... even naked as I was.

A delicious shiver ran down my spine when Rogue's consciousness brushed against mine in a psychic caress. Despite his best efforts, I perceived his repressed worry through our connection. I returned it, trying to make myself reassuring while keeping a stoic expression on my face.

My stomach dropped as soon as the doors parted before me. For rows of ten vertical stasis chambers created a passage in front of the elevator—two rows on each side. Within, a Zombie Soldier stood with his eyes closed. Fully armored, a pair of blasters hanging on their belts, and a tactical bracer on their forearm, they were ready to jump into battle the moment they were activated. No glass door trapped them in. At the edges of the large room, lining the walls, close to one hundred more chambers stood empty.

CHAPTER 14
SHURIA

Forcing myself to appear nonchalant, I moved forward, struggling not to glance at the top left corner of the room where the camera was located. I wanted to look over my shoulders at the team following me for reassurance but couldn't risk giving away their presence if we were being observed. The dampening effect of their stealth shield snuffed the sound of their footsteps, making the eerie silence in the room—aside from the soft hum of the stasis chambers—even more ominous.

Technically, the cameras should be under our control. But until we were able to access their control board, we couldn't be certain.

Reklig's voice resonating in my mind through our psychic group startled the fuck out of me. I shouldn't be so on edge. I'd been on many missions before. However, walking around as a naked human male, surrounded by mindless clones with resurrection abilities would unnerve anyone. That they all bore Giles's face made it all the more terrifying.

"Are these Shells of Dalton?" the Scelk asked. *"Did that sick fuck give himself soul-transfer powers?"*

"No," Rogue replied. *"I do not pick up any Gomenzi*

Dragon DNA from them. They are Zombie Soldiers. My scanner detects a control chip in their brains. They are just clones.

"Why the fuck would he clone himself?" Reaper asked.

"Decoy," I said with a sense of dread as understanding dawned on me. *"If there are hundreds of him communicating with us from various locations, we'll never be able to pinpoint the real one. He'll continue to escape us while we chase after clones."*

A plethora of curses filled our psychic chat. I stopped in front of one chamber.

"Should we disable their chip right now or secure the rest of the base first?" I asked.

"Neither," Commander Hulax suddenly said, his voice tense. *"There's a Worker approaching."*

I froze and jerked my head towards the door at the other end of the room, straight through the rows of Zombies.

"Reklig?" I asked, trying to remain calm.

"She has a control chip, which hinders my ability to read her thoughts," he replied. *"But she's hopeful. She knows there's someone here who shouldn't be."*

Turning to face the door, I braced for what would follow. Still, Reklig's words lifted a great deal of tension.

Moments later—which felt like an eternity—the doors opened in front of a Kryptid Worker. She barely took two steps into the room before stopping dead in her tracks. Her jaw dropped, and her multifaceted eyes widened. The small mandibles framing her mouth quivered in the typical fashion that expressed distress or powerful emotions for her species. Although she rapidly schooled her features, I didn't miss the shock, disbelief, panic, and then disappointment that flitted in quick succession on her face.

"M-Master Dalton… You've returned," the Kryptid female said.

Although her words expressed the obvious, she worded them as a question.

"Master?" Rogue repeated in our psychic group. *"That vermin makes the Workers call him Master?"*

Despite the anger hearing her calling me that had stirred within me, I remained stoic.

"Yes," I replied, matter-of-factly.

"She has an implant," Rogue said telepathically. *"If it is the same one Khutu used on his Workers, be careful what you ask her. Anything that would be deemed a betrayal of Giles will inflict extreme pain to her."*

"Noted," I replied.

"Is... Is something wrong? Have you forgotten something?" the Worker asked, casting a meaningful glance at my naked body before locking eyes with me again. "Why are you undressed?"

"I ask the questions. Why are you here?" I asked.

She blinked, looking confused for a second. "Oh! The sensors detected a presence here. There shouldn't be anyone awake in this room."

"Why didn't you check the cameras?" I insisted.

The Worker cast a nervous glance at the camera in the top right corner, another air of confusion crossing her face.

"She's crushed," Reklig said. *"She was hoping for a rescue and now believes some sort of system malfunction misled her. As for Giles's sudden return naked, she thinks some of the modifications he's done to himself are affecting his mind like they did Khutu."*

"This camera appears to be defective. I will fix it right away," the Worker replied.

"Stay camouflaged, let me handle this. Shuria, play along," Hulax ordered in our psychic group before dropping his stealth shield. "That can wait," he then said to the female.

The Worker gasped and took a step back in shock. Her back leaning against the door that had closed behind her, she pressed her palm to her chest. For a brief moment, I feared my companions had all misread the Kryptid female. Then shock gave way to awe and joy. The Worker's small mandibles trembled frantically. In species like mine or humans, it would have translated as quivering lips and eyes misting with incredulous happiness. But Kryptids did not have the ability to cry.

"Commander Hulax... It's you! It's really you!" the Worker said in a shaky voice. "But..."

She cast a confused look at me. I didn't reply and kept a neutral expression.

"You have a control chip?" Hulax asked, although he worded it as a statement.

Once more, the female glanced at me, seeming both baffled and fearful.

"Answer his questions," I ordered.

She blinked rapidly, clearly struggling to make sense of what was happening. But Hulax's plan made sense. So long as she believed she was operating in accordance with her *master's* wishes, she would be spared the torture of the implant punishing her for betraying him.

"Yes, I do," the Worker replied.

"The other Workers as well?" he asked.

"Yes."

"Who else is here with you?" Hulax continued.

The female cast a nervous glance my way, her mandibles working some more. She scratched the back of her hand with two of her five long fingers—a clear sign of nervousness, if not distress. Kryptids never itched as chitin scales covered their entire bodies.

"I... I'm not sure how to answer that, Commander. If you are referring to the standard definition of people, there are four other Workers, yourself, and Master," she said hesitantly.

"And not *standard* people?" he insisted.

This time, the female stared me straight in the eyes, a frown creasing her brow. I could see her wheels spinning as she started putting two and two together. Hulax had no reason to ask her questions Giles would be able to answer. That could only mean one thing…

"She's on to me," I told everyone in our psychic group.

"Maybe it's time to reveal ourselves," Reaper replied.

"Forty clones here, a brooding Scelk Queen, and a siren. The others are still unhatched eggs, non-functional experiments, or functional ones in cryogenic stasis, mostly used for their DNA and to further our research," the Worker said, her gaze never straying from me.

"What do you mean by siren?" Hulax asked.

"Why are you asking me?" the Worker retorted with a challenge in her voice. She gestured at me with her head. "You should ask him. But then, he's not who he seems, right?"

"You are correct," I replied, shifting back into my natural form.

The Worker recoiled again. Her shocked reaction, similar to the one she had when Hulax came out of stealth, quickly gave way to a delighted but calculating expression I knew too well. My stomach churned as dreadful memories of my early days of being experimented on flashed through my mind.

"Two-thirty-six!" she exclaimed in an elated voice, a glimmer of recognition in her eyes.

My anger immediately flared. It took all of my willpower for me not to pounce on her. "Shuria," I hissed through my clenched teeth. "I'm no longer one of your fucking experiment numbers."

The Worker flinched, a guilty look flashing over her face. I didn't remember her being one of the Kryptids who had worked on me. But then, I had little memory of those days aside from the constant pain and the screams of my sisters in my ears.

"Apologies, Shuria," she replied in a chastised tone. "I didn't expect a Mimic with our Commander."

"Or the rest of us," Reaper said, dropping his stealth shield, the rest of our team dropping theirs as well.

While I'd expected the Worker to be stunned again, the sheer horror on her face immediately had all my senses on high alert. With a certainty I couldn't explain, I knew she didn't fear they would harm her. But something about their presence terrified her.

"Not you... You can't be here!" the Worker whispered as if she'd seen a demon.

"Why do you—?"

I never finished my question.

The soft white light that illuminated the room turned orange, and an alarm went off. Simultaneously, the green lights on the stasis chambers of the Zombie Soldiers turned to red.

The feminine voice of an artificial intelligence resonated through the com system. Although I couldn't be certain, I suspected her message was broadcast throughout the underground base.

"Vanguard intruder detected. Emergency lockdown initiated. All defensive units activated."

"Reaper, we've intercepted an alert emanating from the base," Madeline said through our psychic group.

"We're under attack. Do not let any signal leave this planet, and try to shut down their defense system," Reaper replied.

He then refocused on the rest of us.

"Zappers!" he shouted, activating the energy shield of his armband.

Flapping their wings, both he and Rogue took flight, the four-meter ceiling giving them a bit of room to launch their attack. Reaching in the pouch hanging on their hip, the two brothers grabbed a handful of coin-sized disks, tossing them over the rows of standing stasis chambers like one would throw grass seeds on their lawn. The disks immediately scattered, each one seeking a target.

Simultaneously, the Kryptids took on a defensive position, forming an oval with their backs to each other. Shields raised, they extruded their arm blades, while reaching for their own Zappers.

I ran to the Worker to protect her as the emergency lock down had visibly sealed shut the doors to both the lift and to the hallway leading to the rest of the underground facility.

"They won't hurt me," she breathed out.

She truly didn't seem afraid for her life. Of course, they would recognize her as one of the staff. To my shock, the awakened Zombie Soldiers also didn't seem interested in the Kryptid Soldiers, Reklig, or me.

Their eyes snapped open, instantly alert. They stepped out of their stasis chambers, jerking their heads up to stare at the Dragons. Completely ignoring the Kryptids right in front of them, the Zombies raised both their blasters to shoot at the brothers flying overhead.

"What the fuck?" I whispered, baffled.

But even as the words left my lips, a terrible suspicion took root at the back of my head. Any intruder should have initiated this response, unless they featured in the list of authorized species. Since Kryptids worked in the base, Hulax and his Soldiers wouldn't trigger the defense system. Giles had a Scelk Queen here who had given birth to many hatchlings before he sent them out to his minions. So Reklig, as a Scelk, also wouldn't set off any alarm. That I had shown myself without causing any adverse reaction from their security system could only mean that Mimics, too, had been added to the safe list.

The siren the Worker mentioned?

All such considerations fled my mind as the Zombies unleashed a barrage of blaster shots at the two brothers. Had they been on the floor, they wouldn't have survived the onslaught. But their energy shields, facing down towards the room, absorbed the shots. I didn't need to look at the interface of their shields to know their integrity was quickly dwindling.

Thankfully, this wasn't even a fair fight. At the same time the Kryptids and I opened fire on the Zombies—with our blasters set to the highest stun—the Zappers worked their magic. Following their simple programming, each coin-sized disk flew to one of the Zombies. Their basic evasive maneuvers allowed them to dodge the Zombies' attempts to shoo them away. As soon as they made contact with their target's temple, they set off a localized electro-magnetic pulse that instantly fried their mechanical brains.

One by one, the clones fell to the floor, blood trickling out of their noses and ears. A white foam immediately formed around the bleeding areas, bubbling with a sizzling sound.

"Rogue!" I exclaimed running towards him as he and his brother landed.

I internally flinched for this unprofessional display. The women of the Vanguard didn't fuss over their mates like that during a fight. But I couldn't help it.

"I'm fine," Rogue said in a reassuring tone when I reached him.

He absent-mindedly caressed my cheek before crouching next to a Zombie to scan him. I silenced the urge to examine the wounds Rogue had sustained where the blaster shots had grazed him. A few of his black chitin scales had been torn off. By Vanguard standards, they were superficial wounds, but I couldn't help feeling all worked up about it.

"Remove their weapons and inject them with the Zombie virus as soon as the foam fades," Reaper ordered, leaning down to take the blaster from a clone even as he spoke.

The foam showed their resurrection power at work. It healed at extremely high speed whatever damage they had sustained from both the Zapper electrocuting their mechanical brain, and blaster shots we'd fired at them. With that regeneration ability, we could behead one of these clones and the head would reattach itself to the body before the heart would start beating again.

The Vanguard would wish to study those clones, and maybe even use them as vessels for the Scelks being hatched in this base. Therefore, Reaper asked us to wait a couple of minutes for the Zombies to fully heal before we permanently took away their ability to regenerate like this. Rogue, Victoria, and Liena had devised such a virus when Wrath first encountered the Jadozors—the creatures from whom Khutu had derived this power.

"It's not over," the Worker said in a trembling voice.

We all turned to look at her with the same inquisitive and confused expression.

"We disabled their mechanical brains," I said in a reassuring voice. "These clones are only empty Shells now."

The Worker shook her head and pressed herself against the door, as if she wished it would swallow her whole.

"No. They're not. It's not over," she replied.

Before I could further question her, a clone lying a couple of meters in front of me suddenly opened his eyes. His far-too-aware gaze glided over me before settling on one of the Kryptid Soldiers. The clone immediately took on an aggressive expression.

That's impossible!

Zombie Soldiers were soulless vessels. Without a mechanical brain, there shouldn't be any consciousness animating it. What the fuck was controlling this one?

"Watch out!" I shouted, raising my blaster towards the clone.

Even as I fired, total mayhem erupted in the room. One by one, the clones awakened, immediately attacking my companions. This time, they didn't focus only on the two brothers, but on Reklig and the Kryptid Soldiers as well.

"Kryptid intruder!" a clone said with Giles's voice. "Eliminate the threat!"

The one Rogue had been crouched in front of no sooner

opened his eyes than his right hand flew to my mate's neck. Simultaneously, he pulled a dagger from its sheath on his left thigh and attempted to stab Rogue in the kidney.

"NO!" I shouted, as I shot the clone in the face.

I shouldn't have worried. Rogue not only effortlessly blocked the clone's stabbing attempt, he also broke the wrist of the hand attempting to choke him like one would crumple a piece of paper. The clone's face all but disintegrated under the violence of the shot. Blood and gore sprayed all around, immediately followed by the bubbling foam of his regenerative ability. Freakier still, the scattered flesh fragments started crawling back towards the clone's destroyed face, as if drawn by a magnet, to merge back together.

I had read about it in the reports Wrath, Legion, and Chaos had sent back from their missions, but seeing it happening right before my eyes took it to another level I had not quite been ready for.

Despite our individual greater strength and abilities, the Zombies outnumbered us three to one. In their unexpected second attack, they had managed to kill one of the Kryptid Soldiers and grievously injured two more.

With his shield raised before him, Reaper dragged one of the wounded Kryptids inside the circle they had formed to protect each other's backs. The other one had fallen closer to me. The clones still ignored the Worker and me, not considering us a threat.

Their mistake...

"Morphing," I mind spoke in our group.

While the Kryptids and Dragons held up their shields as a defensive wall, spitting mouth darts, stabbing with their forearm lances and scorpion tails, I initiated my transformation into a Septhoron. Although it fared better underwater, the giant creature, vaguely reminiscent of a squid, would allow me to deal with multiple Zombies at once.

Despite the gaping injury that had the Kryptid Soldier's dark blue blood spilling out from his side, he released the Stingers Rogue and Toksi had worked on. They would sting the Zombies in the neck or ears to deliver the virus most closely to the brain, and more specifically to their pituitary glands, which largely controlled their regeneration ability. Simultaneously, our other companions had dropped their virus canisters—the size of a hand grenades—to the ground. The virus sprayed out with a soft hiss, filling the room.

We just needed to hold off the Zombies long enough for the virus to flood their systems and stop their regeneration before they could kill all of us. I watched helplessly as Rogue and the others inflicted fatal blows to their attackers, their arm blades punching right through the Zombies' chests or faces, and the tips protruding on the other side. Once they yanked their blades back out, the Zombies would fall to one knee. The movement of their blood spilling out would slow down, then in defiance of gravity, start climbing back inside the wound as white foam formed around it, stitching the skin back together.

Although Chaos had discovered that regeneration burned down the lifeforce of the Zombies, aging them before their time, it would take hundreds of deaths for them to start showing any signs. The Dragons and Kryptids would falter from exhaustion long before the Zombies did.

Forcing myself to focus on my shifting, I embraced the burn of my body remodeling itself. Unlike taking on Giles's appearance—who was a humanoid like me—the Septhoron required a complete metamorphosis. A white fog descended before my eyes as I lost control of most of my senses. Shifting left me completely vulnerable while it lasted. My companions bearing the onslaught gave me the time I needed.

As my senses slowly returned, I reveled in the power of the eight tentacles that served me as both arms and locomotion system. Three-meters-long each, with a diameter of twenty-five centimeters, the tentacles ended with hand-like grappling hooks with seven clawed-fingers. A small slit at the center of each 'hand' could open for a spear to stab and inject with a lethal poison whatever it held or touched. Dark, impenetrable scales covered the upper half of my tentacles, shielding glands that coated them in a venomous acid powerful enough to inflict horrible blisters on contact, and would even melt skin and flesh right off the bone if exposed to it for an extended period.

A long, flat, and wide tail trailed behind me. It not only allowed me to propel myself forward in a quick burst, but it could also be used as a deadly weapon. I could use it to whip at target with enough strength that the paddle would instantly shatter the bones of most creatures on impact. But better still, the flat side could wrap around a target, and from the bumps on its surface, countless fifteen-centimeter needles would jut out, turning the victim into a sieve like an iron maiden.

As I completed my transformation, I took a second to regain my bearings. On top of having to adjust my balance in accordance with my new weight distribution, I also had to adapt to my new vision. Septhorons had a huge, flat, circular head with eyes all around its circumference, giving it a 360 view of its environment. The head split in half right in the middle on its entire length to reveal its mouth.

"Brace!" I ordered my companions through mind speak.

Pushing a bone-chilling screech, which sounded like nails on glass, I dragged my new body on the floor, propelling myself forward at dizzying speed with my tail. As I had hoped, my scream drew the attention of the Zombies, distracting them long enough to give our side a slight edge.

In almost perfect synch, Rogue and Reaper flapped their bug wings enough to hover over the others. Then they spread their wings and spun on themselves at a slight angle. The viciously sharp edges of their deceptively thin and translucent wings instantly beheaded the Zombies in front of them. They landed seconds later, raising their shields again to reform their protective wall with the others.

But with a savage flick of my tail, I swiped six of the Zombies trying to brutally break through to Commander Hulax. They flew off to the side, some of them crashing against the stasis chambers nearby, the others smashing against the wall further back in a mess of broken limbs.

Realizing I was now the biggest threat, the Zombies turned their attention to me, only to get impaled by my companions' arm blades or get their heads exploded by mouth darts. The eight others that almost got to me ended up speared at the end of the grappling hooks of my tentacles. For a split second, my heart skipped a beat when a ninth Zombie charged me. I would never have time to turn around to thump him with my tail. As opening my mouth split my head in half, I parted it only wide enough to be able to spit out acid without blinding me too much as to what was happening directly in front of me.

But I never had time to spit out a single drop.

A giant blade punched right through the back of the Zombie, shooting out through his chest before recurving upward. The Zombie flew backward, only to have his neck snapped by Reklig. I realized then that the Scelk had used his bladed tail to harpoon my would-be attacker away from me.

The tide had turned. Effortlessly holding the eight Zombies up in the air at the end of my tentacles, I pumped them full of acidic venom through the spears in the palms of my hands. I then tossed them across the room to catch eight more enemies. By then, my team had maimed or grievously incapacitated the others. With the virus finally taking effect, the white foam appeared a lot thinner, its sizzling fizzling out long before the most severe wounds were fully healed.

Just as I was about to toss the Zombies I currently held in my grappling hands, they suddenly stopped fighting to free themselves. The handful of other badly injured clones struggling to get back on their feet to continue the fight also stopped, their eyes glazing over with a vacant stare.

"What's going on?" Hulax asked.

But even as the question left his lips, he jerked his head towards Reklig, like the rest of us did. Massive waves of psychic energy were emanating from the Scelk as he stared at the clones, flabbergasted.

"They're not mindless," Reklig whispered in disbelief. "They do not have a soul, but they have a controllable organic mind. I've never touched anything like it before."

A soulless, controllable mind?!

The faces of my companions reflected the shock I felt. Scelks could mind-control absolutely any life form that possessed some levels of intelligence. Extremely basic creatures that relied on instinct—like the Swarm Drones and Jadozors—were too primitive to obey compulsions.

We turned to look at the Worker. Huddled up near the doors, she was sitting on the floor, her arms wrapped around her folded legs, pressed to her chest. Her entire body trembling, she stared at us with eyes wide with fear.

"Secure the clones," Reaper ordered. "We need to find out what else Giles has been up to here."

I carefully placed the clones I still held down on the floor. Rogue turning his attention towards me had me instantly feeling self-conscious about my monstrous appearance. But my perfect mate smiled and winked at me. How the fuck did he manage to make me feel sexy even morphed into a giant nightmarish squid?

"Rogue, see which clone can be salvaged," Reaper said, tension filling his voice. "We need a thorough analysis and especially to find out how self-aware they were or not." He cast an assessing look towards the Worker. "Then I want the control chips off the Workers ASAP. We need to know everything that has been happening here."

"On it," Rogue replied.

He gave his brother a stiff nod and made a beeline for one of the less damaged clones. I shifted back to my normal form.

Reaper carefully advanced towards the Worker. She jumped to her feet, eyes wide like saucers, and further pressed herself against the wall. Despite how she'd pissed me off by calling me by the experiment number they'd originally given me, my protective instinct surged to the fore. Reaper wouldn't harm her, but she didn't know that for sure and was clearly terrified.

"It's okay," I told the Worker before Reaper could speak. "You are safe. No one here will harm you."

She glanced at me, her eyes filled with fear and hope, and took a sidestep to the right, closer to me. I doubted she even realized she'd done so. Still, it warmed my heart in a way I couldn't explain that she would seek my protection.

"Shuria is correct," Reaper said in a soothing voice. "You are safe among us. We're here to free you and the other Workers. My name is Reaper. What are you called?"

Her breath still quick and shallow from fear, she cast a look over Reaper's shoulder at the Kryptid Soldiers and Commander Hulax busy with the clones. She relaxed a little seeing them working hand in hand with Rogue and Reklig.

"Zu... Zuno. My name is Zuno," she replied nervously.

"Okay, Zuno. Can you stop the alarm?"

She vigorously shook her head. "No. Unless the threat has been eliminated, only Master Dalton can," she said, her gaze flicking my way.

Understanding immediately dawned on me. So long as the Dragons remained alive inside the base, the alarm would remain active. I glanced around the room for any visible sign of a bioscanner. Zuno pointed a skinny, chitin covered finger towards the left side of the room.

I made a beeline for it, finding a workstation I had not noticed before because of the stasis chambers hiding it. I quickly morphed my upper body back to match Giles's appearance and deactivated the alarm. It wasn't until the siren shut off that I realized just how loud and obnoxious it had been.

As I walked back to Reaper and the Worker, I shed the superficial shift to reclaim my normal form.

"No, there are no other threats beyond," Zuno said to Reaper, no doubt in response to a question. "We had not expected anyone to ever come here, let alone be able to disable the phoenix."

She cast a meaningful glance at the inert Zombies.

"Giles is about to get hit with a lot of things he had not expected," Reaper said in an ominous voice that whipped my bloodlust into a frenzy.

I was looking forward to destroying this would-be despot with the same pleasure I derived from us killing Khutu.

CHAPTER 15
ROGUE

A million thoughts raced through my mind as I attempted to stabilize one of the few surviving clones the best I could. We'd messed them up too thoroughly. The ones Shuria had injected with her venom were lost causes. Even now, their flesh was literally melting off their bones in a thick sludge.

Shuria...

Witnessing the power she wielded had taken my breath away. Without her intervention, I probably would have died along with a couple more Kryptid Soldiers before the virus took effect enough for us to win. While they would have been permanently gone, I at least could have been reborn in a new Shell. But dying seriously sucked.

I couldn't help a shudder at the stoicism with which the Kryptids handled their three fallen—the grievously injured ones having succumbed to their wounds moments ago. As soon as Madeline and Martha arrived with the hover stretchers, we placed the two surviving clones on them, a dome closing over their still form so they'd remain in stasis until I could perform a complete analysis on them.

That task completed, I hastened after Reaper, Hulax, Shuria, and Reklig, who had headed out into the other sections of the base only a few minutes prior. Madeline tagged along to download whatever data we could recover from the computers.

The doors opened on a large hallway. To my relief, despite the Workers seeming to be the only scientists here, no membrane covered the walls. By the great distance between each door—none of them bearing any visible locking mechanism—I easily guessed at the considerable size of each room behind them.

Upon our approach, the first door on the left swished open. My jaw dropped at the sight of the massive nursery revealed to us. Rows upon rows of round holding cases filled the left and right sides of the rectangular room. Each case, the size of a table wide enough to seat ten people, contained about twenty large Scelk eggs. A thick dome covered each of the cases. I couldn't tell if the devices served as incubators or cryogenic chambers. But a single look at the eggs confirmed they were ready to hatch. Inside large cryogenic tanks eerily similar to giant aquariums, at least one hundred Scelk hatchlings were kept in stasis, about ten per tank.

However, it was the creature sitting near the back wall that claimed my full attention. I had never seen such a large Queen before. On average, Scelk Queens measured between sixty to seventy centimeters wide, with their legs outstretched, and about twenty-five centimeters high, which was more than double the size of a regular Scelk bug. But this one was at least a meter wide. Unlike her hatchlings, the Queen didn't have the long, spiked tail that her offspring used to attach to the nervous system of their host through their spines. Instead, a large gelatinous sac writhed behind her with the hundreds of eggs still maturing.

Standing before the raised bed she was lying on, Reklig was gently caressing the swollen chitin dome that spanned the length of her back, and which contained her massive brain. The modified Scelks, as manipulated under my sire's orders, were essentially a huge brain on six spindly legs with a long tail.

By the psychic energy emanating from him, I suspected Reklig was attempting to soothe the Queen. If not for her egg sac rooting her in place, I didn't doubt Reklig would have cradled her in his arms like one would a distressed child.

"Is she all right?" I asked as we approached our companions.

Hulax's expression left little to the imagination as to his feelings about the Scelk Queen and her eggs. He stared balefully at the moving tableau of Reklig reassuring the Queen while she clung to him.

"She's scared and exhausted, but otherwise unharmed," Reaper replied.

"Why exhausted?" I asked, casting a glance at Zuno.

She nervously rubbed the side of her right mandible before answering. "Unlike Kryptids, Scelk Queens need to rest after laying a certain number of eggs. Ideally, five days of rest after every hundred eggs. They are somewhat similar to human females who need time to recover after delivering an offspring, but on a much larger scale. She drains a lot of her own resources feeding those eggs and requires pauses to restore her strength."

"When was the last time she rested?" I asked, already guessing what type of infuriating response I would get.

"One month," Zuno confessed sheepishly. She paused, choosing her words carefully, hinting she was looking for a way to give us more information that wouldn't trigger the punishment mode of her implant. "We needed as many eggs as possible ready to be hatched quickly. Therefore, we give her high nutrition supplements and an inducer to force her to continue laying."

It was my turn to choose my words to ask a safe question. "And how long before she can take a break?"

Zuno hesitated. "Her egg reserves are almost depleted. Scelk Queens are born with an average of one hundred thousand eggs. By the time they reach maturity, they have about thirty thousand viable eggs left. And they steadily lose more over time. In her case, we had to harvest ten thousand of them for… research. She only has a little over two thousand eggs left—at least a third of which will be lost. She was expected to lay until the last one."

I clenched my teeth. Giles had planned on milking her to her last breath. A Scelk Queen usually died within days of laying her last egg—once she'd exceeded her usefulness. The same anger reflected on my companions' faces.

"Can you stop the forced laying?" Reklig asked, echoing my thoughts.

"Stop, no," Zuno replied carefully. "However, if she's not given another inducer injection, once the effects of the current ones wear off, it will be up to her when next to lay eggs again. Well, after she emptied her current sac."

"And what of all these eggs?" Hulax asked in a tensed voice while gesturing at the round casings filling the room.

"They are ready to hatch, but kept in cryo-stasis," she said warily.

"Why not hatch them?" Hulax insisted. "And why are there hatched ones in those tanks?"

Zuno closed herself off, a strained expression descending over her insectoid features as she rubbed her temple.

"Maybe we can save these questions for after Zuno's implant has been removed," Shuria intervened in a disapproving tone.

The grateful look the Worker gave my mate warmed my hearts. Shuria was a natural protector. It shone in every one of her actions. I couldn't wait to see what a wonderful mother she would be to our offspring.

"Agreed," Reaper said. "Let's go see what else Giles has been up to, in here. Time isn't on our side if we are to counter whatever sick plan he has set in motion."

And that worried me the most. The 'sentient' clones would require all my attention in the next few days. We didn't randomly kill innocent people. But these clones didn't possess a soul. Did they qualify as people? How self-aware were they truly?

My innards twisted at the thought that the rebel leader could possibly have devised a way to create an endless supply of sentient soldiers with only a small amount of his own DNA.

Distraught by these disturbing thoughts, I followed my brother and the others outside of the nursery. Having finished dealing with the clones, Martha, Madeline, and the Kryptids joined us. We entered the next room a few meters down the hallway through the door on the opposite side. My blood drained from my face as I took in the spectacle that awaited us.

The gigantic space looked like a smaller replica of Khepri's Incubator where Xian and Dragon Shells were created. Although the ceiling here was much lower than on Khepri, they still had about one hundred spherical incubators hanging from the ceiling. Within each, a clone of Giles huddled in a fetal position with tubes connecting to its spine. Lining the wall, at least twenty more clones stood in cylindrical tanks filled with some kind of liquid. A breathing mask covered their mouths and noses. Unlike the ones overhead, the clones floating in the tanks appeared to have achieved full maturity whereas the others were still in the early stages of their gestation.

No one but the Xians, Dragons, our psychic women, and a very limited number of scientists with high security levels could enter the incubator. So how in the world had Giles known what kind of configuration we had in order for him to replicate it?

And yet, as much as this troubled me, it was the smaller containment chambers sitting on the tables in the center of the room that claimed all of my attention. Fighting a sense of dread, I hastened ahead of my brother, circling around the examination tables that surrounded the research island in the middle.

"You've got to be fucking kidding me," I hissed as I closed in on the island.

Standing in front of one of the containment chambers, I stared in disbelief at the small, fleshy mass in its center. The familiar reddish-brown tissue, crisscrossed by a network of blood vessels, heaved almost imperceptibly.

Reaper stopped next to me, a concerned expression on his face in response to my demeanor. "Membranes?" he asked, warily eyeing the contents of the three dozen chambers on the island.

"Not membranes," I ground through my teeth before looking at Zuno with an accusatory glare. "They're fucking organic AIs. Is that what you're stuffing those clones with?"

I felt horrible seeing Zuno squirm in response to my anger. She only obeyed whatever order Giles had given her. Following this path made sense in more ways than one for a narcissistic psychopath like he was. But it was also a terrifying prospect. We hadn't had a chance to explore the extent of that AI's autonomous ability to think and make decisions. On organic ships, the Kryptids had always created AIs with very specialized functions. How far had they managed to push this one?

Far enough to be deemed sufficiently intelligent for a Scelk to control.

That was terrifying.

"They have both a mechanical brain and an organic artificial intelligence," Zuno replied nervously. "In case of software or mechanical malfunction, or if a signal cannot be sent to them, the phoenixes could function on their own, until communication can be re-established."

"What is its learning capacity?" Hulax asked, intense displeasure visible on his features.

"Infinite, Commander," Zuno said in an apologetic tone. "It is trained then continues to learn on its own."

"Trained in what fields?" Hulax insisted.

After a moment's hesitation, Zuno gave him a strange look. "We train them the same way we trained you, Commander."

"Shit," Shuria whispered.

I gave her an inquisitive look before turning back to Hulax. "What does that mean?" I asked.

"It means advanced combat, sabotage, strategic warfare,

psychology, negotiation, navigation, and general science, to name a few," Hulax growled before refocusing on Zuno. "Is Giles the only model or are there more?"

"You can see here everything related to this project," Zuno replied carefully, waving a hand at the room.

"Which means this is the only model," I said with relief. "Madeline, download all the data and all the settings on the devices."

"On it," Madeline replied.

"Martha, get samples of everything, including the fluids in those tanks," I continued.

"You got it," Martha said.

Two Soldiers stayed with the women, both to provide protection in case things turned bad—not that we expected any other incident—but also to help them move the clones around if needed.

The rest of us proceeded to explore the other areas of the underground facility. We wasted little time checking the next few rooms. Smaller in size, they served as a dormitory for the Workers, storage, cafeteria, meeting room, hygiene room, and machine room.

We did pause in the secondary storage area. Temperature controlled, this one contained dozens of cooling units, each one filled to the brim with hundreds of small vials. I instantly recognized them as the serum derived from Xenon's blood. It confirmed what one of the repentant rebels had revealed to Chaos's team on Aurilia. Giles was hoarding the serum essential to prevent premature aging from using the Zombie's regeneration ability. Now that they could no longer milk Xenon for his blood, every ounce was precious. And clearly, Giles didn't want to share.

Naturally, we would relieve him of the entire supply.

To my surprise, Zuno urged us to visit the ship hangar before the remaining room across from it at the end of the corridor when Reaper made as if he would go there. A strong sense of unease engulfed me when I caught the nervous glance she cast at my female. Whatever that room contained, she feared Shuria's response to it. The Worker's mention of 'siren' immediately came back to me. Considering what we had seen so far, it terrified me to even speculate as to what Giles's demented mind had concocted.

Much too small to have hosted some of the largest Kryptid vessels, the hangar still contained a handful of ships, including a fighter, a chaser, a couple of Coalition shuttles, a Spitter, and the Kryptid equivalent of a chaser. A single glance sufficed to know that the Kryptid ships had been modified or at least tampered with.

"Did a lot of Kryptid vessels come through here?" Reaper asked, his underlying meaning clear.

"No," Zuno replied, looking relieved. "These were enough for our purpose."

"Let's see what remains in the last room," Hulax said with obvious annoyance as he stared at the Worker. "All this dancing around in order to get proper answers is a waste of time. We need to remove that chip from her."

While I wholeheartedly agreed with the Commander's sentiment, I also suspected that it wouldn't be as easy as he seemed to think. As I highly doubted that Giles would have given regeneration abilities to his slaves, removing the control chips would require extreme care to avoid inflicting permanent brain damage to the patients. Zuno and her companions held a wealth of knowledge that could turn the tide in this war.

As we headed out of the hangar and approached the last room, Zuno's nervousness came back with a vengeance. Although she made commendable efforts to keep a neutral expression, her aura shouted her fear and trepidation. I stood closer to my female, ready to support her if needed. By the tension Shuria also displayed, I wondered if she had a hunch or shared my suspicions. My mate possessed a great analytical mind and an impressive sense of observation. Little escaped her notice.

"The other Workers are in that room. They are scared," Zuno said, her lingering fear audible in her voice.

For a split second, I wondered if that had been the real reason she had delayed entering that room. But I quickly dismissed that thought. By now, she knew we meant them no harm.

The door no sooner parted than the familiar scent of saltwater slapped me in the face. Before I even set foot inside the room, I already knew that it contained some kind of large aquarium or pond. Sure enough, a floor-to-ceiling reinforced glass wall divided the room in half. Beyond it, a humanoid female lazily swam in slightly greenish water.

"No," Shuria whispered, her voice filled with pain, anger, and betrayal as she pushed past Reaper to go stand in front of the aquarium.

I followed in her wake, ready to intervene if needed, but didn't otherwise try to hold her back. Thankfully, the Kryptid Soldiers moved towards the four Workers looking on the verge of fainting from panic as they squeezed one against the other in the far right corner of the room. Judging by the five workstations, examination tables, and various scientific paraphernalia on the counters, whatever work they were performing in this room seemed to be a priority.

As the Workers didn't represent a threat, I dismissed them from my thoughts and refocused on the female swimming inside the aquarium. She was fully naked. While her skin bore the distinctive swirly ridges of a Mimic's undars, she looked like a Middle Eastern human, with long black hair and a tan complexion. The siren, who had been gliding away from us, suddenly jerked her head towards Shuria. Her expressionless face perked up.

Flapping her joined legs like a mermaid would her tail, she

approached the glass wall to stare at my mate. Her features overwhelmed by emotion, Shuria pressed her palm against the glass. The siren frowned as she examined it before casting a confused look at Shuria. She then looked at her palm, her frown deepening. Understanding dawned on me as I noticed the webbing between her fingers.

Just as I was about to speak, Shuria figured it out as well and extruded her webbing. The siren's face lit up at that sight, and she pressed her palm against Shuria's through the glass. She continued staring at their hands until psychic energy started emanating from my mate. The siren looked up, jerked her hand back, then started swimming backward, as if suddenly wary of us.

"What happened?" I whispered to Shuria.

She didn't respond. Teeth clenched, her entire body vibrating with barely repressed anger, Shuria continued staring at the siren until she curled up at the far back of the aquarium on what resembled some large spongy plants.

The murderous glare my female then leveled on Zuno sent a cold shiver down my spine. I tensed, ready to intervene if Shuria attacked. The Worker all but withered from fright.

"What the fuck did you do to her? What is she?" Shuria hissed. "She has Mimic DNA, but she's not one of us, and her mind is a wreck. WHAT THE FUCK IS SHE?!"

"Calm, love," I said in a soothing voice while gently caressing her back.

The way Shuria stiffened at my touch, I feared for a second that she would slam her elbow into my side to shove me away. Closing her eyes, she took a loud and deep breath to rein in the fury boiling beneath the surface.

Continuing to gently caress Shuria's back, I psychically brushed against the siren's consciousness—or whatever she possessed that would qualify as such. My stomach roiled at the alien nature of her mind. I had not attempted to mentally connect with the Zombie Warriors earlier after Reklig had confirmed being able to mind control them. But I didn't doubt for a minute that they had created this female in a similar fashion.

She didn't have a soul.

Or should I say 'it'?

Anyone with high enough psychic powers could look at the manifestation of one's soul inside their psychic void. It was a metaphysical space in the brain, usually a dark space at the center of which the colorful lights of one's soul danced in a more or less spherical fashion. People with psychic levels ranging from rank three to five—the highest achievable by most species—could create a shield around their soul which made it look almost like a metallic sphere. The women of the Vanguard all had to be a minimum of rank four, which manifested by a silver sphere. The rare rank five psychics like Ayana, Liena, and all the mature Scelks, Xians, and Dragons possessed a golden sphere. This siren had nothing: not even a void to peer into.

"That's Salma Dalton," Madeline said in an ominous tone. "Or rather what I believe to be a disturbing attempt at recreating her."

"Dalton," Reaper echoed, his shock reflecting mine.

"She was Giles's wife, and an extremely brilliant mathematician. She cared little for fame and turned down many prestigious positions to follow her husband instead while he climbed the ranks. He was madly in love with her," Madeline added with a sad expression. "As you can guess, she died during a Kryptid raid. Actually, that's not accurate. Their infant daughter *was* killed, but Salma was never found. She went missing along with several other women of fertile age."

"I never heard of this," I said. "There was no such mention in his file."

"It probably got edited out," Madeline said with a frown. "I know of Salma because I had studied a lot of her theorems as we use them in many modern programming algorithms. The scientific community greatly mourned her disappearance."

"When did she pass?" Reaper asked.

"A little over six years ago," Madeline replied.

"Six years ago?" I repeated. "Based on Legion's report, this would be around the time Giles began building his rebellion. Could his wife's death have been the triggering factor?"

"I don't give a fuck what the triggering factor was," Shuria hissed. "I want to know what she is and what they're doing to her."

Despite the harshness of her words, I didn't take offence. She was not attacking me but simply falling victim to her emotions and likely a great deal of PTSD. There was no question in my mind that seeing this siren brought back the dreadful memories of her and her sisters trapped inside similar tanks and aquariums while being experimented on.

"From what I've been able to gather from Zuno's mind, the siren is Giles's desperate attempt at recreating his wife," Reklig said in an appeasing tone, devoid of his usual taunting and mischief. "As you accurately stated, she's not a Mimic—at least not a pureblood. She's something closer to the Xians. The Workers have spliced her with a high percentage of Mimic DNA. The organic artificial intelligence is being trained with Salma's memories and personality."

"But why Mimic DNA?" Shuria demanded angrily.

"There weren't enough pure samples of the woman's DNA to grow a new body," Zuno said timidly. "A Mimic can perfectly replicate any appearance, mannerism, and voice. But Shells grown in an incubator are soulless."

"And that's how you justify torturing her?" Shuria shouted.

"We're not torturing her!" Zuno exclaimed, clasping her hands nervously in front of her. "She doesn't feel any pain. Master Dalton wouldn't have allowed it. In truth, she doesn't feel anything."

Zuno winced as she spoke those last words. The defense mechanism of her control chip had likely kicked in, giving her a slight punishment as a warning that she was close to crossing the line.

Her response did not surprise me. While I didn't pretend to be an organic AI expert, I knew enough about them to confirm that they never developed emotions like we did. In more ways than one, they were like the Kryptids, driven by instinct and primal responses. I didn't know that—even with the organic AI merging with the brain and nervous system of the shell—this siren could ever develop an actual personality that wasn't simply the illusion of a very advanced artificial intelligence.

I cast an assessing look at the four other workers huddled fearfully in the far corner of the room. We needed to know everything they did. One thing was certain, Dalton was even crazier than my sire had been.

CHAPTER 16
SHURIA

Saying I felt distraught by what we had discovered inside would be quite the understatement. Finding messed up shit in a secret lab no longer surprised me—I'd expected it. But discovering the Mimic, or siren as they called her—called *it*—struck me hard.

Memories of my past traumatic experiences came flooding back. I felt nauseous, my hands shaking as images of the siren bearing my sisters' faces instead kept flashing before my mind's eye. Shaking my head to clear my thoughts, I refocused on my current task of destroying the still incubating clones of Giles hanging from the ceiling.

Rogue had requested that we do not damage the fully mature ones that floated upright in the tanks lining the walls. As these ones had already received an organic AI, further discussions were pending as to what fate awaited them. Deep down, I believed the decision had already been made but that my mate mostly wanted a few flawless clones to study and analyze.

I had no issues killing the clones, even the mature ones, had I been given that order. But I struggled with the idea of doing the same to the siren. Even though she wasn't a real Mimic, it felt like I had failed yet another sister. It didn't matter that she'd only been spliced with one of us. Upon entering the room, I had felt the bond of kinship that every Mimic experienced when in the presence of another. Granted, it had not been anywhere near as strong as what I felt in the presence of my other sisters, but it had been there, nonetheless.

With the last immature clone destroyed, I exited the incubator room to return to the aquarium. All around me, the Kryptid Soldiers moved crates and devices back to our ship. Standing at the end of the hallway, I hesitated between entering the aquarium or delaying further by joining Madeline in the ship hangar. She was recovering data and samples from the Spitters' AI as well as any data related to the modified Kryptid vessels. But there was no point delaying the inevitable. The faster I recovered samples of all the research in the aquarium, the sooner I could get away from this place.

Right now, I just wanted to go back to my quarters and snuggle with Rogue. But even if I rushed through my current assignment, I wouldn't be able to seek the comfort I needed from him. My mate was up to his eyeballs juggling with all the insanity we had found here. Between studying the experiments and freeing the Workers from their control chips, Rogue would have little to no time for me. With the war looming near, we needed to make full use of every possible edge today's discovery could provide us with. So my pathetic needs would have to take a back seat.

For the next thirty minutes, I forced myself to ignore the siren while packing the biohazard crates with various vials, specimens, and tissue from the cooling units and containment chambers. The weight of her stare on me felt like a living entity.

I picked up the final crate, intending to leave the room and head back to the ship. But with a will of their own, my feet led me straight in front of the aquarium. The siren kept swimming lazily. Although she continued to stare at me, I didn't know that she was truly seeing me. There was a vagueness in her gaze. It took me a moment to realize her swimming pattern would alternate between drawing a horizontal infinity symbol before doing the same but this time vertically. With each revolution, she would switch the way she swam from flapping her joined legs like a mermaid, to doing a breaststroke, or alternating the movement of her legs. There didn't seem to be any particular meaning to this behavior, but it still intrigued me.

"Shuria?"

Martha calling out my name had me nearly jumping out of my skin. I had been so lost—not to say hypnotized—observing the siren that I had not heard my teammate entering the room.

"Yes?" I replied, trying to regain my bearings.

Martha didn't say anything, studying my features instead as she approached me. I shifted uneasily on my feet, an irrational sense of guilt and embarrassment washing over me.

She gave the siren an assessing look before glancing back at me with a serious expression. "She's not a Mimic," Martha said in a soft tone.

I stiffened and averted my eyes. Teeth clenched, I tightened my hold around the crate in my arms, pressing it against my chest as if it were a shield to protect me against things I didn't want to hear or deal with.

"She's just a Shell with an artificial intelligence," Martha continued, her voice filled with empathy. "She's not one of your sisters. That siren does not feel like you and I do."

My eyes flicked towards her as a mix of hope, anger, and a great deal of confusion warred within me. "You can't be certain of that," I countered weakly.

"Yes, I can." The firmness and conviction in her voice hit me like a boulder. "She's no different than a liveship's AI."

"But she got frightened when I tried to touch her psychic mind," I argued.

Martha shook her head. "No. That wasn't fear—or at least

not the way you and I define it. You startled her when you did. She is an organic AI. She does not mind speak. Like with the liveships, the cryptids communicate with them by sending them wireless transmissions. This siren is only used to receiving training subroutines when it comes to mental communications. Otherwise, they will verbally speak to her. She would have perceived your telepathic contact as a communication malfunction. Her self-preservation program kicked in, prompting her to remove herself from the proximity of the source of the malfunction to avoid further defects."

I swallowed hard and glanced back at the siren. Martha's explanation made sense. I had lived surrounded by organic membranes or traveling in liveships long enough to know that they all functioned based on a series of instinctive responses to their environment and interactions. No matter how much she looked like a person, like one of my people, she was merely a droid with an organic artificial intelligence instead of a mechanical brain.

Martha gently caressed my shoulder in a soothing motion and gave me a sweet smile. "Let's get out of here."

I returned her smile, grateful for her supportive understanding, and followed her back to the ship. As we rode the lift up to the main floor, I silently thanked the Maker for these unexpected blessings that now seemed to befall me. During the months leading to the final war against Khutu, I had often observed with envy the sisterly interactions between the women of the Vanguard. Never in a million years would have I imagined I'd be so openly welcomed and granted the same kindness and inclusion. To think I had kept myself isolated all this time because I didn't believe myself deserving.

With the area secured, Thanh had landed our ship right outside the cluster of cabins. We hurried inside, Martha being a good sport at keeping up with my fast pace, no doubt guessing I just wanted to be done.

To my dismay, just as we were organizing the crates in our ship's hold, Reaper called a meeting. I'd had enough of this day. If cuddling with my mate was not on the table at this time, curling up in bed would have been a far more acceptable alternative than further discussing the shit show we were currently wading in.

Groaning inwardly, I made my way to the meeting room with Martha by my side. Half the team was already there when we entered, Commander Hulax and Madeline entering last. I settled next to Rogue, who immediately took my hand in his. My throat tightened, and I once more found myself pathetic that such a simple gesture would affect me so much, giving me the mental boost I so desperately needed right now. As much as I loved to have been returned to my original self, I wished I hadn't become so emotionally fragile. A part of me missed the tough, ruthless, no holds barred assassin I had previously been turned into.

"I know you're all very busy, so I'm going to keep this short," Reaper said as soon as everyone was present. "I have sent a message to Chaos, Legion, and Doom, giving them a quick update about what we found here. Considering the great distance, those messages will take a while to reach them. Steele will take everything here worth keeping back to Khepri and destroy the rest. But he is still four days away. We cannot wait that long for him to arrive. I want us gone by end of day tomorrow so that we can swiftly return to Kryptor."

"But what if Giles or another rebel returns in the meantime?" I asked.

"I will have Martha set up some defenses," Reaper replied. "But that will not be enough. As we need whatever knowledge the Workers possess, we cannot leave them behind."

"Especially considering it will take a while to free them of their control chips," Rogue added with a dejected expression. "They've included a set of nanites with advanced regenerative subroutines. Every time we start unraveling the chip, the nanites kick in to repair them. This means we have to use a more aggressive protocol, which causes swelling in the brain. Therefore, we have to significantly slow down the process to allow them to heal between each treatment to avoid permanent damage."

"How much time are we talking about?" Reaper asked.

"Days," Rogue replied in an apologetic tone.

Reaper cussed under his breath, his sentiment reflected on every face.

"Can't the Scelk just read their knowledge directly from their minds?" Commander Hulax asked.

Although he had not spoken with any contempt or aggression, his wording nonetheless rubbed Reklig the wrong way. Not for the first time since the Vanguard came to warn us of the impending attack, I kicked myself for never trying to teach the Kryptid some basic bedside manners in the time I spent living amongst them.

"What I can read is fairly limited as the control chips impede my abilities. I could force the issue but not without inflicting serious pain if not potentially fatal damage," Reklig replied, his tone a little frigid. "What knowledge they can share with us is far too valuable to put in jeopardy over impatience."

"I agree," Rogue said. "Anyway, we have tons of files and data to read through in between phases of removing the implants."

"Which brings us back to who we should leave behind," Reaper said.

"My Soldiers can stay until Steele arrives," Commander Hulax offered. "They can use the rebel's Kryptid chaser to return home once the Vanguard has arrived."

"If you wouldn't mind, that could be a good solution." By the way Reaper spoke those words, it had clearly been his hope from the start.

"I'm not sure I'm comfortable with that option," Reklig countered, his spine stiff with tension.

The glance he cast in the Kryptid Commander's direction made no mystery as to his underlying meaning.

Hulax's features immediately hardened. "My soldiers will not harm your *Queen*."

My own hackles rose upon hearing the disdain in his voice. If he was trying to reassure Reklig, he was doing a pitiful job of it.

"Why the fuck should I believe you?" Reklig hissed.

Hulax waved a dismissive hand. "Whatever my personal thoughts about your species, our Queen and General have deemed you allies during this looming war. I will not jeopardize this truce or disobey my hierarchical superiors. We will *not* harm your Queen."

When Reklig continued to stare at Hulax, making no effort to hide his dubious expression, the Commander huffed with annoyance. "If my word does not satisfy you, Scelk, then read my thoughts, and let us stop wasting time on this topic."

To my shock, Reklig slightly recoiled, shock at the unexpected offer quickly followed by a sliver of embarrassment. The Scelks were quite sensitive about people doubting their honesty whenever they promised not to read them or pledged to behave respectfully. Being called out for doing unto others—especially a species who he knew was strictly controlled by hierarchy—had to seriously sting.

"That won't be necessary," Reklig grumbled, averting his gaze with a grumpy expression.

"I insist," Hulax said, his tone icy. "We have bigger issues to deal with, and I will not have you distracted by ridiculous worries. Read me and let us be done."

"Go ahead," Reaper ordered sternly, when Reklig appeared to want to argue further.

The Scelk bared his teeth as he glared at our leader. Reaper sustained his gaze unflinchingly. With a frustrated grunt, Reklig gave a sideways glance at Hulax. The way the tension in his shoulders loosened and shame flitted over his features confirmed

Reklig had complied. He gave the Kryptid Commander a stiff nod.

"Now that it's settled, I need you all to wrap up whatever tasks you have to do as swiftly as possible," Reaper said. "Manage your time however you see fit. Just make sure you're ready to go by tomorrow evening. If no one has questions, you're dismissed."

He didn't have to say it twice.

To my pleasant surprise, instead of heading back to the Infirmary, Rogue accompanied me back to our quarters.

"I have done all that I can do for the Workers until they have healed," he explained when I questioned him. "I will go back in a few hours and repeat that process at least a couple of times throughout the night. It's a good thing I'm properly trained in surviving on a few power naps. I also have a few analyses running. The report should be ready for review at about the same time I will resume work on removing the control chips. But for now, I'm more interested in knowing how you are doing. Are you okay?"

My heart melted, and my throat constricted from the genuine concern in his voice and in his eyes as he studied my features. Nodding, I pressed myself against him.

"I've had better days, but I'm fine. I'm dealing with a bit of PTSD, but nothing I can't handle. That siren brought back a lot of bad memories. Still, I'm relieved that you're here, safe, and unharmed."

Rogue smiled, his arms wrapping around me. He kissed the tip of my nose before nuzzling me. "And that's largely thanks to you, my mate. You were absolutely badass in there," he said, the pride in his voice turning me upside down.

"Badass?" I challenged, to hide both how flattered and embarrassed I felt. "I think monstrous and freaky would be more appropriate qualifiers."

"Lethal and impressive would be more accurate," he countered in a teasing tone. "Frankly, I must admit a certain amount of envy when I look at what you can do."

I laughed at the sheepish way in which he pronounced those last words. "You have absolutely nothing to envy. I turn into weird creatures, but you can transfer your soul into a new Shell. Now *that's* badass. I'm just grateful to have you. You are everything to me."

"As you are to me, Shuria."

Our lips met in a soft and tender kiss, filled with the deeper feelings steadily growing between us. After today's traumatic events, I had just wanted the comfort of my mate's presence and the safety I always felt when embraced by his muscular arms. But a familiar flame lit low in my belly.

I melted against Rogue, my fingers slipping into his hair as his hands glided the length of my spine. A shiver coursed through me as I parted my lips to welcome his invading tongue. I loved the feel of its slightly rough texture as it swirled around mine.

Rogue broke the kiss and leaned his forehead against mine.

"I never want to lose you," I whispered, my voice full of emotion.

Lifting his head to study my features with a world of tenderness in his eyes, Rogue placed a gentle hand on my cheek and brushed his thumb over my bottom lip.

"You never will," he assured me. "I'm yours, always and forever. You're everything I want."

Yeah, I was greedy for reaffirmation, even though my mate was doing wonders by steadily reassuring me of his feelings for me. Despite how illogical this continued to feel to me, I no longer doubted Rogue's sincerity. I'd just grown addicted to hearing him say he was mine. The pride with which he claimed me and the joy he seemed to genuinely feel at being mine was intoxicating.

"Show me," I whispered, my eyes flicking to his plump lips before locking gazes with him again.

The air of pure lust that descended over Rogue's features had my stomach do a couple of somersaults. He trailed his hands down to the curve of my hips, pulling me closer to him.

"Gladly," he growled, his lips crashing onto mine once again.

I moaned into his mouth, my hands getting to work on ridding him of the Vanguard pants and shirt he'd slipped back on before starting to work on the Kryptid females. I couldn't help but stare at him, devouring the sight of his chiseled abs and broad shoulders covered in dark chitin scales. My mate was the perfect combination of strength and gentleness. I was still naked, but for my bracer, which he swiftly rid me of.

Rogue lifted me up, carrying me over to the bed, then laid me down. His eyes never left mine as his hands roamed over my skin. How I loved being completely exposed to him, vulnerable to his every touch.

The cinnamon scent of his pheromones filled the air, making me instantly throb with desire. Moisture pooled between my thighs and my inner walls throbbed with the need to be filled. Even though I wanted Rogue inside me now, I'd learned he wouldn't be rushed into anything. He loved subjecting me to long preliminaries, wresting many orgasms from me before he took his own pleasure. But I also loved pleasuring him. The thought of the feel of the rippling ridges of his cock over my tongue and the cinnamon bun flavor of his self-lubricant on my taste buds had my nipples instantly perking out for attention.

Rogue's lips trailed down my neck, nibbling and sucking on my sensitive skin. I moaned softly, arching my back into his touch as his hands slipped below my navel. Without hesitation, I opened for him, parting my legs to give him better access. With two fingers, he immediately started teasing the seam of my sex. I lifted my pelvis, hungry for deeper contact. Rogue chuckled smugly, as he sucked on the little nub of my right breast.

The heat between my legs intensified as he dipped two fingers inside me. A strangled moan escaped me as his touch on the sensitive bundles of nerves lining my inner walls sent electric sparks coursing outwards throughout my body. Our species was created for pleasure, probably to compensate for our low birth rates. The fact that ninety percent of Mimics were also born females –although we could spontaneously switch gender if our male population fell too low—certainly played a part in us having so few offspring.

But right now, my focus was on the insane pleasure Rogue was giving me. Unlike him, I had no qualms chasing bliss. I ground my pelvis against his hand as he continued taking me to the edge. His mouth and the claws of his free hand teasing the undars on my side and belly were driving me insane. Thanks to his pheromones heightening the sensitivity of my nerve endings, the sensations provided by each nip, lick, and scratch were multiplied a thousandfold.

I didn't fight the wave of ecstasy that swept me away. Shouting his name, I raked my claws on each side of the bone spikes lining Rogue's spine. He cried out with that deep growly voice of his. The almost feral sound resonated in my core, and my legs shook as I continued to fly high. Not giving me time to come back down, my lover licked a path down my stomach. My inner walls painfully constricted in anticipation as his breath fanned over my sex, seconds before the heat of his mouth settled on it.

And then, Rogue rewarded me with what I could never stop craving. An almost desperate moan rolled out of my throat as his tongue started pushing inside my opening. Impossibly long and thick, it pushed deeper, narrowing and swelling as it moved in and out of me. I writhed beneath his ministrations, wanting more even as it felt like too much. The rough texture of his tongue rubbing against my sensory receptors had me falling apart in no time again.

Head rolling from side to side while endless strings of blissful moans flowed out of me, I clutched the tips of Rogue's crescent moon-shaped horn with both hands. Despite my mind feeling on the verge of fracturing, I tugged on his horn, keeping his face between my legs while he continued making love to me with his tongue at a frantic pace.

When my third orgasm slammed into me, I felt boneless, my vision blurring and my skin tingling as if my soul was attempting to escape my corporeal vessel. I floated endlessly in a sea of pleasure, my senses too overwhelmed to fully comprehend what was happening. It was only once the burning heat of Rogue's muscular body settled over me that I realized he had stopped feasting on me.

Although still dizzy, I spread my legs wider to express my eager consent, my inner walls quivering with need. As much as his tongue and fingers made me see stars, his cock just wrecked me. Hard and thick, it filled me to the brim. His ridges rubbing against my inner walls sent me over the edge in only a few thrusts. And his stamina was just out of this world.

I occasionally still had to partially morph to welcome him in without having to give my body time to adjust to his girth, but this time, I didn't. Like Rogue, I enjoyed a bit of pain. He had me so wet and so relaxed that, combined with his natural lubricant, my body quickly accepted him. His hiss of pleasure in my ear as we became one had lava rushing through my veins.

Our hands and lips were all over each other as we moved in perfect sync, our moans mingling. Just as I was readying to topple over again, Rogue suddenly pulled out of me. Stunned, I barely had time to register the mischievous grin on his face, laced with a feral hunger that liquified my insides, before he spun me around, putting me on my stomach.

After my initial yelp of surprise, I realized what he wanted. Pushing my hips back, I gave him a view of my curves, inviting him to take me from behind.

He didn't hesitate.

With one powerful thrust, he rammed himself in. I cried out at the exquisite pleasure-pain and extreme fullness of his possession. One hand grabbing my hip in an almost bruising hold, Rogue cupped one of my breasts with the other, squeezing my nipple hard enough to give it the sting I loved. He immediately set a punishing pace as he pounded into me. The scales of his chest rubbed against my back, sending shivers of pleasure down my spine.

A bolt of lust exploded in the pit of my stomach at the feel of his breath on my neck. I moaned in anticipation of what would follow. Seconds later, I detonated as he sank his fangs in the crook of my neck, right below my gills. Since we'd first become intimate, Rogue had steadily become bolder in his lovemaking, his initial nips growing more intense until they became full on bites.

A part of me lamented that he hadn't injected me with his bonding hormones. As it was permanent, he wouldn't do so without my express consent. I was more than ready to permanently bind myself to him.

But the endless waves of ecstasy crashing through me wiped away any such thoughts. My mate wrested one orgasm after the other from me. Although he joined his voice to mine a few times, his searing seed shooting out into me, Rogue didn't stop wrecking me. By the time he finally collapsed, I had lost count of how many times I had screamed his name.

Destroyed, I let him gather me into his arms. My head resting on his broad chest, I listened to the thundering sound of his twin hearts while his consciousness wrapped lovingly around mine.

CHAPTER 17
ROGUE

The journey back to Kryptor proved incredibly grueling. By the time we called it a day, Shuria and I were usually too exhausted to spend any kind of bonding time together. Trying to remove the wretched implants from the Workers felt like attempting to remove the mines from a field with no detection equipment. I wasn't running blind, but I might as well have been. For all his faults, Giles had been diligent in making sure the Kryptid females could not turn on him and free themselves in his absence.

The nanobots in the control chips repaired them faster than the ones I had sent in to unravel them. With the Zombies, it had not been an issue as the localized EMP we unleashed on them fried the entire system. But we couldn't use that on the Workers as it would instantly kill them, and they did not possess the regeneration ability that made it okay to zap the clones. I only made progress by sending small electric discharges locally, strong enough to stun the nanobots into inaction. While it didn't last long, the nanites I introduced immediately after both chewed away at the implant and healed some of the damage and swelling inflicted on the Workers' brains.

In between that, I analyzed the rebel research we had recovered, continued assisting Toksi and Rakma as they pursued their efforts to build up the defenses around their homeworld, and ran tests on Giles's clones. The latter consumed a large part of my time. If he was indeed disseminating several of his clones out there, if we could tap into their system, we could take over controlling them.

On the fifth day of our journey, I eradicated the last repair nanobots inside the Workers. Within two hours after that, I fully unraveled the remnants of their control chips. Needless to say our entire team had loads of questions for them. Although each female provided some answers, Zuno remained their main speaker, no doubt because she was the oldest amongst them.

Unfortunately, yet unsurprisingly, they had little information regarding Giles's actual plans. He only shared with them instructions for specific tasks, rarely anything that hinted at his greater goals.

"We mostly created the foundation that their engineers and scientists would then use as a base to further expand on," Zuno explained. "Occasionally, we had vidcalls with off-worlder scientists to explain some of our research and the logic we followed for our creations. It was akin to providing training and mentoring."

"What kind of questions?" Hulax asked. "I am particularly interested in what they were working on regarding the clones of the rebel leader."

Zuno shook her head with an apologetic expression. "Oh no, Commander. We never discussed Giles's clones with the others. He specifically forbade us from alluding to that project or the siren with anyone outside this base. Most of the more recent questions revolved around the Scelks. It would go from new hatchlings, protecting themselves from getting mind controlled, the best ways to pair the Scelks with a new host, and dealing with the involuntary hosts fighting their bug."

I couldn't help but notice she no longer referred to the rebel leader as Master Dalton. That pleased me tremendously, further confirming he had lost his hold over her without the chip.

"Why did they more recently focus on the Scelks?" Reklig asked. "What were they focusing on before?"

"Prior to that, it was questions about the Jadozors. They were the biggest project that the rebels had been working on. Once your alliance started building up towards the final battle against Khutu, they escalated preparations. They barely allowed us to rest until we stabilized the regeneration ability. Sadly, we never got it fully functional on nonhuman species, which is why all the clones are human."

"Why?" I asked with undisguised curiosity. "Why did it not work with other species?"

"Humans are far more adaptable. They have proven compatible for mating and reproduction with multiple intergalactic species. Their DNA is easier to manipulate. We also had decades of working with humans and studying them as General Khutu's brides."

Zuno stiffened, a sliver of fear flitting over her features as soon as those last words left her mouth. I didn't need to look in the mirror to know what furious expression I displayed. I could have done without this reminder of what experiments my father had performed on our mothers to make them compatible with him and so that they would pass on to us the rebirth abilities of the Xian Warriors.

Indifferent to my anger—also reflected on my brother's face—Hulax further pressed the Worker. It was a good thing, too, as my emotional response would not change the facts of the past and would not provide us with the insights we needed to prevent further bloodshed.

"But what of the clones?" he insisted. "What was their purpose? Why did he create a separate model of himself? And why the secrecy?"

Despite how upset I felt, I almost intervened to tell him not to bombard her with so many questions at once and allow her to respond. Surprisingly, Zuno did not appear distraught by this barrage of questions.

"Initially, they were meant as testing canvases for Giles," Zuno replied. "As one of the Workers in the General's secret bases, I had witnessed some of the negative secondary effects Khutu sustained from all the experiments he had demanded we perform to enhance him and expand his lifespan. Giles wanted to make sure any modification we gave him had been tested and proven to be safe on identical copies of him."

My brows shot up upon hearing those words. It not only made sense but also proved him to be even more thorough and calculated than my insane father had been. Remembering what monstrosity Khutu had become in his last days still sent icy shivers running down my spine.

"So they were nothing more than expendable test subjects? He had no other plans with them?" I asked in a dubious tone.

While I had no reason to doubt that Giles had initially requested their creation as guinea pigs, the organic AI seemed a step too far.

Zuno hesitated. I didn't believe she was attempting to be deceptive but rather trying to form a coherent response to express her interpretation of Giles's intentions.

"He never gave us any insights as to his broader plans for those clones," the Worker said carefully. "He merely requested that we make them self-sufficient in case their mechanical brains were hacked or malfunctioned. However, he did ask that they should behave in a way that they could be mistaken for him."

"Why?" Hulax asked.

"He didn't say," Zuno replied with a shrug. "We believed it was for his own safety. Giles had begun displaying very paranoid behavior. He no longer wanted anyone coming to the base after his huge argument with Cemara and Trogar."

"Cemara and Trogar?" Reaper echoed. "Who are they?"

"I understand that they were his co-leaders. We rarely saw them, and never interacted with them. Cemara, a Lenusian female, was an expert in nuclear fusion. Based on some of the research Giles demanded that we provide her with, we suspect she was building weapons for them. Trogar, a Tegorian male, mostly came to collect the vessels we had modified, freshly hatched Scelks, and any samples to be used in another facility's incubators."

Madeline's fingers were already flying over the keyboard of her laptop, no doubt to bring up any service record still on file about them.

"What was the nature of the argument?" Reaper asked.

"We do not know. The Lenusian female was extremely angry. She stormed out of the conference room shouting that it was going too far, and that she would not be part of it," Zuno said. "The Tegorian seemed just as angry, but mostly distressed. His last words to Giles were that he no longer recognized him, and that he should be careful before he completely lost himself."

"When did that happen?" I asked.

"A little over four months ago."

"What happened next? Did they mend their rift?" I asked.

"We never saw them again. I believe he killed them," Zuno said matter-of-factly.

I recoiled while stunned gasps erupted around the table.

"What makes you say that?" Hulax asked.

"Beyond the fact that they disappeared overnight, Giles demanded that we train the sirens to mimic them," Zuno replied. "The three of them together held regular video conferences broadcast to the rebels. Since they were gone, he needed viable replacements for those events. This convinced us that they were dead. Why else did they not reveal that it wasn't them in those calls?"

"In the video Legion sent us from the base on Ostruria,

Cemara and Trogar sat by Giles's side," Madeline said pensively. "But they never said a word. Giles did all the talking."

"They spoke very little as the sirens' AI hadn't been sufficiently trained yet," Zuno explained.

"Sirens?" Shuria echoed, emphasizing the plural. "Where are the other ones? We only saw the one mimicking Salma."

"They died," Zuno said, once more in a very casual tone. "Many of them died as we tested various grafts to the organic AI. Giles wanted us to figure out a way to make it self-aware, like a person. But that was not possible. Sure, with enough training, we could get it to behave almost like a person, but it was still only advanced algorithms. He had convinced himself that we could achieve something similar with the sirens as with the Scelks. But the Scelks are born sentient. They already have a soul. The host only allows their cerebral activity to expand beyond the limitation of their smaller bug brain. But their personalities are unique. They are not programmed."

"If so many died, how come there was only the one in the aquarium?" I challenged. "Shouldn't there have been more incubating?"

Zuno nodded. "Normally, we always had three or four backups," she conceded. "But after four-twenty-four died, he told us not to grow any new sirens. He would get extremely upset every time one of them died. We were to focus on enhancing his clones and making them more sentient first. In the meantime, we had to keep four-twenty-six happy and train it with memories of Salma based on dream walks he recorded for us. But he did take four-twenty-five—the only other remaining siren—with him when he left."

We exchanged glances, a variety of thoughts as to why he had taken a siren—some less charitable than others—running through our minds.

"He made his peace with the fact that he couldn't recreate his wife and settled for what he could," I mused out loud.

"No. He is obsessed with recreating her," Zuno said with conviction. "Seeing the sirens dying or suffering unintended mutations triggered him. I think it made him relive the death of his wife. He wanted to make sure future experiments on them would have a greater chance of success by experimenting on his clones instead. Which was a flawed assumption. The same way the Jadozor graft didn't react well on non-humans, an organic AI that would perform well on his clones wouldn't react the same way with the sirens, who are made of a variety of splices."

"You didn't warn him of that?" I asked.

Zuno shook her head with an almost malicious expression. "He didn't ask. We followed his instructions."

Reklig snorted, a similar evil glimmer in his eyes. "Malicious obedience... I approve."

"That is all fine and well," Hulax interrupted, his mandibles clacking with annoyance. "But it doesn't give us any insights as to what Giles's plans are. You said he was growing paranoid. Why? If he had eliminated his co-leaders and had the sirens to mimic them, what did he have to worry about?"

"We have our suspicions but cannot say for sure," Zuno replied sheepishly. "We overheard some discussions about unrest before his co-leaders vanished. Many of the rebels had serious issues with Scelks being added to their ranks. When the Vanguard took an official stance against the attack on Kryptor, more people became nervous. Then the fallout with Cemara and Trogar occurred around the same time we started receiving requests about how to handle cases of involuntary hosts fighting their Scelks. We believe they were used to silence increasing vocal dissenters. A few days later, we received tons of serum vials, which Giles demanded we preserve at all costs, and figured out a way to produce more."

"He must have feared for his life," I said pensively. "Despots often have body doubles in case of assassination attempts. If the rebels were discovering how he had screwed them over, they would want blood. But are we to understand that using the Scelks is what turned Cemara and Trogar against Giles?"

"Oh no! They were in favor of using the Scelks. It was something else they strongly disapproved of. But we don't know what," Zuno said.

We continued questioning the Workers for a while longer. Although they gave us some great insight as to what had transpired, Giles had done too great a job of keeping them in the dark about his plans. He had locked the good stuff in his computer hard drives and encrypted files.

Despite Madeline being a formidable IT specialist, she couldn't hack into the files without triggering a self-destruct defense mechanism. Both the drive and files required his authorization code. Although Madeline continued to work on it, we held little hope of success. But without his code, we would remain blind as to his plans.

However, an urgent request from Chaos and Legion shifted our priorities. They needed a way to hijack the AI of the Kryptid vessels currently used by the rebels. Zuno and her team had designed those artificial intelligences and the control chips they had attached to them. Working closely with Bane, they designed a new command that would force the existing membrane to rewire itself to completely reject the control chips. It would consider them as dangerous foreign bodies to be destroyed for its own protection. Through the same type of long-range, organic com systems used by the Spitters, we could direct the vessels to behave according to our commands instead.

Just then, Chaos threw a second curveball at us. They were en route to the rally point with the Scelk Clones from Aurilia, who Nevrik convinced to join our side. They had every reason to believe a handler awaited them at their destination. Initially, the Scelk clones each possessed control chips to keep them under Giles's thumb. Naturally, Chaos's team had freed them of it. They intended to board the rebel vessel, pretending to still be under their control so that they could take it over in a Trojan horse type of attack. But with the chips disabled, they would be quickly found out the first time their handler issued a command to the control chips and that they failed to respond to it.

Therefore, working alongside the Kryptid females, I had a blast devising an organic com system that would behave like a receptor, informing them of any command issued through the control chip so that they could pretend like they were obeying its compulsion.

However, this work also gave us some extra ideas, especially the one to hijack the liveships' AI. A few quick tests confirmed that so long as we could tap into the frequency of the signal controlling the clones' AI, we could hack it and take control of the clones. The thought of using Giles's own puppets against him had a thrill running down my spine.

As we made our final approach to Kryptor, my jaw dropped at the sight of the defenses they had been busy setting up. A swarm of Spitters flew around the planet, their numbers so great they looked like a planetary ring. This many of them could wipe out an entire fleet, including motherships and battlecruisers. But they remained very weak vessels independently. A single electromagnetic pulse could destroy them all. At least, the rebel ships would have to get very close to the swarm for the EMP blast to work. That meant they would need to take on a lot of damage before they could get in position. Spitters were expendable. The rebel fleet, not so much.

As we penetrated the planet's atmosphere, I stared in awe at the spectacle that welcomed us. Hovering spheres littered the sky. Once the battle began, they would link to each other with energy beams, forming a protective shield over the city. Below, lining the top of the bridges interconnecting the Kryptid buildings, countless Bombardier Beetles stood at the ready. Numerous new hills had cropped up around the perimeter. During our training before the war against Khutu, we'd been spanked multiple times by sandworms in the simulations the Scelks had prepared for us. As tall as skyscrapers, their massive mouths filled with needle teeth, the sandworms could swallow most smaller ships, bite a chaser in half, and make a serious dent in a frigate.

In the days that followed our return to Kryptor, Vanguard ships began to arrive to bolster the defenses of the planet. Fury's team was the first to show up after investigating Hehiri. As suspected, the rebels had abandoned the base. They had used it as a clone production factory, but there was nothing left, not even samples or schematics. The only clue they found from the production reports of the machines was that over one hundred thousand clones had been produced. It was a terrifying number. Even with all the defenses we had set up, with this many troops, a significant number of clones would likely land on Kryptor.

Accordingly, Xians, Dragons, Scelks, and Creckels trained with the Kryptids for battle on the ground alongside Nastarex beasts. Shaped like a beach ball with legs, those freaky creatures could burrow underground to travel far and wide and shoot out underneath their unsuspecting target. Aside from their two speared arms, the four horns adorning their backs could extrude into additional telescopic arms with dagger tips. On top of the two spears framing their mouths, an even longer and sharper one could shoot out of their mouth to sting their victims and inject them with a digestive acid that would liquefy their insides in seconds. A series of bumps forming a ring around their heads actually released a hallucinogenic gas that would make the target paranoid and make them see horrible things that did not exist. Naturally, one of my first tasks had been making sure to create an antidote that would be effective for all the different species members of the Vanguard.

Watching my mate training alongside these beasts unnerved me more than I would ever admit out loud. It sucked all the more that I wanted to train with her but had far too many scientific duties to handle.

And then everything happened at once.

We received the call that Chaos, Legion, and Wrath had reached the rebels' rally point. Under the circumstances, we were as prepared as reasonably possible. All we could do was wait with bated breath for the outcome of their raid on the ship carrying the thousand Scelk Clones meant to act as the vanguard of the rebel attack. With their mind control abilities and their regeneration powers, if our three teams failed to get these Scelks under control, things would turn quite ugly. It would take a while to disable their control chips and let them heal before we could flood them with the Zombie virus to remove their regeneration abilities. In that time, they would have enough of us in their thrall, turning us into standing targets that they could effortlessly massacre.

Therefore, Chaos's and Legion's teams had to succeed. Otherwise, we would be forced to eradicate these Scelks without giving them a chance to heal and then be redeemed. I didn't even want to imagine how the current Scelks, within the Vanguard, would react to this. In the meantime, all we could do was get ready for an imminent attack.

To our dismay, barely thirty minutes after they began the raid, Ayana contacted Doom through mind speak to warn him that the rebel fleet had jumped into warp.

They were coming.

From their current position, it would take hours before they reached us at the highest warp. The primary concern was that the entire fleet had not gathered at that one rally point. Others were incoming from different locations. We did not know how close or far away that would be. Barely an hour later, we detected the first rebel ships approaching. They had repurposed stolen Kryptid vessels. Unfortunately, they weren't the ones from Chaos's rally point.

We immediately sent the rewiring signal to hijack the artificial intelligence of those vessels. But as they needed to be within a certain range for this to work, the Spitters forming a defensive ring around the planet stirred into action long before any rewiring could start occurring.

The battle had truly begun.

CHAPTER 18
SHURIA

Heart pounding, I settled in one of the battle stations of our chaser. Martha, Reklig, Reaper, and Rogue occupied the other four. Sitting at the Science Officer station, Madeline ran scans and coms, while Thanh piloted our vessel under Doom's command. Our leader hated not being on the ground with the Creckels. For now, Stran led the other Creckels. But I suspected that once the fight reached the ground, Doom would make us join the fray.

I never feared battle before. Who cared about death when you had little or nothing to live for? My gaze flicked towards Rogue sitting on the opposite side of the deck from me. Waves of love swelled within as I admired his noble profile. Where people saw a baby face, I saw the sweetest, most beautiful male in the universe. And he wanted me, the real me. Today, I had everything to fight for.

Heavy silence filled the room, only disturbed by the discreet hums and beeps from our navigation equipment as our chaser flew over the city.

"Twenty Kryptid frigates are closing in on the planet," Madeline said, her eyes glued to her monitor.

"On screen," Doom ordered.

An insert displaying Madeline's monitor appeared on the giant screen of the vessel, allowing us to see the approaching fleet in space without blocking our view of what was happening right outside our vessel.

"My long-range scans reveal few crew members on board," Madeline continued while her fingers flew over her keyboard. "But I'm detecting tons of Jadozors."

Even as she spoke those words, the closest frigates suddenly opened their hangars. To our shock, each one released a few dozen Spitters.

"Shit!" Madeline exclaimed while typing frantically.

Martha, our weapons expert, was also typing furiously on her keyboard.

"This is going to be a problem," Madeline said, as the rebel Spitters rushed towards the Kryptid ones surrounding the planet. "We did not account for this."

"What didn't we account for?" Doom asked. "We knew they had Spitters."

"Yes but we only planned on rewiring their AI so that we could take control of them," Madeline explained. "We never programmed our own Spitters to recognize the rebel versions as threats to be shot down. They will ignore them."

As if to confirm her words, the Kryptid Spitters scattered, flying right past the rebel ones on their way to attack the frigates. As soon as they were surrounded by a large enough number of our Spitters, the rebel ones set off massive EMP blasts, simultaneously knocking out hundreds of our small ships. Curses resonated throughout the room. As we had the foresight to change the hue of our Spitters so that we could avoid friendly fire, we easily recognized how many had been affected by the blast.

"The Kryptids are sending new orders to their Spitters to take out the rebel versions," Madeline said. "It should only take a couple of minutes."

Despite being a quick response to the situation, the EMP blasts made a significant dent in our defenses. Still, between our own Spitters swarming the rebel frigates, aided by the Vanguard and Kryptid fighters also attacking them, the enemy vessels started sustaining some critical damage.

"What the fuck are they doing?" I muttered as the frigates started spreading wide instead of clustering together to focus fire on our ships.

It didn't take me long to realize they were spreading our forces. A shiver ran down my spine as a sea of Jadozors spilled out of the frigates. They, too, scattered, a fraction directly attacking our vessels fighting in space, the others making a beeline for the planet.

To our dismay, as our troops gave chase to the apparently fleeing frigates, five battlecruisers dropped out of warp and rushed the opening thus created by the frigates' diversion. As they barreled forward towards the planet, they also released Spitters of their own to clear the path of our allies charging them.

We readied for battle, our weapons hot as the Bombardier Beetles started shooting from the surface. The blueish-white missiles streaked the skies as they raced towards the frigates and battlecruisers entering Kryptor's atmosphere. All of them released more Jadozors, the giant pterodactyl-looking beasts flapping their double sets of wings with frightening eagerness.

Thanh flew our chaser closer to one of the Jadozor entry points. Along with our Kryptid allies, we released the Stingers that the Workers had been busy growing over the past few weeks. No bigger than a golf ball, with small translucent wings, a Stinger carried the Zombie virus that would eradicate the regeneration abilities of the creatures. As soon as it came in contact with a target, its dart would shoot out at the speed and strength of a bullet, able to even punch through metal, before delivering its payload.

As the scales of the Jadozors were nearly impenetrable, the Stingers had been programmed to target one of the three vulnerable spots of the Jadozors: the narrow strip of tender flesh alongside their spines, their eyes, or inside their mouths. Most of the Stingers aimed for the spines, two or three of them finding their marks in the same creature.

We chased after the Jadozors getting closer to the protective net, unloading photon torpedoes at them. The proximity sensor suddenly went off, warning Thanh that she was flying too close to it. She moved our ship back down to a safer distance. The Bombardier Beetle missiles exploded in the air in the Jadozors' flight path, permeating the area with the virus. Moments later, the floating spheres littering the sky started glowing. They shot out light beams, which connected them in a shimmering net.

Blinding lights from the ground twisted my insides. They were missiles shot by the Electric Beetles, a breed variant of the Bombardiers. Unlike the latter, the Electric Beetles didn't fire plasma, but a high voltage missile that electrified the protective net over the city. I remembered them far too well from the final battle against Khutu. Back then, they hadn't electrified a net, but had instead created electric walls between two missiles, causing countless Coalition vessels to be instantly fried or destroyed.

With morbid fascination, I watched the Jadozors getting within proximity to the net get instantly zapped with such a lethal charge that some of them literally exploded. Others had a limb or wing torn off, white foam instantly forming only to fizzle out in seconds due to the amount of virus floating in the air. My heart soared as countless creatures went up in ashes, their broken forms falling back to the net only to disintegrate.

However, this moment of elation was short-lived.

Three of the frigates clear the planet's atmosphere, firing on all cylinders at the net. A quick scan revealed there were only a handful of clones onboard, with hundreds of Jadozors. Using a typical Kryptid tactic, the rebel vessels headed straight for the net, crashing into it one after the other, suicide style. The electrical surge fried all the vessel's systems. This staggered onslaught destroyed the floating nodes in that area, creating the perfect breach for the battlecruiser trailing the frigates to squeeze through.

The disabled frigates plummeted to the ground while the remaining Jadozors they still carried flew out to rampage through the city. Countless turrets in the highest buildings unleashed a barrage of fire on the incoming menace. Simultaneously, a volley of Stingers took flight, darkening the skies like a swarm of locusts closing in on the Jadozors. But our focus was on the battlecruiser.

Along with other Kryptid chasers, we fired everything we had at the larger vessel. Having infiltrated our defenses, the battlecruiser regurgitated multiple smaller ships, from shuttles, to fighters, to chasers, each one darting in opposite directions. Sandworms shooting out of the mounds they hid under swallowed several of those vessels whole. A few of the rebel ships crashed into them or were sent careening to the ground when smashed by a vicious swipe of the creature's cylindrical upper body.

Although the situation might have seemed dire, this wasn't even a fair fight for the rebels. Countless shuttles landed on the ground, vomiting a sea of Zombie Soldiers. But even before their vessels touched down, glimmering Zapper discs flew towards their destination. The discs exploded as the clones disembarked, frying their control chips. In a scene straight out of a nightmare, I watched the clones trampling over their fallen in an effort to invade the city, only to be zapped or shot, creating a trail of bodies.

Despite the white foam indicating the Zombies regeneration kicking in, the clones still didn't stand a chance. In an explosion of dirt and dust, an army of Nastarexes shot out of the ground, stabbing the helpless zombies, spraying them with their hallucinogenic gases to make them unable to coherently battle, and injecting them with their liquefying acids. More Stingers joined the fray to neutralize their regeneration abilities. And all around, the Creckels chased down the few clones who had survived all other defenses, turning them into sieves by firing the dagger-like darts under their scales at them.

It was a massacre. At least, it was soulless clones dying. We could only hope that the sentient rebels would see this and rethink pursuing this attack.

Overhead, new spheres had replaced the damaged ones, closing the holes in the net. Unless they had a new weapon we had not accounted for, they would never achieve their goal. Without the Vanguard's early warning, and had the rebels retained control over their Scelks, we likely would have lost.

As if in response to the thoughts crossing my mind, Doom stopped talking mid-sentence while giving us battle commands. His face went slack as psychic energy swirled around him. A savage grin stretched his lips moments later. He scribbled something down before addressing us.

"Ayana just contacted me," Doom said. "They won the battle and secured the Scelk Clones."

We responded with a collective victorious roar. The emotion on Reklig's face messed me up. His species rarely showed soft emotions or vulnerability. But with their extremely low population numbers, knowing that we'd managed to spare a thousand more of their own was a blessing.

"They're obviously not ready to fight by our side, so Chaos and Wrath are taking them back to Khepri. Legion and the rest of his team are coming to join us. They spoke directly with Giles, who attempted to blow up their ship. He failed miserably thanks to us having taken over control of the vessel's artificial intelligence."

More cheers greeted his words while I cast a proud glance at my mate for his part in helping achieve this outcome.

"Linette is sending us a recording of that conversation, that we are to broadcast on all frequencies to the rebels," Doom continued. "It will take a moment for the recording to reach us. Giles used an authorization code in that recording to set off the self-destruct on their vessel. Madeline and Rogue, I want you to use it to see if it will allow you to unlock his files."

"Fuck, yes!" Rogue said, shooting to his feet from his battle station.

Tapping a few instructions on his armband, Doom transferred the code he had transcribed to Madeline and my mate. They both left the room as we continued raining death on the invaders.

CHAPTER 19
ROGUE

In my eagerness to settle behind my workstation, I nearly fell off my chair by sitting too close to the edge. My fingers flew over my keyboard, pulling up the encrypted files whose content continued to elude us. Holding my breath, I plugged in the authorization code that Doom had communicated to us, bracing for yet another disappointment. When the words "authorization granted" flashed on the screen, the shout of victory that escaped me rivaled the roar of the most feral beasts in the galaxy.

"Oh, my God! It worked!" Madeline exclaimed. "It freaking worked!"

Although she laughed at my over-the-top reaction, Madeline buzzed with the same excitement coursing through me. Working side by side in the engineering room, we started going through every single file that had previously been locked to us, only pausing for half a second to inform Doom of our success through mind speak.

While Madeline was working on quickly organizing the files by category to make reading through them more efficient by order of priority, I dove headfirst into all the scientific and medical communications he'd exchanged with the rebel bases.

Less than twenty minutes later, we called the others for assistance. With the war already ongoing, time was of the essence. If these files contained anything we could leverage to help the odds lean in our favor, then we had to identify it as urgently as possible.

As much as Doom hated being away from the action, he didn't hesitate to pull us out of the battle. Shortly after the entire team started skimming through the files, Madeline squealed with delight, drawing our attention.

"I just found the master list with the hailing frequencies to all the rebel vessels," she said excitedly. "It will make it easier for us to target their com systems and try to hijack their AI. But more importantly, it will allow us to track them easily. All we have to do is to send a subtonal signal to their vessels, which their com will dismiss as noise, but which will give us their position in real time."

"I can work on that," Reaper offered.

"Do it," Doom said with a predatory glimmer in his eyes. "This will be perfect to make sure we can reach every rebel when we broadcast the video Chaos's team captured of Giles."

As if in response to that comment, our own com system beeped before the artificial intelligence informed us of an incoming message—the video recording. As much as I wanted to continue plundering the secrets hidden in Giles's files, I watched the video with the rest of the team.

"This is great," Doom said, although a frown creased his brow as he intensely pondered on something. "But we should edit it, only keep the most relevant and impactful parts, and add a message of our own within."

It made sense. While the recording in itself was very incriminating—Chaos having been masterful in taunting Giles into confirming some of the worst crimes he had perpetrated against his own followers—it wouldn't be as powerful without adding a bit of context. With the rebel fleet that had jumped from the rally point still on their way here, we had every incentive to try to sway them before they joined the battle. Most of the troops on those ships were real people, former allies we'd fought alongside, not clones. We still hoped to keep casualties amongst them to a minimum, and ideally to none.

After a brief discussion we agreed on what the content should be.

"Shuria," Doom said turning to my mate, "put together a montage of the footage we gathered with our body cams, and the surveillance system on Wyngenia. Showing what Giles has been up to in his secret lab should make many rebels reconsider their allegiance."

"On it," Shuria replied.

"Martha, you can edit the recording Linette sent us while I write the script," Doom continued.

"You got it," Martha said, her voice filled with excitement.

As much as I would have wanted to partake in that little project, I was too busy following a disturbing thread in Giles's communications. The answer felt within reach but kept eluding me. By the increasingly aggressive tone of the message exchanges, especially with the Lenusian female Cemara, Giles had been keeping secrets from his co-leaders. Cemara had gotten wind of it, but Giles kept giving her the runaround every time she tried to pry. Unfortunately, nothing in the messages I'd read so far gave even the slightest hint as to what it could be about.

I couldn't say how much time had lapsed since they started working on that montage. It felt like seconds. Then Doom stood in front of the camera with which Martha would record him.

"If you're ready, I will patch the signal through to the rebels," Reaper said to our team leader.

"Go ahead," Doom confirmed.

The green light on the camera turned red, indicating the recording had begun.

"This message is for every member of the rebel coalition. My name is Doom. Most of you know me well as we have fought together to protect our allies for decades against a common enemy. It saddens me that we should stand on opposite sides today. Therefore, this is an ultimate plea to end this madness before more useless bloodshed occurs and honor the peace that we have earned at the cost of far too many lives over a far too long period of time. Many are saying that the Vanguard has turned on the Coalition, but that is impossible. You created us to have a single purpose: protect our allies. And that is what we are trying to do right now."

The strangest pride filled my hearts as I listened to Doom speaking. He always hated anything related to diplomacy. He enjoyed being in the field, cracking skulls and taking names. And yet, time and time again, he had proven himself a great ambassador for our cause.

"You have been misled, conned into following the same type of monster that we have spent the past hundred years trying to eliminate," Doom said in a passionate tone. "Giles Dalton is as bad if not worse than Khutu. He doesn't care about you or your losses. He merely uses you for his own goals with total and complete disregard for your welfare and the consequences of his actions. To him, you are pawns, expendable bodies to be used in the way he deems most efficient for his purpose. But do not take my word for it. I will let you hear it from his own mouth. And while you're at it, take a good look at his eyes. He's not human anymore. He is experimenting on himself like Khutu did."

With that, Doom nodded discreetly at Shuria. My mate immediately played the first segment of the recording Lynette had sent us, and which Martha had edited.

"Dear Chaos," Giles said with an obnoxiously sweet voice, "once again, you and your Vanguard come meddling where you have no business. I had warned you to stay out of my affairs while we finished a job you were all too lazy or too weak to complete. But no. There you are again. Too bad for you, you're too late. A fleet of staunch defenders of the Coalition are razing Kryptor to the ground and exterminating the bugs you didn't have the balls to wipe out. You have proven the Vanguard no longer has a purpose. I guess it is time I also put you out on retirement."

"We are doing exactly what we were created to do," Chaos replied in a stern voice. "You, on the other hand, have become exactly the same monster we've been fighting for nearly a century. How many of your gullible followers know that you have been secretly implanting them with control chips? How many know that you've been lying about the side effects of regeneration? Are they aware that every time they use it ages them before their time? How many know that you've sacrificed as Scelk hosts anyone who had the nerve to challenge your demented plans?"

"I am *nothing* like Khutu!" Giles hissed. "I am saving the galaxy from future genocides. Soldiers know that sacrifices must be made in a war. They volunteered for this holy crusade. And as their leader, it is my duty to take whatever means necessary to ensure our victory."

"By using the same means you decried when General Khutu used them?" Chaos challenged. "By turning yourself and others into abominations? And worse still, by doing so against their will and unbeknownst to them?"

"I will not justify my choices or actions to the likes of you," Giles said haughtily. "You lost my respect the minute you started welcoming vermin amongst your ranks, and once your members started lying with bugs and monsters."

In the recording, Giles had not bothered hiding his now naturally oversized irises, which Zuno claimed he did when interacting with other rebels. It was the only visible sign of his mutation.

"Bugs and monsters?" Doom echoed when the recording segment ended. "You lift your noses at the Dragons and the

Scelks because of the way they were created. But the Coalition created *us* the same way. Are we to be deemed monsters as well? We do not control how we are born. We only choose who we want to be, and how we will behave. They *chose* to join our side and fight for peace and freedom for every member of the Coalition. And still you shun them? Without the Scelks and the Dragons, half of my brothers who fought with us on Zekuro would have met a permanent death. They are heroes!"

My throat tightened upon hearing those words. The Xians and the women of the Vanguard had never made a secret of their gratitude. But hearing it verbalized to the entire rebel force touched me deeply. By the look on Reklig's face, he shared the sentiment. Doom wasn't kidding by claiming we'd spared countless Xians from a permanent death. After our defection, we'd gone to Zekuro with the Vanguard to free the surviving Mimics. The Xians—led by Wrath and Rage—had been trapped like fish in a barrel with psychic disruptors preventing our Soulcatchers from retrieving the souls of the Warriors. Between the Swarm Drones and the Kryptid Soldiers firing at them, the Xians would have perished in mass numbers. My brothers and I went in, flying them out of the trap so that the Soulcatchers could rescue the souls of the dying once we cleared the disruptor range.

"The real monster is your leader," Doom continued. "The immortality he promised many of you is a lie. Everything comes at a cost. What cost, you ask? Every time you die, every wound you receive kicks in your regeneration power. And every time it activates, it consumes your life force, aging you before your time. It is subtle at first, but the more you use it, the more severe the injury, the faster you're burning yourself out. In order to avoid those terrible side effects, you need a serum."

While Doom spoke, Reaper displayed an overlay of his monitor on the room's giant screen, showing some of his chatter being intercepted in the rebels' various chat systems. The shock and outrage from the comments confirmed many of the rebels had been unaware of this.

"Those of you who volunteered probably noticed that you're no longer getting your shots," Doom said matter-of-factly. "The reason for this is simple. That serum was derived from the blood of my brother, Xenon. Giles had him trapped in one of his secret bases, milking him daily to replenish his stash. We have freed my brother. Your dear leader has therefore decided to hoard the remaining stash for himself."

As he spoke that last sentence, Shuria broadcast the footage we had taken of the room filled wall to wall with serum vials. The chatter went into overdrive, between those demanding those reserves be seized and shared, those expressing doubt as to whether we were lying, and those seeming totally confused.

"But the worst part is that a lot of you, many of whom you may not even be aware of, have been coerced into receiving the regeneration graft. It was done to them against their will because they had dissented or challenged some of the more extreme plans Giles had put in motion," Doom said, anger and contempt seeping into his voice. "Again, do not take my word for it. Hear it directly from the mouth of one of your former teammates."

This time, Shuria played a recording of one of the rebels rescued on Aurilia.

The redhead male looked to be in his late fifties. He was broad-shouldered and in top physical shape, like a fitness model or a member of an elite military corp. Along each side of his neck, three round scars indicated where the claws of the Scelk bug that Giles had intended to take control of him had previously attached to his nervous system.

"Hello, friends. My name is Joseph Brenner. Many of you know me or at least have seen me over the past couple of years. I'm hardly recognizable today, am I?" he said in a dejected tone. "I turned twenty-six just a little over three weeks ago. But as you can see, I now have the body of a man nearly sixty years old.

This is a result of me being one of the first volunteers of the phoenix program. That regeneration ability was flawed. Dalton knew it but never told us because he needed us to comply."

A part of me felt sorry for the male. Granted, he had volunteered to gain extra powers in the pursuit of a questionable goal. That did not justify Giles hiding from him and the others such vital information that would have undoubtedly kept many of them from subjecting themselves to something like this.

"The serum that he was giving us was never about preventing a rejection of the graft. All it does is slow down the horrible effects of the regeneration on our bodies. As long as you don't get wounded, and especially if you don't die, you will be mostly fine," Joseph continued. "But Giles's treachery didn't stop there. I've been quite vocal about what I think of the Kryptids and of their creations who have joined the Vanguard. When I found out that our dear leader had created more Scelks, I loudly expressed my displeasure. Too loudly, it seems. To shut me up, Dalton decided that I should get better acquainted with the bugs."

He pulled sideways on the collar of his shirt to expose more of his neck and shoulder line. With his other hand, he pointed at the round scars by his neck.

"One night, I went to bed. The next day, I woke up with Scelk claws stabbing my spine and neck. Dalton had volunteered me as a fucking host for the bugs. He condemned dozens of us to the same fate. To add insult to injury, Dalton had the scientists give us control chips so that once the Scelks killed our souls, he would be able to make them obey him. The worst part of it all is that the only reason I'm still alive today is that Nevrik, one of the Vanguard Scelks—one of the monsters I feared—convinced the hatchling bugs who were taking me and the others over to set us free. He explained to them that it was wrong to kill a person just to appropriate their bodies."

His voice choked as he spoke those words, a moving mix of shame, gratitude, and betrayal battling for dominance on his features. This was a powerful testimony which resonated with the rebels, as clearly displayed in the chatter. I had never heard of Joseph Brenner. But based on the comments and reactions from the rebels, he had been a highly respected member of their movement.

"The Dragons and the Scelks are not the monsters, Dalton is. I know some of you are currently thinking the bugs must have brainwashed me or are making me say this through compulsion. Don't take my word for it. Use your own eyes and your own intelligence to look at the facts," Joseph continued, his voice stern. "Look around you and ask yourself where are your former friends who expressed any challenge against Giles? How many of them were suddenly assigned to a different post never to be heard from again? How many of you were *accidentally* given a regeneration graft shortly after you demanded answers or argued with some of the plans? With the serum, Dalton holds you by the balls. At first, he blackmailed us into compliance just to get our dose. Now, he can no longer even spare that carrot. *He* is the enemy."

The broadcast of Joseph's recording ended, Doom taking over again.

"Giles is not who you think. Whatever argument he sold you on in order to launch this unwarranted attack against the Kryptids, they were lies," Doom said. "He is just another Khutu, looking for ways to enhance himself so that he can rule over the galaxy. We found his secret lab, and this is what he's been working on."

This time, Shuria showed the incubator room where Giles's countless clones had been maturing. In the video, the clones were still intact.

"Why would anyone need to make so many clones of themselves? Unless you are a Dragon or a Xian with the ability to soul transfer, there's no reason. Unless it is so that he would have safe guinea pigs to experiment on before performing the enhancements on himself once they've been validated. And you helped him secure the Kryptid research he needed to achieve his goals. When his co-leaders realized what madness was taking over him, they challenged him. So he got rid of them and had his own genetically created form of Mimic species fool you into thinking that Cemara and Trogar were still standing by his side."

Shuria displayed footage of the siren swimming around the aquarium. Those who knew Salma immediately commented about it, many of them finally acknowledging that he had gone insane.

"Stand down," Doom commanded. "Enough people have died. We fought and bled side by side for years towards a common goal. Are we seriously going to start killing each other now? And all this to serve the demented goals of a single man? Let there be peace, not more hatred, lies, and subservience to the bigoted ambitions of a madman. There is still time. Your Jadozors are getting obliterated, and your Zombie Warriors are getting wiped out."

Without giving any glimpses of our defenses, Shuria showed some still images of the carcasses of the rebel vessels that had crashed near the city, as well as the piles of corpses and ashes of the Jadozors and Zombie Soldiers.

"If you come here, you will join them in a senseless death," Doom warned. "The Kryptid defenses are formidable. They have honored the truce, and *we* will honor our pledge to protect all our allies. You have survived the war, do not come die here for a narcissistic psychopath. Stand down and turn back. Persist and there will be no mercy."

Martha ended the transmission.

"Well done. For someone who hates diplomatic bullshit, you're quite efficient," I said to Doom in a teasing tone.

"Of course, I am. I don't have to like something to excel at it, like I do at everything else," he replied in the same tone.

We all laughed, slightly reducing the tension in the room.

Doom indeed excelled at pretty much everything, although he was best known for being unkillable. While he would shamelessly boast about his combat skills, teasing his brothers for being overly squishy in comparison, he was otherwise rather humble and the sweetest soul.

In the minutes that followed, part of the team monitored the chatter and tracked the rebel vessels. Using the broadcast signal, Madeline had successfully located each of the vessels. She also sent the rewiring program to take over control of the few remaining Kryptid vessels commandeered by the rebels. However, the message had been effective. Quite a few Coalition vessels dropped out of warp, some becoming stationary while others greatly reduced the speed at which they were coming here. We could only hope that intense discussions were taking place among the troops that would result in the majority standing down. My only concern was that infighting could turn into further bloodshed among themselves.

Focusing on unraveling the thread I had found in Giles's communications, I distractedly listened to the conversations between Doom and the rest of the team.

"Have you found any trace of Giles?" Doom asked. "I had expected him to block our signal to his minions. The way he's grown paranoid and has been controlling everything, I cannot imagine he wouldn't be spying on what is happening on his vessels."

Madeline shook her head with a dejected expression. "Unfortunately, there's still no sign of him. I had expected the same. This complete silence is quite strange. That said, I found the algorithm he used to hide the origin of his coms through various relays. We cannot use it on prior communications as he jumped through too many relays. We can only go so far back. But the next time he communicates with us, we will be able to send a snitch signal in return to narrow down his position. We just need to keep the communication open for at least four minutes."

"Excellent work, Madeline," Doom said warmly, which had Reklig puffing out his chest with pride at his mate. "Let's just hope that vermin contacts us sooner than later."

But I realized that we had a much bigger problem looming over our heads.

"Martha, I need you to come have a look at this," I said, my voice filled with tension.

Every head turned my way while Reaper's Soulcatcher made a beeline for my workstation. I increased the size of my holographic monitor to give her a better view of the schematics I had found in one of the messages between Giles and Cemara.

"You're the weapons expert. But am I reading right that these are the schematics of a planet killer?" I asked.

A collective gasp rose around the room. Martha pulled a chair, all but shoving me out of the way as she took over my keyboard. The horrified look on her face confirmed my worst suspicions.

"Yes, this looks like it was based on some nuclear fusion research that had been banned many years ago. It had initially been meant to help the mining industry deep drilling into extremely hard cores. But some studies revealed the technology actually acted as self-burrowing nuclear missiles. Even simply using it for commercial purposes would literally destroy the planet."

"Oh God, that actually explains it," Shuria said with dread. "I did some research on Cemara. She was a highly regarded nuclear physicist. Of course, Giles would have wanted her expertise to complete the work on this technology. Could they have fallen out over that? Although she was clearly in favor of killing the Kryptids, was blowing up their planet a step too far for her?"

I shook my head. "From what I'm reading, she seemed on board with developing this specific part of the project. But I believe he had other targets in mind as well. And that seemed to have become the point of contention. The communications are too brief and too vague to give proper insight into what was brewing behind the scenes. But why do that at all? Why waste all the troops they're sending in if they had the technology to simply blow up the planet?"

"Fair questions," Doom said. "But even if they disagreed on the other targets, I agree that not using it on Kryptor makes no sense. Their goal is to eradicate the entire species. Nuking their planet would achieve that without risk of failure. We must be missing something. And especially why he had to go so far as to eliminate both of his co-leaders. But the biggest question right now is figuring out where he intends to launch these missiles from, assuming he's going to do it at all."

"Actually, these schematics could help us pinpoint the launch coordinates," Martha said, excitement permeating her voice. "I believe these three marks are the intended points of impact. If I read this right, each one would be staggered. This means the missiles would be sent back-to-back from the same cannon, instead of simultaneously from three different launchers."

"Yes!" Madeline exclaimed with the same enthusiasm. "We should be able to triangulate the point of origin from the data on these schematics."

"Good," Doom said, his eyes sparkling. "Find me that ship. We need to take out the trash."

Martha hesitated before shaking your head. "There is no guarantee that he would launch those missiles from his ship," she explained cautiously. "Beyond the fact that those weapons were deemed too dangerous for the stability of the planet, they were banned because they can travel through space and be launched from a different planet. Conflicting worlds could destroy each other without sending out a single vessel."

"Are you fucking kidding me?" Doom exclaimed, his shocked disbelief reflecting the one felt by everyone else in the room. "How far away can they shoot this thing from?"

"I do not know the exact distance," Martha replied sheepishly. "I just remember reading about this technology because it had everyone in the weapons development community in an uproar. While the general consensus was in favor of banning the technology, a few people were intrigued by the potential and wanted to pursue it. But the main discussions were about countermeasures. As further development of the technology had been forbidden, I don't know that anyone ever pursued countermeasures. That said, perfectly timed anti missiles could help protect the planet. But we cannot blow them up. We need to neutralize them on approach. Even in space, if they explode too close to the planet, the radioactive fallout will wreck its atmosphere."

"You two find out everything you can about those damn missiles and the best way to counter them," Doom said to Martha and me. "Madeline, Reaper, find me those coordinates. We need to warn the Kryptids."

CHAPTER 20
SHURIA

I had barely finished communicating our discovery to the Kryptids when Reaper let out a string of curse words. Stunned, we glanced at him only to notice the dismay on Madeline's face.

"It's Umbra," Reaper whispered in angry disbelief. "The bastard is launching the attack from Umbra."

"Are you fucking kidding me?" Rogue hissed in response to his brother's statement.

I felt the blood drain from my face while the others stared at the two siblings with confusion.

"Umbra is a dead planet not too far from here," I explained, flabbergasted by the shameless gall of the rebel leader. "It is where the Dragons lived in secret before the Queen knew of their existence."

"Rumors had begun spreading," Rogue explained with a disgusted expression. "To avoid us getting discovered and to better keep us under his thumb, Khutu had demanded we move to Zekuro with our mothers and young siblings. It gave us the opportunity to defect with everyone we loved."

"This is actually a good thing," Doom said pensively. "If it was your homeworld, you will know the place. It beats going there blind. We must go at once."

Everything started moving at the same time. Thanks to Ayana's unlimited psychic range, Doom was able to communicate with her instantly about what was happening. Legion agreed to meet us directly on Umbra instead of coming here as the rest of the Vanguard and the Kryptid forces had the situation under control.

Daeko immediately assigned tons of Workers to set up countermeasures and anti-missiles to protect the planet. With Martha's help, they labored diligently on setting up a magnetic system that would slow down and eventually stop the missiles until they could be recuperated and disabled. An additional disruptor system would be included to cut all communications to the missile to prevent remote detonation, should Giles realize yet another one of his plans was getting thwarted.

Forced to make a slight detour to avoid the battle still raging in the sky and on land, we quickly left Kryptor's atmosphere. Guilt gnawed at us as we left, especially seeing a few more rebel vessels drop out of warp to join the battle. Among them, we identified two Kryptid vessels that the rebels had stolen. They had been part of the fleet at the rally point where Chaos had raided the ship transporting the Scelk Drones. For a brief moment, we enjoyed the show of our rewiring program on those vessels' AI.

Under the command of our Kryptid allies, they redirected the two ships to attack a rebel battlecruiser, their crews unable to stop that friendly fire as they no longer controlled their vessels. We jumped into warp on our way to Umbra when the lights of the rebel battlecruiser started flickering. The unexpected close-range fire from two formerly allied frigates had inflicted serious damage and wrecked its power and propulsion systems.

A part of me wanted to feel sorry for the rebels thus getting killed. But they had joined that rebellion of their own free will. I wanted to believe none of them were under the duress of a control chip. Our scans didn't indicate the presence of Zombies onboard their vessels. These had to be the hardcore fanatics that nothing would sway. After all, their other allies had slowed the speed at which they were coming here or stopped altogether while reassessing their stance following our broadcast.

But I dismissed them from my thoughts to refocus on the important mission that awaited us elsewhere. With still an hour flight to our destination, we continued to plunder the rebel leader's messages and files while also preparing for battle.

"Fuck me!" Rogue exclaimed. "I've found the answer we were looking for." He projected his monitor's display onto the giant screen in Engineering. "This is an infiltration plan to access the Well of Knowledge."

"Maker!" I exclaimed, shock and horror coursing through me. "Of course! How did we not think of it first? They recorded absolutely everything that has ever been researched, built, accomplished by their people in the Well of Knowledge. Every blueprint, every methodology, every weakness is there for the taking. In the wrong hands…"

I didn't need to finish my sentence.

"This means he will not launch the missiles just yet," Rogue reflected out loud. "This is too great a wealth for him to destroy before having done everything in his power to secure it first. I would take a wild guess that he was hoping to infiltrate once the rest of his fleet had reached Kryptor and the battle was at its apogee. Everyone would be too busy fighting to notice him sneaking in."

My blood turned to ice. "No… not him. He will send in the siren he took with him when he left Wyngenia. Bioscanners cannot detect Modified Mimics as intruders. We literally fool any device into thinking we truly are the species or person we pretend to be. If he sends her in as a Worker, no one will question her presence."

"Excellent work," Doom said. "Keep digging for anything else. I will warn Daeko."

The Kryptid General didn't dally. On top of sending reinforcements to guard the Well of Knowledge, he forbade all access to that room until the rebel attack was over—no exceptions. Anyone attempting to enter would be detained for interrogation and be treated with extreme prejudice should they try to resist.

We found nothing else of consequence aside from getting a better understanding of what had been transpiring over the month of Giles's descent into madness. From the various communications we found, he had indeed been growing increasingly paranoid, fearing to be deposed. The growing number of people challenging his plans and decisions exacerbated that sentiment.

One thing had become clear, while the rebels wanted revenge for the loss of their loved ones and the destruction of their home-worlds, they were not okay with the experiments their leader had been running. They had no problem appropriating the technology ill-begotten by the Kryptids and turning it against them. But enhancing it, pushing it further went a step too far. In his efforts to silence dissenting voices, Giles had fueled the movement against him, becoming the catalyst of his own demise.

That fear had prompted him to move up the timetable of his invasion. It had been such a long time in the making, had he maintained the calculated and deliberate pace he had followed for the past six years, he could have blindsided us even more and likely gotten the upper hand.

As Umbra's silhouette loomed in the distance, we started preparing for the raid, and discussed our plans once we landed.

"We should split our forces in there instead of merging with Legion's team," Rogue said. "There are two secret passages that we could use to infiltrate the base without Giles ever suspecting our presence."

"Secret passages?" Doom echoed.

Reaper nodded. "Yes, that's a good idea. As you know, we were a dirty secret that had to be kept from the Kryptid Queen. We couldn't live on Kryptor for fear our existence might be discovered. Should our location have ever been found out, we had planned secret exits so that we could flee with our infant siblings undetected. The chances of Giles having discovered them are slim to none. We built them specifically so that they would not show up on any scanner. The doors leading to those passages are nearly impossible to detect, and even more impossible to open if you do not know exactly how to proceed."

"That sounds like a plan," Doom said with enthusiasm.

"Legion's team should take the left tunnel," Rogue continued. "It's a bit longer, but they don't have a Scelk as they left Tremak with Chaos to help look after the young Scelk Clones they rescued from the rebel ship. The right passage will take us in faster, and Reklig can help us get things under control while the others catch up."

"How many exits are there?" Doom asked.

"Aside from the secret ones, only the ship hangar. Technically, there also are the ventilation shafts, but you need wings to exit through them or know how to activate the hover platforms, which I once again highly doubt Giles will know how to do," Rogue said.

"Then we need to lock the ship hangar's exits so that we can trap him inside," Doom said pensively.

"Agreed. We can remotely disable the controls to the hangar as well as shut down the base's power grid from a central location," Rogue replied. "Kate and Madeline could handle it while we secure the rest of the place."

"Kate and Madeline?" Reklig asked, casting a worried look towards his mate.

"It will be safe for them," Rogue replied reassuringly while leaning back in his chair. "We designed the entire base around the fact that we have wings. It was an added layer of protection for us as the Kryptid Soldiers can't fly. It provided us with many places our young siblings could shelter in or escape through without the Soldiers being able to follow." He turned back to Reklig. "You lived there with us. You couldn't access the machine rooms because you didn't have wings back then. But both you and Xenon have blessed your mates with wings. Those sections are extremely hard to access otherwise."

Reklig nodded, mollified.

"But how will we know what to do and where to go?" Madeline asked.

"I can run a dream walk with all of you to show you what the base looks like," Reklig offered.

"Good idea," Reaper said. "We should ask Dread to do the same for his team."

After communicating this plan to Legion, we all comfortably settled in our chairs before Reklig pulled us into the dream walk. It would never cease to amaze me how realistic the experience was when Scelks created a virtual world and drew our consciousness into it. It was even more intense than in the fanciest holodeck. Everything from tastes, smells, sensations rivaled what one would experience in the real world.

In this instance, Reklig walked us through the entire base, while Reaper showed us how to operate the manual overrides once the power would be out.

We began our descent into Umbra's atmosphere almost at the same time as Legion's vessel. As we closed in on the base's location, Thanh ran a scan to assess what kind of threat awaited us. We had not expected the numbers it revealed.

"Holy shit!" Thanh exclaimed. "I'm picking up one hundred Zombies, eight Scelks, three Mimics, and one Lenusian female."

"What the fuck?!" I exclaimed. "Didn't Zuno say that Giles only took one siren with him?"

"They must have created more sirens elsewhere, on a

different base," Rogue suggested.

"I guess that's possible," I replied with a frown. The thought of dealing with more sirens, even knowing they weren't actual people, made me feel sick to my stomach. "But I suspect the Lenusian female is Cemara. Zuno never saw Giles execute either of his co-leaders. Could she be cooperating after all?"

"It wouldn't surprise me if she was indeed working with him on his nuclear project," Reklig said pensively. "But it may not be voluntarily, especially with those eight Scelks with him."

"Are they going to be a problem?" Doom asked.

"I highly doubt it. From the information Zuno shared with us—and she was completely honest based on the knowledge she actually possessed—these Scelks will also be young like the ones Chaos found. As a mature Scelk, I will have no problem controlling them all."

"Good," Doom replied. "It makes even more sense now for us to be the first ones infiltrating so that we can handle them instead of Legion's team. Once we get in there, kill all the Zombies and sirens. Spare the Scelks and, if possible, Cemara as well."

With our plan of action set and everyone ready, we headed towards the shuttles with which we would land inside the smaller escape docks at the end of the secret passages. As we entered the ship hangar, Rogue grabbed my hand and pulled me aside, startling me. We stopped at a corner near the maintenance equipment, a panel protruding from the wall providing us a bit of privacy from prying eyes.

I gave him a questioning look, but my heart skipped a beat upon seeing his expression.

"I'm sorry we haven't had much time to spend together over the past few days," Rogue said, sounding a little nervous. "My timing is probably not ideal, but I can't keep it to myself anymore."

I swallowed hard, my stomach fluttering with hope, anticipation, and an eerie sense of surrealism.

"When I came to Kryptor, I merely expected to help put an end to the reign of terror of yet another would-be dictator. Instead, I found you. No words can express how beautiful and perfect you are to me. Just being in the same room, breathing the same air you do makes me happier than I ever could have dreamt possible."

Tears pricked my eyes while emotions swelled within me. Rogue carefully took both my hands in his, his thumbs gently caressing my knuckles. He cleared his throat, appearing just as emotional but also quite vulnerable—a strange look for such a strong and massive male. It gave his baby face an even sweeter and more innocent edge.

"What I'm trying to say is that I don't need my Dragon to tell me you are the one. I'm falling desperately in love with you. And when this mess is over, I want us to bond. I want us to truly be one, to see my scales adorn your shoulders, and touch minds with our son growing inside you. I want to spend the rest of my days with you if you would have me."

By the time he stopped talking, happy tears were freely rolling down my cheeks. The silly male, how could he be this nervous about how I would respond? Didn't he see how crazy I was about him, too?

I closed the small distance between us, my eyes locked with his. "The Maker only knows what I did to deserve you. You are so far beyond anything I ever thought I deserved or could have hoped for. Do you have any idea how wonderful it is to see myself through your eyes? Back when I barely knew you, I'd already been in awe of you. And now that I've gotten to know you, I know that I could never have wished for a more perfect male. The way you look at me, talk to me, touch me, make me feel like the most precious treasure in the universe is an addiction I never want to live without. I love you, Rogue... Not because your Dragon says I'm supposed to, but because you touched my heart and soul like no one else ever will. I want to bond with you and spend the rest of my days making you and our children happy."

"My love," Rogue whispered, pulling me into his embrace.

His consciousness penetrated mine as we kissed, the power of his love wrapping around me at a spiritual level. In that much too brief instant, we truly felt as one.

A part of me wanted to kick his butt for choosing this moment to declare himself. I had known—or at least strongly believed—that he was getting ready to do so for a few days now. Although I still worried that his bonding fluids modifying me could sever our connection, completing our union was worth the risk. Everything was too right between us to turn sour now. But I wanted to revel in this moment of bliss, not force my mind back to the mission ahead.

Still, knowing what a beautiful future awaited us gave me an even greater incentive to kick ass during this raid, and safely return.

With much reluctance, we broke the kiss. He caressed my cheek, and ran his thumb over my lip, the infinite tenderness in his eyes making my knees wobble.

"Let's go spank a villain," he whispered.

I snorted and nodded. "Let's…"

Hand in hand, we went to join the others who patiently waited for us inside the shuttle. They hadn't heard our conversation, but a single look at our faces had to be revealing. Their friendly, happy, almost fraternal expressions touched me deeply.

Whatever doubt might still have lingered in my mind died in that instant. Khutu's monster no longer existed. I was Shuria, a proud Mimic and beloved mate to the wonderful Rogue. These people were my new family who had accepted me for who I was, just the way I was.

After all these years of pain and solitude, I finally belonged…

CHAPTER 21
ROGUE

I'd never considered myself the impulsive type, yet the stunt I had just pulled—asking Shuria to bond with me as we were heading out for a potentially deadly mission—certainly qualified as such. And I didn't regret it for one second.

No words could ever describe what it felt like to be in love and for that love to be reciprocated. Touching her soul, basking in the purity of her emotions and affection was a drug I wanted to indulge in day in and day out. The thought of seeing her stomach swell with our child filled my hearts to bursting. I couldn't wait to see our son.

But I couldn't help wondering if he would inherit some of his mother's traits. In all prior unions between a human woman and either a Xian or Dragon, the offspring had always come out fully like his father. The only visible contribution of the mother could be found in his facial features. Would our son have gills? Would he be able to morph like Shuria?

Humans didn't have any particular powers to transfer to their children other than psychic abilities. We systematically enhanced those abilities with the enzyme we had introduced in their diet since we first formed the alliance with Earth. The prospect of that journey of discovery also thrilled me. I didn't care what abilities our children would have or not. I just wanted to hold this living embodiment of the love between Shuria and me.

Our shuttle approaching the cliff face of the eastern secret hangar forced me to chase away those pleasant thoughts and focus on the mission. Yumi and Ayana had remained on board Legion's ship, while Thanh and Jessica had remained on board ours. They would shoot down any ship that tried to escape, run interference if needed, and block any attempts at external communications. The rest of us were down here to deal with this mess.

Umbra was a dead planet. Like Kryptor, the landscape resembled a desert but in dark-gray and charcoal color instead of the ocher and burnished sand tinge of the Kryptids' homeworld. But we didn't have breathable air here. Nothing grew outside, nothing thrived.

Building this lair for us to raise our hundreds of young siblings had been quite the challenge. But it had also been a smart decision —one of many—of our oldest brother, Bane. No one would have thought to seek us out here. Carved directly into the rock formation, it had taken years to make it comfortable enough so that we no longer had to live trapped inside one of our father's breeding ships, at the mercy of the Workers' and Soldiers' constant abuse.

Without us taking them directly to the entrance, our team would have never discovered it. The striations of the rock face, including the overhang, made it impossible to see the openings unless you approached it at exactly the right angle. We flew right through the energy field that shielded the docking bay beyond.

A strange nostalgia gripped my hearts as Reaper landed the shuttle. In many ways, we were coming back home. As painful as our lives had been under the thumb of our father, Umbra had been a haven where we had found some measure of peace and even happiness.

No doubt sensing the emotions coursing through me, Shuria rubbed my back in a soothing fashion, her claws gently raking the sides of the bone spikes lining my spine. I gave her a tender look of gratitude, my hearts warming with love for my female. I leaned down and gave her vertical gills a teasing lick before kissing them.

She chuckled, playfully elbowing my ribs while pulling away from me. It was particularly ticklish for her, depending on which angle I licked her gills. Otherwise, it was extremely erogenous. But now was not the time to turn her on. Once this mission was over, there would be plenty of naughty times between us as I made sure we were properly bonded.

The room seemed smaller than I recalled. It was large enough to accommodate a dozen shuttles and a couple of chasers. The other docking bay where Legion's team was landing could only contain half as many vessels. Considering we had over seven hundred siblings, every vessel completely packed would have been required to evacuate everyone. I only thanked all the powers that be that it never came to that.

Although we had taken away almost everything when the general had forced us to move to Zekuro, we had left a couple of shuttles, all the oxygen masks, and UV ray suits on the racks lining the walls.

As we disembarked, Reaper and I couldn't help the smug smirk on our faces as the rest of our team—excluding Reklig, who knew better—looked around in awe at the more or less squarish space. Even though we'd shown them the hidden entrance in the dream walk, they were still failing to see it. Just like outside, the striation of the rock made it nearly impossible to see the seam of a door. We hadn't bothered polishing any of this, having roughly carved everything, except for the ground which we had reasonably evened out so the ships could sit level. Despite our departure, nearly four years ago, the room seemed frozen in time, the ventilation system having spared it the musty scent of long abandoned places.

Reaper came to stand in front of a seemingly inconspicuous section of wall. Like Doom, Shuria, and me, my brother was naked, but for his weapons and accessories. We were still in our normal form, but he extruded his scorpion tails before pointing a finger at the two barely noticeable holes in the wall, located a little over a meter above our heads. He aligned the hollow tips of his scorpion tails' stingers with the holes and shot a dart in each with deadly precision.

Pride surged through me at my baby brother's performance. Granted, we trained at an early age to master our aiming accuracy with our darts, but Reaper had always excelled in everything combat related. Aside from us sharing the same mother, he had always been my friend, and one of the nicest, most honorable people I'd ever known.

The wall shifted with a slightly grinding sound, the massive set of doors parting, finally revealing their position.

"Should you ever need to re-enter the base through here, the manual override is located on the wall over there," I explained, pointing at it before indicating a small rock spike that almost looked like a miniature stalagmite in front of it. "This spike is the marker. Just draw the letter D for Dragon using the shape of the Kryptid alphabet, and it will do the same thing."

"Hopefully, there won't be any need for us to return here," Reaper said, grimly.

"Agreed," I said as we entered the long hallway beyond the open doorway.

It was carved even more roughly than the ship hangar. As the latter was located much lower than the base, we had dug the corridor at a relatively steep incline. Wide and high, it allowed us to transport large items through it and also to fly without bumping our heads on the ceiling. In fact, we hardly ever walked through here.

Reaper, Reklig, Madeline, and I extruded our wings. My beautiful mate partially morphed to grant herself a pair of translucent bug wings similar to my own. For some dumb reason, that warmed my hearts. My brother turned to look at Doom with a shit-eating grin. As a Xian, he was the only one in the raiding party without the ability to fly.

"In my arms, sweetheart," Reaper taunted. "I will fly you to my lair."

"Fuck off," Doom grumbled, making us all laugh.

My brother was a brat. He loved teasing the Warriors, especially Chaos, who had all but adopted us after he'd found out that his original Soulcatcher had been our mother. Despite Doom's seemingly harsh response, he was merely playing along. We'd flown him and his brothers on more than one occasion.

He lifted his arms. Reaper and I flanked him, each hooking an arm under his before we took flight. The swooshing flapping sound of Madeline's and Reklig's bat wings almost buried the discreet buzzing of our bug wings. Although Legion's team had a similar hallway to cross—and a longer one at that—they'd have no problem doing so. Xenon, Viper, and Kate all had wings. And the three Mimics accompanying them could also partially morph to fly. Between them, they had plenty of options to carry Legion.

In no time, we crossed the five hundred meters to the end of the tunnel, which curved up into a vertical shaft. Once again, we showed our team how to manually activate the hidden platform that could serve as a lift if needed, before flying up to the first level. There, no hidden mechanism prevented us from opening the secret door. A standard panel hung on the wall by the camouflaged door.

"This is where we part ways," I told Madeline while we hovered in front of the door. "You remember the way to the power central?"

"I do," she replied with confidence. "I'll see you guys in a bit."

She turned to her husband, who drew her into his embrace. They exchanged a passionate kiss before parting ways. My hearts melted seeing the striking tableau they formed, with Madeline being a stunning albino of African descent, and Reklig being a mature Scelk with a muscular Janaurian host. He watched his mate continue flying up the shaft to the upper level of the base, love and worry mixing on his features.

"She'll be fine," I said reassuringly.

He grunted in a non-committal fashion.

"The coast is clear on the other side," Doom said, his eyes glued to the interface of the scanner on his armband.

Nevertheless, we all activated our stealth shields. I waved my hand in front of the access panel, and the door quietly glided open, revealing the main dorm room. Our youngest siblings slept and played here. Had we been attacked, they would have had an escape right there while the rest of us held back the invaders.

Thankfully, that never came to pass.

My hearts constricted as memories flooded through me as we crossed the now empty space. It had been one of the few rooms that we had properly finished and polished so that the young ones would have a safe and beautiful space to dwell in. When we'd left Umbra at our sire's command, we'd taken everything with us, including their beds and toys. The only thing that remained was the life size mural Bane had drawn on the walls, representing each of our mothers.

Love flooded through me at the thought of our oldest brother. He had sacrificed so much to protect us and give us what happiness he could. He had selflessly taken on a leadership role he had never aspired to. In many ways, this mural embodied everything that Bane was: someone who saw beauty and goodness even in the grimmest places and brought it forth to share with the world.

Under different circumstances, I truly believed Bane would have become a renowned artist.

We had saved images of this mural, and of the countless other sketches and illustrations he had drawn over the years. But being in the presence of this original one moved me deeply.

We exited the room into a large hallway. Two more doors a couple of meters ahead gave access to the other two dorms where us older siblings had slept. Although the scanners claimed them to be empty, we still confirmed it by entering and having Reklig psychically scan the rooms to make sure no one hid within using stealth mode.

As we cleared the mess hall on our way to the training room —where our scanners indicated the presence of the eight Scelks —Legion informed us through mind speak that his team had just reached the end of their secret passage. It led to the storage located next to the classroom and a short distance from the main ship hangar, where the Zombies all seemed to be gathered.

That seriously concerned me. Unless they had set up the stasis chambers of the Zombies in the ship hangar, the only other explanation I could think of for their presence there was that they were preparing for departure.

"We have a problem," Reklig suddenly said as we closed in on the training room. "My scan doesn't show that these Scelks have regeneration abilities. But they definitely have control chips. That means we cannot use the Zappers without permanently killing them."

Doom muttered a curse under his breath. "Can you control them while we disable the chips?"

"I should be able to do it, but it will be difficult. The chips will interfere," he replied with a concerned voice. "The problem is that if we try to subdue them, they will send out a warning."

"We can ask Thanh to activate a local disruptor to block out any signal outgoing from this room," Shuria suggested. "That will give us the time we need to disable the devices."

Reklig gave my mate a grateful smile. "That should work. It'll be even easier if you grab them with that squid thing you morphed into on Wyngenia."

"No!" I interjected forcefully. "If they have their bladed tails, they will butcher her."

"It's okay, sweetie," Shuria said, caressing my chest in a soothing gesture. "The scales of a Septhoron are bullet proof. It will take many, many blows for them to successfully pierce through. It just means you all have to move really fast, knocking them out."

"But how?" Reklig insisted. "It took days to release Zuno from her control chip. Should we sedate them?"

"Actually, we should be able to simply deactivate them with a standard hacking device," I replied in her stead. "As far as we know, Giles doesn't know that we broke into his files using his authorization code. If he hasn't changed it, we should be able to disable the chips and change their access code. This will give us plenty of time to remove them later, once we're done with this mission."

"Sounds good," Doom said, giving me an approving look. "And if he has changed the authorization code, we'll just sedate them. Everyone, get in your battle form."

We complied, Reklig taking the least time as he simply had to extrude his tail as an extension of his spine, sharp blades jutting out along its outer edge, and the tip ending in a vicious dagger that could decapitate an enemy with a single swipe. Reaper, Doom, and I finished second. And my mate, with her complete metamorphosis finishing last. The dampening effects of our stealth shield had sufficiently muted the crackling sound of us shifting not to betray our presence. Before we were even done, Thanh mind spoke to us, confirming she had blocked all communications to and from the training room.

As our women of the Vanguard loved to say, Shuria looked absolutely badass in a terrifying way. The creature was at least three meters tall and twice as wide. And yet, like a cat, she would have no problem squeezing through the door. It still baffled me how self-conscious my mate became whenever she morphed into a monster in my presence. She simply did not understand how in awe I was of her. No, that beast was not sexy. But knowing that it was my female wielding such power made it a wonder to behold.

"You're kind of hot with tentacles," I privately mind spoke to her.

I felt her amusement and relief through our psychic connection. *"Glad to hear it, because I intend to use them on you the next time we're in private."*

The powerful wave of lust that surged through me took me by surprise. Obviously, I was absolutely not turned on by her Septhoron form, but I could think of at least a dozen sentient species with tentacles that I wouldn't mind her morphing into while we played naughty. I'd done enough research on Mimics to know how kinky they tended to get. I'd been eagerly waiting for Shuria to feel sufficiently comfortable with me to get her freak on. She'd soon find out that I would be a willing participant in pretty much anything she could come up with.

"Looking forward to it, my love," I replied in a tone full of promises.

Doom opening the training room door put an end to our banter. A part of me wanted to feel guilty about flirting with my female in such serious circumstances, but I didn't feel bad for failing miserably at it. I was too happy and in love. For all that, I immediately went into battle mode the moment we walked in.

In less than a second, I registered a million things about the scene that greeted us. The first thing that struck me was that the eight Scelks training inside had generic human clones as hosts—not one of Giles's clones. It shouldn't have surprised me. Such a narcissist could never bear having his likeness taken over and subjected to the will of another. He enslaved others but would be a slave to no one.

The second thing I noticed was the lingering redness around their shoulders and spines. Added to the swollen bulge of their bug's back indicated that they were early in the process of merging with their hosts. They still heavily relied on the cerebral functions of their original brain while fusing with their new human body. Nevertheless, they had merged enough to grow a tail. Seeing how narrow they were, these young Scelks had likely reached the stage for their tails to extrude barely a handful of days ago.

All males and bare chested, they'd been in the middle of combat training when we barged in. Judging by the staves in their hands, I didn't believe they had yet achieved very high levels. The same startled expression settled under eerily similar faces. Despite that, slight differences were already noticeable between them. As Chaos's team had reported, even when given an identical clone, as the Scelks merged with their hosts, their respective DNA increasingly manifested itself through unique traits that grew more evident over time. Even now, I could see that one of the Scelks here would eventually end up being blonde, while another was growing a square jaw.

But their stunned expression quickly gave way to aggression, mixed with confusion. I didn't doubt for a second that they had attempted to raise the alarm, only to find the signal through their control chips blocked. With angry snarls, they charged us, their bladed tails raised, and their claws out. They'd barely started moving when their steps faltered. They blinked, shaking their heads like one would to fight against dizziness while powerful waves of psychic energy swirled around the room.

In a battle of wills, Reklig was forcing them to submit to his compulsion. However, unlike with the Zombies, we couldn't waste too much time if we wanted to avoid them suffering brain injury from the chips trying to coerce them into acting otherwise.

They didn't have regeneration to heal back. Shuria swooped past us, her thick tail propelling her forward at dizzying speed. Disoriented by Reklig's mind control powers, the young Scelks failed to dodge her tentacles as they wrapped around their waists, ensnaring them.

Reaper, Reklig, and I flew towards them to place hacking devices on their temples. Simultaneously, Doom shot them with his blasters set at medium stun. It would not knock them unconscious or harm them, but they would fight less, and it would especially dampen their efforts and accuracy at stabbing my mate with their bladed tails. They still tried to but were as effective as a drunken person attempting to walk in a straight line. Even their claws proved useless against the thick scales of Shuria's tentacles.

Just like when we hacked a lock, we accessed the interface of the devices that immediately connected with the control chips of the Scelks. Half-dazed, they tried to fight us without success. This time, instead of running a decryption algorithm on the devices, we immediately entered Giles's authorization code. Moments later, the first Scelks went limp.

For a split second, I feared something had gone wrong, and we'd somehow injured them. Then I noticed Reklig had landed a couple of meters from Shuria. He stood completely still, his face slack. I realized he was dragging them into a dream walk to avoid having to physically restrain them while explaining the situation to them.

Giles had probably not bothered trying to indoctrinate them against us and merely relied on the control chips' compulsion to keep the Scelks in line. But their species possessed a form of hive mind. They would follow the lead of one they could acknowledge as their alpha, for which Reklig more than qualifies.

We considered shackling them after Shuria carefully placed them on the floor but decided against it. She shifted back into her natural form while we waited after the Scelks. It took a few more minutes before Reklig and the younglings emerged from their dream walk.

"You will remain here quietly while we secure the rest of the base," Reklig said in a tone that brooked no argument. "You will not try to harm, read, or control any member of the Vanguard. Remember that we will only allow you to join us, your Queen, and the other hatchlings of your clutch if you behave and prove that we can trust you."

"She truly lives?" one of the young Scelks asked, the underlying emotion in his voice taking me by surprise.

I had never known a newborn Scelk to show love or empathy. But then, from what Zuno had told us, Giles had not indoctrinated these Scelks to feel hatred and lust for blood. He had been content to bend them to his will through control chips. It was going to be fascinating to see how they would evolve when raised in a normal and healthy environment from the start.

"Yes, your Queen lives," I said in a gentle tone. "She's no longer forced to lay and is enjoying a much-deserved rest to regain her strength."

"Rogue is correct," Reklig said. "You have read me and know I speak the truth. I would not deceive you. Stay here and wait to be evacuated. If you see any trouble, contact me through mind speak."

"Yes, Alpha," the same young Scelk said, the others nodding their ascent.

Normally, I would have felt more comfortable locking them inside the room. However, Reklig's confidence in the fact that they would behave was all the reassurance we needed. You couldn't lie to a mature Scelk. Even the secrets of your subconscious, things you didn't realize you wanted to do deep down, would be exposed should he probe your mind.

As we headed for the door, Madeline's voice resonated in our psychic group.

"I have reached the central control. I am now locking the exit gates of the main hangar," Madeline said.

"Excellent," Doom replied. "Wait until we have reached the hangar to lock us inside with the Zombies. After that, you and Kate can evacuate the Scelks currently waiting in the training room. They will expect you."

"Understood," Madeline said.

"I have reached the power central," Kate said. "I will need a few more minutes to isolate the specific sections we want to shut down. Someone found this room and made some changes compared to what Dread showed us in the dream walk. They have added what I believe to be a couple of missile launchers."

"Understood," Doom responded, echoing Madeline. "Keep us posted."

"Doom, get ready for all hell to break loose," Legion said. "We're right outside the hangar. Join the party as soon as you can."

"On our way, brother," Doom replied. "You know I never missed a good battle."

We chuckled as we rushed towards the hangar in a half run. Our team leader was indeed a battle junkie who loved boasting about how long he could last without needing to transfer into a new Shell. His record had been over three years in the same body before he died. The rest of us were lucky to last more than a few months of steady fighting before keeling over. Jessica spent more time soulcatching other Warriors than the one she was officially assigned to. But she was fine with it, taking great pride in being paired with the Unkillable Doom.

CHAPTER 22
ROGUE

The alarm going off had us increasing the pace. We shifted back into our battle forms even as we ran, except for Shuria who remained in her normal form. As morphing took a bit longer for her, it made sense for my mate to delay until she had assessed the situation to decide which creature would be most effective under the circumstances.

A familiar roar in the distance turned my blood to ice.

Is that a Gomenzi Dragon?

On top of being extremely rare, these almost mythical beings represented one of the highest percentages of the splices that had gone into our creation. Smart, extremely loyal, and long-lived, they had passed each of those traits to us, on top of the soul transfer ability. Had Giles somehow captured one of them for his demented experiments?

But I instantly rejected that thought. Our scans would have detected his presence. It then dawned on me it had to be a Mimic in Legion's team or Giles's sirens.

The sound of battle grew louder as we turned the last corner to the hangar. Straight ahead, through the parted doors, we got the first glimpse of complete mayhem. Standing side by side, their backs to the entrance, Legion and Xenon, their shields raised before them, were shooting their blasters and mouth darts at the swarm of Zombies rushing them. A Creckel was bowling through the masses in her ball form, keeping them away from the Warriors. She would stop and get on her paws just long enough to shoot the darts under her scales at the Zombies. Then she'd roll up into a ball to trample them at high speed all over again. She was one of Shuria's Mimic sisters, but I didn't know which one.

Flying overhead, my brother Viper was raining death on the Zombies with both his tails and mouth darts and throwing Zappers at the enemy. Reaper, Reklig, and I took flight, dashing forward to join him, while Doom and Shuria ran behind. We burst inside, taking advantage of the high ceiling to sweep through the room, unloading our Zappers and Zombie virus on the clones.

All of them resembled Giles.

My gut told me he wasn't among them. As if to confirm my suspicions, one by one, the Zombies collapsed as the Zappers fried their mechanical brains. It was hard focusing on them with not one but two Gomenzi Dragons fighting at the far right of the entrance, in front of the staircase leading to the control room.

Two other Mimics, morphed into Creckels, were fighting them, closing up in their ball form whenever the Dragons would spit fire. Although I couldn't deny Creckels were formidable combat creatures, that the Mimics had chosen this form had initially confused me. But it now made sense. When balled up, a Creckel could resist almost any type of damage, even a nuclear explosion right next to them. No other creature could boast such immunity. Apparently agreeing with her sisters' choice, Shuria also morphed into a Creckel and joined the battle against the dragons.

Moments later, the hangar's entrance doors closed shut behind us, locking us in. It made me uncomfortable to the extent we had a few mortal members in here with us—my mate being at the top of that list. But I could get us out with the manual overrides.

Shuria assisting her sisters finally gave them the edge they needed. She would roll at high speed straight into one of their targets, ramming them in the side to either make them rear back or knock them over. The other two Creckels would then whip their tails forward, launching a barrage of darts from under their scales straight at the vulnerable underbellies of the dragons.

Even knowing they weren't real Gomenzi Dragons, it twisted my insides hearing them roar in pain as they swiped their massive paws and dagger claws at the Mimics. I didn't know whose idea it had been for the sirens to take on this form, but I suspected it had been an order from Giles. What greater cruelty than to force us to kill a fundamental part of ourselves, the core splice that defined us and everything we stood for?

It was a mercy that the Mimics took care of them while we mowed through the clones. Despite their great numbers, we didn't give them much chance to recover from their wounds. The Creckel knocking them down significantly helped us avoid getting overwhelmed. While the Zombies attempted to dodge her rolling attack, we unloaded our blasters, shot them full of darts, stabbed them with our scorpion tails, and decapitated them with the sharp edges of our wings.

That didn't mean we didn't get a few close calls of our own. With so many of them firing at us, I had felt the burn of a couple of shots grazing me. Even with my energy shield, I could only cover so many angles at once. But with their mechanical brains disabled, this became almost insultingly easy thanks to Reklig being now able to take control of their minds, unimpeded—if their organic AI even qualified as that.

Reaper, Reklig, Viper, and I landed, forming a wall with Xenon and Legion. Our shields raised before us for extra caution, we pushed forward, striking and gutting our enemies with our arm blades as their regeneration abilities gradually fizzled off.

Giles had made a grievous strategic error common to most leaders whose only combat experience was logistics and not actual battle on the ground. He had erroneously thought that numbers trumped quality. That would have been true had Wrath not discovered the Jadozors when he did and had Legion's team not stumbled on the Zombie Warriors early enough for us to devise these countermeasures. The clones could aim and fight well enough, but they were no challenge for seasoned warriors like us, whose entire existence had been shaped around our ability to obliterate anything that stood in our way.

The same could be said for the sirens. Yes, they could morph into some of the most lethal creatures in the universe, but that didn't make them adept at fighting as one of them. And those two were failing miserably at leveraging the immense powers of a true Gomenzi Dragon. The Mimics—modified by my father—had undergone strenuous training, which they had pursued and refined long after they had escaped his tyrannical reign.

"Reklig, do you sense Giles?" Doom asked, grunting as he swiped his scythed blade at a clone, splitting him in half from the top of his head to the middle of his chest.

Hardly any white foam bubbled from the dreadful wounds. He collapsed on top of another clone, their spilled blood making the stone floor slippery.

"He's over there," Reklig said, jerking his head to our right. "I believe he's inside the control room with the Lenusian. We need to get there quickly. I can't read him, but she's terrified of whatever he's doing. She has a chip, which makes her harder to read. But I think he's trying to launch the missiles."

Even as he spoke those words, Reklig kicked a clone in the chest, sending him flying backward while simultaneously stabbing his bladed tail straight in the face of another enemy. It pierced right through, exploding the back of his skull in a shower of blood and gore.

"*Kate, status?*" Legion telepathically asked her in our psychic chat.

"*I've disabled the missile launchers and cut the power in all the sections other than our path back to the secret passages,*" Kate replied. "*Madeline just entered the eastern tunnel with the Scelks. The only way out for anyone who doesn't know the manual overrides is through the secret passages. Should I cut the power in the hangar as well?*"

"*No, let him keep the illusion he's still in control,*" Legion said with a malicious edge in his voice. "*Good job. You can head back to the ship.*"

"*Acknowledged.*"

Just at that moment, one of the two Gomenzi Dragons fell over, writhing in its death throes. Its size shrank as it reverted to the original form of the siren. With all four Mimics turning to the other dragon—the one who had been helping us with the clones having joined her sisters—it keeled over in seconds.

"Reklig, Doom, Rogue, with me," Legion ordered as the Mimic charged the remaining clones. "Xenon, find out what they were loading in those ships."

While Reaper and Viper helped the Mimics finish dealing with the clones, we followed Legion as he ran past the corpses of the sirens. We climbed the short flight of stairs, carved directly into the rock, which led to the control room. The reflective glass had prevented us from seeing inside. As soon as we opened the door, my hearts seized with horror at the familiar tingling followed by a falling sensation as a veil of darkness descended before my eyes.

I'd been dragged into a dream walk.

The alien feel of the consciousness trying to control me belonged to a Scelk. By the power of its compulsion, it was much older than the younglings we had just released in the training room. How had we missed the presence of another Scelk?

My vision returned only to find myself alone in the middle of a desert. I fought the panic that wanted to overtake me as a million horrible scenarios flashed through my mind as to what could be happening to my body in the real world. Focusing instead on the techniques we had trained in to escape an imposed dream walk, I visualized and created my own exit.

I'd barely started shaping my doorway when an excruciating pain tore my psychic mind to shreds. The ground fell from under me, and I tumbled through the void, the psychic pain shifting to an even worse physical one through my chest. I shouted as my consciousness crashed back into my body. A bright light blinded me, and a familiar hand on my shoulder dragged me backward.

As my vision cleared, I realized I was on my knees, blood pouring out of the piercing wound through my left heart.

"Rogue, get up!" Reklig shouted.

His shield raised before us, he was blocking the attack of a nightmarish creature hovering over us. That was an Erkentar, not a fucking Scelk. How in the world had it mind-controlled me?

Clenching my teeth through the pain, I shot up to my feet. Even if my left heart completely failed, my right one would allow me to continue fighting until either the battle was won or this Shell died. By the slightly disoriented look on Doom's and Legion's faces, they had also just emerged from being swept away. I could only surmise that Reklig had ripped us right out of that dream walk, causing the psychic bruising I felt, then activated our psychic disruptors. If not for him, we'd probably be dead or dying.

"I don't know what this creature is. It's not an Erkentar. It's not a Scelk, and yet it's both," Reklig mind spoke in our group, sounding confused. *"I can't control it."*

Raising my left arm before me, I deployed my energy shield

and rolled out of the way a split second before the Erkentar would have speared me with one of its extensible lances.

The horrendous creature resembled a dark red gas cloud. Six shadow tails trailed behind it and could be used as whips or cords to either restrain or strangle its victims. All around its round body, its lances—reddish, spike-like tendrils—waved around in wait. In the blink of an eye, the Erkentar could extend them over a four-meter distance, making them harder than titanium to stab at a target. Once it found its mark, the tip would open up inside the body like a grappling hook to inflict maximum damage when it yanked its lances back out.

In between them, dark circles indicated the location of its vents through which it released an extremely toxic fume. On contact with skin or any tissue, the gas triggered excruciating blisters. Inhaling it provoked critical internal damage that usually resulted in death by suffocation as the blisters made it impossible to breathe. On that front, our only blessing was that the fume lost all its potency within seconds of being exposed to oxygen. It served as an unforgivable close-range defense mechanism for the creature.

Killing it would prove quite the challenge, even for seasoned warriors like us. You could only defeat an Erkentar by inflicting lethal damage to its brain. The problem was locating its head, which could be described as a black dome framed between a tiny set of arms with two clawed fingers. Once it felt under attack, most of the Erkentar would dissolve into a gaseous form and fold in on itself to hide its vulnerable head in the cloudy mass. You had to strike blindly, hoping for a lucky hit. But you couldn't linger nearby, or it would melt the skin right off your bones with its fumes or turn you into a sieve with its lances.

We launched into a deadly dance with the Erkentar as our puppet master. We couldn't get close enough to it. Every time we lunged, it would stab at us, whip us back with its tail, or gas the fuck out of us. I even tried activating my stealth shield to sneak up under it, while Legion and Xenon harassed it. But it didn't fool the Erkentar. I barely had time to jerk my head right to avoid having a lance punch right through my face. But I failed to dodge one of its tails viciously whipping me.

The sting felt more like a searing blade slicing me in half. I flew backward, crashing against the wall by one of the consoles. Although it knocked the wind out of me, it saved me from the fumes the Erkentar had released almost simultaneously.

As I jumped back to my feet, discreet movement at the edge of my vision and a soft whimpering sound drew my attention. Curled up in a corner of the room, Cemara trembled in fear. Our gazes met, and her eyes flicked to the console on her left between us. I glanced at it and felt my blood drain from my face.

"Kate, cut off all power to the hangar. They've initiated a silent self-destruct sequence!" I ordered in our psychic group.

"Right away!" Kate replied.

Seconds later, the power went off in the hangar and adjoining control room, plunging the area in darkness, aside from small emergency lights. With us all possessing night vision, we could still see clearly... including the fact that the console was still counting down towards self-destruction.

"FUCK!" I hissed out loud. "It must be linked to a secondary system. This place will blow up in fifteen minutes. Can you turn it off?" I asked Cemara, already guessing her answer.

She pressed two fingers to her right temple, confirming my fear: a fucking control chip.

"Reklig and the Mimics must leave at once. Kate, too," I said in the group.

"Go, now!" Doom ordered.

"Madeline?" I asked.

"The Scelks and I are boarding the shuttle," she replied.

"Where the fuck is Giles?" Legion hissed. *"Did he already escape?"*

"No," Reklig replied telepathically. *"He's still here. I can't locate him, but he's in the hangar."*

"Reklig, take the Lenusian with you," I said out loud, gesturing at her with my head.

He complied. Still looking terrified, Cemara didn't resist when he picked her up and flew out of the room while we distracted the Erkentar to cover them. The wretched creature appeared to know and anticipate each of our moves. It even seemed to be baiting us, making itself look open, only to try and impale us with its lances.

"Why hasn't Giles left?" Reaper asked. "He has to know the self-destruct is active."

Like my brother, I didn't doubt for a minute he had ordered Cemara to launch it. So why remain in harm's way? In direct response to our questions, Giles's voice resonated through the console's com system.

"I would have long been gone, since you vermin can't seem to stay out of my business," Giles said in a voice filled with venom. "But you brought me an unexpected present that I simply cannot leave without. Considering you thieves have taken away my serum, it is only fair that I replenished my stock right from the source. Thanks for sparing me the trouble of having to chase him throughout the galaxy."

"The only thing you'll find here is death," Xenon hissed.

"Oh no, my dear little serum factory," Giles said in a sickeningly sweet voice. "Remember that you're only still alive thanks to me."

"No, I'm still alive thanks to the Vanguard. I'm going to enjoy watching you die painfully," Xenon vowed.

Even as he spoke those words, the Erkentar swooped down on him, three of its lances darting in his direction, followed by a thick cloud of fumes. Xenon grunted as huge blisters swelled on the side of his face not covered in protective scales. White foam immediately covered them as his regeneration kicked in. Reaper,

Legion, Viper, and I rushed the creature to allow Xenon to heal. But once again, the wretched thing turned into gaseous form and spewed more fumes, forcing us to back away.

"Aww, did that hurt? Don't worry, it will soon be over," Giles said in a taunting voice. "And while your buddies are respawning in their Shells, wherever your vessel is at, I'll come and gather your healing body, my sweet little Xenon."

Understanding finally dawned on me. Whatever self-destruct Giles had initiated, the entire base wouldn't collapse from it, only kill any life form within. Maybe some form of radiation. Once our women captured our souls, between the time it took us to be transferred into a new Shell, gear up, and run back here, Giles would casually claim his prize and fly out of here.

Or so he thinks...

"There's no point for us staying in here to die and play his little game," Reaper suddenly said in our psychic group. *"The clones loaded planet killer warheads in two other ships. We can get out of here and set one of them off. Giles will be trapped here in a hell of his own making."*

"Let's do it," Legion concurred. *"But this damn thing..."*

"I will charge it and stay with it, taking all the damage. You go in right behind," Xenon ordered.

The rage with which he mind spoke those words made it clear Xenon was out for blood. My hearts went out to him. He would endure an insane amount of pain to give us the edge we needed. But then, that's why we were the Vanguard: suffering and making sacrifices to protect others.

Having become the perfect mix of Xian and Dragon since his rebirth, Xenon deployed his bug wings, similar to ours. He dashed forward, throwing himself at the Erkentar, shooting darts through his mouth and both of his scorpion tails, and slashing at the beast with forearm blades. Poor Xenon roared in agony as the Erkentar's lances speared through him, the sharp tips protruding through his back before splitting open like a grappling hook.

Five of the creature's tails wrapped around his limbs, restraining him. The sixth one closed on his neck, visibly trying to snap it.

Blood poured out of Xenon, coloring the foam forming around his wounds. Despite the excruciating pain he undoubtedly felt, he balled himself into a fetal position while flying down, dragging the Erkentar to the floor. As soon as it released its fumes, we charged, as it would take it five to six seconds before it could spit more of it.

Although it felt like time had slowed to a trickle, only seconds had gone by since Xenon had attacked. Seeing us all rushing it, the creature violently yanked its spears out of our brother, literally ripping his guts out in the process.

But that hadn't been fast enough.

Although it turned back to its gaseous form, with Reaper, Legion, Doom, Viper, and I striking it with both our forearm blades, shooting our darts, and stabbing at it with our scorpion tails, we finally hit our target. Doom's blade was first to get stuck in the cloudy mass the Erkentar had turned into. I felt my right scorpion tail make contact next. Then all of us just kept slashing while the creature emitted an ear-splitting shriek.

The gaseous mass fell to the floor. To our surprise, no white foam formed around it. Then it struck me: we'd filled the hangar with the Zombie virus. It would have come into the control room, permeating the air once we entered. Assuming this Erkentar had possessed regeneration abilities, the virus would have disabled it by now.

"What have you done?!" Giles shouted through the com. "Salma!"

Salma? Why is he calling the creature by his dead wife's name?

The question answered itself as the Erkentar morphed into its original form. My hearts seized at the sight of a siren with a Scelk bug fused to its spine. The scientist in me wanted to grab it and bring it to the ship in all haste for later study, but we had other priorities. I shifted back to my normal form and picked up Xenon, who hovered between life and death while his body regenerated. Reaper and Viper flew out, no doubt to rig the planet killer missiles.

"What we did is defeat you, again…" Legion replied to Giles. "Half of your army defected once we exposed what you were up to. The others are getting wiped out as we speak. We have found and destroyed all the bases you usurped and eradicated the abominations you created. Like Khutu, you will be remembered as a failed narcissistic psychopath with the blood of countless innocents on his hands. It is a blessing that the real Salma will never see what a monster you've become."

"I'm going to fucking kill you!" Giles shouted.

"What you're about to do is get a taste of your own medicine," Doom said. "In case you haven't noticed yet, there is no escaping for you."

Giles went quiet, but we didn't wait for his response. Time was ticking, and none of us particularly wanted to get another taste of death.

"Everyone, move out," Legion ordered through our psychic group.

I was already flying out of the hangar when I heard Giles's faint voice shouting through the com. He had no doubt tried to open the hangar door only to finally realize he was locked out. Behind me, the footsteps of Doom and Legion resonated loudly as they ran after me on our way to the second secret passage located in the storage room and through which Legion's team had entered. Although it was a longer distance to their ship, it was closer than the passage through the dorm.

"We're coming, my love," I mind spoke to Shuria.

Her joy and relief through our mental connection quickly shifted to worry. I kicked myself for it. She would feel my pain. And right now, the pain from my dead left heart was growing exponentially from the strain of carrying Xenon.

"*All is well. I've only got a flesh wound,*" I said reassuringly.

"*You're a terrible liar. Come back quickly,*" she replied, her love pouring freely through our link.

It spurred me on further. I landed in front of the plain wall section inside the storage room. Catching up, Doom took Xenon from me while I manually activated the hidden door. Viper and Reaper flew in behind Legion just as I was summoning the hover platform that would serve as a lift.

"Forget that," Reaper shouted. "We'll take them down."

He picked up Legion. Just as I was reaching for Xenon in Doom's arms, his eyes snapped open, and he glanced at his brother.

"I'm good," Xenon said. "Remind me not to do this again any time soon."

We snorted and flew down the shaft, Viper picking up Doom. Relieved of my burden, I flew more easily. We'd barely begun our descent when the sound of a loud explosion reached us.

"*Still forty-five seconds left on the self-destruct,*" Madeline said in our psychic group. "*Giles is firing at the hangar's doors to force them open. We're standing by to shoot down his vessel if he succeeds.*"

"*It won't work. The only missiles powerful enough to destroy them would obliterate half of the hangar and wreck his own ship,*" I replied smugly.

"*That's a relief. If—*"

Madeline didn't finish her sentence. A loud whooshing sound resonated in the distance. The air around us shifted. For five seconds, it felt as if we'd been caught in a vacuum where the oxygen, sound, gravity, and even time itself had been sucked right out. Then everything returned to normal.

"*A ship blew up,*" Madeline said. "*The planet killer is activated. Get out fast. We cannot stay in range for too long. I have no idea how much time we have before this thing blows up.*"

She didn't have to say it twice. With Viper and Reaper

carrying Doom and Legion, Xenon and I led the way, flying as fast as we could through the long passage to the secondary secret hangar. Four more times, we felt a tremor followed by the unnatural five-second stillness. Each instance appeared to occur at a twenty-second interval.

We rushed inside the shuttle. Reaper dashed for the pilot's chair and took off before we even finished taking our seats. As soon as we were airborne, Madeline hailed us to confirm with a status report.

"Giles is still trapped inside the hangar. You guys will want to see this when you get here. He may have been a monster, but I wouldn't wish that death on even the worst of my enemies," Madeline said grimly.

A part of me couldn't wait to see how he was getting his comeuppance, while the other oddly mourned the second death of the planet that had sheltered my brothers and me for so many years. I didn't love Umbra. Too many bad memories were linked to that period of my life. And yet, it had also hosted the few times of happiness my younger siblings and I had known.

Cracks and fissures were already appearing, zigzagging like lightning bolts on the surface of the mountain range we had built our base in. Clouds of dust and debris floated above them in defiance of gravity. In a way, this final death of a dead planet marked the ultimate closure of this chapter of our lives and the beginning of a new one.

As we had traveled aboard a single shuttle, we all came to our vessel, even with Reklig and the Mimics, we felt better having a couple of warriors present with those young Scelks in our vessel.

As soon as we landed in the docking bay, Shuria ran to the shuttle. She nearly knocked me off the ramp in her impatience to get to me. Although pain flared under the impact of her brutal embrace, I happily returned it, only to have her guiltily pull away from me.

"You're injured! We must take you to the infirmary right away!" Shuria exclaimed.

"It can wait, my love," I said in a gentle tone. "I want to see what's happening with Giles."

"But—"

"No buts," I interrupted softly, but firmly. "I'll probably need a new Shell, anyway. Come, my love."

Despite her obvious desire to argue, Shuria swallowed back the words burning her tongue and slipped an arm around my waist in support as we followed the others out of the hangar.

Once we got on the deck, the spectacle that awaited us on the giant screen took my breath away. Madeline had connected to the base's camera system. The grainy image indicated the device would soon cease to function under the effects of the planet killer. As was common inside ship hangars, we used cameras made to sustain exposure to space, extreme temperatures, as well as high velocity impacts, be it from a vessel crashing inside the docking bay or from the debris following an explosion.

But this was at another level.

The ship that had contained the missile had exploded outwards, its gut open like nightmarish petals made of twisted metal. From within, a blindingly glowing light pulsated for five seconds, causing objects inside—including the smaller ships—to levitate for that duration before falling back down on the floor. Each time, new cracks appeared on both the room and its content, some ships caving in on themselves.

However, it was the lone figure stumbling through that apocalyptic landscape that retained all of my attention. Giles's clothes had completely burned off his back. Any metal equipment and accessory he had been wearing had melted into his skin. White foam bubbled all over him as he regenerated at an accelerated pace. But before he could fully heal, the white light would pulsate again, hitting him with another radiation blast. Half of his skin and muscles appeared to melt right off his bones. Followed by what looked like welts. I couldn't say for sure because of the regenerative foam engulfing him.

The twenty-second reprieve between blasts only allowed him to heal enough to crawl a short distance towards the door, barely three steps. I stared in morbid fascination at the endless loop of agony he was trapped in.

"How? Didn't the virus kick in?" I asked.

"The radiation burnt it out of the air," Madeline said. "Giles didn't come out of his cloaked ship until after the missile went off. He'd still been trying to blow the doors open. But the second blast of the planet killer fried his weapons system. He's likely trying to exit the hangar to flee through whatever passage he now knows you guys used."

"He will never make it," I whispered, shocked to find myself feeling pity for him. "With his regeneration powers, it could take days, maybe even weeks of him going through this endless loop before he permanently dies. Judging by the speed at which he regenerates, he used the serum recently. How long before the planet collapses?"

"It won't be quick," Martha said grimly. "These missiles are not meant for surface explosion. They are designed to burrow deep, all the way down to the core of the planet, then start destabilizing its integrity from within. I doubt that the current setup will allow it to destroy the entire planet. I suspect it will wreck only a portion of the sector before the missile becomes too damaged to continue to function. Being buried inside the core would have provided it with the stability it needs, like a tight sheath. But right now, every time it pulses, the ship it's sitting inside of levitates then slams back down on the floor."

"This truly is hell," Madeline said with a shudder. "He will continue to burn alive, heal just so that he can burn some more until he's exhausted his life force."

"Can he escape?" Doom asked.

"No," Madeline said with conviction. "No ship can approach

his location without getting destroyed by the effect radius of the blasts. The structure is collapsing. Even if a rescue team managed to get within range to search for him through the rubble, life support is gone inside that base. There's no oxygen. In the time it would take them to dig him out, he'll either already be dead, or will have suffered such intense accelerated aging that he'll be but a few breaths from permanent death. He's done."

"Good. Then let's get back to Kryptor and finish this mess," Legion said. "Madeline, broadcast the footage of his demise to the remaining rebel fleet. It's time for them to know their leader is no more."

"You got it," she replied.

With that, Legion, Viper, Xenon, and Kate returned to their own ship, the Mimics remaining with us to be with Shuria, who they had not seen in far too long.

CHAPTER 23
SHURIA

The journey back to Kryptor was bittersweet. As soon as Madeline began broadcasting the video of Giles's horrible demise, more than half of the rebels still fighting fled the battle. The others appeared to go into a suicidal rage, throwing all caution to the wind to cause as much death and destruction as they could to the Kryptids. By the time we arrived, the battle was mostly over.

The few stragglers received no mercy. While we would have spared their lives, imprisoning them instead, it was not the way of the Kryptids. Daeko ordered his troops to obliterate them all. As much as we disapproved of this course of action, we couldn't deny him this right, considering they had invaded his home world with the intent of slaughtering his people.

Still, he made his displeasure very clear that we had not brought back Giles's remains. Obviously, he couldn't expect us to go try to dig him out with an active planet killer. The footage of the rebel leader caught in an endless loop of burning alive somewhat mollified him. But he still gave us a fair warning that his people would monitor Umbra until all seismic activity stopped so that they could recover whatever remained of him and make certain he wouldn't resurface again.

As for Kryptor itself, it fared even better than we could have ever hoped for. The defenses more than held. Our early preparation with the Zappers and Zombie virus had basically ended the invasion before it even started. Without them, the Kryptids wouldn't have stood a chance.

They still sustained losses, including Bombardier Beetles, Nastarex, Sandworms, and a few hundred Soldiers. By Kryptid standards, those numbers were negligible. As for the Vanguard, aside from a number of warriors requiring to be transferred into a new Shell, and a few of the women and Scelks getting slightly roughed up during particularly brutal skirmishes, we didn't register any casualties. Many ships would require some major repairs, but that was nothing in the greater scheme of things.

I was beyond ready for this day to be over, but we still needed to deal with Cemara. On our trip back to Kryptor, we had removed the control chip Giles had put on her. However, we delayed fully interrogating her until things had settled here. Either way, we wouldn't have had time beforehand.

We sat in the same conference room we had previously used inside the Queen's palace for our prior meetings. Daeko and Commander Hulax were present, the Queen having once more joined us through the vidscreen to proceed with the interrogation. Cemara sat at the end of the table, her hands shackled, and an expression that reeked of resignation and defeat. I didn't know what fate awaited her, but if the Kryptids had their way, she would be executed.

For what felt like hours we grilled her about the entire rebel operation, her role in it, their key contacts, which planets or government secretly supported them, their sources of funding, and what their ultimate goals had been. Knowing she couldn't fool a Scelk, and that full cooperation might earn her a more lenient sentence, she held nothing back.

Half of the names she shared, we had already identified through Giles's communications. But some of those she revealed turned out to be a complete surprise. It would be a massive diplomatic mess dealing with some of the culprits who had worked in the shadows to facilitate this rebellion. It was all the more complicated that the Vanguard didn't actually possess jurisdiction on specific planets beyond the rights afforded to us during missions sanctioned by the Coalition. All that could be done in cases involving high-ranking political figures was to expose them publicly and let their respective leaders and the galactic community decide.

"Whatever caused the fallout between you and Giles?" Doom asked at last.

She heaved a sigh, an air of disgust descending over her reptilian features. "He became crazy. I don't know if it was the result of all the modifications he was performing on himself, or if it had always been there. A part of me thinks he had just stopped bothering to hide his true agenda."

"Which was?" Doom insisted.

"Bringing his late wife back to life. Turning back the wheel of time as if a hundred years of bloody battles could simply be undone. Giving himself the power to never be at the mercy of other people's protection."

She said those last words while casting a meaningful glance at our team leader.

"Which part specifically made you clash?" Legion asked, a sliver of annoyance seeping into his voice at her continued vague responses.

"He was diverting our resources on the sirens and wasting the Workers' time trying to make a clone sentient," Cemara spat out with anger and bitterness. "Had he not wasted so much time on a project that every scientist—including the Workers—had repeatedly warned him could not be achieved, we would have been ready long before any of you started raiding the secret bases. You would have never seen us coming before it was too late."

I stared at the Lenusian female in disbelief. "Is that really what you want to be saying right now?" I asked, incredulous.

She shrugged, the same resigned expression settling on her face. "I'm already dead. If the bugs don't execute me, the Vanguard will throw me in a cell where I might as well be dead. And assuming you send me back to my home world, my government will make an example out of me to avoid taking on any blame for their part in this. And in the highly improbable possibility that you would set me free, those whose names I have ratted out will seek to punish or end me. So, as you can see, I have nothing to gain or lose by speaking my mind."

A wave of pity swept through me. Her assessment was accurate. In her shoes, I would likely also no longer care and hope for a swift death.

"This entire rebellion was about making the Kryptids pay for what they had done," Cemara said angrily while casting an accusatory glance in turn at Daeko, Hulax, and Queen Xerath. "You keep hiding behind your so-called hive mind and blind obedience to hierarchy to justify why you allowed Khutu to perform the greatest genocide in the history of this galaxy. And yet, the minute the very survival of your colony was threatened, you suddenly grew a backbone. You challenged his authority and raised your blades against him until you brought him down. You are not victims—you were complicit."

I shifted uneasily in my seat, loathed to admit the validity of her arguments as similar thoughts had crossed my mind too many times in the past.

Far from being offended or shamed by her accusations, the three Kryptids merely observed her with the curiosity one would cast over a strange creature.

"You have nothing to say?" she hissed when the silence stretched. "No excuses? No lame defense to justify decades of lying to your own Queen and facilitating scientific horrors on innocent species who had never represented a threat to your people?"

"We do not owe you any excuse or justification," Xerath replied in a factual fashion. "Daeko and I were not born when this war started. Those who came before us were misled into believing those innocent species were in fact a threat to us. Could we have acted sooner? Yes. Why didn't we? There are too many reasons to list them all. But what would be the point? Laying blame will solve nothing and will not 'turn back the wheel of time' as you said so eloquently. Whatever wrongdoings occurred, all we can do is learn from them and strive to avoid history repeating itself."

Cemara emitted a disgusted sound while glaring at the Queen with contempt. "Typical politician platitudes. Instead of taking responsibility and making amends, you just dismiss all the pain and suffering your people caused with promises of doing better in the future?"

Xerath tilted her head while studying Cemara's features with an almost amused expression. "You off-worlders waste so much energy on pointless emotions. What would groveling and begging you for mercy accomplish? Nothing. But your bitterness has brought about the death of hundreds if not more of your own people. The war was over. They could have gone back home to rebuild. Instead, you fueled more aggression that entirely back-fired. Had your plan succeeded, and had you destroyed my people, would it have brought back those you lost? Whatever satisfaction you might have derived from that temporary victory, it would still have left you hollow and empty."

The Queen's gaze roamed over her birthing chamber, her expression unreadable. And yet, I knew Xerath well enough to recognize what would be deemed as powerful emotions in other species.

"Do not doubt that my people have suffered. We also faced

extinction. You deem us complicit, but what we are is survivors. Unlike you, we are bound by our genetic compulsion to obey even when our better judgment suggests we shouldn't. But when your entire world is on the verge of collapse, the visceral need to fight for that last breath, to cling desperately to life will overcome even the most powerful compulsion. We fought back when we did because we finally could and absolutely had to. Whatever you may think of us, we are not predators. The war ended, we moved on. *You* attempted to rekindle it. We thwarted your efforts. And now, once again, we are moving on. We are not the aggressors. You are."

With those words, Xerath ended the communication. A heavy silence descended over the room while a million different emotions flitted over Cemara's face. For a split second, I believed the Queen had managed to get through to her and made her see the futility of revenge under these circumstances. But the Lenusian's expression hardened, her resolve renewed in her belief of the self-righteousness of her stance. There would be no changing her mind. Her loss had been too great, her pain too deep to ever allow her to see the Kryptids as anything other than the monsters who had destroyed her life and who deserved to be obliterated.

The interrogation continued a little while longer, this time mostly to confirm what other targets Giles had been planning on destroying with the planet killers. Unsurprisingly, Khepri—the homeworld of the Vanguard—would have been next to ensure we could never threaten the dictatorship he intended to instate.

By the time it finally ended, little remained unanswered. Giles had tapped into the suffering and discontent of Coalition members in their most vulnerable time to rope them into a foolish venture that only prolonged their torment. I didn't know what would become of Cemara, but she wouldn't die at the hand of the Kryptids. Xerath had rendered her verdict: they were moving on.

I headed back to my quarters, that I now shared with Rogue, distraught not to have him by my side. Once again, duty kept him away. As it would probably take him a few hours, I decided to go soak in the tub. After the wondrous tub I had enjoyed on the Vanguard vessel, this one paled by comparison. But the salts Rogue had given me made-up for it.

I sank to the bottom, inhaling deeply through my gills. Eyes closed, I let my spirit drift, Enjoying the rejuvenating effects of salt water on my skin. In a few days, once everything here was sorted, we would head back to Khepri. I hadn't fully thought out what I would do with my time.

Every woman of the Vanguard was a highly skilled professional, with tons of degrees in one field or another, many revolving around sciences, information technology, psychology, or politics. Granted, there were those who were simply masters in specific disciplines, like Linette being unrivaled when it came to piloting any type of vessel.

Unlike the others, I didn't possess a degree of any kind. I had no particular mastery of anything that could contribute to the advancement of the Vanguard in times of peace. All I knew was how to fight. Other tasks, from hacking, to tracking, and everything else in between, I could perform decently. But it wasn't anything that a novice with basic training couldn't also achieve.

I had pulled my weight during this mission. Now I needed to figure out how I could be useful again while waiting for the next one. Images of the future that awaited me with my mate invaded my every thought. My throat tightened at the vision of a small Dragon infant with his father's beautiful black scales and Deynian horn, and my stormy eyes.

Once again, the question that had plagued me since the moment Rogue had claimed me as his mate came back to the fore. Would any child of ours inherit part of my mimicking abilities or would he entirely be a Dragon?

My mind further drifted as countless scenarios of Rogue and

I raising our child, spending romantic evenings together, flying side-by-side over the Dragons Rise, and making love by the Mistral River flashed before me.

It took me a moment to realize the fingers caressing my lips were not part of my daydreaming. My eyes snapped open and locked on the beautiful face of my mate staring tenderly at me.

I exhaled as I emerged from the water, my skin warming with the emotion Rogue's presence always stirred in me. Maker, the way he looked at me like I was the brightest of stars in the sky.

He leaned forward and kissed me, his lips so soft, so gentle, so reverent against mine that tears welled in my eyes. This male loved me. I didn't understand why, but I praised the Maker for it. He broke the kiss and took my hand. As he rose to his feet from his crouching position, he helped me up. Only then did I realize he, too, was fully naked. Rogue pulled me into his embrace, lifting me out of the tub. Unlike the one onboard the Vanguard chaser, this one wasn't recessed into the ground, but merely sitting on top.

Arms wrapped around his neck, the bone spikes on his shoulders gently poking at my upper arms, I drowned in the dark depths of my beloved's multifaceted eyes. I brushed my lips against his, nuzzled him, then buried my face in his neck to deeply inhale the unique scent that was all his and that always made me feel safe... at home.

To my shock, a different spicy scent tickled my nose. It wasn't the cinnamon aroma of his pheromones, but something rarer... more special...

I jerked my head up to look at him in shock. He smiled, his expression filled with a world of love and possessiveness that made me melt from the inside out. Lips quivering, I let him carry me back into the bedroom. The fragrant scent of night thimbleweed permeated the room. Rogue had scattered them everywhere. The edges of their white petals glowed in reaction to the darkness otherwise filling the space.

"How?" I whispered in shock and awe.

"I asked Steele to bring them from Khepri after he dropped Xenon's DNA there and came to join us for the battle," Rogue replied in a soft tone. "I wanted this to be done right... if you still consent."

A lone tear of joy ran down my cheek as I nodded, the silliest grin on my face. "I do. I most certainly do."

"My love," Rogue whispered before reclaiming my mouth.

On a Mimic's wedding night, the couple always surrounded themselves with night thimbleweeds during their coupling. It represented the blessing of the Maker shining on their union, and the light that would keep at bay the darkness in troubled times. I couldn't believe Rogue had not only informed himself of our customs but also gone out of his way to make sure he could honor them on this most sacred night between us.

He carried me to the bed, laying me carefully on top of the mattress before joining me. No wild and unbridled passion animated us just yet. It would come. For now, we were rediscovering each other, our hands caressing our naked bodies as our tongues mingled. My mate didn't rush through any of it, his lips worshipping every inch of my body.

My skin tingled as his pheromones awakened my senses, sending them into overdrive. Maker, the way the rough texture of his tongue glided over the sensitive buds of my nipples had electric sparks coursing through me. He laid a trail of kisses down my chest, his hands teasing me as they slipped between my thighs.

When I didn't part the veil of scales hiding my modesty, Rogue stopped kissing my pelvis to look up at me. I held his gaze with a mischievous expression, a challenge in my eyes. I liked a bit of roughness and when he displayed his dominance. It made me feel the good kind of weak in all the right places.

Once more, my mate delivered.

His face took on a menacing expression that had my nipples

hardening and my toes curling. He bared his teeth at me. My stomach did a backflip when the tips of his canines descended into sharp fangs. A shiver of anticipation coursed through me. Rogue loved to nip at my skin, and I loved a biter. He'd shown me glimpses of his fangs before, but never displayed them in their full glory until now. And tonight, for the first time, he would not just pierce my skin with them, he would also inject me with his bonding hormones.

An eager fever warmed my skin as he lowered his head towards my pelvis in a threatening fashion. But it was the sight of his scorpion tails extruding from his back and curving over his shoulders towards my face that undid me.

A bolt of lust exploded in my nether region, my inner walls palpitating as he grazed my cheek and the side of my neck with the ball of his right scorpion tail. The vicious needle of its tip pointed away from me. His fangs stabbed at the delicate flesh around my navel, tearing a strangled cry out of me. Rogue bit hard enough for a solid sting but not to break skin.

I parted my veil, a moan rising from my throat as my mate sank his fingers inside me. My ollia—the sensitive ridges lining my inner walls—immediately responded, pleasure pulsating throughout my nether region. I reached for the left tip of his Deynian horn with one hand. But lightning fast, Rogue wrapped his right scorpion tail around my wrist, immobilizing it. Saying that turned me on would be quite the understatement. I attempted to grab the other tip of his horn with my free hand, expecting him to restrain it as well. To my shock, he ignored it, his second scorpion tail wrapping around my neck instead.

My gasp turned into a moan as it tightened its hold, although not enough to suffocate me. Eyes locked with mine, Rogue accelerated the movement of his fingers moving in and out of me. Lips parted, my free hand clenching the soft fabric of the blanket covering the mattress, I breathed increasingly loudly as my pleasure quickly built towards its crescendo. As I neared completion, my mate suddenly pulled out his fingers, replacing them with his impossibly long tongue, sending me over the edge.

I cried out, my hips gyrating in the throes of bliss while Rogue continued to make love to me with his tongue. Even as I flew high, a plan began forming in my mind. Knowing my mate —generous lover that he was—as soon as I came back down, he would work on giving me at least a couple more orgasms before he sought his own pleasure. But if we were going to permanently bond tonight, we needed to do so having shown our true selves to each other.

Rogue starting to carefully rake his claws over my undars signaled he had realized my climax was ebbing away, and he was initiating round two. I released the blanket and grabbed the right tip of his Deynian horn, yanking his head back. Seeing the crazy length of his tongue once more made my toes curl and my legs turn to jelly. The lingering sensation of how insanely good it felt inside almost made me reconsider my course of action.

But Rogue tightening his scorpion tail around my neck while he growled menacingly spurred me into challenging his dominance. I held his gaze unwaveringly with an air of defiance as I welcomed the pain of a partial shift. My mate's eyes widened first in shock then in understanding as tentacles quickly extruded from my waist and hips.

Flipping us around, I forced him onto his back, then climbed on top of him, still morphing. The Drimik—a sort of kraken— were a popular species to impersonate among my people. Although I'd never enjoyed that kind of play yet, I'd been counting the days until I finally could. Heart pounding with a mix of fear and excitement, I studied Rogue's features for any sign of discomfort or disgust.

A wave of love swelled in my chest when his gaze smoldered. Rogue smiled in a lascivious fashion, his scorpion tails releasing me before resorbing into his back as he yielded to me.

Maker, how I loved how powerful it made me feel that such a magnificent male would give himself over to me... *only me.*

Like he had previously used his scorpion tails to immobilize me, I did the same with my tentacles, this time restraining each one of his limbs. I considered wrapping one around his neck as well but skipped that. I loved biting his neck, right below his earlobe. The way he reacted to that turned me on beyond words.

Unwilling to resist temptation, I buried my face in his neck, kissing, licking, and biting. His chest vibrated with a rumbling purr in response. When I lifted my head to claim his lips, the sensuous smile of his face vanished. Rogue recoiled and jerked his face away from mine, his body tensing.

My stomach dropped, a fear I had thought long buried coming back with a vengeance. Did morphing in an intimate setting confuse his Dragon? Did it sever his connection with me?

"Not your face," Rogue said, his voice strained. "You can morph into anything you want, but I must always be able to recognize you. When we make love, I do not want to look at any other face but yours."

I melted from the inside out, emotions too powerful to define overwhelming me. Without a word, I shed the Drimik facial features I had taken on but kept the five thick and ropy appendages dangling from my head, which acted as their version of hair.

The look of pure love that settled over Rogue's face as he smiled totally wrecked me. "There she is, my beautiful mate."

"Do you have any idea how much I love you?" I whispered in a choked voice.

"Show me," he whispered back, his searing gaze boring into mine.

And show him, I did.

I reclaimed his lips, my hands roaming over the firm muscles of his chest while my tentacles spread over his limbs. The suction cups flattened over his skin and scales. They emitted a subtonal pulse that instantly had Rogue crying out as pleasure blasted through him.

We often referred to the Drimik as sex deities. They didn't lie when they claimed to be able to make their partner climax with a touch. Each pulse felt like liquid ecstasy coursing through every cell and nerve ending.

In seconds, Rogue was trembling beneath me, an endless string of moans tumbling out of him. I kissed and licked every inch of him, loving the power I held over him as he lay helpless, with no other choice but to take everything I gave him. Before my hand even reached the apex of his thighs, my mate parted the scales of his loin plate. His hiss of relief at his cock finally being freed blended into another throaty moan. The powerful cinnamon scent of his pheromones and natural lubricant struck me hard, making me instantly wet and achy.

I had meant to torture him with pleasure, wresting one orgasm after the other from him like he always did to me, but Rogue had other plans. Even shackled by my tentacles, my mate was trying to top from the bottom. His chest vibrated with his mating song, and he released even more of his aphrodisiac pheromones, driving me insane with lust. My skin felt on the verge of combusting, and my inner walls contracted painfully with the need to be filled.

With a furious shout, I impaled myself on his length, welcoming the burn of this brutal penetration. But it had sufficed for me to win the unspoken challenge between us.

Rogue threw his head back against the mattress and roared his release, his burning seed shooting inside me. A triumphant grin stretched my lips as I rode him hard. But soon all thoughts of competition faded from my mind as my own climax built within me. Even as he came down from his high, Rogue thrust upwards into me, grunting as the sensuous pulses of my tentacles once more pushed him towards the edge.

The room spun when a violent orgasm swept me away. My

mate joined his voice to mine as I shouted in bliss. I vaguely felt his seed shoot into me again. But time and space had lost all meaning as I flew high. When I started regaining my bearings, I was on my back, Rogue lying on top of me.

At first, I thought he wanted to take control of the next round. However, a single look at his beautiful face and his serious expression made me realize the time had come. Through the sparks of pleasure lingering through me, a swarm of butterflies took flight in the pit of my stomach. My throat dry with anticipation, I locked eyes with him, eager for what would come next.

"I want to bond with *you*," Rogue said, his voice deep and gravelly.

He didn't need to explain further for me to understand his meaning. I nodded and morphed back into my natural form. He smiled with infinite tenderness, his fangs descending while he studied my features as if he couldn't believe I was real.

"I am yours, Shuria. Now and always."

"And I am yours, Rogue, all yours, until the Maker calls us back to the Well and beyond," I said.

He kissed me. It was slow, deep, and devoid of the unbridled passion that had just animated us. His lips traced the path along my jawline, down the curve of my neck, before settling over the fleshy part of my shoulder. I felt them part seconds before the sharp tips of his fangs pressed against my skin. My arms tightened around Rogue's back, fear and excitement warring within me as I clamped down on the negative thoughts attempting to rear their ugly heads.

My shout of pain as his fangs pierced my skin quickly turned into a cry of ecstasy as bliss in its purest form raced through my veins. I felt Rogue insert himself inside me, his chest vibrating against mine with his mating song. Then his consciousness brushed against my psychic void.

Drowning in a sea of pleasure, I welcomed him in. I dropped

all my defenses, including the psychic shield that sheltered the dancing lights of my soul. A tidal wave of love swept me away when Rogue's consciousness merged with mine as our bodies moved harmoniously in the most ancient of dances. There was no beginning, no end. We were one.

EPILOGUE
SHURIA

Two days after Giles's demise, Doom's team—with me in tow—prepared our return to Khepri. Legion and his team would linger to iron out the final details with the Kryptids and coordinate the efforts to track down the rebels and whatever stragglers might lurk in Kryptid space.

To our surprise, several rebels turned themselves in. Finding out they all had regeneration abilities explained that otherwise irrational behavior. They didn't want to age before their time. Knowing it could be reverted was worth the risk of facing the consequences of their actions. Unsurprisingly, the majority claimed to have received the graft against their will once they realized the error of their ways and tried to abandon the rebellion. We couldn't prove it either way, not that it was our decision to make. We would heal them—if only to limit the number of 'immortal' potential enemies out there—before turning them over to the authorities of their respective homeworlds.

I couldn't deny feeling tense throughout the journey home. Things were beyond perfect between Rogue and me. But I couldn't shake the fear that our bonding process would mess things up for us. And yet, the hours turned into days, and days into the three weeks it took to reach Khepri, my new home. The only symptoms that manifested themselves during that period were the legendary maddening itching bouts every female mated to a Dragon or Xian endured as she gained her mantle.

And what a magnificent mantle it was.

All around my neck and shoulders, black chitin scales made their appearance, making me look every shade of fierce and regal. They contrasted beautifully against my dusky blue skin, giving me a tough yet elegant edge. Rogue performed regular tests—mostly at my insistence—to make sure everything was as it should be. It amused him as he felt my insecurities had long lost any reason to persist. Still, he played along, understanding I really needed that reassurance.

His Dragon never turned away from me… from us.

The day we landed on Khepri, I feared I would faint from panic. The long-dreaded moment of truth was finally upon us. Rogue had already informed Bane of our union. He had reassured me that his brother had expressed nothing but happiness for us. But did he mean it or simply played along out of the goodness of his hearts?

My pulse racing, I nearly squished Rogue's hand in panic as we walked down the ramp of our vessel. Bane and Tabitha already waited for us inside the docking bay. My mate's consciousness brushed against mine, his love flooding through our mental connection. I gave him a psychic nudge in gratitude.

I didn't fear for my relationship with Rogue. Whatever welcome—or lack thereof—I received from Bane and Tabitha, I was finally confident in the undying strength of the bond between my mate and me. Rogue wouldn't leave me because of his sibling's disapproval. But they were extremely close. I wanted us to be one big, united family and to leave the past where it belonged.

"Brother!" Bane said with a beaming smile while staring at Rogue.

My mate gave my hand a little squeeze before releasing it in order to exchange a hug with his brother. The obvious love between them moved me deeply. I kept my gaze locked on the two males, not daring to glance at Tabitha, whose stare weighed heavily on me. After Bane released him, Rogue turned to Tabitha to hug her as well.

"I see you've returned in great company," Bane said in a gentle voice, his intense gaze leveled at me although he addressed his brother.

Rogue released Tabitha to look at me with a possessive pride that had my heart swelling with love for him. He slipped an arm around my waist and drew me against his side.

"The best possible company," Rogue replied happily.

"Welcome home, Shuria. Welcome to the family. You got the good one," Bane said, the warm and affectionate way in which he spoke those words wrecked me.

I'd meant to put on a brave front, to be apologetic without groveling. Instead, my dumb ass got overly emotional. My lips quivered while tears welled in my eyes.

"I'm sorry," I blurted. "I'm so sorry I hurt you."

"Hey! None of that," Bane said in a gentle but firm voice. "You have nothing to apologize for."

To my shock he drew me into his arms to console me. I didn't bawl, but welcomed the soothing motion of his hand caressing my hair while I regained my composure.

I pulled away, feeling mortified. "Wow, that is *not* how I had intended for this to go."

The three of them chuckled. Rogue wrapped his arm around my waist, a tender expression on his face as he kissed my temple.

"Actually, we kind of owe you one for killing him," Tabitha said in a slightly teasing tone.

My jaw dropped, and I gaped at her, confused. Bane snorted then nodded in agreement, baffling me even more.

"I captured his soul and had to remain with his brothers until he could be transferred into a new Shell," Tabitha explained in a friendly fashion, her face taking on a wistful expression as she continued. "Without that, I would have returned to my ship with Chaos, and who knows how long it would have taken before Bane and I could be reunited and bond? For three years, we'd only been two ships passing each other in the night."

My throat constricted, I gave her a grateful smile. "Although that had not been the plan, I'm glad it worked out that way," I replied with a nervous laugh.

She smiled before sobering. "There is no need to apologize. I get being deeply hurt and heartbroken by someone who had never meant to hurt us. But then it makes finding your true soulmate all the more magical."

Tabitha turned to look at her mate with an air of pure adoration, her fingers brushing over the black scales at the base of his Deynian horn. She turned back to look at me.

"You are embarking on the most wonderful journey of your life. Do not let past regrets tarnish it. You are home, you are loved, and we couldn't be happier to have you as part of the family. Welcome home, Shuria."

I couldn't say which one moved towards the other first, but Tabitha and I ended up hugging, my stupid eyes prickling again.

"But don't think that takes you off the hook of being put through your paces as does every new recruit of the Vanguard," Tabitha said in a playfully menacing way as she released me.

We laughed, the weight of the world having been lifted from my shoulders.

In the weeks that followed, we began building our new life amidst quite a bit of confusion and turmoil. It wasn't between us, but between the Vanguard and the rest of the galaxy. It had shocked me to find out that the leaders of the Vanguard had been seriously discussing the possibility of parting ways with the Coalition.

They had been created to bring peace to the allied planets but also to every other planet under threat from external forces. While the main menace had been General Khutu, it had always been understood that once that war ended, they would remain neutral peacekeepers to help handle all the other conflicts that had torn apart the various members of the Coalition before they had to shift their focus on a greater common enemy.

But after a hundred years of endless bloody battles, the Coalition had grown to perceive the Vanguard as their personal attack dogs. They expected obedience, for the Vanguard to jump, go fetch, or sit when so ordered according to the whims of the various parties. The rebellion had made it even clearer what unrealistic expectations each planetary government had where we were concerned.

Long-standing feuds that had been put on hold while the entire Galaxy fought the Kryptids had recently resumed. Each party now demanded the Vanguard side with their cause against their opponent. Barely veiled threats and less-than-subtle blackmail abounded as members of the Coalition implied they would cut off all the resources they had been supplying the Vanguard with, including ending the psychic training programs on their respective planets. Without this training, the Vanguard wouldn't be able to recruit the wonderful women that made the entire program viable, from Soulcatchers, to Portals, to Shields.

Without their women, Xian Warriors and Dragons were no more than highly enhanced Soldiers. At least, Dragons like my mate possessed a special edge to the extent that, so long as their Shells were within psychic range, they could self-transfer to a new vessel upon death. Xians couldn't.

But that threat didn't faze the Warriors. Although they had not planned for this specific situation, the Vanguard had spent the century of war against General Khutu building their homeworld into a self-sufficient ecosystem. Thousands of families had gone through stringent security background checks before being allowed to settle here to work in the various fields necessary to sustain our needs. From farming, to construction, to advance technology, any industry that could be found on a regular planet could also be found here.

As for the threat of ending the program, those governments would undoubtedly face major backlash from their population, angry to be deprived of such an opportunity. But even if they nevertheless banned such training, nothing would prevent potential candidates from traveling off world to pursue their dreams. Many already did, seeking entry in the schools reputed for having the most graduates qualifying for the Vanguard. Either way, enough planets wanted to remain in the Vanguard's good graces that the handful of blackmailers weren't worth losing any sleep over.

In the end, Chaos and Legion held the referendum they had been alluding to since the end of the war against the Kryptids. In a unanimous vote, every citizen of Khepri, from the members of the Vanguard to the civilians who worked here, decided to make our independence official. We wouldn't be the hired thugs some governments wanted us to be, but we also wouldn't act as vigilantes. Our job was to enforce the peace and protect the vulnerable and innocent. We would do so, heedless of political machinations, like we had done with the Kryptids.

As for me, my career took on a most unexpected turn. Ayana, Legion's mate, ended up taking me under her wing. Based on my part in fanning the flame of rebellion amongst the Kryptid Workers, and my advisory role at Queen Xerath's side, Ayana became convinced I would be the perfect ambassador or political liaison to negotiate peace and truce treaties with guerillas and warring factions.

I laughed at such a preposterous suggestion. But according to her, I had something she—as the Vanguard's main ambassador—and other diplomats didn't have. I was a true survivor, having faced not only the very real prospect of my own death at the hands of a genocidal maniac, but also the threat of extinction of my entire species. This allowed me to empathize with those factions in a way none of them could, and that inspired trust—the essential foundation for any chance at successful negotiations.

It wasn't a full-time role, my services only being needed for specific situations. But saying I ended up enjoying it would be quite the understatement. It didn't hurt that my mate gladly tagged along when I set off on such missions.

But my primary duties lay elsewhere, right here on Khepri, as beast master and combat trainer. I started teaching our young Mimics in basic defense and combat, so they'd never be helpless like we had been when the Kryptids raided our homeworld. It then extended to the other members of the Vanguard, both the women and the Warriors.

I was a living, breathing encyclopedia of the most fearsome creatures in the galaxy. With my modified sisters—now also fixed like me—we provided real-life scenarios where they could train fighting against the creatures, instead of approximated simulations. Rogue particularly enjoyed being able to get a close view of some particularly vicious beast without risking having his head bitten right off… not that I didn't sneak in a nibble or two.

After five months settling into this new life, I was getting ready for a pre-mission training session. With the end of the war, pirates and slavers had become a plague. Tabitha, whose analytical skills would never cease to amaze me, had pinpointed what she believed to be their base of operation where slaves and contraband were stashed. Vicious beasts dwelling in the area blocking its only access served as natural defenses against their will. This training aimed at rehearsing strategies to disable the beasts without unnecessarily killing them.

Standing naked between my sisters Herina and Deisha,

Doom's and Rage's teams waiting to jump into action, we began morphing.

Or at least I tried.

While my sisters easily started turning into fearsome beasts, my entire body shut down. I froze, shock and disbelief coursing through me. I tried again, my morphing abilities present, but muted. Wanting to make sure I wasn't imagining things, I attempted a partial shift, growing a pair of diaphanous wings similar to those of the Dragons.

They extruded without any problem.

A choked laugh escaped me as tears of joy welled in my eyes.

"Shuria?" Doom asked with a worried expression.

"I can't morph," I whispered, my voice incredulous. "I can't morph!" I repeated, laughing and crying at the same time.

"Why? What's wrong?" he asked, clearly baffled as to how to react to me saying what he had to deem terrible news but doing so while laughing.

He likely thought me mad, but I couldn't stick around to answer. Flapping my wings, I flew out of the room located in the Training Center. I burst out of the seashell-looking, off-white building, and soared in the sky. For a split second, I considered using Khepri's bubble transport system—glass spheres that traveled through underground tunnels at great speeds. They could have gotten me to the Research Center located inside the HQ, but that meant a slight detour and possibly having to wait for a free bubble to come to my station.

I had no time for that.

Shooting through the sky like a bullet, I crossed the short—but endless—distance to the HQ. As I dove towards the entrance, the doors parted for a group of Warriors exiting the building. Not wanting to slow down, I nearly knocked the Warriors out of the way as I squeezed past them, shouting an apology. Only once inside did I land to avoid hurting myself on the ceiling, high though it was.

People moved out of my way, all of them gaping at me as I ran past them as if a Drone Swarm was hot on my heels. I veered right into the hallway leading to the Research Center, almost crashing into a Xian I hadn't seen coming. Mumbling another apology, I spun around him to pursue my mad dash forward.

I finally reached my destination, annoyed to no end with having to wait for the bioscan to grant me access to this restricted area. As soon as the doors parted, I irrupted inside the room, shouting my mate's name.

"ROGUE!!"

I jerked my head left then right, dismissing the other scientists working at various workstations, all of them staring at me in shock. Then I finally saw him, halfway through the back, next to Victoria—Doom's mate.

"Shuria? What's wrong?" Rogue asked, discarding the datapad he was holding onto the counter next to him before hurrying towards me.

I advanced a few more steps towards him before stopping, overwhelmed by emotion. "I can't morph. I can partially shift, but I can't morph."

Stopping in front of me, Rogue grabbed my right hand in his left, and cupped my cheek with the other, an air of concern on his face as he studied my features.

"You can't morph? What—?"

He froze, his entire body stiffening. For a beat, his eyes went blank. Then understanding, shock, disbelief, and utter joy flitted in quick succession over his face.

"You can't morph!" he whispered. "My mate…!"

He picked me up by the waist, lifting me like I weighed nothing, and pressed his face against my stomach.

My yelp of surprise gave way to a happy giggle as he spun around, making me slightly dizzy.

He finally lowered me, not to put me back down on my feet, but carried me to an adjoining room to lay me down on an examination table. Having anticipated our needs, Victoria was already setting things up for a sonogram.

Moments later, the confirmation we received exceeded all expectations.

"Congratulations," Victoria said in a sweet voice. "You're expecting twins."

~

In the weeks that followed, I couldn't decide if I wanted to kiss Rogue or smack him. As expected, he went into overprotective mode, his brothers and my sisters also joining the fray. Twins were extremely rare both among Mimics and Warriors. In fact, Raven, Doom's firstborn son, was the only Warrior to have sired twins. But while we knew what to expect from the union between a human and a Warrior, we were walking blind with my pregnancy.

Naturally, I underwent so many exams—most of which I had requested to make sure everything was still fine—that I might as well have taken up residence in the infirmary. The babies were doing great, even though they were on the smaller side—which wasn't uncommon for multiples. We couldn't see much about them as they kept hugging each other. But we could glimpse the tiny bumps that would grow into their Deynian horns, and a mix of scales and undars on their limbs.

I felt beyond restless as the weeks stretched on. Training had been part of my daily routine for so many years, being forced to remain idle proved more challenging than I expected. Although I could still do partial shifts, as a pregnant Mimic, I could not morph as it required completely rewiring my internal organs to match those of the creature being emulated. That would kill any potential fetus. Therefore, that ability automatically shut down the minute we conceived.

I channeled that excess energy into preparing our house by the Mistral River to receive our two babies. Impatience gnawed at me to see them playing with the other young Dragons, Xians, and Scelks. I only hoped my genetics wouldn't set them too much apart. As the date drew near, I spent an increasing amount of time in the water. On a few occasions, I even spent the entire night sleeping underwater. That made me wonder if our children would be more aquatic than land bound.

Through it all, Rogue proved over and over again what a perfect mate he was, going so far as to sleep by my side on the riverbed while wearing an oxygen mask.

When the time came at last, night had already fallen over Khepri. I was lying in the shallow part of the river in front of our house, cuddling against my mate. My Mimic sisters were swimming in the water while humming a welcoming chant as we waited. They remained at a respectful distance to grant Rogue and me some privacy. Countless night thimbleweeds floated on the water, bathing the darkness in a dreamy light.

Delivery wasn't a long or painful process for us. The minute the child was ready to come out, we simply relaxed our pelvic muscles, distending them through a partial shift, to let him or her out. We just needed to wait for the youngling to initiate the process.

And then the first one did.

Rogue moved from my side to kneel in front of me, water rising to the middle of his chest.

"He's crowning!" Rogue whispered, a look of wonder on his face.

Hands extended, he caught our firstborn, holding him almost fully immersed for a few moments longer until he stopped breathing through his gills and shifted to his nose. As was standard with young Mimics, he didn't cry, content to cough a couple of times before emitting a soft cooing sound.

"He's beautiful," Rogue said, his voice choked with emotion. And beautiful he was.

I took him from my mate, staring at our perfect little bundle with awe while Rogue reached for our second child making his entrance into the world.

His skin was the perfect mix of his father's gray complexion and my dusky blue shade. He possessed far fewer black chitin scales than his father, but they were woven in a stunning pattern along the ridges of his undars. He didn't have mandibles; just the most adorable heart-shaped mouth, and stormy eyes like mine. A smattering of black scales framed the sides of his cheeks and forehead, where the rounded tips of his crescent moon shaped Deynian horn timidly poked their heads.

He reached for my face, and a teary laugh escaped me at the sight of the fine webbing between his tiny fingers. I caught his hand, kissing his palm before pressing it against my cheek. Glancing up at Rogue, my heart filled to bursting at the mesmerizing tableau of the love of my life bonding with our second twin.

As I gazed back at our firstborn, my wistful smile froze on my lips. I had meant to check if he had webbed toes as well when my brain finally registered that he didn't have a loin plate like a Dragon or Xian, but a veil… a thin one…

"No way!" I whispered in disbelief.

"What?" Rogue asked, worry audible in his voice.

I didn't answer right away, wanting to confirm my suspicion. Pressing the tip of my finger right below the baby's umbilical cord, I traced a path downward over the veil. The infant instinctively parted it open.

"Maker! She's a female," I breathed out in shock before glancing back at Rogue. "Our firstborn is a female!"

"That's impossible," Rogue said, just as stunned.

But she was indeed a girl, as was her identical twin. Where the majority of Mimics were born females, Xians and Dragons could only sire males. Saying this changed everything was the understatement of the millennium.

At first, we believed my Mimic DNA had been dominant and that, aside from some cosmetic traits of their father, our daughters were fully like me.

We couldn't have been more wrong.

Storm and Tempest turned out to be full-fledged Dragons with soul transfer ability and my morphing powers. Saying my girls took badass to a whole new level couldn't even begin to do them justice. My fears of them not fitting in with the other children never came to fruition.

Sitting on a bench in one of the gardens of Skogoth—the Scelk city located on the opposite side of the Mistral River, I watched the children chasing after a ball. Their squeals of delight filled the scented air carried by a soft breeze. Little Xians, Dragons, Scelks, and Mimics were playing together. We had all been created to exterminate each other. Instead, we had become one big family.

We weren't monsters. We weren't abominations. We were the Vanguard.

THE END

KRYPTID QUEEN

KRYPTID SOLDIER

BOMBARDIER BEETLE

SEPTHORON

NASTAREX

ERKENTAR

SCELK

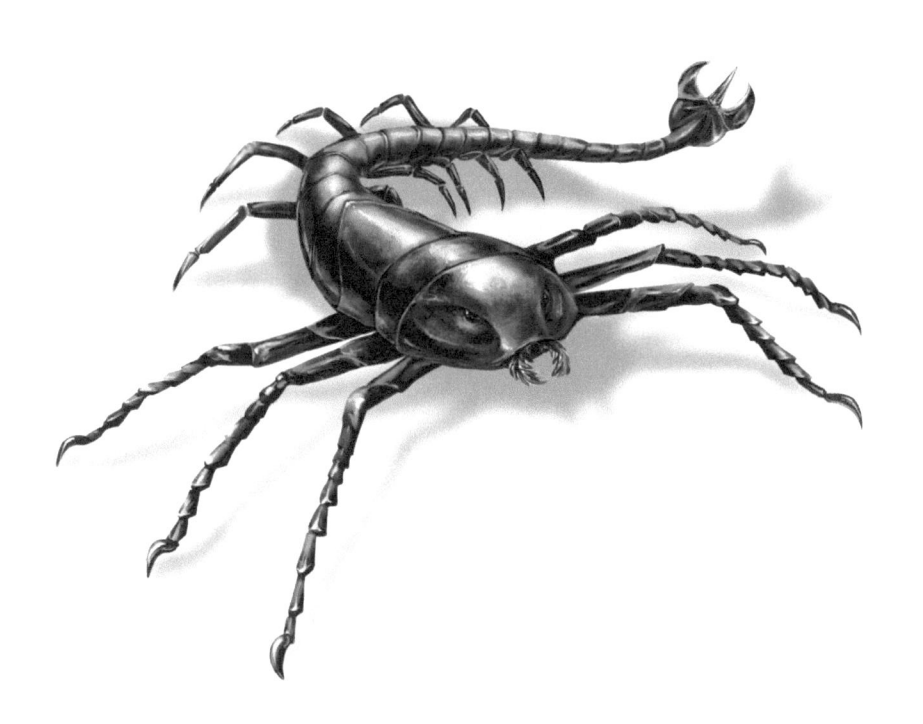

JADOZOR

GOMENZI DRAGON

STORM

ALSO BY REGINE ABEL

THE VEREDIAN CHRONICLES
Escaping Fate
Blind Fate
Raising Amalia
Twist of Fate
Hands of Fate
Defying Fate

BRAXIANS
Anton's Grace
Ravik's Mercy
Krygor's Hope

XIAN WARRIORS
Doom
Legion
Raven
Bane
Chaos
Varnog
Reaper
Wrath
Xenon
Nevrik
Rogue

PRIME MATING AGENCY
I Married A Lizardman
I Married A Naga
I Married A Birdman
I Married A Minotaur

ALSO BY REGINE ABEL

I Married A Merman
I Married A Dragon
I Married A Beast
I Married A Dryad

THE MIST
The Mistwalker
The Nightmare

DARK TALES
Bluebeard's Curse
The Hunchback

BLOOD MAIDENS OF KARTHIA
Claiming Thalia

VALOS OF SONHADRA
Unfrozen
Iced

EMPATHS OF LYRIA
An Alien For Christmas

THE SHADOW REALMS
Dark Swan

OTHER
True As Steel
Alien Awakening
Heart of Stone

ABOUT REGINE

USA Today bestselling author Regine Abel is a fantasy, paranormal and sci-fi junky. Anything with a bit of magic, a touch of the unusual, and a lot of romance will have her jumping for joy. She loves creating hot alien warriors and no-nonsense, kick-ass heroines that evolve in fantastic new worlds while embarking on action-packed adventures filled with mystery and the twists you never saw coming.

Before devoting herself as a full-time writer, Regine had surrendered to her other passions: music and video games! After a decade working as a Sound Engineer in movie dubbing and live concerts, Regine became a professional Game Designer and Creative Director, a career that has led her from her home in Canada to the US and various countries in Europe and Asia.

Facebook
    https://www.facebook.com/regine.abel.author/

Website
    https://regineabel.com

Regine's Rebels Reader Group
https://www.facebook.com/groups/ReginesRebels/

Newsletter
http://smarturl.it/RA_Newsletter

Goodreads
http://smarturl.it/RA_Goodreads

Bookbub
https://www.bookbub.com/profile/regine-abel

Amazon
http://smarturl.it/AuthorAMS

Made in United States
Troutdale, OR
08/14/2023